"Please forgive my necessary deception," Victoria whispered. Fresh tears stirred her silky lashes, and her green eyes were wide with confusion and innocent desire.

Sebastian's passion ignited with the quickness of a striking match. "So lovely," he said softly and lifted her face up as he lowered his.

He slipped his arm around her small waist and slowly pulled her against him. Deepening his kiss until her sealed lips became limpid and opened willingly, he lingered in the sweet nectar of her innocent response, tasting, teasing, until he thought he would go mad.

Victoria's senses reeled as his gentle play turned demanding. She pressed wantonly against his hard body as though searching for a release from the heat that threatened to consume her. . . .

HEARTFIRE ROMANCES

SWEET TEXAS NIGHTS (2610, $3.75)
by Vivian Vaughan

Meg Britton grew up on the railroads, working proudly at her father's side. Nothing was going to stop them from setting the rails clear to Silver Creek, Texas—certainly not some crazy prospector. As Meg set out to confront the old coot, she planned her strategy with cool precision. But soon she was speechless with shock. For instead of a harmless geezer, she found a boldly handsome stranger whose determination matched her own.

CAPTIVE DESIRE (2612, $3.75)
by Jane Archer

Victoria Malone fancied herself a great adventuress, but being kidnapped was too much excitement for even Victoria! Especially when her arrogant kidnapper thought she was part of Red Duke's outlaw gang. Trying to convince the overbearing, handsome stranger that she had been an innocent bystander when the stagecoach was robbed, proved futile. But when he thought he could maker her confess by crushing her to his warm, broad chest, by caressing her with his strong, capable hands, Victoria was willing to admit to anything. . . .

LAWLESS ECSTASY (2613, $3.75)
by Susan Sackett

Abra Beaumont could spot a thief a mile away. After all, her father was once one of the best. But he'd been on the right side of the law for years now, and she wasn't about to let a man like Dash Thorne lead him astray with some wild plan for stealing the Tear of Allah, the world's most fabulous ruby. Dash was just the sort of man she most distrusted—sophisticated, handsome, and altogether too sure of his considerable charm. Abra shivered at the devilish gleam in his blue eyes and swore he would need more than smooth kisses and skilled caresses to rob her of her virtue . . . and much more than sweet promises to steal her heart!

Available wherever paperbacks are sold, or order direct from the Publisher. Send cover price plus 50¢ per copy for mailing and handling to Zebra Books, Dept. 3227, 475 Park Avenue South, New York, N.Y. 10016. Residents of New York, New Jersey and Pennsylvania must include sales tax. DO NOT SEND CASH.

San Francisco Surrender

Donna Fletcher

ZEBRA BOOKS
KENSINGTON PUBLISHING CORP.

ZEBRA BOOKS

are published by

Kensington Publishing Corp.
475 Park Avenue South
New York, NY 10016

First printing: November, 1990

Printed in the United States of America

Prologue

San Francisco 1873

There was no place to hide; the voices grew louder, more distinct. The small urchin was grateful for the fog that rolled in every night off the San Francisco Bay covering the wharf along the Barbary Coast. At least it provided some anonymity.

Silently the creature hunched down beside a stack of crates that waited for morning's boarding. Soundlessly shifting position to better hear, the sharp ears caught the sturdy voice of a man and the sweet tongue of a woman.

"Come on, luv, let's go back. This isn't anyplace for the likes of you. It's dangerous."

The tall gentleman dismissed her suggestion with a wave of his hand and stumbled slightly from side to side. "There's nothing to fear, my dear Lola, I'm quite capable of protecting you."

"I don't have any doubts about that, luv," she cooed, slipping her arm through his, "but you've heard the stories about—"

"Nonsense," he interrupted, snatching his arm away from hers to stumble against the numerous stacks of cargo. "The dastardly fellow wouldn't dare attack me. Why, I would thump him on the head and thrash him soundly before he even had a chance to attack."

Lola giggled at his false bravery.

"Why, I'll skewer him with his own dagger," the man boasted, demonstrating his proficiency with an imaginary sword. He swung and pivoted in grand style. When he completed his display of swordsmanship he gallantly bowed before her.

It was at that precise moment that the urchin decided to make a move, and within seconds a shiny blade was strategically placed between the startled man's legs.

"Stand up real slow, mister, or you'll never enjoy a woman again," whispered the raspy voice.

The man did as he was told. A fine film of perspiration broke out across his brow as his unknown assailant moved the blade slowly, producing a tear in his expensive black trousers. The hard steel was pressed warningly against his thigh. His body shook with fear and once again the raspy voice cautioned his actions.

"My God," the man choked, "whatever you want is yours. Just don't move it any higher."

"Ya purse," the assailant demanded.

He cautiously removed the velvet coin purse from his breast pocket and dangled it over his left shoulder as directed.

"Drop it."

The purse was caught at the same moment the dagger slipped across his thigh. At the mere thought of

6

the damage that had been inflicted, the gentleman slumped to the ground in a dead faint.

George Oliver Stanton opened his eyes to several anxious faces peering down at him. Beyond the curious stares, he caught sight of a brilliantly lit crystal chandelier. His ears picked up the sound of shrill laughter from an adjoining room.

"Are you all right, George?" asked a plump, short gentleman leaning directly over his head and peering wide-eyed into his pale face.

"Of course he is," Lola answered, sitting next to his reclining form on the topaz velvet settee. She placed a cool cloth against his warm brow and favored him with a smile and a tender pat on the arm.

"Wh-what happened?"

Lola's faint giggle filled the smoky air. "Nothing to worry about, luv. You've just crossed paths with the Serpent, that's all."

The men roared in robust laughter.

"Did he leave his mark on you, George?" cried one.

"Of course he did," remarked another. "The Serpent's sting isn't deadly, but thank goodness it's accurate."

George felt the heated sting of embarrassment creep up and stain his cheeks. His hand quickly assessed the damage done to his trousers and thigh. The wound wasn't deep, just a slight cut near his groin.

He pushed Lola out of the way and sat up straight. "This is ridiculous. Something must be done about this insufferable thief."

"With all the problems plaguing the waterfront, do you actually think the authorities care about one small thief?" asked the plump man.

"Well, Jacob, if the authorities won't do anything, perhaps we should," George said.

Several men laughed and snickered at his suggestion.

"And who do you suppose is capable of handling the task?" called out another man.

George furrowed his brow, giving considerable thought to who would be the most logical candidate. His mind finally focused on one person. Of course, many found it difficult if not impossible to deal with him, but if approached in the appropriate manner, perhaps the man would prove willing. The gentleman—if he could be called that—did not require monetary inducement. He was reported to be one of the wealthiest men in San Francisco.

His mind made up, George leaned back against the settee and smiled. "I know the perfect man."

"Who?" asked Jacob.

"Yes, who would be capable of such a task?" questioned another.

"Don't keep us in suspense, George, who is it?" another voice insisted.

George's grin broadened. "The Dragon."

Chapter One

"Sebastian Blood!" Percy English shouted.

The sailors, who were hoisting the giant rope nets filled with cargo on to the deck of the ship, stopped and turned their heads. The man who had been addressed did not move, or even acknowledge the summons.

"Sebastian Blood!" Percy shouted once more and marched toward the man, swatting at people in his path as though they were irritating flies.

Sebastian remained as he was. Only when Percy stood directly behind him, his breath fanning the rich black material of the large man's waistcoat, did he turn.

"You wish to speak to me?"

Percy took a step back. The dark blue eyes with their chilling stare said far more than words. "Yes, sir, Mr. Blood."

Sebastian nodded for him to continue.

"I need this job real bad. Don't fire me."

Sebastian glared at the fellow, whose towering height easily matched his own.

9

"I've got to sail, Mr. Blood, I've just got to."

Sebastian quirked a dark brow in irritation. "You should have thought about that before smashing the Hades Saloon to pieces."

"I-I lost my head. It won't happen again."

"Too late, Percy," Sebastian said and casually stepped around the bearlike man. A sharp tug at his coat sleeve forced him to stop.

Percy realized his mistake instantly and released the dark material as though it were a hot branding iron scorching his callused hand. No one touched the Dragon. No one.

"When you learn to control your liquor, come see me," Sebastian said. He dismissed the man without even a backward glance.

Sebastian continued on, ignoring the ever-present chaos of the wharf. Merchants argued over shipments. Chinese men shuffled in and out of the crowd conversing in their fast, pointed language; the pungent odor of raw fish and manly sweat permeated the area.

He hastened his pace wanting to reach his office early. His long muscular legs vaulted to the wooden walkway and he hurried his stride as he checked his gold pocket watch for the time. Snapping it shut with a forcible click, he swiftly turned the corner. The next second he was stumbling backward. A small street urchin was plastered against his silver gray vest. He grabbed the ragamuffin by the shoulders to steady himself as well as the boy.

"In a hurry?" he asked.

The lad muttered several unintelligible remarks before looking up.

Sebastian was confronted by the widest, greenest eyes he had ever seen. They were startling in contrast to the smudges of dirt that marked the thin face.

"Out of my way, giant," the boy demanded.

"An apt description," Sebastian said. The lad reached just below his chest.

The boy squirmed against the tight hold the huge man had upon him. "Let go."

"When I'm ready," Sebastian demanded, roughly shaking him to quiet him down. "That's better."

A slight grin spread across the dirty face and sparkling white teeth peeked between full lips. "I don't take orders from the likes of you."

"You don't have any—Damn!" Sebastian howled as a small booted foot caught him square in the shin.

The boy was free in a flash. He wasted no time in disappearing into the crowded street, leaving an angry Sebastian staring after him.

"Smart-mouthed hooligan," he muttered as he walked on, favoring his sore leg.

A few minutes later he entered the two-story brick building that housed Blood Enterprises, a joint venture owned by him and his father.

Several men were busy scanning maps and charts on their desks, but each took a moment to call out a friendly greeting that Sebastian returned in kind before disappearing behind a closed door at the rear of the room.

"There's a gentleman here to see you. And he has no appointment," Ben Shavers said. The short elderly gentleman had been Sebastian's personal secretary for the last five years. He ran the office like a stern captain

11

piloting a ship.

Sebastian grinned at Ben's annoyance. "Who is it?"

"George Oliver Stanton."

Sebastian was familiar with the name, but not the man. He was well known for his love of women and gambling, in that order. "Very well, tell him I'll see him in a moment."

George tapped his gold-tipped cane on the floor as he waited for Sebastian Blood. The man had nerve making him wait.

"Mr. Stanton."

George jumped, startled by the deep voice.

He was about to stand and offer his hand when Sebastian stepped around the chair and walked behind his desk, seating himself in the large leather chair.

"Mr. Blood," George said, amazed by the height and width of the man, "I was hoping you'd help in ridding the waterfront of a perverse character."

Sebastian remained silent waiting for him to continue.

George shifted uncomfortably in his seat. "I'm referring to the Serpent."

"Is it safe to assume you have been a victim of his?" Sebastian inquired. The rush of color to George's pale cheeks answered his question.

"Something must be done about him," George demanded, pounding his cane on the floor.

Sebastian stood and walked to the front of the desk. He leaned against the corner, pushing his black waistcoat back to rest one hand on his hip. "And why

12

should I be the one to do something?"

"Well, you are referred to as the Dragon, aren't you? And, of course, you spent many years with those barbarians, the Japanese. All things considered, you're the most likely one to handle the matter."

Sebastian's finely sculpted features locked in anger. "Get out."

George stood to face him. "But-but . . ."

"Out!"

Sebastian slammed the door on the rapidly retreating figure. He had often met men similar to George Stanton, men who believed that because their families were socially acceptable, they were superior to the rest of society. He was sick of their self-righteous attitudes. The only reason he was admitted into their intimate circle was because of his money and their curiosity. And the only reason he joined their snobbish group was to shock them even more.

He laughed, thinking of all those fine upstanding gentlemen whose wives tried to seduce him at every party he attended. If half of them realized how much their wives enjoyed coupling, there would be no reason for their nightly visits to Madam Champlain's. Sebastian eased himself into the large chair behind the desk and smiled as he recalled the unique talents of one such wife.

But George Stanton did have a point. Many of the Serpent's victims had been his own friends and associates. Perhaps it was time he became involved.

Ben Shavers intruded upon his thoughts. "Your next appointment is in ten minutes, sir."

Sebastian nodded. "Ben, I want you to spread some

news around the wharf. Make sure it spreads quickly. I'm hoping it will resolve the matter without any further action on my part."

"What is it you want made known?"

"The Dragon wants to meet the Serpent."

The urchin ran faster, heedless of the clouds of dirt erupting in the faces of the people passing by. Late. Late again. This job was a necessity, a definite necessity.

The small boots hit the steps with a thud and took them two at a time. The door swung open and with a rush of gushing air, the lad flew up the stairs.

The garish gold carpeting muffled the noise of his worn soles as he raced along the second-floor corridor searching for one room in particular. The bottom of threadbare trousers almost met that of the carpet when rushing feet skidded to an abrupt halt. A thin hand reached for the brass doorknob as the other hand knocked.

"Where have you been?" Lola demanded, swinging the door open and drawing the person in with an unexpected flourish. "Oh, never mind, it doesn't matter. There's something important we need to discuss, Vic."

Vic nodded and waited patiently for the distraught woman to continue. Lola paced back and forth in front of the big brass bed across which were strewn numerous wrinkled articles of clothing. The buxom redhead grabbed a thin cigar from the marble-topped dresser, lit it, then pushed a mound of ruffles to the side before sitting on the messy bed. "Why, in heaven's name, did you attack the man I was with last night? I thought we had an agreement about you staying away from my clients."

"I didn't have any choice. It was late and I needed the money for today. It won't happen again, Lola. I'm really sorry."

The fiery redhead sprang off the bed shaking her head in frustration. "That's the least of your worries, Vic."

"What do you mean?"

Lola drew on the end of the thin cigar and inhaled deeply before releasing the heavily scented smoke. "The Dragon means to stop you. He's let it be known on the streets."

"Bloody hell," Vic mumbled, collapsing back against the closed door.

"You must cease your nightly trade," Lola pleaded.

"I can't—and you know why."

Lola crushed the half-finished cigar in a glass dish and walked over to Vic. "You have no choice. The Dragon knows too many people. They'll find you."

"I'll be careful."

"It will make no difference," Lola insisted.

"I need the money."

"Find another way, Vic."

"There is no other way."

Lola reached for the handkerchief tucked between her bulging breasts, dipped it in the water, and began to gently wipe at the dirt on Vic's face. "And what happens when he captures you, strips you bare for a whipping, and discovers your secret?"

15

Layers of dirt faded away to reveal pale, tender skin. "I won't let him capture me."

Lola shook her head. "But what if he does? How do you intend to explain to the Dragon that the notorious Serpent, the skillful thief, is actually an eighteen-year-old female?"

Vic slumped dawn as she leaned over him, her hands...

Chapter Two

Vic slumped down along the door until she was sitting on the floor. She leaned her head back and closed her eyes, but not before a lone tear slipped unchecked down her cheek.

Lola had met Vic Chambers six months ago when he had brazenly carried the "help wanted" sign into the house. He had announced to Madam Champlain that he could handle any job the woman wanted done. The other girls had laughed at the scrawny little beggar, but he soon proved his worth and the sight of him in patched trousers, an oversized frayed shirt, and worn boots had become a familiar sight in the bawdy house.

Lola had been taken in by the lad's determination and they became fast friends. It wasn't long before she discovered that the bold boy was actually a frightened girl.

"I have some money tucked away for emergencies, you're welcome to it," she offered.

"Thanks, but I'll manage," Vic said, wiping her teary eyes with her sleeve.

"You could work here in another capacity," Lola suggested as she had many times before.

Vic shook her head. "No, it's bad enough I've been forced into thievery to provide for Beth. I won't add to my sins."

"Vic, we're not talking about the police who are paid handsomely to look the other way. We're talking about the Dragon."

"I'll be careful."

"And I'm telling you it won't be enough," Lola insisted.

Vic stood; her hand clutched the brass doorknob. "It will have to be. I have no choice."

She was out the door before Lola could respond, hurrying down the steps to begin her daily chores. She buried herself in each menial task attempting to drive the bitter memories from her mind.

Cruel fate had forced her into her present situation. A carriage accident had taken her parents' lives leaving her and her ill sister Elizabeth under the guardianship of her father's half brother, Tobias Withers. Victoria discovered all too soon that he expected certain favors from her. If she didn't comply with his wishes, then he'd just satisfy himself with Elizabeth.

She had to flee and she did, taking her ill sister with her. Making certain no one would find them, she disguised herself as a boy and soon discovered she was better off. There were no jobs for women that paid decently. And with the influx of Chinese workers and the labor union problems, there was barely enough work for a man. She had taken odd jobs, but still the money wasn't sufficient to care for Elizabeth. The doctor's fee, the medicine, room and board—there just

18

wasn't enough money.

"Hey, Vic, bring me some fresh water," Rosy called from the second floor.

"Sure," she called back and hurried to the kitchen. She was lucky to have this job. At least it paid for the room and board. It was the doctor's fee and the cost of the medicine that hurt her the most.

She shook her head, recalling the strange twist of fate that had solved her problem. She was on the wharf late one night, finishing up her job of cleaning fish at Louie's Place. She had gone out back to empty a bucket of water when she heard a noise in the alley. She quickly reached for the dagger she kept tucked in her boot for protection.

It was a drunken gent who had lost his way. He was stumbling from side to side. Vic reached out to steady him. The man yelled and threw his purse at her. She realized that he had thought she was a thief. She had tried to run after him, but he had vanished. The money had provided Elizabeth with medical care for a month. It was then she decided there were only two ways to make the money she needed. Thievery or prostitution. Neither appealed to her. Both were wrong, yet she had no choice. She found it impossible to sell her body, for, in a way, if she had given in to her uncle's demands she would have been doing just that. Thievery seemed the lesser of two evils.

Of course she hadn't meant to cut her first victim. She was so frightened and he so nervous that it just happened. It was afterwards she realized that it was a good way to aid in her escape. The men were so upset by the small cut that they stood frozen to the spot, giving her time to make a hasty exit. It was after a few robberies that she was dubbed "the Serpent." The talk on the waterfront was that the fellow was so quick with a knife that it was like a serpent's fangs striking.

Vic finished her chores for the day and hastily left the house. She maneuvered her way along the crowded walkway, cutting across the street without looking. She didn't see the carriage careening down upon her, but she heard the driver yell and froze in her tracks.

The horses protested in being brought to a sudden halt. The large black man had his hands full in bringing them under control.

Vic couldn't move. Her eyes were focused on the horse only inches in front of her. The stallion pounded the dirt with his hoof, again and again. The dry dust rose up, stinging her nostrils. Fear held her frozen and she envisioned the thick hoof coming down upon her head.

"What the devil?" She heard a man yell and looked up.

"You!" Sebastian shouted from the window of the carriage and flung open the door.

Vic remembered the man from their early morning encounter. "Stay away, giant," she screamed.

Sebastian stopped, shocked by the boy's command. "I do as I please, lad."

"So do I."

Sebastian smiled at his boldness. "Aren't you a bit young to be working in this area?"

Vic threw her shoulders back with more bravado than she felt. "I can take care of myself."

Sebastian doubted that. The lad was too thin. His eyes were too big and curious for his round face. "A gust of wind would blow you away."

"Unless horses stomp me first."

"Then watch where you're going."

"Always do."

"I think not," Sebastian said, stepping forward.

Vic took two steps back and raised a clenched fist. "I'm warning ya."

Sebastian laughed. "And what do you expect to do with that puny thing?"

"This," she said, kicking him square in the shin for the second time that day.

Sebastian hadn't expected that and let out a howl. Vic ran in the opposite direction.

The sound of laughter drew his attention away from the lad who had disappeared around the corner. "You find something amusing, Daniel?" he asked.

Daniel nodded slowly still snickering, but trying to control it. "The boy, sir."

"He's one lad I intend to get my hands on and when I do I'm going to—"

"Have to catch him first, sir."

Sebastian shot the man a murderous glare. "Home, Daniel," he snapped, and climbed into the carriage.

Vic didn't stop until she reached the white clapboard house where she and Elizabeth lived. She sat on the steps leading up to the small porch and took deep breaths. She didn't know who the giant was, but she certainly didn't want to run into him again.

She brushed the dusty dirt from her clothes and stamped her feet before entering the boarding house. She had been lucky to find this place so close to the waterfront, yet clean and safe. She ran up the two

21

flights of steps and flung open the door at the end of the hall.

"See, I told you he'd be here any minute," Mrs. Kenny said to the frail girl in the bed.

Vic went straight to her sister's side. "Are you all right, Beth?"

"Yes, but you're late. I was worried," she answered in a soft voice.

"No need for you to worry," Mrs. Kenny ordered. "Your brother takes good care of you."

"I know," Beth said, looking up at Vic with regret.

Vic reached for her hand and squeezed it reassuringly.

"I'll send supper up in an hour," Mrs. Kenny said and left the two alone.

"She's so good to me," Beth said. "She comes up here every afternoon when she finishes her chores and sits with me."

Vic didn't have the heart to tell her that she paid Mrs. Kenny extra money to look after her. Her sister felt she was a burden enough. That information would only add to her worries. "She's a nice woman."

Beth nodded. "I love to hear her speak of Ireland. Sometimes I can almost see it."

"Have you taken your medicine?" Vic asked, picking up the bottle and noticing that it was almost empty.

Beth shook her head and stuck out her tongue. "It tastes horrible."

Vic laughed. "But it helps." At least she hoped it did. Beth wasn't coughing as much, although she was pale and continued to lose weight. Her light brown hair that was once so lustrous and wavy was now limp and lifeless. Even her green eyes, so like Vic's, seemed to have lost their vibrancy. She certainly didn't look her fifteen years. She looked more like a sickly twelve year old.

"Let's get you washed up before supper," Vic said, reaching for the water basin and pitcher.

Several hours after supper Vic tucked the quilt around her sleeping sister. She turned down the flame on the globe lamp and tiptoed to the door. She hadn't planned on going out tonight. The Serpent only struck every couple of weeks. Unfortunately, the man she had robbed last evening had had a pitiful amount of money. She had felt awful after stealing it as she always did. Now it was necessary to go out again. Beth needed more medicine and the doctor would be paying her a visit soon. Vic walked out the door saying a quick prayer that their dire circumstances would soon change for the better.

The fog was more dense than usual that evening, providing Vic with a thick blanket of protection. Cautiously she made her way along the notorious waterfront. Too many men and women disappeared all too frequently along this strip of unfavorable establishments. She found herself a niche between two barrels and waited for her next benefactor.

Dr. Aaron Samuels had just completed a visit to a nearby saloon where two sailors had had a disagreement. A rather nasty one. He had finally finished stitching the two and was returning to his carriage.

The Serpent watched the man carefully. He was of average height with a thatch of red curly hair. There was nothing unusual about him. Then her eyes caught sight of the familiar black bag. A physician. Perfect,

23

she thought, just perfect.

In seconds Dr. Samuels was standing dead still with a blade pressed against his thigh. "I'm afraid you're wasting your time," he said in an unthreatening tone.

"I'll be the judge of that," came the raspy reply. "You're a doc, right?"

"Yes, but I don't have any money on me."

"Don't want no money."

Aaron was surprised, then realizing what the thief was after he spoke directly. "I carry none of the drugs you're looking for."

"Don't want any of that stuff. I need the medicine that helps the coughing sickness. You know, the kind that a person can't stop once it starts."

"If you require medical attention, I'd be glad to help."

"That's a laugh, Doc. The law would swoop down on me in a flash. It's not for me anyway. It's for a friend."

"I see," Aaron said, not actually believing the unlikely tale. "I have some in my bag."

"Can't let you put your hands down, so drop the bag. I'll fetch it myself."

"How will you know the correct medicine to choose?"

"I can read," she snapped, almost biting her tongue for supplying him with even a small shred of information regarding her identity.

Aaron was surprised by his assailant's knowledge. So the Serpent wasn't the ignorant creature everyone thought him to be. "I'd appreciate it if the medicine was the only thing you took from my bag."

"Fine with me, Doc. Don't want any of that other stuff anyway."

24

Aaron felt the knife move slightly as the Serpent reached down into the bag to grasp the bottle. He felt the light slip of the blade cross his thigh. Then he heard the sound of scurrying feet in the distance and knew he was once again alone.

He reached down for his bag and checked the damage done. It wasn't much of a cut, or a tear. He could have both mended in no time. He finished the walk to his carriage and climbed in . He was about to go home when a sudden impulse made him change direction. He headed toward Rincon Hill.

Jenny lay contented in Sebastian's arms. Her brow held a fine film of perspiration. Her lips were slightly swollen from too many ardent kisses and her body ached pleasantly in all the right places.

"Are you all right?" Sebastian asked, pushing the damp tendrils of dark hair away from her closed eyes.

Jenny purred like a contented kitten and snuggled closer to his nakedness. Her body tingled and she admonished herself for wanting him again. In her profession she couldn't afford to have favorites, yet she measured every man she serviced up against the Dragon. And there was definitely no comparison. Where his body was hard and taut, others were soft and weak. Where he caressed and cajoled, others demanded and took. He was a man who had mastered the art of making love and Jenny had never met anyone with his precise expertise.

Voices raised in excitement drifted up from below causing Sebastian to slip from the bed and Jenny to cast a petulant smile.

"Don't fret, pet. As soon as I see what the disturbance is about I'll return and satisfy your insatiable thirst for me."

Jenny giggled and watched with unabashed pleasure as he slipped into a deep brown floor-length robe he had taken from the closet. He walked over to her, kissed her gently on the lips and left the room.

Sebastian tightened the gold cord around his waist and descended the curving staircase in annoyance. He focused his attention on the Japanese woman who had run his home so smoothly for the last ten years. "Akiko."

The small, thin woman approached him slowly. Her precise steps were more of a shuffle than a walk. Her head was bowed in submission as she had been taught so thoroughly many years before. "Sebastian-san, I'm sorry for the disturbance. Samuels-san is in your study. He has been robbed by the Serpent."

Sebastian released a fusillade of Japanese words that caused Akiko's eyes to widen in surprise. He whirled around and headed for the study. His echoing shouts in Japanese bounced off the rich teakwood walls. Several frightened servants found themselves falling over each other as they hurried to move out of his path.

"Aaron!"

Aaron jumped out of the high-back leather chair he was sitting in. "You have a strange way of entering a room, Sebastian."

"The Serpent robbed you," he stated instead of questioning.

"Yes—"

"That's it, I've had enough. The fellow's days are numbered."

"I really wonder if he can be captured. He's quite adept at his trade."

Sebastian grinned. "No one is that elusive."

Akiko entered the room silently carrying a red lacquer tray on which sat two handleless cups and a teapot. The porcelain set held an intricate design of a blue dragon. She placed it on the oval table in front of the chairs and bowed to Sebastian before leaving the room.

Aaron quickly helped himself. "Never liked tea until I tasted this stuff."

"Akiko prepares it quite well."

"So you have your sights set on the Serpent," Aaron said, leaning back in his chair and sipping the soothing liquid.

"The Serpent will be taken care of by week's end."

Aaron saw the determination in Sebastian's deep blue eyes. There was no stopping him when he got that look. "If you say so. Enough talk of the Serpent. What about a game of cards?"

Sebastian smiled and stood. "I have much more interesting entertainment waiting upstairs for my return."

Aaron laughed. "Then by all means don't let me keep you."

Sebastian walked toward the door. "Stay and finished the tea. And, Aaron, I meant what I said. By week's end the Serpent will be no more."

Sebastian entered his bedroom and went straight to the bed where Jenny lay waiting for him. He opened his robe and let it slip from his body. Jenny smiled and drew the cover back, inviting him to join her. He eased down next to her, taking her in his arms. His lips

27

brushed across hers lightly before traveling down her neck, over her shoulder, to her breast.

"Oh, Sebastian," she moaned, and they were soon lost in a world all their own.

Jenny slumbered in complete contentment while Sebastian stood by the window staring out into the night. His arms lay crossed over his bare chest. His nakedness seemed not to bother him, nor would it have disturbed the sleeping woman. She was accustomed to such a state of undress.

The dark-haired beauty was one of Madam Champlain's private stock, only available to certain influential people. Sebastian sought her out when he felt the need. Particularly since she was permitted to discreetly visit a client's home upon request.

Sebastian turned and the reflection of the full moon cast a ghostly image across his stern profile. The Serpent had returned to haunt his thoughts.

He had learned in his youth not to allow his emotions to rule. He recalled the first time he had met the mighty warrior who had taught him so well. He was a young lad of ten and had just suffered a terrible blow to his ego. A younger boy had given him a sound thrashing and he was livid with rage as well as tears.

The short, powerful samurai had grabbed him by the nape of the neck and in rapid Japanese assaulted him with a tongue-lashing for allowing another to witness his emotions. Their strange relationship had flourished after that chance encounter and Sebastian soon learned to defend himself with nothing more than his bare hands.

28

The samurai had warned him that when a warrior did not possess his sword he had to rely on an alternate method of self-defense. Hence, he learned karate, meaning "empty hand."

Sebastian had worked diligently on mastering the art. Over the years he had become skilled in the art that his old friend had warned him was "necessary to sustain one's dignity."

Now his dignity was being challenged. He would call upon his skills to bring the matter to an abrupt end. Sebastian's finely sculpted lips turned up ever so slightly at the corners as he tasted the pleasures he would receive in besting the fellow at his own game. The trap would be set. The Serpent would fall directly into the hands of the Dragon.

Chapter Three

Vic massaged the temples of her throbbing head with her fingers. The stubborn headache refused to go away. It had been with her ever since she had discovered the doctor she had robbed last evening was a close friend of the Dragon's.

The pain grew worse as Vic continued her chores. She knelt on the foyer floor scrubbing the white marble tiles that required constant attention. Her hands were red from the hot water she used to maintain the clean shine Madam Champlain insisted upon. She had worked her way up from the back of the hall and was almost finished.

She scrubbed harder hoping to push the nagging problems from her mind. She tried to weigh the urgent needs of her sister against the Dragon's thirst for revenge. She just couldn't find a solution to the perplexing problem.

Lighthearted laughter intruded upon her thoughts. It had been a long time since she had reason to laugh, much too long. Not stopping to weigh the consequences of her rash action, Vic stood. She picked up the pail and tossed the dirty water across the remaining unwashed tiles.

Startled cries echoed through the establishment. Vic realized she must have wet some of the girls and possibly the customer they were greeting. Her emotions were still running high. She straightened to her five foot two inch height, braced her hands on her hips and raised her head with a sharp snap.

She met the solid chest of a large man. A tiny warning signal sounded somewhere in her mind, but she refused to listen. Instead she threw back her head and prepared to assault the Goliath with a few choice words.

"You!" Sebastian yelled.

Vic was stunned to see the man she had kicked in the shin twice, but it didn't prevent her from speaking. "I've got work to do, mister, so make your choice and get out of my way."

Once again, startled cries escaped the girls' lips.

"Jenny, please tell Madam Champlain I wish to speak with her," Sebastian said, staring at Vic.

Vic stared back finding it difficult not to be nervous. His dark blue eyes appeared to dance with a fiery amusement as though he were enjoying this encounter.

"Don't be harsh on the poor lad," Rosy said, playfully running her slim hand up and down his dark vest.

"You're in for it now," giggled another girl near Vic's ear.

Vic tensed and watched as Rosy hung all over the huge man. Her fingers continued to play along his flat midriff before moving up to caress his cheek.

"Fool," came the harsh whisper in her ear. "don't you know who he is?"

Vic glared at May, the young Chinese girl beside her.

"Look at him, Vic. Look how handsome he is. How big. How powerful."

Vic felt her stomach rumble.

"Fool," May whispered again. "Do I have to tell you, or should I just say there's a tattoo on his right forearm of a fire-breathing dragon?"

Vic didn't need her to say anymore, although it took her a few seconds to accept the fact that the Dragon stood before the Serpent.

Sebastian was fascinated by the defiant ragamuffin. Twice he had run across him and twice he had slipped through his fingers. Even now when his defeat was imminent he still had the courage to speak out. It was obvious from his patched clothing that he was one of the orphans living off the streets. His puny size attested to his lack of food. Yet there was a certain beguiling innocence to his brilliant green eyes and a vulnerability to his features that stirred a protective instinct in Sebastian.

Madam Champlain bustled into the room, her plump form wrapped in mounds of pink ostrich feathers. "My dear Sebastian, whatever is the problem?" Her hazel eyes caught sight of his partially soaked trousers and shoes and the empty bucket. "Why, you stupid boy," she yelled, raising her chubby hand.

Sebastian grabbed her hand before it could connect with Vic's pale face. "I have no wish to see the lad abused."

"But he must pay for his insolence," she insisted.

"I agree."

32

"Perhaps a few days work without pay will teach you a lesson," Madam Champlain said to Vic.

Vic's head drooped in defeat. She was trying so hard, so very hard to care for Beth. If she lost even one day's wages she wouldn't have the money to pay the doctor when he visited. A single tear slipped from her eye and fell to splash against the tip of her worn boot.

Sebastian was disturbed by the lad's strange reaction. He hadn't meant to upset him. He just felt he needed to be taught a lesson in acceptable behavior. He waved his hand in the air silently dismissing the girls and Madam Champlain.

"If you have a problem, lad, perhaps I can help."

Vic refused to look at the man. "Have you ever been hungry?"

"On occasion."

She raised her head. A single tear glistened on her dark lashes. "I mean real hunger. The kind that gnaws at your stomach till you want to throw up, only there isn't anything inside you."

"No, I've never known that kind of hunger."

"I have . . . many times."

Sebastian reached into his pocket. "I have some—"

"I don't want your charity!" she screamed. "I just want to be left alone so I can do my job."

"I understand your anger, but don't direct it at me," Sebastian said. "Lay the blame where it's due. Where's your father and mother? They should be taking care of you."

"My mother and father aren't any of your business," she shouted.

"Don't raise your voice to me," he ordered, confused by the boy's hostile attitude.

33

"What seems to be the problem?" Lola asked from the doorway.

Sebastian smiled at the redhead who had entertained him on many occasions. "The lad's lack of good sense got him into trouble."

"I got plenty of good sense, Dragon," Vic said.

Lola watched Sebastian's features glow with fury. Nobody called him the Dragon to his face. He took a step toward the lad.

Lola, wanting to avoid trouble, stepped in front of him. "He's young and has a foolish tongue."

"He's also going to have a stinging backside," Sebastian said, grabbing Lola by the arms and gently pushing her to the side.

She clung to his arm. "Don't, Sebastian. The boy has enough problems."

Vic, realizing her error, picked up the bucket and scrub brush and ran to the kitchen. The Dragon's strange blue eyes followed her all the way down the hall.

"Who is he?" Sebastian asked, watching the small retreating figure slip behind the door.

Lola let go of his arm and shrugged her shoulders as if unconcerned by his question. "His name is Vic. I don't know where he lives, but I do know he works hard to provide for his ill sister."

"Tell Madam Champlain not to punish him. I don't wish to be the cause of him failing to provide for his ailing sister."

Lola was relieved. "That's decent of you."

Sebastian stood, smiled, and kissed her lightly on the cheek. "Have you ever know me to be decent without a reason?"

"What do you mean?"

"The lad fascinates me, although I don't know why. I intend to keep an eye on him."

"Whatever for?" Lola asked.

"I'm not sure," he said and walked to the front door.

Lola watched him leave. The door closed silently behind him. She wondered why a man of his status and wealth would concern himself with the likes of a defiant street urchin.

What was even more puzzling to Sebastian was that he was wondering the same thing.

A soft sigh escaped Beth's dry lips. Her hand made a valiant attempt to reach for the water glass on the table next to the bed. The slight effort proved too much. Her hand fell weakly against the rose-colored quilt.

"Beth, I've told you not to exert yourself," Victoria scolded. "Just tell me what you want and I'll get it for you."

"You do too much already."

Victoria picked up the water glass and slid her hand under Beth's head. "Don't talk nonsense."

She sipped the cool liquid. "You work so hard. All I do is lie in bed all day being more of a burden on you."

"I won't stand for this, Beth," Victoria scolded earnestly. "When you're feeling better it will be your turn to pamper me. Now, I insist you get some sleep. It's getting late."

Victoria tried to ignore the fact that her sister might never be healthy again. She shivered, hating the thought of losing Beth. She was all the family she had left.

Beth was too weak to argue. She slipped into a fretful slumber.

Vic finished putting the clean clothes away that she had washed and hung out to dry yesterday. She had hoped to mend the other trousers she owned tonight, but she had to go out. She hadn't planned on taking up the Serpent's identity again so soon, but Mrs. Kenny had to fetch the doctor quickly today for Beth. His visit had used up all the money. He would return tomorrow to check on her and there was no coin left to pay him.

She walked toward the door. Her shoulders drooped from the weight of the burden she carried.

"If only there were another way," she whispered, closing the door behind her.

The lonesome moan of the distant foghorn punctuated the heavy mist that swirled along the harbor. It brought a rare smile to the Serpent. Most people hated the fog, but to her it was a friend who appeared in time of need. And tonight she felt extra needy.

An uneasiness chilled her. The repeated blasts of the foghorn only added to her unusual nervousness. She had the uncanny feeling that someone was out there waiting for her. Her pragmatic senses told her to cease tonight's unlawful activity, but the need for money held her firm.

She moved along the quiet dock looking for a hiding place. She found a good spot between two boarding crates. She crouched down and began her wait.

The sound was so faint at first that Vic had to strain her ears to hear it, but it was there. She had just about given up, having spent the last three hours bent in a most uncomfortable position.

She moved slowly as the voice grew louder and more distinguishable. Her feet were the first to gather life back into them. Her legs soon followed. By the time the boisterous drunk was upon her hiding spot she had managed to regain the use of her stiffened limbs.

The fancy gent was wobbling from side to side obviously well saturated with liquor. His deep voice was raised in raucous song interrupted by spurts of laughter at his own amusing, singsong tale.

Vic scanned his form finding it difficult to measure the man up since he was constantly weaving and bending over with laughter. At least his black formal attire attested to his wealth.

Uncertainty caused her to pause a moment. Realizing that this was probably her last chance for the evening, she made her decision fast. She slipped from between the crates and crept silently up behind him. "Don't move."

The man froze. Then, with deliberate slowness, he straightened to his full size. He threw back his wide shoulders and raised his head. The girth and towering height of him made her suck in her breath, and a low rumble erupted in the pit of her stomach. She had no need to see the imposing man's face to know his identity. It was the Dragon.

"Do you know who I am?" Sebastian said. No trace of drunkenness was evident in his clear strong voice.

"Nope, and I don't care." Show no fear, she kept repeating silently, show no fear.

His large body stiffened in anger. He attempted to turn and face his assailant, but Vic moved fast, pressing the blade firmly against his thigh.

"Don't move," she warned again.

Sebastian took a deep breath and released it slowly. He required total control of his emotions to trap this elusive fellow. And capturing him was exactly what he intended to do.

"Give me ya purse and make it quick. I don't got all night."

"My pleasure," Sebastian murmured, feeling victory close at hand.

Vic didn't have time to think, only react as the heavy purse was tossed with great force back toward her head. Instinctively, her hand flew up to catch it while she moved the blade to leave her mark. But at that precise moment Sebastian attempted to turn, and the dagger's sharp edge sliced deep into the thick muscle of his thigh.

An animal-like growl started deep in his chest before spewing forth in an earth-shattering rumble. The thunderous roar filled the late night air, vibrating along the waterfront.

Vic didn't waste any time. She vacated the area with much haste.

Sebastian reached for his handkerchief and pressed it firmly against the bleeding wound. When his ears caught the sound of his assailant scurrying away, his anger gave way to rage. "I'll find you," he shouted into the heavy mist. "Do you hear me, Serpent? I'll find you if it takes me forever."

His vengeful screams continued to fill the night air. Vic pressed her small hands against her ears to muffle his awful threats as she moved along the otherwise quiet street. She stayed close to the buildings, slipping every now and then into an alley upon hearing the sound of fast-approaching footsteps. Her heart hammered in her chest and breathing was difficult.

She finally reached the edge of the waterfront. Making certain no one was about, she ran with lightning speed. Sweat trickled in her eyes and she wiped it away with her sleeve. Her eyes stung. Her chest felt tight, but still she ran.

Arriving at the boarding house, she flew up the steps and didn't stop to take a breath until she was safe behind her locked door. She wrapped her arms tightly around her nervous stomach and sank like a dead weight to the floor.

Time seemed suspended as her tears flowed freely. Finally gaining control of her taut emotions, she wiped her red swollen eyes. She noticed the early morning light peeking through the curtans of the solitary window. She remained seated on the floor while she fought to open the strings of the pouch she had been clinging to.

She tilted the heavy bag, spilling out the contents. Her heart caught in her throat as she released a pitiful moan. There on the floor in a heap lay a mixture of pebbles and stones.

"You're fired!"

"Fired?" Vic repeated, not sure she heard Madam Champlain correctly.

"That's right," the plump woman said, and popped another chocolate into her mouth.

"Why?"

"Because I hired someone who'll work cheaper."

"Is he Chinese?"

"Yup, them foreigners'll work for almost nothing."

Vic wanted to tell her that anyone would work for almost nothing when they're hungry and couldn't find a job, but the words would have been wasted on the greedy woman.

She walked out of the room. The smell of stale cigars and cheap perfume trailed her. What was she going to do? She had planned on asking Madam Champlain for an advance on her pay. The doctor was due to visit Beth today and there was no money. And he wasn't the generous kind.

"Vic."

She stopped and glanced into Lola's room. The buxom woman was resting against a mound of pink ruffled pillows. "You heard?" she asked.

Lola shook her head and patted the spot beside her. "What are you going to do?"

Vic sat down. "I don't know. After what happened last night, I can't go back on the street."

"I heard. The news is that the Dragon's furious. It took ten stitches to close the wound."

Vic winced. "I didn't mean to cut him so deep, but he shouldn't have moved."

Lola reached out and pushed back the sable brown curls falling across Vic's forehead. She ran her fingers along the side of her round face and cupped her chin in her hand. "You're young and untouched. Men would pay handsomely for the privilege of possessing you. And once caught in those wide, enchanting eyes of yours they'd be lost. You could demand anything and get it."

Vic pulled her head away and stood. "I can't do that."

Lola sighed, worried over the innocent girl's fate. "Then what, in heaven's name, will you do?"

Vic squared her shoulders and raised her chin. The idea had been in the back of her mind, nagging at her. She thought it ridiculous at first, but the more she considered it the more it made sense. "I'm going to ask the Dragon for a job."

"What?"

"You heard me."

"Are you crazy?"

"No. I need the money and what better place to hide than the Dragon's lair?"

Lola sat up and gave the strange idea thought. "You know, you may be right."

"Right or wrong I need a job," Vic said, and headed for the door.

"Vic, perhaps you should wait until tomorrow to approach him. He's probably still angry over last night. Besides, he most likely hurts like hell."

"Can't wait. Doc is due to see Beth today. Take care, Lola."

"You make sure you let me know how you are, alright?" Lola called as the waif disappeared out the door.

"You'll be hearing from me," Vic shouted back as she hurried down the stairs.

Vic sat at the end of the long bench. Her feet barely touched the floor. She was glad she had washed up before coming here. Of course, there was nothing she could do about the sorry state of her patched clothes, but at least she wasn't dirty. Her face shined, although

41

she could have done without the slight blush that covered her cheeks. Her hair was clean and hugged her face in soft curls. She even managed to get hold of a lemon and use the juice to rub on the back of her hands and neck so she'd smell fresh.

The three men sitting on the bench had frowned as she walked past and sat at the end, but the Dragon's secretary, Ben Shavers, had been kind to her. He had told her that Mr. Blood was extremely busy and that if she wished to wait he might be able to see her when he was finished with his appointments. Vic waited.

After a couple of hours she found herself feeling drowsy. She tried to fight it, but not having any sleep last night didn't help. She soon drifted off into a peaceful slumber.

"He's been waiting for the last three hours," Ben informed Sebastian as they both looked down at the lad. His small form was stretched out upon the bench and one arm hung to the floor.

"He's so thin," Ben said, "and hardly big enough to take care of himself, let alone work here."

Sebastian stared at the boy. His full lips were slightly parted and had a rosy glow that matched his cheeks. Dark lashes curled up along his closed eyes and his hair tickled the edges of his small ears. One trouser leg was bunched up displaying a skinny calf.

Sebastian shook his head. There were too many scrawny lads like him living along the waterfront. Hungry and homeless, deserted by parents, or worse, sent out by them to beg or steal. "Wake him, Ben."

Ben shook the boy gently. "Wake up, lad. Wake up."

Vic woke with a start, lost her balance, and rolled right off the bench to land on her hands and knees.

"You wanted to see me?" the strong voice commanded.

Vic knew instantly whose shoes her face was practically plastered against. She stood quickly, straightening herself. "Yes, Mr. Blood."

"Follow me," he ordered and turned abruptly.

Vic trailed behind him. Several of her footsteps matched one of his. He closed the door to his office and told her to take a seat.

The room was large. Actually, everything in the room appeared large to Vic, but then to one of the Dragon's size the furniture was appropriate.

"So you want a job?"

Vic sat straight. "Yes, sir. I'm a real good worker. Don't take no time off. I show up every day."

"Come here," Sebastian said and walked around to the front of the desk.

Vic obeyed. She stood before him, trying to hide her nervousness. She tilted her head slightly to peer up at him and was surprised to see a stern expression. Perhaps Lola was right; she should have waited.

"Hold out your arm."

With a bit of reluctance she did as he ordered.

He raised his right hand and squeezed her soft arm. She let out a small yelp.

"As I thought. No muscle," he said, returning to his chair behind the desk. "Tell me just what type of work could you possibly do for me when you don't have the strength of a kitten?"

"I could run errands."

"I have messengers."

43

"I could keep your office clean."

"I have cleaners."

Vic felt her only hope of making any money fading away. She was desperate. She held her chin high and spoke. "Mr. Blood, I got a real sick sister that needs lots of doctor's care and medicine. I lost my job at Madam Champlain's and I got no way of making money. The doc is due to see my sister today. If I don't have the money, he won't even look at her. I'll do any kind of work you have. I may not look strong, but I am."

Sebastian stared at the lad. His wide eyes looked close to crying and his bottom lip stuck out ever so slightly, quivering as he spoke.

"Where do you and your sister live?"

"At Mrs. Kenny's boarding house."

A thought came upon him quickly. Sebastian didn't understand why he was even considering it. He usually wasn't given to helping every poor soul whose path he crossed. Yet the lad seemed so pathetic that he, somehow, felt compelled to help him.

"I need someone to assist my housekeeper and driver with chores. Do you think you can handle that?"

"Yes sir, no problem. I can do whatever they want done," Vic answered with relief.

"You've got the job on one condition."

Vic stared at him.

"Being part of my staff requires you live at my home on Rincon Hill. Your wages include room and board. Since your sister is ill and requires medical attention, I will provide a larger room for you both. If you wish to take on extra chores, I'll make certain she receives good medical care."

Vic hadn't counted on living in the same house as the

44

Dragon, but the offer was too good to turn down. At least Beth would be safe and taken care of. She had to accept. "Agreed."

"Good. I'll send my driver Daniel to pick you and your sister up," he said and stood. "Gather your things and be ready around three."

Vic held out her hand. "Thanks."

Sebastian took it, feeling several calluses on the soft flesh. "No thanks necessary. Just do your job."

"I will. You can count on it." Vic smiled and walked out the door.

Chapter Four

"Remember, Beth, I'm your fifteen-year-old brother," Victoria warned, slipping her sister's thin arm around her shoulder and helping her to the only chair in the room.

Beth slumped back against the wooden spindles of the rickety seat. "How can we be certain this Mr. Blood will treat us fairly? Perhaps he's like Uncle Tobias." She shivered at the mention of her uncle's name.

"He's nothing like him. He's wealthy and handsome. And has a line of women waiting eagerly to please him. Believe me, he's not the type to do us harm." Vic didn't add her fear of him discovering her Serpent identity. Beth knew nothing of it and she wanted to keep it that way.

"Do you think Uncle Tobias is still searching for us?"

Victoria frowned as she folded the last of their clothing into the tapestry satchel. "He'll never stop searching. He's too greedy. He wants everything he can take from us, and there's no way in hell I'm going to allow him that pleasure."

"Victoria, really. Your language. What would Mama say?"

She knelt before Beth, grasping her fragile hands in hers. "Beth, Mama and Papa are gone. I'm the only one left to provide for us, and I intend to do just that—no matter what the cost."

A lone tear escaped the ill girl's weary eyes and slipped down her cheek. "I-I worry about you."

Victoria wiped away the tear. "There's no need to worry any longer. I'll be working for Mr. Blood."

Beth's thin lips barely had time to produce a small smile before she was seized by a fit of coughing. It took several minutes before the attack passed. She sighed heavily, fighting to control her labored breathing.

Victoria knelt in front of her, holding her hand. She squeezed it tightly as though her grasp would keep Beth safe. "Are you all right?"

Beth nodded.

Victoria stood. "I must hurry. Mr. Blood's driver will be here soon and I don't want to keep him waiting."

"Why do you think this man is being so charitable toward us?"

"Perhaps it's good for the Dragon's image."

"The Dragon?"

Victoria's hand flew to cover her open mouth, then dropped away swiftly before she spoke. "Beth, you must never call him by that name. Please promise me."

"I'll remember. Don't worry," she answered, concerned by the panic flooding her sister's widened eyes.

Victoria released a sigh of relief and picked up the satchel, placing it on the floor near the table.

A pounding knock vibrated the door. Beth and

Victoria glanced at one another and nodded their readiness.

Vic swung open the door expecting to see the black driver, Daniel. Instead the Dragon stood there. His large form filled the doorway. A slight smile tickled at the corner of his mouth as though he wasn't certain whether he should look pleased or stern. He seemed to make a fast decision, and his handsome features lit with a breathtaking smile.

"Are you ready?" he asked.

Vic found it difficult to speak. This was the first time she had really noticed his features. They were striking. They appeared sculpted by a master artist. His narrow nose, his fine lips, his strong jaw all were too perfect to have been formed any other way. Even his dark wavy hair that whispered along the back of his gray collar seemed tailored expressly for him.

Vic shook her head, realizing she had been standing there staring at him. "Ready. We're all ready."

"Good," he said and walked past her into the room.

Vic scurried around him to stand in front of Beth as if in protection.

Sebastian stopped where he was and watched as Beth peered around her sister to glance at him. She giggled.

Vic swung around and frowned at her.

"I'm sorry, Vic, but he's so big and you're so small. You could hardly stop him from doing as he pleased."

Sebastian laughed. "Your sister appears to be the more intelligent one of the family."

Vic ignored his remark and introduced Beth. "This is my sister Elizabeth Chambers." She made certain to use their assumed surname.

Sebastian's gallant bow brought a smile to Beth's pale face. "It's a pleasure to make your acquaintance, Miss Chambers."

"Thank you, Mr. Blood."

"Please, call me Sebastian."

"Sebastian," she repeated as if testing his name. "Everyone calls me Beth."

He nodded. "Beth."

She was suddenly seized by a fit of uncontrollable coughing. Vic moved instantly to her side.

Sebastian stooped down in front of her. He slipped his large hand over her fragile one offering her comfort. "I have a friend who is an excellent doctor. Perhaps you would allow him to examine you?"

Beth nodded her approval, too exhausted to speak.

"Good," he smiled, patting her hand, concerned with the look of fatigue that had overtaken her so quickly. "Now let's get you moved and settled."

Vic reached out to help her sister, but the Dragon's hand firmly grasped her small wrist. He was standing once again. He loomed over her like a menacing bird of prey.

"I'll see to your sister. You see to the baggage."

She tried pulling her hand free, but his grip was steadfast and strong. "I can take care of my own. I don't need your help."

Sebastian dragged the scrawny boy to the door. "Can you managed to carry her down those stairs, for she is certainly in no condition to walk."

Vic studied the steep stairway and then her sister. She faced the Dragon with a proud toss of her head. "You best be careful with her."

Sebastian smiled at the lad's boldness and loosened

his hold. "I won't let anything happen to her."

"I'll be watching you, to make sure."

"Don't you trust me?"

Vic had heard similar words before. Her uncle had assured her the day of her parents' funeral that Beth and she could trust him. She learned the truth quick enough. "I don't trust anyone."

Sebastian caught the note of disdain in the lad's voice. "There may come a day that you need to rely on another's trust."

"I got myself, that's enough."

"Perhaps, but if that day should ever come, I do hope you'll realize I can be trusted . . . with anything."

Vic could see by the intensity of his look that he didn't give of his trust lightly. And at that moment she was glad she was befriending the Dragon and not making an enemy of him. "I'll remember."

"Good, now get the baggage so we can get your sister settled as quickly and easily as possible."

Vic turned to do as he directed.

Sebastian walked over to Beth and stretched out his strong arms. "With your permission?"

She smiled her approval and was instantly snatched from the chair up into his powerful arms.

"Make certain you get everything, Vic," he called over his shoulder as he easily carried Beth out of the room.

Vic struggled with the two satchels and one box while muttering to herself. Her small booted feet were having a hard time judging the steps since she couldn't see over the bundles. The worn soles inched their way to the edge of each step then down to the next. It was a slow process, but she managed.

50

"Inch, inch, step down," she muttered repeatedly.

The howling screech tore right through her. "Oh, my sweet Beth, I'm going to miss you!" Mrs. Kenny cried out.

That did it. Vic lost her balance. Her feet went out from under her and the packages went flying through the air. She found herself tumbling down the whole flight of steps, coming to rest in a most undignified position at the Dragon's feet.

"Damn." She heard him mumble before she felt his hands grab her around the waist and hoist her up off the floor. He pulled undergarments off her head and stockings from the front of her shirt.

"Are you all right?" he asked, tugging a yellow ribbon from her hair.

Vic felt dazed and shook her head gently as though trying to clear away the fuzziness. "I-I think so."

Sebastian frowned. "I don't." He took Vic by the arm and sat him down on the steps. He then proceeded to feel her arms for broken bones.

Vic was so stunned from the fall she simply sat quiet while the Dragon's large hand roamed her thin arms. It wasn't until his fingers moved down to her ribs that she realized the danger.

"I'm fine," she yelled, pushing his hands away and jumping up. Her fast movement was a definite mistake. Her head spun, and she fell forward right into his arms.

Sebastian held the lad around the waist attempting to steady him. "My God, you're nothing but skin and bones. Don't you ever eat?"

Vic felt the sting of his words. She ate when she could, or when money allowed. Besides, she was a female and a small one at that. She panicked at the thought of him discovering her identity and pushed herself away, hoping to grab the banister for support. It didn't work. She missed it and toppled forward.

Sebastian grabbed the boy by the back of the shirt and spun him around, none too gently. "Sit down," he ordered.

Vic plopped down on the bottom step. She was afraid he would touch her again and the cloth she used to bind her breasts was coming loose. She didn't need him to discover that.

"Don't you watch where you're going?" he asked.

"My hands were full and the baggage isn't that light."

"Perhaps you aren't strong enough for the work I require of you."

Vic stood. "I'm strong enough. Don't worry about that."

Sebastian's hand reached out and grabbed Vic by the back of the head, holding it firm as he tilted it back and turned it slightly to the side. "That's a nasty bump you got," he said, touching the bruised and swollen lump over Vic's right eye.

Vic didn't move, not that she could. The Dragon's hold was too strong. But it wasn't that. It was the tenderness of his touch and his warm breath that tickled the tip of her ear that held her firm. She felt strange, a good kind of strange, and she wanted to cling to the odd feeling as long as she could.

"We'll have my friend Dr. Samuels check it tonight," he said and moved away. "I'll have Daniel take care of the bundles."

"No! No, I can do it," she said, bending down to gather the clothes. "I'm fine, just fine."

"Very well, but I'll have Daniel give you a hand," he

52

said, and walked to the carriage.

She shoved the clothes into the satchels with Daniel's help. She tripped twice over her own feet, falling once and barely catching herself another time, as she hurried to the carriage.

Rincon Hill sat south of the city. The area offered a generous view of San Francisco Bay and was far enough removed from downtown to avoid the noise of the boisterous city, yet close enough by carriage for the men to ride to their offices.

Vic had heard talk of the beauty of the stately houses, but never had the opportunity to frequent the area. She wasn't prepared for the elegance of the homes that passed by the carriage window. She was awed by their manicured appearance and shocked that she was actually going to reside in one.

The shiny black carriage turned into a circular driveway and halted in front of one of the larger, more impressive homes. The three-story structure was bathed in the late afternoon sun which cast a soft glow across it. The deep blue of the house was accented by stark white shutters embracing numerous windows. A wide stone walk marked the way to the veranda that disappeared around the sides with wild red roses clinging tenaciously to it. It was a home that stated its wealth in elegant silence, and Vic found herself impressed by the Dragon's lair.

"See to the baggage, Vic, while I help Beth," Sebastian ordered.

Vic looked to her sister and seeing that Beth was comfortable with the Dragon helping her, she did as she was told.

She hurried to take the satchels from Daniel, feeling uneasy by the odd way he stared at her. She was about to lift the box into her already overburdened hands when Daniel placed his hand on her arm stopping her.

"I'll carry that, son."

"Thanks, but I can make it."

Daniel shook his head. The thin lines fanning the corners of his eyes deepened as he squinted several times before he spoke. "No, you can't. I don't know what's going on here, but I've taken care of Mr. Blood's horses for the last ten years. And I always mind my own business, no matter how crazy things may seem."

Vic widened her eyes and stared incredulously at the rambling man. Did he know she was a female, and if so, how?

"Come on, son, Mr. Blood is waiting, and I have a feeling that for your own safety you should stay on his good side."

Vic followed Daniel into the house like a lost puppy having found someone to console her. She couldn't understand why she felt safe with this man, but she did.

"Akiko," Sebastian called, standing in the entrance hall and continuing to cradle Beth in his arms.

Daniel left the box next to Vic and nodded at her before leaving. A faint smile touched her lips in silent thanks just as her eyes focused on the Oriental woman walking toward Sebastian. She wore a pale peach silk kimono and bowed her head submissively as she stopped before the Dragon. When she raised her head her dark almond-shaped eyes held a hint of sensitivity. Vic relaxed instantly, knowing this gracious woman posed no threat to her.

54

"Akiko, this lovely girl in my arms is Beth Chambers. The scrawny lad behind me is her brother Vic."

Vic couldn't help but childishly stick out her tongue at him. Akiko smiled at his small show of defiance.

Beth became nervous that her sister would make matters worse with her boldness and sought to distract the Dragon. "Your home is elegant."

Vic heard her remark and had to agree. She had often heard rumors that the Dragon was one of the richest men in the city, and now she could believe the tall tales.

The large house bespoke of wealth, yet stated it quietly. A marble-topped table was the main focus of the entrance hall. Its cabriole legs defined its rich elegance. A crystal hurricane vase with an array of freshly cut flowers sat in the center, adding to the subtle beauty of the room. White marble tiles gleamed from the rays of the setting sun filtering in through the diamond pane windows of the front door, and the highly oiled teakwood walls were accented with several Japanese paintings.

Vic turned her head hastily surveying the rooms to the left and right. She caught a quick glimpse of a large parlor and a formal dining room, but the most impressive sight was the wide oval window in the wall of the center landing that divided the staircase to the left and right. Vic was certain it provided the viewer with a magnificent sight of the San Francisco Bay.

Sebastian finished issuing orders to Akiko and walked toward the steps. "Akiko is in charge of my home. Whatever chores she gives you, you will do."

He continued up the steps, stopping halfway up. He

turned and looked directly at Vic. "Do you have any problem with that?"

"Nah. Why should I? If you say she's the boss, that's good enough for me."

Sebastian was glad to hear that the lad was not prejudiced against Orientals. God knew there was enough of that going around, but he refused to tolerate that narrow-minded attitude in his home. "While I make certain your sister is settled, Akiko will show you where you can bathe, then you may join us."

"Look, Blood," Vic snapped. He could order her in what chores to do and she'd obey, but she wasn't about to let him take the care of her sister out of her hands.

"What did you say?" Sebastian asked in a deadly calm tone.

"You heard me," she continued, dropping the satchels and walking up to stand beside him. "I've been tending to my sister for a long time. I don't want anyone else doing it for me. After I get done taking care of her, I'll take a bath. But I care for my sister, understand?"

Vic followed Sebastian's murderous glance to her finger which she hadn't realized had been poking him in the arm the whole time she had been speaking. She hastily pulled it away, tucking it behind her back.

"I admire your devotion to your sister and I won't stand in your way of caring for her, but *never* make the mistake of calling me Blood again and *never* poke me."

Vic swallowed the lump of fear that had lodged in her throat and nodded her head several times in reply.

"I'm glad we understand each other," Sebastian said and turned to continue up the stairs. "Get the bags and follow me."

Vic did as she was told, flying up the steps as fast as the baggage would allow. She halted in front of the room she had seen Sebastian enter.

"This is beautiful," Beth said as he placed her on the fourposter bed.

Vic glanced around the room. It was beautiful, but it certainly wasn't a servant's room. "I thought the staff lived downstairs."

Sebastian helped Beth off with her blue cape, placing it on the ebonized maple chair near the window. "Normally they do, but I felt your sister would be more comfortable up here. Your room is off this one, not as large, but adequate for your needs."

Vic watched her sister's face light with a smile as she took in the whole room. The walls were papered with a pattern of tiny pale roses and a deeper rose color highlighted the bedspread and heavy drapes. An Oriental rug in an intricate design of soft greens and creamy beige circled the polished floor. Across from the bed was a fireplace trimmed in marble tiles and set off by a mahogany mantel which held an array of various ceramic birds.

"Thank you so much, Sebastian. It's so lovely," Beth said.

"I'm glad it pleases you, but there's no need to thank me since your brother pomised he'd work hard, earning your right to be here."

"You bet, I'll work hard," Vic boasted. "I'm not afraid of hard work. I'll earn our keep."

"I have no doubt you will," Sebastian said with a smile.

Vic eyed the Dragon skeptically. She couldn't allow herself to trust him, not yet. Especially when she looked into those midnight blue eyes of his. They were so intense. It was almost as though he could see right through a person. She unconsciously rubbed at the cloth that bound her breasts, fearing he could see it as well as her true gender.

"Shall I have a bath prepared for the young lady?" Akiko asked.

Vic looked at her in alarm before realizing she was speaking about Beth. She hastily dropped her glance to the floor hoping the woman hadn't caught her blunder. "If you could just tell me where I could fetch a basin of hot water, I can see to Beth myself."

Akiko tilted her head slowly from side to side as though in confusion. "The requested items will be brought to you."

Sebastian walked over to the bed and slipped Beth's frail hand in his. He kissed it gently. "It has been a pleasure meeting you, and I look forward to becoming better acquainted. I'll have your meal sent up and see you later when my friend Dr. Samuels arrives."

Beth smiled her appreciation.

"Vic, a moment of your time," he said, holding the door open for the lad to join him in the hallway.

Vic followed reluctantly.

"You'll make certain you take a bath, after which I wish to see you in my study."

"Fine with me," she said and watched him walk down the hall. His sleek strides were filled with sheer power, from his muscular legs to the width of his broad shoulders that warned one of his brute strength. She recalled the numerous seamen on the waterfront who frequently removed their sweat-soaked shirts as they worked. Their arms and chests were a mass of taut muscles, although a few had thickening waists from their constant consumption of ale.

She fantasized, for one brief moment, the Dragon stripped naked to his waist. He lifted heavy crates. The sweat glistened off his sinewy muscles. No fat marred his strong frame. His belly was flat and lean and tempting to a woman's eye.

Vic shook her head, scattering the disturbing thoughts. She turned to enter her sister's room when a vision of the Dragon half-naked rose up before her. His dark eyes glared at her. His mouth wore that strange smile and his large hands reached down toward her. She let out a yell and ran into the room, slamming the door behind her.

Chapter Five

Akiko returned as Vic was adjusting the covers around Beth who had drifted into a restful slumber.

"May I prepare your bath now?" she asked.

Vic absently tugged at the oversized shirt she wore. "Will I have privacy when I bathe?"

"If you wish."

Vic glanced at her sister. She slept soundly. The blue ribbon she had tied in her brown hair earlier was still in place. Beth had insisted she leave it there so when the doctor came she would look presentable.

"Will the doc be here soon?" she asked, wanting to be there when he examined her.

"He will arrive within the hour."

Plenty of time, she thought. "I just have to get clean clothes." She knelt in front of the bed where her satchel sat and pulled out a tan patched shirt and brown trousers. She didn't allow Akiko to see her sneak in a clean white strip of cloth that would bind her tender breasts.

Akiko studied her movements and shook her head gently.

Vic willingly followed her down the steps and to the rear of the house into a large kitchen. Two young Oriental girls were busy cleaning the already sparkling room. They smiled at her as she entered.

Vic returned their friendly greeting and continued to follow Akiko until she stopped inside a large room that held an enormous wooden tub. It was an odd room.

Across the wall where she had entered, on each side of the door, was a row of pegs. One row held thick, sturdy pegs with wooden buckets hanging from them. The row on the other side of the door held thinner pegs presumably for clothes. Off to the left, opposite the large round tub, was an area with raised wooden slats almost like a separate section of the floor. On the slats were two low stools and a place where buckets sat filled with steaming water.

Akiko satisfied her curiosity by explaining the room was fashioned after the bathing rooms of Japan. The bather sat on the stool and washed then rinsed himself with the water from the buckets before climbing into the huge tub to relax.

Vic eyed the woman with uncertainty. She couldn't very well undress in front of her, yet the whole idea of bathing in such a strange fashion sounded too inviting to pass up. "No one will disturb me?" she asked, clinging tenaciously to her bundle of clothes as well as her identity.

"I will make certain no one enters, but," Akiko added, quickly, "I cannot keep Sebastian-san from entering if he wishes."

"Is he busy?" Vic asked, longing to soak in the steaming water.

"He is attending to a business matter in his study."

"I'll make sure I hurry."

Vic hastily stripped as soon as Akiko closed the door. She unwrapped the cloth that had bound her full breasts, breathing a sigh of relief. Her fingers gently brushed across her irritated nipples. She squinted her eyes with their tenderness. She hoped the warm water would help soothe their raw condition.

She generously lathered the sponge with the bar of softly scented soap. It was a light, sweet aroma almost like that of a rose about to blossom into maturity. She scrubbed hard, removing the fine dust of dirt that covered her. She ran the sponge over her narrow hips and across her flat stomach. She paused, her hand pressed flat over her belly. She wondered if she would ever marry and bear her husband children. She shuddered recalling her uncle's disgusting touch. But that was different. Perhaps with a man she loved it would be a pleasant experience. He would be kind and caring, guiding her into womanhood gently. Dreams, she thought, that's all they are, or ever will be.

She poured the warm water from the bucket over herself, making certain she rinsed thoroughly. She shivered as she hurried up the three steps to enter the steaming water. Her feet touched the smooth bottom. She submerged herself completely before standing and leaning back against the side. The water rested just above her rosy nipples. She felt the aches and pains of her sore joints ease away.

"Akiko, I want to speak to him. Now move," came the impatient voice of the Dragon.

Vic was stunned. The closed door was the only thing separating him from her and her nakedness. There was no time to climb out and dress. She was certain he'd pounce in the room any second. She ducked lower under the protection of the water as the door flew open, slamming solidly against the wall.

"Why do you need privacy?" Sebastian demanded, marching into the room.

Vic didn't know what to say. What possible reason could she have for wanting to bathe alone? If she learned one thing while working on the waterfront it was that men didn't care who saw them naked.

"Well, has the water plugged up your ears, or are you going to answer me?"

She thought fast. "I-I-I have this scar I don't like anybody seeing."

"From a fight?"

"Yup, from a fight. And I won," she quickly added, feeling she might as well make herself appear a brave lad instead of a coward.

Sebastian stepped forward. "Then you should be proud of it and not ashamed to let anyone see it."

"It's ugly," she said, squishing up her face in disgust.

"That doesn't matter. Where is it? Let me see."

"No! No!" she screamed as he took several steps toward her. "It's much, much too ugly. If you had one like it, you wouldn't want anyone to see it."

"But I have a scar too."

Vic stiffened and felt her stomach muscles tighten.

"And it is ugly. As a matter of fact, it's still healing. And unlike you, I'm sorry to say, I didn't win the fight."

No, he hadn't. She had, the Serpent. "Well, you can't always win. Someone has to lose."

His eyes darkened, if that were possible, and his expression grew serious, deadly serious. "I always win, Vic. The fool who cut me will find that out

63

soon enough."

Vic couldn't speak at all. The lump of fear in her throat prevented it.

"Now, show me this scar and tell me the story behind it," he said, stepping closer.

Two more steps. Two more steps and he'd be close enough to see her breasts.

"Sebastian-san," Akiko said, halting him. "Samuels-san is here and is most anxious to speak with you."

"Thank you, Akiko. Tell him I'll be right there," he answered and turned his attention back to Vic. "Our story telling will have to wait until another time. You better hurry and dress. The doctor will be seeing to your sister directly."

Vic shook her head in agreement and was still shaking it after the Dragon had left the room. It took a few minutes to calm herself down. Then realizing Beth would want her there, she dressed quickly and flew up the stairs. She came to an abrupt halt inside the bedroom. The two men looked up in surprise at her brusque entrance.

"Aaron, may I introduce Beth's brother, Vic."

Vic felt more secure clothed and walked over to the doctor, her hand extended. "Glad to meet you, Doc. Mr. Blood tells me you're a real good doctor. I really appreciate you seeing my sister."

"I'm only too glad to have your charming sister as my patient, Vic," Aaron said, shaking the boy's hand rigorously.

"Dr. Samuels was about to begin his examination. I suggest you and I wait downstairs," Sebastian said, taking Vic by the arm and directing her toward the door.

"Vic," came the pleading voice from the bed.

All eyes turned to the ill girl.

"I'm sorry, Sebastian," Beth said, "but I fear examinations and would prefer my brother present."

"As you wish, Beth," he said, releasing Vic and leaving the room.

Twenty minutes later, Vic and Dr. Samuels left Beth resting comfortably while they joined Sebastian downstairs in his study.

"Take a seat, I'll only be a minute," Sebastian said, pointing to a group of chairs in front of the mahogany-trimmed fireplace. He was seated behind a large rosewood desk writing in a ledger.

Vic took a seat in a leather wing-backed chair. She felt lost in its size since her feet were unable to touch the crimson and beige Persian carpet covering the floor.

Aaron poured himself a liberal portion of brandy from the decanter on the desk before taking a seat opposite Vic.

Sebastian soon joined them sitting in the chair next to Vic. "Well, Aaron, I'm sure the lad is anxious to hear about Beth."

Aaron swallowed another generous gulp before speaking. "Beth is very ill."

Vic nodded. She didn't need a doctor to tell her that.

"I wish there was something I could do for her."

Vic felt a flutter in her stomach and her heart began to pound. It was like the feeling she experienced the day she learned of her parents' death and it frightened her. "Isn't there medicine that'll help her?"

Aaron shook his head. "The medicine can only do so much."

"What are you saying, Doc?" she asked, fearing

65

his answer.

Aaron looked to Sebastian, who nodded, as though encouraging him to go on. "Vic, I'm afraid Beth's condition is far beyond my help."

"What d'you mean? Tell me!" she demanded.

"Beth only has two, perhaps, three months left."

Vic sprang out of the chair. Her breath locked in her throat. She gasped for air, but none would come. Her chest tightened in pain. She couldn't lose Beth, she just couldn't. She struggled to breathe, but still no air filled her lungs.

"Vic! Vic!" The voice shouted her name over and over. Powerful hands gripped her small ones pulling them away from her throat. A glass was forced between her lips and she swallowed the burning liquid. It did the trick. She was coughing and breathing in seconds.

Tears streamed down her cheeks. "Beth," she murmured.

Sebastian took a deep breath. He felt awful for the boy. Even though he had just met him, he could tell the lad and his sister were close, very close. He placed his hand on Vic's shoulder, offering what support he could. "I'm sorry."

"I never-never expected this," she sobbed, always fearing her sister would not get well, but never thinking she would die.

"I wish I could offer you more hope," Aaron said.

Vic lifted her head proudly. Her pint-sized frame stood ramrod straight. "Thanks, Doc, for being so honest. Now if you don't mind I'd kind of like to be alone."

She walked slowly to the door. She grasped the brass doorknob, but hesitated a moment before turning and directing her remark to the Dragon. "I'll do any work you give me. I'll work my fingers to the bone if you just let me spend extra time with my sister."

Sebastian curled his hands into tight fists as they lay draped over the arms of the chair. He agonized over the boy's plight and the courage it took him to request a favor. "You may take as much time as you like, Vic."

"I don't want any special treatment," she snapped, her pride evident in the proud toss of her head.

Sebastian admired his courage. "I'll make certain Akiko assigns you chores that will enable you to see your sister often."

Vic continued to hold her head high. "Thanks," she said and left the room.

Sebastian uncurled his fingers and released a frustrated sigh.

"I understand how you feel, Sebastian," Aaron offered, pouring another, much-needed drink. "The lad has pride. It's difficult not to envy his determination even if it does get in his way at times."

Sebastian couldn't help but smile at the truth to his words. "He's full of pride all right, and stubborn as a mule."

"Sounds like someone I know."

"Are you insinuating that I'm stubborn?" Sebastian asked with a slight grin and a raised brow.

"Stubborn and prideful. So you should get along with the boy famously. Of course, that is, unless your similar natures clash."

Sebastian's expression suddenly grew serious. "There's nothing that can be done to save Beth?"

"I'm afraid not. She has consumption and it's in the advanced stage."

67

Sebastian felt regret for the loss of one so young and innocent. The one thing he could do for Beth was make certain her brother fared well after her passing. "Then do all you can to make her comfortable. In the meantime, perhaps you can help me fatten the lad up and make a strong man out of him. He's such a puny runt for his age."

Aaron nodded in agreement.

Neither man realized the impossibility of the task before him.

Chapter Six

"Victoria, I'm so glad you're working for Sebastian," Beth said, sitting up in her bed and supported by numerous mounds of embroidered pillows.

Victoria agreed with a halfhearted smile as she placed their breakfast plates on the silver serving tray to take down to Akiko. They had been residing with the Dragon for two weeks, and while Victoria admitted Beth benefited from the move, she felt otherwise.

Sebastian was always ordering her to eat more at meal time and constantly correcting her speech. It was downright frustrating.

She tried to stay out of his way, but he continually stalked her. She did make certain he wasn't home when she bathed, fearing a recurrence of their earlier confrontation in the tub.

He was true to his word though. Akiko had provided her with many chores centering around the second floor. She would often stop in to visit her sister, not that she needed the company. Dr. Samuels was there at least every other day and Akiko made numerous trips to her room as well as Sebastian. Many times Vic backed out of the room not wanting to disturb the rich deepness of the Dragon's voice as he read from a book to Beth.

The only job she could have done without was the two-day-a-week duty in the carriage house. She was instructed to help Daniel. Even though the man tried to find chores that were easy for her, Sebastian always managed to show up demanding that the lad be given strenuous work to help develop his muscles. Daniel never opposed his boss, but after he left Vic would find the black man mumbling to himself until he finally ordered her to rest while he completed the task.

"I have carriage house work this morning, Beth, so I won't see you until later today."

"All right, Vic. I'm awfully tired anyway," she sighed and closed her eyes to sleep.

Vic carried the full tray down to the kitchen and managed to sneak out of the house without running into the Dragon. In a few minutes he would be leaving for his office and she wouldn't need to worry about his unnerving presence.

She made her way around back to the carriage house. The building housed two carriages as well as prized horses. Everything was well maintained. Daniel saw to that as Vic had quickly learned. She also discovered he had been in Mr. Blood's employment ever since the Dragon had prevented him from being shanghaied. She had tried without success to find out more of the tale, but Daniel was adamant about supplying her with further detail.

"Not for your tender ears," was all he would say.

She laughed to herself. She knew that he knew she was a woman, yet neither would openly admit it. It was a strange relationship they had formed, but she cherished it.

Daniel was waiting for her as usual. "The back stalls need cleaning today," he instructed, handing her a pitchfork.

"Fine with me," she grinned.

"Don't you ever complain?" he asked.

"Won't do me any good, so there's no point in wasting time crying about it."

Daniel laughed and shook his head.

"Vic!" came the echoing shout of the Dragon.

Vic grimaced. She thought she had successfully avoided him.

Sebastian entered the stable with a package wrapped in brown paper tucked beneath his arm. "You'll be coming with me to the office today. I need you to run some errands. I took the liberty of buying you some decent clothes." He handed the parcel to her. "Put these on now so we can leave. I'm already late for my appointment."

Vic took the package from him and opened it. She took out a pair of black trousers, a white cotton shirt, and a black jacket. The size of the garments was small. They would fit her perfectly—too perfectly. She was certain once she slipped into them there would be no mistaking her gender.

"I won't wear them," she said, holding them out to him.

Sebastian was prepared for the boy's refusal, having become familiar with his damnable pride. "They're not

71

a gift. You can pay me back out of your wages."

"I can't afford them. I need to save my money."

"These aren't expensive, and you can't continue to look like a ragamuffin."

Vic's hand involuntarily rubbed at the patched and worn garments she wore. She didn't need reminding of her sad state of attire. It was bad enough having to dress like a boy, but it was far worse wearing such pathetic clothes.

Sebastian silently cursed himself for his insensitive remark. He saw the look of utter despair cross the boy's face and wished he had held his sharp tongue. "Take the clothes, Vic."

Vic knew there was no possible way she could accept them and, besides, she needed all the money she could save.

"I need my money to bury my sister. I won't see her in a pauper's grave. She'll have a Christian burial."

The bitter taste of defeat was not to Sebastian's liking, though he had no choice but to accept it. Even if he offered to pay for the girl's interment, Vic would never agree. "As you wish."

"Do you still want me to go with you to the office?"

"Of course I do," he snapped, irritated by the boy's assumption that he was ashamed to be seen with him.

Vic shrugged her shoulders and followed him to the front of the house where Daniel had driven the carriage. She approached the front to climb up by the smiling black man.

"You'll be riding inside with me today," Sebastian announced, holding the door open for him.

Vic mumbled beneath her breath and Daniel chuckled.

"Did you say something?" Sebastian asked, climbing in behind him.

"Nah, I didn't say anything," she answered, knowing any other reply would be futile. She slid over to the corner opposite the Dragon, purposely straining her neck out the window and making a display of watching the sights so she needn't converse with him.

Sebastian relaxed against the tufted cushion bending his knee and bracing his boot not far from the boy. He studied him with a keen eye. The lad was a sly one. Sebastian had tried since the pair's arrival to discover any shred of information pertaining to their past or other family members. Neither brother nor sister would speak of their family. They always managed to conveniently avoid the subject. No matter though, his investigators were looking into it and would provide him with information shortly.

The carriage stopped. Vic hastily jumped down, holding the door open for Sebastian. He no sooner stepped down than a high squealing female voice called out his name.

"Sebastian, darling, you've been a naughty boy," a blond woman of fair height scolded. She walked briskly toward him and slipped her arm possessively around his.

"Lydia, you look lovely as usual," he said, patting her hand and making her blush with that devouring smile of his.

"Sebastian," she sighed, stroking her fingers slowly along his coat sleeve.

73

Vic was sure she'd be violently ill. The stuffed peacock before her was making an utter fool of herself. All those blue feathers and ornate jewels made her look ridiculous.

Lydia smiled while toying with the buttons of Sebastian's vest. "We haven't had an intimate supper for two lately, darling, and I do so miss your splendid dessert."

Sebastian released a faint chuckle. Lydia enjoyed the art of sex, as she referred to it; nothing was out of her realm of pleasure. And he didn't need to worry about her demanding marriage. Her father had bought her a titled husband. A recent fad of the wealthy. They were to be married in an elaborate affair in September.

"I've learned a few new tricks, darling, and I'm desperate to try them out on someone who isn't a prude."

"I don't need convincing, Lydia. And if you don't cease rubbing against me, I will drag you to your father's storeroom, lock the door, and fill you with myself . . . and not merely just once."

Lydia laughed with delight and squeezed his arm. "I love your naughtiness and if Father wasn't expecting you, I'd insist you carry out your threat."

"Sebastian," Howard Hodgeson called, walking in short rapid strides toward the laughing couple.

"Thursday evening, eight o'clock. Daniel will pick you up . . . and don't keep me waiting," he whispered before accepting the outstretched hand of her father.

Vic made her way to the corner of the building and leaned against it, sending invisible daggers toward the

74

Dragon's heart. "Why, he's no better than a tomcat," she mumbled, kicking a stone with her booted foot and sending it flying.

"Vic," Sebastian called, "don't wander off."

"Got yourself a street urchin to help you?" Howard asked, directing the influential man into his building, while his daughter clung possessively to his arm.

Vic glared in anger at the older man as he disappeared inside. "Hope your daughter looks exactly like you when she gets older," Vic said, "full of gray hair, a mustache, and a pot belly."

She caught the twitch of laughter that touched Daniel's lips after she spoke. He smiled as he passed her, walking into the warehouse with a few of the men he had become acquainted with on other visits.

She frowned at being deserted and deliberately stomped off to visit her own waterfront friends. Her hasty departure proved a soothing relief to her frustration. She talked with several friends, filling them in on Beth's condition and finished her excursion at Louie's.

Louie was a rough seaman who had abandoned the seas to run an eating establishment near the docks. It wasn't a place frequented by society, but Vic was safe there since Louie was her friend and also the first person who had agreed to hire her upon her arrival in San Francisco. He had taught her how to clean the fresh-caught fish and had often provided her with much-needed food.

Vic felt renewed after visiting her old haunts. She happily munched on the delicious fish Louie had wrapped in newspaper and insisted she take to eat, scolding once again that "you're too thin."

She hastened her steps after realizing how long she had been gone and hoped that Sebastian hadn't finished his meeting with Mr. Hodgeson just yet. She muttered to herself how highly improbable that was since the peacock more than likely still had her claws in him. Why the thought disturbed her, she couldn't say, but it did.

A quick sigh of relief escaped her lips as she rounded the corner and saw the carriage still waiting with no sign of Sebastian or Daniel in sight.

She leaned against the same corner of the Hodgeson Warehouse as before and looked as though she had never budged from her spot. The fish she continued to eat was the only evidence of her departure.

Her ears picked up the sound of scurrying feet before her eyes spotted the small urchin that was fast approaching. He rooted himself in front of her, staring at each morsel of flaky white meat Vic popped into her mouth.

His face was smudged with dirt, and his eyes held a faraway vacant look. Vic couldn't swallow another bite. She remembered that expression all too well. It was one of ravenous hunger. She had experienced it many times herself. The gnawing pain, the dry mouth almost tasting the food one smelled, yet couldn't afford to buy.

She handed the remainder of the fish to the young boy. He grabbed it, shoveling the food into his grimy mouth as though he hadn't eaten in days, which Vic was almost certain he hadn't.

She watched his pitiful actions and shivered. It was

as though he were her mirror image. The tattered clothes, the smudged face, they brought back all her anguish and fear. Tears swelled, blurring her vision, but she quickly wiped them away upon hearing the fast approach of heavy footsteps.

A large man came barreling around the side of the warehouse. His extra weight caused him to huff and puff from exertion and his cheeks to flame. "You little beggars get away from here. I don't want you bothering decent folk."

The young boy scurried away like a frightened animal, but Vic didn't move.

"I told you to get," the man said, raising his hand in warning.

"No!" Vic shouted, angry at the man's lack of compassion toward a hungry child.

"You get, boy, or I'll give you a good wuppin'."

Vic stood firm even though the man stepped toward her. "I'm not going anywhere."

The man's entire face grew bright red and he snorted several times. "Get!" he screamed and reached out giving Vic a hard shove.

She fell on her backside in the dry dirt. Quickly she scrambled to her feet and brushed at her pants. The smug grin on his face was what did it. It caused her to lose her temper. She charged at him like a raging bull, head bent and aimed for his protruding gut. She hit her target. He spewed out a burst of air.

The commotion began to draw a crowd, but Vic paid no heed. Her anger at the injustice to the small boy, and her own sorry state of affairs was too much for her to endure.

The large man glanced quickly about and saw that he was being made to look like a fool, and by a little beggar. He raised his hand and landed a swift and striking blow to the side of Vic's mouth.

Vic went sprawling backward, again landing in a cloud of dirt. Blood trickled from her split lip and her head spun from the unexpected blow.

The man wasn't finished with the arrogant lad who had made such a fool of him in front of so many people. He held his aching gut with one hand and picked up a heavy board with the other, swinging it as he approached the boy.

"I'll teach you to attack your betters!" he shouted for the benefit of the anxious crowd, raising the stick to deliver a sound thrashing.

"I wouldn't do that if I were you." The warning was issued in such a deadly calm tone that it made even Vic's blood run cold.

An instant hush settled over the gathered crowd and all eyes turned to stare at the Dragon. His powerful body stood rigid and his midnight blue eyes glowed with suppressed anger.

"Mr. Blood," the man said, trying to smile, but he was shaking too had to produce a grin. "I didn't know the lad belonged to you."

"Do you often attack the street urchins?" Sebastian asked, walking over to Vic and extending his hand to help him up. Once Vic was on his feet Sebastian took hold of his chin, tilting it back to study the damage done. His eyes narrowed dangerously. His lips locked in anger as he caught sight of the blood trickling in a steady stream from the lad's split lip.

"Are you all right?" Sebastian asked in a tightly controlled voice. His fury was rapidly mounting, and he was doing his best to keep a firm hand on it.

Vic could only shake her head in response. She had never seen such a murderous glare in his eye before and it frightened her.

He took a clean white handkerchief from his breast pocket and pressed it against the boy's bleeding lip.

"Ouch," Vic yelped.

"Damn," Sebastian added. With a more gentle touch he wiped the blood away.

Vic's eyes widened into misty pools.

Sebastian roughly grabbed his chin and spoke in a harsh whisper. "Don't ever let your adversary see you cry."

Vic wiped her eyes with her sleeve, and matched his murderous glare with one of her own.

"That's better," he said and turned to face the man who had dared to harm the lad.

"Honest, Mr. Blood, if I had known the boy was with you I would never have touched him," he pleaded.

"An honest mistake, Sebastian. You can't fault Casey for that," Howard Hodgeson added, not wanting one of his best workers hurt.

Sebastian impaled the two men with such a threatening glare that Howard turned pure white and Casey shivered.

"He," Sebastian said, pointing to Vic, "belongs to me."

A thick silence hung in the air. The crowd focused their attention on the Dragon and waited . . . expectantly.

79

The movement was so quick it couldn't be seen. If Vic hadn't been there to witness it with her own eyes she never would have believed it happened. Sebastian's hand slashed out so fast striking Casey that even he was shocked by the amount of blood that ran onto the fat man's shirt from the wide gash the Dragon's swift blow delivered.

"No one touches what is mine," he emphasized.

The crowd mumbled in hushed whispers, their terror-filled eyes planted firmly on the Dragon.

"Daniel," he called and the black man hurried to open the door to the carriage. Sebastian grasped Vic by the arm and propelled her toward the waiting vehicle. The crowd hastily parted, clearing an ample path for the feared man.

Sebastian helped Vic inside, practically hoisting him in in one swift motion. He slammed the door and ordered Daniel to drive home.

The startled crowd was left murmuring in frightened whispers of the Dragon's barbaric abilities.

Vic was relieved when they returned to the house, although she still feared repercussions from the incident, especially since Sebastian hadn't spoken one word after entering the carriage. He just sat there staring at her with an alarming glare that made her shiver.

"Akiko, hot water and a clean cloth," he demanded upon entering the foyer. He reached for Vic grabbing his arm and forcibly dragged him into the study.

He pushed the startled boy into the large leather chair and ran his fingers through his dark hair before pushing his waistcoat back and bracing his hands on

80

his hips. "Care to tell me about it?"

"Nope," was her only reply.

His thick brows arched in annoyance. "No . . . no? You become embroiled in a common street fight with a man five times your size and you have the audacity to refuse to tell me why?"

"Yup."

Sebastian moved across the room in a flash until he was standing in front of the boy. He leaned over, bracing his large hands on each arm of the chair and brought his face close enough for their noses to touch. "Let me rephrase myself. I'm not requesting the information, I'm demanding it."

Her brilliant green eyes were riveted to his midnight blue ones. "I'm not going to tell you."

The muscles in Sebastian's face tightened. He gripped the arms of the chair turning his knuckles an angry white. What was the matter with the little fool? He could have been seriously hurt or, worse, killed, yet here he sat defying him in all his glory. The boy had gall.

"It isn't going to do you any good to try an' scare me, 'cause I'm not going to tell you," she adamantly informed him while forcing her churning stomach to keep its contents.

The Dragon emitted a low growl before pulling away. He addressed Akiko in a clipped tone when she entered. "See to his face and make him soak in a hot tub."

He stormed toward the door speaking in a tongue that Vic didn't understand, although it brought a smile to Akiko's face.

81

Sebastian abruptly stopped at the door and turned. "Vic."

She looked up at him and wisely held her tongue.

He continued. "Someday I'm going to give you what you so richly deserve, and I intend to enjoy every blow I deliver to your backside."

Vic opened her mouth to retaliate.

"Say it, Vic. Say it and give me just the excuse I need," he demanded, his threatening glare promising immediate repercussions.

She clamped her mouth shut, folded her arms across her chest, and stuck up her chin in defiance.

He released a groaning yell. "Someday, Vic. By God, someday." And with that he stormed out of the house, his departure evident by the echoing slam of the front door.

"Come, I'll see to your needs in the kitchen," Akiko instructed. Vic followed willingly.

Vic felt more at ease having the Japanese woman tend her and she relaxed under her gentle ministrations.

Akiko repeatedly cleansed the cut with warm water while speaking. "It is not wise to defy the Dragon."

Vic was startled by her reference to Sebastian's infamous nickname. She listened intently as the woman continued.

"He is a strong and influential man and also a fair one. He would help you with any problem."

"Somehow I doubt that," she answered. The memory of the night she had slashed his thigh was still vivid in her mind.

"He would help you," Akiko insisted. "He helped me."

"How?" Vic asked, patting her tender lip with the towel.

"My father wished to sell me to a powerful shogun. He was a man known for his cruelty to the concubines he kept, but the amount of wealth he offered for me prevented my father from seeing his true nature."

Vic was appalled by the idea that Akiko's own father would sell her to a man to be used as he wished. She listened intently as Akiko continued.

"A close friend of mine told Sebastian-san of my problem. He offered my father more money than the shogun. My father didn't hesitate. I was on the next ship leaving Japan with my new master."

"You make it sound as if he owns you," Vic said, failing to speak in the boy's uneducated tongue.

"He does. He paid my father a great deal of money for me. I am his property to do with as he wishes. He is an extremely fair master, though. He offered me my freedom, but where would I go? I possess more freedom belonging to the Dragon."

Vic understood perfectly. Society wouldn't accept Akiko because she was an Oriental. At least by being part of Sebastian's household she was treated with respect.

"Come, you will soak in a hot tub so your body will not ache later on," she directed.

Vic followed her, suddenly finding herself interested in learning more of the Dragon's past. "How long did Sebastian live in Japan?"

Akiko's graceful movements never faltered as she prepared the tub and spoke. "His father brought him there when he was five years old, in 1845. The only port open for trade was Nagasaki and only for Dutch merchants."

"He's Dutch?" she asked, while mentally calculating his age to be thirty-three.

Akiko shook her head. "No, but his father speaks fluent Dutch, Spanish, and Japanese. He worked for a Dutch trader and settled at Nagasaki with his young son since his wife had died two years before."

"Then the stories are true? He was raised in Japan?"

"Yes, he returned ten years ago to form Blood Enterprises, a trading company owned jointly by him and his father. They are the major importers of Japanese merchandise. Even though trade is now open with Japan they are still able to acquire many items other merchants cannot."

"His father is still living?"

"Yes, he lives in Japan and operates their office there. Sebastian-san journeys once every two years to visit."

Vic was so absorbed in all the information she was learning about the Dragon that she forgot to wait for Akiko to leave the room before beginning to undress. She worked on her buttons absentmindedly. Her mind filled with images of Sebastian as a child growing up in a foreign land. She pulled open her shirt without thinking.

"Have you injured yourself?" Akiko inquired, pointing to the thick strip of cloth that bound her breasts.

Vic gasped and snapped the shirt closed. "I-I—"

Akiko spoke softly, putting an end to the young girl's nervous stammering. "Why do you hide the fact you

84

are a female?"

Vic's first response was to deny it, but she was tired of hiding and pretending, and she felt she could trust Akiko. "If you promise not to tell anyone, I'll explain all the messy details," she said, with no intention of revealing her Serpent identity.

"I promise."

Vic breathed a heavy sigh and plunged on. "My parents were killed in a carriage accident and my father's step-brother, Tobias Withers, was left as guardian over the estate. My father had acquired vast holdings across the country, and although we weren't wealthy, we wanted for nothing. He left my uncle in charge to protect us from unscrupulous men, only he wasn't aware of how unscrupulous his step-brother had become."

She shuddered as the haunting memories grew vivid in her mind. "Shortly after my parents' funeral, my uncle made his intentions clear. He-he wanted me in his bed and the things he planned on doing to me . . ."

Victoria paused, finding it difficult to continue. Several minutes passed before she found the strength to go on. "He detailed his intentions in such vividness that it made my stomach turn. It was then he attacked me. I fought and managed to get away. That night I took Elizabeth and left the house forever. The Chambeau sisters became the Chambers brother and sister."

She rested her head back against the tub and wished the soothing heat of the steaming water could wash away her sad memories as easily as it washed away her aches and pains.

"Sebastian-san would help you if you would confide in him," Akiko said.

"I can't, Akiko. I can't," she repeated in a hushed whisper. She shook her head recalling the awful threats of revenge the Dragon had screamed at the Serpent that fateful night.

"You cannot hide behind boy's clothing forever. He will learn soon enough."

Vic heard the truth in the astute warning. Eventually the Dragon would learn her secret, perhaps through an accident, or through a fault of her own. It mattered not. As long as her charade lasted until her sister's demise . . . then she'd be gone.

Chapter Seven

The Dragon's fist pounded the desk, rattling the crystal decanters. "What do you mean you can't find him?" Sebastian shouted. His demanding voice echoed throughout the silent house, sending shivers through a pale Vic.

She moved silently along the hall, her back pressed against the teakwood wall. She stopped by the closed study door and listened. Sebastian had just gone in with two men. A few minutes later the shouting had begun. It was obvious they were delivering news of the Serpent's mysterious disappearance, and she intended to hear every word of their report.

"Mr. Blood, sir, we have searched the entire waterfront. We've had men hiding along the docks. We've set up decoys. There's no sign of the fellow. You must have put the fear of God into him."

Vic covered her mouth with her hand in an attempt to suppress a giggle. Why, the Serpent was under his very nose! Her sudden humor quickly faded when next he spoke.

"I don't care if it takes my entire life. I will find that miserable creature and make him suffer for what he has done to me."

His harsh words made her realize she couldn't hide from him forever. He was a man obsessed with the destruction of the Serpent and for the first time she could understand why. The creature had tarnished his reputation. He had dented his power and credibility along the waterfront.

Vic felt a sudden stab of regret for what she had done to him. A few weeks ago she would have thought herself daft for even regarding the Dragon as human, but she had learned about the man everyone feared, and she saw him differently.

She saw him as the young boy whose father refused to leave him behind when his business took him to a faraway land. She saw him as the child growing to adulthood in a foreign country and raised to respect many races. She saw him as a protector of the weak and less fortunate, and she saw him as a man whose smile could easily ignite a woman's heart.

His towering height and powerful form still frightened her at times, yet she was able to see his gentleness in the way he treated Beth and the way he tried so hard to educate the ragamuffin lad in better manners and proper English.

The door to the study flew open, and Vic hastily plopped herself down in a nearby chair.

"I will expect a weekly report from you, gentlemen," Sebastian said, showing the men to the door.

The two plump men shook their heads in unison, bumping into each other as they both attempted to fit through the front door at the same time.

Vic contained her laughter after catching sight of the Dragon's black expression.

"Did you wish to see me, Vic?"

"Nope, was just wondering what all the yelling was about," she answered.

"Let's just say I have a debt to repay. And I intend to see it paid in full as soon as possible."

Vic's slim fingers clutched the sides of her trousers. A tingle of fear fluttered in her stomach and raced up through her chest. It was impossible for him to trace the Serpent identity to her. Impossible. She had always been careful. No one had seen her face, or even her small size. He had no clues to her identity. Or did he?

She took the chance and asked. "So who is it you owe?"

Sebastian smiled nastily. "The Serpent."

She had to learn as much as she could. She had to know if she was in any danger. "I heard about that fellow. Heard you were looking for him. So did you find him?"

"Not yet, but it won't be long," Sebastian said with such confidence that Vic could almost hear the prison bars slam shut in front of her.

"You mean you know who he is?"

"Not exactly, though I do know he's of short height and lacks strength."

"How do you—"

Sebastian anticipated the lad's question and didn't wait for him to finish. "The way he attacks his victims and the necessity of the cut. If the fellow was large he wouldn't waste his time. He'd have no fear of handling any resistance. The Serpent, on the other hand, guarantees his victim won't move and can't move afterward, thus preventing him from being chased. Actually I admire him in a way."

"You do?" she asked, confused.

"Of course. Lacking size is a deterrent to his profession, so instead, he relied on an even better asset, his wits. He's an intelligent man. His only major error was attacking me."

"Being so smart, he's probably moved on."

Sebastian shook his head thoughtfully. "I don't think so. Something tells me he's still around."

"Why's that? You said yourself he's intelligent. He'd be dumb to stay around here."

"Simple. Once a man tastes fame and power, he can never get enough of it. He'll strike again, and I'll be there waiting."

A chill ran through Vic like an omen. The Serpent wouldn't rise again. There was no reason. She wasn't interested in fame and power, only survival. He had misjudged her character, but then he didn't know the Serpent was a female. Would it make a difference? She wondered.

"We leave for the office shortly," Sebastian said, ending the conversation. "First I want to see how Beth is doing. She's been sleeping the last few times I've tried to visit with her."

Vic frowned. "She hasn't felt too good lately."

"Well, then the best thing for her is rest," he offered, knowing the young girl's condition had worsened considerably, but not wanting to upset the lad. "I'll just be a moment. You make certain Daniel is ready."

*   *   *

Sebastian walked quietly into Beth's room and stared down at the sleeping girl. Her illness was progressing at an alarming rate. The medication Aaron had been giving her no longer helped. Her pale complexion heightened the darkness beneath her eyes and her weight had steadily declined from lack of appetite. The hacking cough racked her frail body almost continuously, day and night. Aaron had tried to warn him of this, but he had always hoped . . .

Her eyelids stirred and opened slowly as though the simple movement were too much for her.

"How are you feeling today, Beth?" he asked, leaning over to place a fatherly kiss upon her forehead.

"Not too well," she sighed, her breathing labored.

He patted her shoulder gently. "Well, you just rest. I'll stop by the bookstore and see if I can find something new to entertain us tonight."

She smiled. "I look forward to it. Is Vic accompanying you to the office today?"

"Yes," he said.

"Vic can be . . . trying at times."

Sebastian laughed lightheartedly. "Trying isn't the word for it, Beth. He's downright stubborn, bold, brash, foolhardy . . ."

"But," she add softly, "she has a heart of gold."

Sebastian leaned closer to Beth. "What did you say?"

"Heart of gold," she whispered, her eyes drifting closed.

Had she said what he thought she did, or had he misunderstood? It must have been her sleepy state and weakened condition that caused her to refer to her brother as "she." He pushed back the soft tendrils of

91

hair that had escaped the confines of her favorite blue ribbon. "Sleep tight, Beth."

Vic's eyes scouted the deck of the ship with excitement. The sailors were busy preparing the vessel for departure. Crates upon crates were being loaded in the hull. Food was being hauled on board and seamen who had been signed on at the last minute were busy stowing their gear below. The exciting bustle of activities was contagious and Vic found herself caught up in the thrill of it all.

She had known one of Sebastian's ships had been docked in the harbor for some time. The men in the office had talked of repairs that were being done to it. Afterwards, it would leave for Japan with its hull full of merchandise.

Vic hopped over the ropes that lay like coiled snakes on the deck. She tilted her head back and watched the huge net rope swing precariously overhead as the men shouted for it to be lowered. They pushed and shoved as they directed it toward the hole.

"Vic, be careful where you step," Sebastian called out.

She waved her acknowledgement of his orders before he disappeared below with Captain Parker.

"Hey, boy, come over here and give me a hand," a heavy man in a sweat-stained shirt called out.

She hesitated.

"Come on, boy. I need you now!" he shouted, reaching overhead to direct the net stuffed with crates.

She scurried over, sensing it was best to do as he asked.

"Push it. To the right. To the right," he yelled at the men helping him. "Get around to the other side, boy, and yell down to Jack to clear right way."

Vic hurried to do as ordered, relieved it was such a simple task. She stepped near the edge of the gaping hole and peered down. Crates were stacked in an orderly fashion and several men were milling about. She cupped her hands around her mouth to give her soft voice more volume. "Jack, clear right way!"

"Clear right way," the echoing voice repeated.

She watched the men move swiftly, still repeating the orders. She smiled, pleased with herself and was about to step back when a screaming shout halted her.

"Snapped rope! Snapped rope!"

Vic looked up. The heavily burdened net was rushing toward her.

She heard her name shouted and in the next instant she was smashed against the Dragon's solid chest and toppled to the deck. His arms hugged her tightly to him as they tumbled over and over before crashing into a stack of barrels. The top barrels swayed back and forth, teetered on the edge for several seconds, then came pitching toward them. Sebastian's one arm remained firm around Vic, pushing the lad against his chest for further protection, while the other arm swung out with a tremendous force, splintering the barrel that was about to hit them into pieces.

Sebastian felt a slight quiver run through Vic's body. He tightened his hold around the lad's waist, disturbed by the fact that it was so narrow. "Are you all right?" he whispered in his ear.

She didn't answer immediately. She felt so protected, so safe wrapped in his arms, that she didn't want him to

93

let go, at least not just yet.

"Vic?" he questioned, concern in his voice.

Her words were muffled against Sebastian's chest, but he heard them. "I'm all right."

"Good," he said and heaved himself as well as Vic up. He held the lad by the shoulders for a few moments to make certain he was steady on his feet, then released him. He questioned his condition once again. "Are you sure you're all right?"

Vic wasn't even certain where she was. There was a ringing in her ears. Her head spun, and her body ached, yet somehow she managed to speak. "Yup."

Sebastian pulled a slim piece of wood from the lad's hair and shook his head. He hadn't realized how thin the boy really was until this minute. There wasn't an ounce of muscle on him. "Are you sure? That was a nasty spill."

"Yup," she said, brushing at her shirt.

Sebastian noticed the tilt to his stand and reached out to straighten him. "Sit down and rest a few minutes. We'll be leaving soon."

She shook her head and did as he said. She didn't think her legs would hold her up any longer anyway. She sat there picking the remaining splinters from her clothing and wondering when the aches and pains would lessen in intensity. She felt as though someone had battered her with a thick board.

"Vic," Sebastian shouted. "Let's go."

She stood swiftly and instantly regretted it. Every muscle in her body screamed at her and retaliated by turning her legs into instant mush. She collapsed to the deck like a dead weight.

Sebastian rushed to the boy's side. He lifted him

some, slipping his arm behind his back.

"Ohhhhh," she moaned in protest.

"Where does it hurt?" Sebastian asked, his hand reaching out to examine the lad's ribs.

Vic's eyes burst wide open and she grabbed for his hand, squeezing his large fingers. "All over. It hurts all over. I'm dying. I'm dying. You've got to get me to a doctor." She knew she was being overly dramatic, but she had no choice. She couldn't let him touch her.

"Captain Parker," Sebastian called, "see to it that Dr. Samuels is summoned to my house immediately."

He gently scooped the boy up into his arms. "Easy Vic. Aaron will have you feeling better in no time."

Sebastian was concerned for the lad. He didn't like seeing him in such pain, yet his annoyance grew with every bump that jostled the carriage and caused Vic to grimace. "If you weren't so foolhardy and listened to my orders, you wouldn't be suffering now."

Vic sent him an evil look.

Sebastian smiled in return. He couldn't help but admire the boy's tenacity. "Perhaps next time you'll listen."

"I listened."

"Really? Standing near the edge of the hole while cargo is being loaded is being careful?"

"The big fellow asked me for help."

"You don't work for the big fellow. You work for me."

"I was just helping out."

Sebastian raised his voice to a near shout. "You do as I order. I thought I had made that clear!"

She snapped forward ready to tell him exactly what she thought when the pain hit. Her eyes widened, her head spun, and she fell forward right into the Dragon's arms.

"Damn," he muttered and as gently as possible returned the boy to the corner of the seat. "Don't try to speak and sit still."

She opened her mouth, but Sebastian cut her off. "Shut up, Vic, and do as I say."

The carriage stopped a few minutes later. Sebastian hoisted a surprised Vic into his arms and carried her into the house. Aaron and Akiko were waiting in the foyer.

"What is it?" Aaron asked, concerned by the lad's pale complexion.

"He took a nasty tumble on the ship," Sebastian answered.

"Take him to the study," Aaron directed. "I'll examine him there."

Vic suddenly realized the danger she was in. The doctor couldn't touch her. He couldn't.

"Perhaps you should take him upstairs," Akiko offered, receiving a grateful look from Vic.

Sebastian agreed and in minutes she was placed on the Dragon's large fourposter bed.

"Let's take a look," Aaron said, and reached for the top button on Vic's shirt.

"No!" she yelled and pushed his hand away.

"Perhaps Vic would feel more comfortable removing his own clothes in privacy," Akiko suggested.

"Yeah, I'd feel better doing that," Vic added quickly.

Sebastian and Aaron walked toward the door followed by Akiko.

"Akiko," Vic called. "Maybe you could help me?"

"If you wish," she answered.

Both men looked at each other, shook their heads, then walked out of the room.

Vic breathed a sigh of relief, but it was short-lived.

"The doctor will return and insist on examining you. You will not be able to prevent it. You must confide in him. He will not betray your trust," Akiko insisted.

Vic wanted to deny her reasoning, but she couldn't. There was nothing she could do. If she refused to allow Aaron to examine her, Sebastian would see to it that she was forcibly held down. Then her identity would be revealed. She had no choice—she had to take the chance with Aaron.

Akiko helped her remove the cloth that bound her breasts, but she kept her clothing on. She felt safer, more in control of the situation while dressed in the lad's disguise.

Aaron entered moments later and approached the bed. "Where does it hurt?" he asked, sitting on the bed next to him.

"Before you examine me, there's something you must know." She shut her eyes tightly for a few seconds, then opened them as the story came pouring out in a fusillade of words, causing the doctor's eyes to widen in amazement.

Twenty minutes later Aaron had finished the examination and was mixing a powder in a glass of water and handing it to Vic. "This should ease the pain. There's nothing broken, just some bruises and bumps. I want you to stay off your feet for the remainder of the day."

"Will you tell Sebastian?" she asked in her refined, educated tongue.

"No," he said, shaking his head. "But eventually he

must be told. You can't keep this masquerade up forever."

"Thank you," she smiled, relieved that her secret was still intact.

Aaron's expression grew serious as he sat by her side. He cleared his throat as though finding it difficult to speak. "You know, Victoria, Sebastian appears the raging tyrant, but he can be extremely understanding. He has influential friends and could possibly help you with your dilemma."

"Can he guarantee my sister's safety?" she asked directly.

Aaron understood. She wouldn't take any chances of Beth's last days being filled with fear and terror. She was happy and content and that was how Victoria intended to see her stay.

"Perhaps later you will be able to confide in Sebastian," he suggested, thinking that once Beth passed on, the young woman couldn't be allowed to roam the streets as a boy, or continue to reside with Sebastian under the present circumstances.

"Perhaps," she whispered. Her eyelids grew heavy with sleep from the drug Aaron had given her. She drifted into a light slumber. Her thoughts centered on making certain Beth received a proper burial in the family cemetery next to their parents. Then, with that important matter finally settled, Victoria Chambeau intended to disappear forever.

"So, no serious damage done?" Sebastian asked, handing him a drink and taking a seat opposite him in front of the cold hearth.

"No broken bones, just some bruises and soreness," Aaron assured him. "You seem to have grown attached to the lad."

"The little devil sort of grows on you. The day never seems dull with him around. He always has a snappy remark or colorful phrase to annoy me with. As a matter of fact, I think he takes great pleasure in defying me."

"He does have a way with words," Aaron smiled, recalling Victoria's refined speech.

"Should he stay in bed?"

"For the remainder of the day and no heavy work for about a week." Aaron thought a moment and revised his orders. "Actually, the boy shouldn't be doing any heavy lifting for several weeks."

Sebastian readily agreed, and Aaron released a grateful sigh of relief.

After his friend's departure, Sebastian instructed Akiko to see to Beth's needs for the remainder of the day. He then proceeded to attend to business in his study instead of returning to the office.

He finished several hours later and decided to see how Beth was getting on without the able assistance of her brother.

His tall form stood deadly still in the doorway when he caught sight of Vic hoisting Beth up to rest more comfortably against her pillows. That he was still experiencing pain was obvious from his pale complexion and perspiring brow.

"Akiko!" he shouted. His full, bellowing voice shook the rafters of the solid house.

The two young women turned, startled by his demanding yell.

Akiko must have flown up the steps for she was there in seconds.

"I did instruct you to see to Beth's care this day, did I not?" he asked, directing his eyes at the lad.

"Yes, Sebastian-san, but Vic woke and insisted on tending his sister."

"Am I still the master of this house, or have I lost my command in the last few hours?"

"I am sorry, Sebastian-san."

Vic had no intentions of standing there while Akiko was being blamed for something that wasn't her fault. "I told you, Mr. Blood. I take care of my sister."

Sebastian walked into the room and stood in front of the lad. His hands were braced purposely on his hips. "You are in no condition to move your sister."

"Vic, what's wrong?" Beth asked, frightened by what she heard.

"It's nothing to worry about, Beth," Vic assured her, itching to ring the Dragon's neck for causing the frail girl needless worry.

"Shall we talk elsewhere?" Sebastian asked, not wishing to upset Beth further.

Vic nodded and followed him from the room while Akiko prepared to feed Beth her supper.

Once in the hallway Sebastian released his anger. "You are in no shape to lift your sister."

Vic found herself unable to become angry with the imposing man. He was expressing sincere concern for the boy and it touched her heart. "I appreciate you caring about me, but I have to look after my sister myself."

Sebastian ran his fingers through his dark hair in frustration. "Don't you ever accept anyone's help?"

"Don't need it."

"What do you need?"

She stared at him a moment, recalling the strength of his arms around her, and the sense of security and safety it had instilled within her. It made her feel good, so very good. It was almost like feeling loved. Love? The thought frightened her. "There's nothing I need," she snapped. "Especially from you."

Sebastian was taken aback by the boy's sudden hostility. "There are many things you need, Vic, but the most immediate one is a good whack to your backside for speaking to me in such a rude manner."

Vic braced her hands on her hips and spoke with a defiant tone. "Don't you think it would be awful cruel to whip my backside right now?"

Sebastian recalled the boy's bruised condition. He certainly had a quick wit and a smart mouth—too smart. "Someday, Vic, I'm going to lay your backside bare to my view and give you exactly what you deserve."

He stormed off down the hall. His hands curled tightly in fists. His wide shoulders were thrown back in rigid anger. He called back, startling her. "Make certain your sister is lifted by Akiko or myself from this day on."

Vic, at first, found amusement in his threatening response, but the vivid picture his warning suggested painted an entirely different image in her mind. She suddenly saw herself sprawled naked across the Dragon's muscular legs. One powerful hand held her prisoner while the other descended slowly to her soft flesh. She shivered at the thought of his touch. The gentle, soothing play of his fingers exploring her intimately.

A moist heat spread through her, centering in the valley between her legs. Her eyes closed as her daydreaming continued. His fingers roamed freely, slipping downward, forcing her legs to spread, forcing entrance to the heat, forcing pleasure upon her.

She was startled by the low, pleading moan she heard and turned crimson when she realized it had slipped from her lips. Her eyes searched the hall hoping no one was about to hear. She was alone.

She stamped her foot in frustration and turned to enter her sister's room, but stopped. Her hand firmly grasped the brass handle. She was confused by her strange feelings toward the Dragon . . . and frightened. It was as though she wanted him to touch her, wanted to feel his hand roam her naked flesh, wanted him—

"No," she silently cried, covering her eyes with her hands to block the image of the Dragon rising naked over her bare flesh ready to—

"Never. Never," she whispered and hastily entered her sister's room.

Chapter Eight

The torrential rain sent people into their homes and caused the waterfront to appear abandoned. It was an oddity for it to rain during the hot, dry summer months, yet it was almost September and the steady downpour had started the previous day and continued into the next with no sign of relenting. People shook their heads over the strangeness of the weather and waited to see what would follow.

Aaron turned his coat collar up and jumped down from his carriage to hurry up the steps to Sebastian's house. He had been expecting this summons for the last few days. Beth's condition had worsened. The pains in her chest had picked up in frequency and the cough syrup did little to alleviate her dry, hacking cough. Her ankles and feet had begun to swell and Aaron suspected her time was drawing near.

"The sky weeps for the young one," Akiko said, assisting Aaron in the removal of his wet coat.

He caught the note of sorrow in her singsong voice and his heart constricted when he spied the grief evident in her almond-shaped eyes. "She has suffered much, Akiko." He wanted to ease her pain, yet he was feeling the same.

"They are waiting upstairs for you," she whispered as though an ominous presence would hear.

He followed her up the long staircase, their feet muffled on the thick carpet as they approached the room.

Akiko opened the door and they entered. A single light on the table next to the bed flickered as in protest, causing eerie images to dance across the walls. The heavy rain pounded against the glass window panes. Vic's small body knelt next to her sister's bedside, holding her frail hand. The sight almost broke Aaron's heart.

Sebastian nodded to his friend. He stood behind Vic and placed a hand on the lad's shoulder to let him know the doctor had arrived.

Vic lifted her face to look at Aaron. Tears marred her pale complexion, and her brilliant green eyes begged to hear something other than the truth.

He stepped around her and leaned over Beth. He touched her face gently. There was no need for him to examine her. Her breathing was so shallow one could barely hear it, and her young, innocent face appeared almost lifeless.

Vic glanced up at him for confirmation of what she already knew. He nodded, not able to find the strength to speak.

She wasn't ashamed to cry. Her tears came freely as she hugged her sister's listless hand to her wet cheek.

Aaron joined Akiko at the foot of the bed and shook his head. A lone tear glided down the Japanese

104

woman's smooth face.

Sebastian stood rigid behind the lad, his stern expression only a mask for the tormenting sorrow that he felt. He wanted to protect the vulnerable boy from the grief he was about to experience, yet he knew that was impossible. So instead he stood near, offering what little support he could.

"Beth. Beth, can you hear me?" Vic cried, wanting to let her know how much she loved her.

The frail girl stirred. Her lashes fluttered. "Mama?" she whispered.

Vic almost choked on her tears. "No, Beth. It's me."

"Mama," Beth pleaded softly.

Vic had no choice. She couldn't allow her sister's last minutes to be filled with fear. She wanted desperately for Beth to hear the familiar voice of her sister, the voice that used to tease her when they were young children, or laugh with her, or cry with her. One moment, one last moment as sister to sister.

She blinked away the tears and spoke in her soft female voice. "It's me, Beth. Your sister . . . Victoria."

The Dragon's hand that rested on her shoulder was quickly snatched away.

"Victoria," Beth murmured contentedly. "I must go."

"I know, Beth."

"Mama is waiting."

"Yes, she is. Beth, I love you."

"I love—Victoria, be careful . . ."

Victoria leaned closer as her sister's words faded. "Beth! Beth!" She dropped her face down next to her sister's and pressed her cheek to hers. "Oh, Beth. How I shall miss you!"

Her tears flowed freely as the agonizing pain of losing a loved one descended upon her. The hurt deepened as memories of their childhood flooded her mind and she realized that now her entire family was gone.

She did not prevent the tears from falling. She welcomed them as a catharsis for the raw hurt that pained her. It gave her resolve to face the urgent problem she had created. She stiffened, raised her head proudly, and courageously turned to face the Dragon.

Sebastian had not moved from his position behind her. He was too stunned by her words to budge. His penetrating eyes scanned her face, the face of a young woman and not that of a ragamuffin lad. Those rich green eyes framed with long luscious lashes still defied him with their proud boldness and glistening tears. He wanted to reach out and pull her to him, to force her to release her sorrow in the comfort of his arms. Instead, he spoke, with a bit more harshness in his voice than he intended. "You're a woman?"

She tilted her head up. "Yes."

His fingers gripped her chin, snapping her head sharply to the left then right as though his close scrutiny would prove her admission true.

She didn't care for the way his eyes narrowed, or how the dark color seemed to glow. And she didn't care to be examined so blatantly. She pulled her face from his grasp. "I had no choice," she said in defense of herself.

"There's always a choice."

"As I asked you once before, have you ever been hungry?"

Sebastian stiffened and gazed down into her defiant eyes. They challenged him, but they also held sorrow.

106

"Forgive me, Miss Chambers. I've been inconsiderate. I'm truly sorrow over Beth's passing."

She nodded, unable to speak. Her sister was gone. She was alone. The thought frightened her and she shivered.

"Akiko, please see to Miss Chambers's comfort." Sebastian instructed.

Victoria acted instinctively. She placed her hand on Sebastian's arm, looked up into his eyes, and spoke in her soft, feminine voice. "Thank you, Mr. Blood, for your kindness to my sister."

Sebastian felt as though a fist had been rammed into his stomach. Her touch was like a gentle caress; her voice was like soothing music. He shook his head as he watched her leave the room. The worn garments hid her feminine curves quite well. Now he could understand the narrowness of her waist, the slimness of her calves, the soft features of her face. And the reason she wore that oversized shirt. He was anxious to learn more about this tiny, dark-haired woman. Especially since she belonged to him.

"Do you know her age, Aaron?" he asked, assuming his friend and his servant knew of the charade since neither had seemed surprised by what had taken place.

"She's eighteen."

"The day you examined her, I can safely assume, is when you discovered her gender."

Aaron shook his head in confirmation. "I gave my word, Sebastian. I couldn't go back on it."

"I understand. I only wish I hadn't been so blind that I couldn't have seen for myself."

Aaron laughed. "She does have a stunning face, especially those eyes. They're so expressive."

"I won't ask you to betray her trust, but please inform her that I am willing to help her since I assume she is in some sort of trouble, hence the disguise."

"I'll deliver your message."

"And when she is feeling up to it, ask her what arrangements she wishes to be made for Beth's interment."

"Why not ask her yourself?" Aaron asked, confused by his friend's reluctance to approach the young woman.

"She will seek me out when she's ready," he announced calmly and walked toward the door. He stopped just before entering the hall and turned to face Aaron. "Whatever Vic . . . Victoria requires make certain she receives."

He didn't wait for a response. He was too accustomed to his orders being followed without question.

Aaron smiled. He wondered if the pint-size female would bow to the will of the Dragon.

Lightning illuminated the night sky and thunder crackled and roared like an angry lion as Victoria slowly descended the steps and approached the closed study door.

Her small hand reached out to knock, but hastily withdrew. Her courage was waning from all she had to endure this day, and if the Dragon refused to assist her in this matter, she knew not where to turn.

She closed her eyes tightly. She couldn't fail her sister. She had to make certain Beth was buried alongside her parents in the family cemetery. If only Sebastian had yelled or raved or did anything but

108

respond with such controlled calmness upon discovering her a female. It was as though it were the calm before the storm and his strange acceptance of her charade frightened her.

She took a deep breath, threw her shoulders back, and with a will born of necessity knocked on the door.

Sebastian called out for her to enter having waited for the past several hours for this moment. He was totally unprepared for the sight of the ragamuffin lad turned refined young lady.

He skillfully disguised his surprise and pleasure, still unwilling to openly display his emotions, yet the picture the small enticing woman presented was enough to ignite his passion, especially since her luminous green eyes still retained their defiance. Her head was held high and proud and she met his intense glare with that of her own.

He couldn't help but admire the trim fit of her black mourning gown. Its high collar ruffles hugged the slim column of her neck and tapered over and around her full breasts to fit firmly at her narrow waist. He wondered how those high thrusting peaks could have been so successfully hidden from his view these many weeks. He silently admonished himself for his lack of perception. How the devil had he allowed her obvious femininity to slip by him?

"Victoria," he said, wishing to end the oppressive silence in the tense room and extended his hand to her. "This is a surprise."

She accepted his hand, unnerved by his gentle tone. "You aren't angry?"

He curled his long fingers around hers and a hot tingle started in his hand, traveling up his arm slowly until the odd sensation caused him to clench his teeth. *Damn the little vixen for getting into my blood so soon.*

"At first, perhaps, but then I realized there must be a very good reason for the disguise. So I thought that I should hear your explanation before I passed judgement."

She was confused by his easy acceptance of her charade, expecting rage and anger at her deceit. "I very much want to explain things, Mr. Blood," she said, finding her fingers locking with his as though with a will of their own.

"Sebastian, please. After all, it isn't as though we're strangers," he said, leading her to the group of chairs near the fireplace.

She sat, reluctantly releasing the comfort of his firm grip. "Sebastian," she began, folding her hands demurely on her lap and trying to avert his chilling eyes.

He couldn't help but grin at the picture of refinement she portrayed. After all, he had seen those small hands fell Casey and had heard that sweet voice sound anything but educated.

Victoria continued. "I require your assistance in seeing that my sister is able to join my parents in the family cemetery."

"I'm at your disposal," he readily agreed.

"Perhaps you should hear what is required of you before you commit yourself," she offered, a touch of the lad's boldness edging her words.

His dark brows shot up, and his grin was almost savagely wicked. "Come, Victoria, do you really doubt my ability to deal with your problem?"

She didn't, but the fear of her uncle having control

110

over her life once again frightened her.

Sebastian didn't miss the flash of alarm that crossed her face. He reached out, covering her small hands that had clamped themselves together into tight fists. "Tell me, Victoria. We shall solve your problem together."

The compassionate glow in his midnight blue eyes was like a beacon in a storm, and she was drawn to its offer of solace. Her tale started with the unexpected death of her parents and proceeded to detail her uncle's guardianship and subsequently his attack.

She purposely omitted the type of weapon she had used to subdue her uncle. She still feared Sebastian learning of her Serpent identity. He may be able to accept her as a female without anger, but never would he accept the knowledge that she was the notorious Serpent.

Sebastian listened as her nightmare unfolded vividly before his eyes. The trembling of her hands beneath his alerted him to the fear that she still harbored toward her uncle and he inwardly seethed with anger.

"You have nothing to fear," he consoled when her story was finished. "I'll handle all the arrangements as well as your uncle."

Victoria expressed her gratitude for his generous assistance in handling the matter, but she had no doubts that her uncle would demand her return. After all, Tobias Withers was her legal guardian and the law was on his side.

She would retain her true identity for the funeral, but afterwards, the ragamuffin lad would help her escape into obscurity.

Sebastian sensed her readiness to run from the fear that she harbored, and he had no intentions of allowing

111

her to slip through his fingers. He had much he wished to learn about her. She had produced an odd, disturbing feeling in him since he'd discovered she was a female. He wasn't certain what it was—annoyance at himself for not realizing her deception, or finding their friendship challenged in a strange way? Could he be friends with Vic, the female, or would he want more from her femininity than just that? Regardless of his unusual feelings, or perhaps because of them, he intended to make certain Victoria remained with him until he chose otherwise. She belonged to him as much as the ragamuffin lad.

Victoria stood and looked down into his dark haunting eyes. Their strong color intoxicated her. She shivered over the intensity of his raw power and try as she might she could not pull her eyes away from his. She felt compelled to look into the very depths that frightened her.

Her body tingled as though small pins prickled her flesh, causing it to heighten in sensitivity. The odd sensation spread throughout her, teasing every nerve ending until she thought she would go mad from the want of something she couldn't quite understand.

She forced herself to speak. Her voice trembled.

"Please forgive my necessary deception."

Sebastian eased himself from the chair and cupped her chin in his hand, gently lifting her face. Fresh tears stirred her silky lashes, and her green eyes were wide with confusion and innocent desire. His passion ignited with the quickness of a striking match.

His finger reached out, catching hold of a lone tear that had begun to travel down her flushed cheek. He raised it to his lips and slowly licked the tiny sparkling drop with the tip of his tongue. "Why do you cry? What is it you're feeling, Victoria?"

She didn't know how to respond. Beth wasn't in her thoughts at the moment, only the peculiar feeling that had continued to penetrate her body and make the Dragon's touch feel like the tonic that could ease her odd condition.

His hand reached out to tenderly brush away the tears that followed. "So innocent," he whispered, and lifted her face up as he lowered his.

Victoria did not retreat in fright as his lips touched hers. They were warm, moist, and welcoming.

Sebastian pressed gently, allowing her to become accustomed to his light, intimate contact. Her body soon lost its rigidness as it succumbed to his command. He slipped his arm around her small waist and slowly pulled her against him, almost lifting her off the floor.

Still she didn't retreat, and Sebastian pursued his pleasure as well as her own. He tempted her with the tip of his tongue, tracing along her sealed lips until they became limpid and opened willingly. He entered and explored the unchartered territory. He lingered in the sweet nectar of her innocent response, tasting, teasing, titillating until he thought he would go mad.

Her senses reeled as his gentle play turned insistent. She found herself wantonly pressing against his hard body as though searching for a release from the heat that threatened to consume her.

Sebastian experienced a throbbing tightness in his loins as her small body pressed demandingly against his. He fought the urge to strip her bare and relieve the torment that had captured both of them, but he was too well schooled in the way of women not to realize that part of her response was from the grief of losing her sister. She was lonely, therefore vulnerable.

He reluctantly ended their kiss, holding her trembling body against his and listening to her heavy sighs as she fought to regain control. There would be other times, he promised himself, definitely other times.

He stroked the soft tendrils of curls that framed her face and spoke almost in a murmur. "You're safe here with me, Victoria. What is mine no one touches."

His statement penetrated the hazy fog she was drifting in and its meaning disturbed her. She pulled away from him and met his eyes with the boldness of the lad. "What do you mean, what is yours?"

Sebastian grinned at her familiar tenacity. "You forget you work for me, Vic."

Victoria thought for a moment, absentmindedly chewing on her lower lip. She had accepted a position with him under the condition that he saw to her sister's needs and it was still necessary for him to see to her burial, so technically she was still in his employment.

"I'll work for you until my sister is safely interred with my parents. After that, I will seek employment elsewhere," she announced with a proud toss of her head. She grabbed the side of her dress, lifting its length from the floor, and turned to leave.

In seconds she felt the Dragon's vicelike grip clamp around her waist. The next instant she was lifted off the floor and turned to face him, her feet dangling in midair.

His controlled, calm speech frightened her since, as usual, his face wore an emotionless mask. "Don't cross me, Vic, or you'll be sorry . . . very sorry."

Victoria swallowed hard. She didn't like the warning

glint in his eyes.

Sebastian held her firm, forcing her to press flat against him. His grin turned sinfully wicked. And he laughed, a deep, throaty laugh that chilled her.

She pushed at his iron-hard chest in a futile demand to be released. "And I thought you were helping me out of sheer generosity."

He lowered her feet to the floor, but held her wrist firmly so she wouldn't flee. "I offer my help because I cared deeply for Beth, and I don't wish any harm to befall you."

"But you said I still work—"

He pressed his finger to her lips to silence her. "If it takes a threat to keep you in my home and under my protection, so be it."

Victoria frowned, realizing his protection was definitely necessary at the moment. "I must insist that I continue to earn my keep while I'm here."

"Why did I expect you to say that?"

"Because I'm stubborn."

"We finally agree on something," he laughed.

"Do I continue to earn my keep, Mr. Blood?"

Sebastian produced a disarming smile. "You shall definitely earn your keep, Miss Chambeau."

Victoria didn't trust the Dragon, or herself, and she feared the coming confrontation with her uncle. It was time to remove the dagger from its hiding place. She had the distinct feeling she was going to need it.

Sebastian made all the necessary arrangements for the funeral. He informed Victoria later that evening that he and Dr. Samuels would accompany her the next morning to Santa Clara and her family home.

He further explained that her uncle had been sent a wire apprising him of their arrival on the eleven o'clock train. He had responded, informing Sebastian he'd await them at the family cemetery for the services. Sebastian stressed the fact that she would be returning with him to San Francisco the following day.

She prayed he meant it.

The unusual rain tapered off during the night and the morning dawned sunny and bright. The sky was bursting in its rich blue color, and the familiar sounds of another day stirred the silent air.

Victoria yawned and stretched under the quilt. She had slept only a few hours. Her sister's passing had finally taken its toll and she had released her grief in tears.

She pushed the covers back and dragged herself from the safety of the bed. There was no use in delaying the inevitable. She would draw on all her strength to face today.

She had retrieved the special mourning gown she had worn for her parents' funeral from the satchel where it had lain crumpled for these past many months. It had been pressed and was hanging in the wardrobe.

Victoria slipped on the soft undergarments she had so desperately missed and winced when the material rubbed her still-tender nipples. It would take more than one day for the soreness to disappear, and she was too embarrassed to ask Dr. Samuels for medication to ease the discomfort.

There was no corset to tie and constrict her breathing

116

since she failed to pack one. It really didn't matter. She had lost several pounds over the year and the black silk skirt trimmed in velvet and silk fringe hugged her slim waist perfectly. The matching basque gently conformed to her full breasts and the high collar was trimmed in plush black velvet. Long form-fitting sleeves reached to her wrists and the black velvet was repeated at the wide cuff. The fashionable bustle rested on her backside and high-buttoned shoes with small heels graced her feet.

The last piece of attire she added reminded her of her precarious situation. She strapped the peal-handled dagger to her upper thigh just in case of an emergency.

Her hair had grown some, but not enough to style properly, so she pulled it up and away from her face with two combs, allowing only a few wisps of curls to fall along her forehead and neck. She placed a black velvet Normandy bonnet on her head and finished her outfit with buff kid gloves.

Victoria held her head high, took a deep breath, and walked from the room to face the day.

Sebastian waited patiently at the foot of the stairs with Aaron. Both men were respectably outfitted in black.

Aaron caught sight of Victoria first, and Sebastian followed the direction of his widened eyes. His heart pounded viciously in his chest as she descended. He felt like a young schoolboy experiencing his first pangs of love, and he admonished himself for acting like such a love-struck puppy. After all, she was just another woman, no different from the rest he had sampled over the years. Then why did he continue to feel this consuming possessiveness toward her?

"Is Beth all prepared for the trip?" she asked, as though her sister would join them any moment.

"She is already aboard," Sebastian answered, extending his arm to her not merely out of courtesy, but for support.

Victoria gratefully accepted. His dark eyes were too earnest in their intentions to refuse. She walked out of the house to end a journey that she and her sister had been on for over a year.

Chapter Nine

The large locomotive spit and hissed as it sat stoically on the tracks. It looked as though it wanted to lunge forward and begin the journey that Victoria wished were already at an end.

She shivered though the day was warm and pleasant. Even the laughter of the children waiting to board the train and the adults in conversation did little to ease her tension. She silently worried over the confrontation with her uncle. Sebastian was powerful, but the law was on Tobias Withers's side and Sebastian was not above the law. She had a dreadful feeling she wouldn't be returning to San Francisco.

She watched the Dragon's tall lithe form move with grace and agility as he walked next to the station-master. His handsome face displayed no signs of emotion, yet beneath it Victoria knew there was a man who could love deeply.

She had seen it. It was hidden, yet there in small ways and the things he did for people. When he met that special woman he would make her his, branding her the

Dragon's lady forever.

She suddenly found herself irritated by the thought. Was it because she wished to be that woman? The one who knew the Dragon intimately, who bore his children, and harbored his love? She shook her head. *Nonsense, pure, nonsense, Victoria.*

"Miss Victoria," Daniel said, drawing her attention away from her all too wicked thoughts. "I want you to know how sorry I am over your loss."

"Thank you, Daniel," she replied, and couldn't help but ask what she had always suspected. "You knew, didn't you?"

"Yes, ma'am. You can't have eyes like yours and not be a female."

Victoria smiled and reached out, placing her hand on his. "Thank you for being such a good friend."

The train arrived in Santa Clara on schedule, an unusual occurrence. Sebastian waited with Victoria while Aaron saw to the coffin's removal. The Dragon was concerned by the silence that had overcome her as soon as they had boarded the train. All efforts of trying to converse with her had failed. Neither he, nor Aaron, could get her to utter a single word and it worried him.

He was use to the brashness of the lad and he rather missed her gutsy ways. Sheer courage and determination were the reasons she and her sister had survived so long on their own and he admired her for it. She needed that bold audaciousness now to fortify herself for what she must face.

120

He slipped his arm around her waist, steadying her as Beth's coffin was removed from the train. She stiffened. His grip tightened, digging into the folds of black material until she could feel his fingers pressing into her skin.

She watched in rigid silence as the highly polished mahogany coffin with shiny brass trim was hoisted onto a wagon. Tears spilled from her eyes at the thoughtfulness of the Dragon, and she closed her small fingers over his, squeezing tightly.

Sebastian leaned over and whispered, "I know, Vic, that you intend to repay each dime." He hoped his playful teasing would ignite some of the lad's stubborn determination. He wasn't disappointed.

"You bet I'm going to repay you," she responded in the boy's uneducated tongue. Sebastian smiled.

Victoria sat safely tucked between the two men as Aaron drove their rented carriage behind the wagon bearing Beth to her final resting place.

Victoria absentmindedly linked her hand with Sebastian, nervously gripping at his strong fingers as the carriage bounced along the bumpy road.

She didn't realize her actions proved her need of him, unknowingly demanded his protection and procuring it, for he silently vowed no harm would come to her.

Aaron caught sight of her desperate actions and Sebastian nodded to him, both men agreeing to defend the tiny woman who had worked her way into their hearts.

The Chambeau residence sat in a small valley. It was a self-sufficient estate and Victoria was proud of it. The house lacked the elegance of the homes on Rincon Hill, but here it was considered one of the most beautiful, with its full wraparound veranda and numerous windows reflecting the morning sun.

Here was where she and her family had shared many happy moments and here was where she would leave Beth to join their mother and father. Then she would be alone. A single tear slipped from the corner of her eye, and she wiped at it with fierce determination. She would not allow her uncle the satisfaction of seeing her cry.

Sebastian smiled. *Good for you, Vic.*

The family cemetery sat to the far right of the home among a group of towering trees lush with foliage and weeping branches. An appropriate spot for such a solemn occasion.

Victoria was surprised to see the many neighbors and friends gathered around the small fenced-in plot, but then her uncle would have to make a display of this, pretending to show his concern and sorrow.

She caught sight of him just as the carriage came to a halt. He stood between Preacher Johnson and her father's attorney, Mr. Fielding. His short pudgy frame was in stark contrast to the two tall men.

He looked somber in his mourning suit. His high stiff white collar made his heavy jowls appear even more pronounced. She was about to turn her gaze away from him when his eyes suddenly locked with hers. She watched as he slowly licked his thick lips as though he was tasting her and enjoying it.

She shivered and shut her eyes tightly against his blatant action, collapsing back upon the seat of the carriage.

Sebastian had caught the suggestive act and it ignited his fury. He contained it only by sheer willpower and the satisfying thought that he'd have his revenge.

"Victoria," he said soothingly. The delicate hand that had clung tenaciously to him all morning reached out to him once again. He helped her down. She straightened her skirt and stood tall as she waited for the procession to begin.

"Thank you," she whispered, firmly holding his hand and walking behind the six men who carried Beth's coffin to her final resting place.

His hand squeezed the one side of her slim waist, reassuring her he was there if needed.

Her eyes stole a quick glance to the stone markers that bore her parents' names. The tears she had promised herself she wouldn't shed involuntarily released themselves.

Her hand refused to relinquish her hold on the Dragon. He and Aaron took up a protective stance on either side of her as they stopped near the preacher.

The unsmiling man walked over to her and mumbled a few words of condolences before returning to his perch between her uncle and Mr. Fielding to begin the service.

Victoria stared at the shiny box. The thick ropes that would lower it into the deep hole were already situated beneath the coffin in preparation.

Her eyes fluttered lightly, hearing her father's distinct voice warn her that life wasn't always fair in its dealing, and it was at those times one needed strength and determination.

Well, Papa, she thought, I guess this is one of those times. She allowed her tears to flow steadily and silently as she bid farewell to her sister.

The preacher ended the service. Friends and neighbors filed passed her offering their sympathy. Sebastian and Aaron stepped aside to allow her to receive them.

Victoria was so engrossed with everyone's sincerity that she didn't notice Mr. Fielding and Preacher Johnson approach Sebastian and Aaron. They walked to a large tree, stopping beneath the drooping branches, and were soon deep in conversation.

The people drifted off into groups, chattering in whispered murmurs. Victoria continued to shake hands and accept condolences. The line grew shorter. She spied her uncle at the very end.

"So, you've finally returned," he snarled. "Although I daresay it was for the benefit of your sister."

"I have no intentions of remaining," she said, and took a step back.

He stepped forward, standing near enough to her so no one could hear. "You have no choice in the matter. I'm your legal guardian. You shall remain under my care."

"Never," she spoke through clenched teeth. "Never will I willingly stay and submit to your disgusting touch."

The pudgy man suffered the indignation of her cutting remark silently. The only indication that her words had disturbed him was the nervous twitch that had centered in his right cheek.

He turned his head casually from side to side to see if

anyone was watching. After making sure no one was, he slowly reached his hand out and grasped her thin wrist. "I do so enjoy force."

Victoria struggled against his tight grip. Her fury mounted at the injustice of all she had endured and without hesitation she reverted to the audaciousness of the lad. "Take your filthy, whoring hands off me."

Tobias's cheeks grew scarlet and he began to sputter. "Why—why, you . . ."

Victoria continued her verbal attack, delivering several well-chosen barbs that not only stung her uncle's pride, but caused his eyes to bulge in shock.

Tobias huffed, puffed, and sputtered at his niece's outrageous remarks. He couldn't stand there and ignore her insolence. He raised his hand, without thought to his whereabouts, and prepared to deliver a stinging blow to her insulting mouth.

"Good heavens!"

"Oh my!"

"Good gracious!"

The startled cries echoed throughout the graveyard as her uncle was suddenly hurtled into the air. His arms flew wildly about him and his hands reached out, grasping, but capturing nothing before he landed with a resounding thud against the hard ground.

The air was knocked from him in a loud whoosh. He fought to regain his breathing, an impossible task since the Dragon's boot was pushed firmly against his throat, preventing any further movement.

Tobias's meaty face brightened like a cherry. He gagged as his hands frantically tore at the black leather boot, attempting to gain his freedom.

125

"Listen well, Mr. Withers," Sebastian said in a loud clear voice for all to hear. "Victoria is my wife."

Tobias stopped struggling and lay still.

Sebastian removed his foot and walked over to Victoria grasping her arm. "Don't fight me on this," he whispered harshly.

She was too shocked to offer a response and even if she were capable of speaking she wouldn't, for the cold look in his dark eyes warned her of his determination.

"I have finally rendered you speechless," he murmured teasingly before releasing his crushing hold on her.

She thought she had caught a slight glimpse of emotion flash across his stern face—a show of admiration for her as though he admired her stamina and intelligence. She wasn't certain, but she held strong to the strange thought anyway.

Sebastian turned as the fallen man was being assisted to his feet by the preacher and Fielding. "My solicitor will contact you in regards to my wife's inheritance. Make certain you're expedient in providing him with the necessary papers. And make certain you vacate the premises by the end of the month."

"You—you can't throw me out of my home," Tobias whined while grasping for air.

Fielding supported the heavy man as much as his lanky frame would permit and tried placating him.

Sebastian looked upon the two men like an adult who was tired of dealing with children. "Gentlemen, I do believe the Chambeau property was entrusted to Withers until Victoria reached a specific age or married, as normally done. Thus, the property automatically reverts to me upon our marriage. Therefore, Withers will vacate *my* property as directed."

"I never gave permission for this union," he shouted, angry at losing his wealth.

"That's irrelevant. The union has already taken place and the marriage consummated." Sebastian turned and focused his penetrating eyes on Victoria, challenging her to deny it.

She become flustered and blushed in frustration.

Everyone present took it as a sign of a new bride who had just discovered her wifely duties.

Sebastian's fine lips curled up slightly at the corners, frustrating her even more, but she wisely remained silent.

He faced the crowd once again, addressing himself to her uncle. "There is nothing you can do to change what has passed. Victoria is mine and shall remain so."

"Perhaps," Preacher Johnson interjected softly, "Victoria didn't freely agree to this marriage. If she had second thoughts, the church could arrange a dissolvement."

"You doubt my word?" Sebastian asked, annoyed by the clergyman's interference.

Preacher Johnson patted his perspiring brow with his soiled white handkerchief. "No, sir. I but wish to hear Victoria openly admit her acceptance of this union."

Victoria hesitated only a moment, for she wondered if being obligated to the Dragon would entail more than she could handle. "I accept Sebastian Blood willingly as my husband."

The preacher nodded his head in satisfaction as well

127

as breathing a sigh of relief.

"Perhaps we should adjourn to the main house," Tobias said, noticing the mourners had lingered to listen to the startling news that surely would be all over town by early morning. He didn't need gossip spreading around. He had enough problems.

He brushed at his dark waistcoat, regaining command of himself. "Let's all go and enjoy the mourning feast that has been prepared. After all, I'm sure Victoria wishes to tell her friends all about her wedding."

Sebastian caught the glint of doubt in the man's eyes. He covered Victoria's hand with his, leaned over, and spoke softly. His warm breath whispered across her face, tingling her delicate skin. "Do you feel up to this, or do you wish to retire to the hotel?"

She couldn't help but grasp at his firm hand and pretend that his words were genuine. Even his eyes seemed to possess an intense desire to comfort her and she shivered.

"The day has been too much for you. We will leave for the hotel at once," he said, disturbed by the way she trembled.

She shook her head. "No, please. I'd like to see the house again and gather some of my personal belongings."

He debated the wisdom of submitting her to more unpleasantries, but bowed to her wishes. "We shall not stay long."

She nodded and forced a slight smile.

"We will join you at the main house after Victoria spends a few private moments alone with her sister,"

128

Sebastian announced, curtly dismissing everyone.

The crowd dispersed, eager to adjourn to the house and have the chance to question Victoria about her secret wedding.

Aaron waited patiently by the buggy.

Sebastian spoke after everyone had departed. "Before you bid a final farewell to your sister, I wish to explain my strange actions."

Victoria lifted her head, tilting it to the side as she gazed up at the man who had proclaimed himself her husband. The tight lines etched around his mouth warned her he would brook no opposition to his decision and her silence demonstrated her willingness to listen.

"Marriage is the only way I can protect you," he began. "Otherwise you will be at your uncle's mercy, and I refuse to allow that to happen. I have a friend who is a judge and owes me several favors. Tomorrow when we return to San Francisco we'll be married and our license will be predated." He didn't find it necessary to add the fact that he had discovered this the morning at the train station. His solicitor had worked on the problem throughout the night and had informed him of the specifications of the Chambeau will just before the train was to leave. It was then he had decided upon the marriage.

"But how can—"

"Money buys anything, Victoria."

"Yes, I suppose it does," she said, realizing that even she was available for a price. After all, he was offering her protection, but what would he demand in return?

He caught the look of doubt and suspicion flash

across her face. He knew now was not the time to discuss what he expected from her. "I don't think we should keep everyone waiting. We can discuss the particulars of this arrangement later this evening."

She agreed, and he walked away to join Aaron.

Victoria glanced down at the coffin. Tears stung her eyes and slipped down her cheeks. "Oh, Beth, we were always there for each other. Now I have no one, no one, but the Dragon."

Chapter Ten

Victoria sat amidst a sea of wagging tongues.

"He's gorgeous," sighed Belinda Dubbins, a young woman whose round shape was being added to by the piece of thick spice cake she was shoving into her mouth.

"You're so lucky," pouted Amanda Jarvis, raising her teacup to her lips.

"Bet you have plenty of babies," giggled Sara Watson and received several threatening glares from the surrounding women for her audacious remark.

Victoria smiled and nodded, not actually hearing any of the busy chatter. She was too engrossed observing the surprising changes that had occurred in her home since her departure.

The family's faithful servants had been replaced by people with unsmiling faces and stiff postures. Their black uniforms with white starched collars and aprons were in stark contrast to the garish furnishings.

Victoria felt a tightness in her chest as her eyes surveyed the once-familiar room. Rich reds and startling gold colors were splashed throughout the parlor. Ornate gold objects filled every nook and cranny. Madam Champlain and the girls would have been right at home among this repulsive glitter, but she wasn't. This house was no longer the sanctuary it was when she was young.

The night she and Beth had fled in terror was when it had ceased being Chambeau property, and she found herself once again wanting to escape.

Her eyes searched the room and caught sight of Aaron trapped in conversation with Mrs. Harding. As soon as the woman had learned he was a physician, she had started bombarding him with complaints of her ailments, most of them imaginary.

Victoria continued displaying her forced smile, her head perpetually nodding as though it were precariously balanced on the tip of a spindle.

She needed to get away from these cackling women. She glanced about the room for Sebastian. It was easy to find him. His towering height and impressive stance drew all eyes to him.

She watched as men surrounded him, hounding him for business advice, and how women openly flirted with him, practically offering themselves on a silver platter.

And to think this man who created such attention was shortly to become her husband. It was a fact she found hard to grasp. She was actually going to be Mrs. Sebastian Blood. A slight shiver ran through her and for one tiny moment she felt a terrifying doubt as to her future.

Sebastian noticed the way she drew in her shoulders and the almost undetectable frown that flashed across her face. She was upset. He quickly stood erect away from the mantel against which he had been casually leaning.

He took a step forward, but Victoria forced a smile, shaking her head as though telling him it wasn't necessary. She was fine.

He nodded and tilted his head slightly to one side as though asking if she were certain. She dazzled him with a grin that brought a sly smile to his lips before he turned to once again converse with the numerous men.

Victoria's grin faded quickly after she excused herself, receiving disappointing glances from the women. She had a strange urge to see her old room and gather some of her personal things.

She walked into the foyer and stopped. A chill suddenly descended upon her. She shivered, rubbing her arms. The odd feeling worsened as she approached the staircase. Her slim hands hugged her arms to her chest. She delivered a silent tongue-lashing to herself for being so silly. Why, she had walked the notorious Barbary Coast in the dead of night, alone. How could she be fearful of climbing these steps?

Victoria forced her trembling hands to grasp the polished wooden banister and placed one foot on the first step. She glanced upward to the silent emptiness. She wished the fog from the waterfront would mysteriously appear and wrap her in its safety.

Her foot hesitantly took one step at a time, climbing slowly, cautiously. What was it she feared? What horrible thing was waiting for her at the top of the steps?

She stopped suddenly. A cold chill embraced her body as that fateful night from over a year ago came tumbling back in vivid detail. She cringed at the horrid remembrance of her uncle's pudgy hands pulling at her clothing, touching her bare flesh, forcing himself upon her.

Her eyelids fluttered closed as she fought to drive the wretched sight from her mind. Her hand firmly gripped the railing for support as she felt a wave of weakness attack her limbs. Her legs wobbled. Her arms shook, yet she was unable to move.

Her uncle had instilled such a deeply rooted fear in her that she couldn't break free of it. It locked around her like a tight-fitting chain. Panic engulfed her as a lone tear slipped down her flushed cheek. Her uncle had succeeded in his domination of her. He had won. She had lost.

Strong fingers glided slowly across her hand that gripped the banister while a muscled arm circled her slim waist until it rested snugly around her middle. It wasn't necessary to see the man's face to know his identity. Victoria gratefully leaned back against the powerful form of the Dragon.

"Relax, love. I'm here," he whispered. His soothing voice shattered the intruding vision.

"Sebastian," she murmured, barely able to speak.

"Hush. It's all right. No one is going to hurt you."

Her eyes remained closed, and she allowed her full weight to rest against him.

His long fingers tenderly caressed her hand that refused to relinquish the hold on the banister. "Let go, Vic," he whispered near her ear. His warm breath fanned the side of her cheek, raising the delicate skin on her arms.

She heard his gentle command, yet she couldn't

make her limbs obey. "I—I can't."

"Listen to me, Vic," he said softly while locking his fingers over hers. "There's nothing to fear. What happened those many months ago is in the past. It's over. It will never happen again. No one will ever hurt you."

She began to loosen her rigid hold. His reassuring words worked their magic until he added something that caused even more fright.

"My God, Victoria, my penchant for revenge against anyone who dares to touch you surpasses that of my desire to end the life of that miserable creature, the Serpent."

Victoria felt a wave of pain stab her chest. Her fingers reaffirmed their tight grip on the banister, clinging to it as though it were a lifeline.

Sebastian's fingers pressed firmly over hers. He had hoped his choice of words would have made her realize just how safe she was with him since she had witnessed many times how powerful his thirst of revenge was against the Serpent. But somehow his statement had the opposite affect on her. She appeared even more frightened than before. And he was at a loss as to comprehend why.

His moist lips lightly brushed her temple. "Trust me," he whispered, attempting to gently pry her fingers loose.

She feared surrendering her total trust to him and clung tenaciously to the wooden railing.

"Let go," he demanded gently, pressing featherlight kisses along her cheek.

She felt torn between two worlds. One promised trust, understanding, and possible love, while the other hatred, revenge, and possibly death. It isn't fair, a small voice inside her screamed.

Sebastian sensed her confusion and took advantage of her weakness. He forcibly ripped her hand from the banister. A wrenching of nails against wood caused him to shudder. He quickly turned Victoria into the comfort of his strong arms.

She pressed against him seeking his protection. His chest pillowed her head and her arms were wrapped tight about his waist.

His hand soothingly stroked her hair while he spoke softly to her. She didn't hear all of his reassuring words, for the dagger, which she had secured to the inside of her thigh, suddenly felt like it was branding its impression into her tender skin.

She turned her face into his chest. Her lips brushed the white cotton of his shirt, and she wished that she could touch his heart and see if there was any room for forgiveness.

He read her demonstrative actions as a capitulation to his request and felt a small victory in an attempt toward winning her total trust. He sensed she harbored doubts, but he was sure of his ability to deal with those. He was troubled, though, by a strange feeling that she carried an even heavier burden. A burden that was laden with fear.

His midnight blue eyes turned almost obsidian as his anger mounted. His thoughts spun in turmoil over his silent suspicions. Had her uncle been successful that night in his attack? Was she ashamed to speak of it to him? He had every intention of discovering if his suspicions were true. And if they were, her uncle would regret the day he set eyes on the Dragon.

"Is she all right?" Aaron asked, standing at the foot of the staircase.

Sebastian turned his head to look at his friend. "She's fine. I'm going to help her gather what she wishes to take, then we'll leave for the hotel. She's spent enough time here and any more would only prove disastrous."

Aaron nodded in agreement. "I'll have the buggy brought around front in about thirty minutes. Will that give you enough time?"

"Plenty," he said, lifting a startled Victoria up into his arms and effortlessly carrying her up the remainder of the steps.

"That way." She pointed down the hall. She rested her head against his shoulder. She was too drained to protest and at the moment she felt relieved to be cradled in his arms, away from all hurt and pain.

Sebastian walked into the room she had indicated and gently lowered her to the carpeted floor. He remained standing behind her in case she found the memories too painful and required physical support as well as emotional.

She stood in complete silence. Her eyes scanned the familiar surroundings. It was exactly as she had remembered it, not an object out of place. It was as though time hung suspended and she had been transported back one year. The pale pink floral wallpaper still highlighted the walls, and the starched white ruffled curtains still covered the three windows. The row of her favorite books remained on top of her small writing desk sandwiched between two iron bookends. Her closet door stood ajar displaying her clothes neatly pressed and hung in preparation for

137

her use.

An icy chill ran through Victoria. This room had been kept in readiness for her return. Her uncle had no doubts about his ability to find her and keep her here. The thought of his sick intentions repelled her. She turned quickly to leave only to crash against Sebastian.

His strong hands instantly seized her shoulders and held her swaying body in command.

"I want to leave," she demanded.

"What about your clothes? Perhaps there are some keepsakes you wish to bring along." His grasp remained firm, and he forcibly directed her into the center of the room. Her small frame was no challenge for his brute strength and it necessitated her obedience.

"Are you frightened of this room because this is where your uncle attacked you?" he asked directly, hoping to shock her into an immediate response.

His tactic worked. She nodded without taking her wide eyes from the bed. She watched in horror as the scene unfolded before her. She lay pinned beneath her uncle's pudgy body. Her nightdress was torn and pushed up, exposing her thighs. Her uncle rubbed against her, his breath heavy and groaning with each thrusting movement. His hands fumbled at his nightshirt. Victoria reached out to the table next to her bed. Her hand touched the cold steel of the dagger—the pearl-handled dagger her father had jokingly given to his wife for a birthday one year. "For protection," he had laughed. Victoria's hand closed around it. As her uncle pushed himself off her to remove the interfering garment she lashed out at him.

"What did he do to you?"

The scene faded with Sebastian's words, but not the

memory. Her uncle had robbed her, not of her virginity, but of her innocence. Gone were her youthful dreams of tender love. She had learned much in this last year living along the waterfront and she wasn't a naive young girl any longer.

"Well?" Sebastian said.

Victoria met the Dragon's determined look with one of her own. "It's none of your business." She walked to the closet, swung it open, and pulled out a large satchel from the bottom.

Sebastian held rein on his temper. "It is my business, Victoria. You are about to become my wife."

She flashed him an angry look as though saying that was his decision not hers. Then she continued packing in silence.

"Answer me," he demanded with an icy stare that was meant to freeze her where she stood.

She walked over to her dressing table and with her back to him she spoke. "I don't wish to discuss it at the moment."

"Really, and when do you think you will *wish* to discuss it?"

She raised her head and stared defiantly at his reflection in the mirror. "Never!"

"That's not good enough for me," he snapped and advanced toward her.

His towering height looked even more menacing in the mirror and she spun around to face him.

"Tell me, Vic. Now!" he demanded.

She placed her hands on her narrow hips and held her head high. She had had enough of people telling her what to do. "What? Tell you what? That my uncle tore my nightgown from my body, that his hands touched me intimately, that he rubbed his—" She broke off choking on her own sobs.

Sebastian's face was rigid. His mouth was clenched tight in anger. His jaw muscles were hard and his dark eyes almost glowed with the blue fires of hell. He knew he should reach out and comfort her, hold her until the dreadful memories faded, but he needed to know. He had to know.

He slipped his fingers beneath her chin and raised her face to look at him. The sobs that racked her body tore at his heart, and her wide, green eyes pleaded for him to stop.

His dark brows drew together. A tiny flicker of sorrow crossed his face and for one brief moment Victoria thought she had touched his heart. But then he spoke. "Did he take your virginity?"

She released a heavy sigh. "Would it matter?"

"Did he?" he demanded, his fingers biting firmly into her chin.

She tried to pull away, but it was useless. His strength was no match for hers, but the defiance of the lad's sharp tongue was. "I not going to tell you, Blood."

Surprisingly Sebastian retained his composure. A smile even managed to emerge from his lips. "Fine, Vic. Then I'll find out for myself." He released his hold on her and walked over by her desk.

"What do you mean?" she asked, fearing she already knew the answer.

"We are husband and wife and as such share a bed. After all, we can't have the townspeople gossiping about how newlyweds sleep in separate beds."

"But we really aren't mar—"

"An oversight that will be rectified by tomorrow

140

evening. We may as well start the honeymoon tonight since I refuse to leave here without a satisfactory answer."

"You can't—"

"I can do anything I want . . . to my wife," he stated bluntly. "Now do I get an answer, or do I discover for myself?"

Victoria didn't know how to respond. At times she seemed to ache for his nearness and other times she feared what the end results would bring. She truly didn't know if she were capable of sharing such an intimate act with him. But there was one thing she was certain of: she didn't want their union consummated tonight.

She lowered herself to the edge of the bed and tossed her head up in defiance of his demand. "I'm still a virgin."

He walked over to her. He reached out and ran his finger lightly along her full lip. It was moist, warm, and aching to be caressed. He suppressed the urge to bend down and kiss it. "Make certain you speak the truth, Vic. If you've lied, I'll discover it easily enough, and then your uncle will have hell to pay."

She pulled away from his touch. It confused her, causing her body to react oddly. "I'm telling you the truth. I can't make you believe me."

How could he explain the strange emotions that tore at him when even he didn't understand them. The thought of someone hurting her outraged him to the point of extreme danger. She belonged to him . . . no one else. And tomorrow evening it would be a lifetime commitment. He hadn't planned on marrying yet, but then he wasn't getting any younger, and he did desire children. Something about this pint-size bundle of femininity touched his heart and ignited his loins. No woman had done this before to him.

"I believe you," he said, caressing her soft cheek with his finger. She tensed against the unexpected flutter of pleasure and he smiled at her innocent response.

"Finish packing, Victoria," he commanded in a gentle tone.

She obeyed without hesitation, needing to keep a safe distance between her racing heart and the mighty Dragon.

Chapter Eleven

Victoria hesitated a moment before crossing the threshold of the hotel room assigned to them. She sensed her fate would be sealed upon taking this final step and doubt suddenly shadowed her mind. She had faced many obstacles before and had managed to come away unscathed, yet she felt this time would prove different. How could she become the Dragon's lady and walk away untouched?

The choice was taken from her as Sebastian's hand cupped her elbow and propelled her into the room. The door closed behind them with a loud click, and she shut her eyes tightly attempting to stifle the overpowering urge to flee.

"I'm afraid these meager accommodations were all that were available," Sebastian said, sensing her apprehension and wishing to ease it.

She opened her eyes and surveyed the Renaissance-style bedroom. He considered this meager accommodations? But then his wealth and position in society had afforded him many luxuries.

She found her attention drawn to the object against the far wall. An intricately carved walnut bed with a primrose quilt and ruffled-edged pillows sat in readiness.

She swallowed the lump lodged in her throat and spoke in a soft whisper, barely able to hear her own words. "There's only one bed."

Amusement registered in his deep blue eyes and the devilish curl of his finely shaped lips proved he had heard every word.

"You can't possibly expect me to sleep with you."

"Victoria, our marriage tomorrow is only a formality. There is no reason why we cannot share a bed this evening."

"I will not share a bed with you," she said, stamping her foot in defiance and worrying that she couldn't prevent this giant of a man from doing as he wished.

"Disobedience from my wife so soon in our marriage," he teased, removing his black waistcoat and throwing it over the chair. "Tsk tsk, Victoria. Shame on you. Don't you know it is your duty to share my bed?"

"When we are married," she said. "Then it will be my duty, but we aren't married *yet.*"

His long fingers unfastened the row of buttons along his vest. "Then what you're saying is that tomorrow evening you will come willingly to my bed."

Victoria's fingers twisted nervously. She wasn't certain if she was capable of that most intimate act shared between a husband and wife, and she feared making a commitment she would not be able to keep.

Her attention was drawn to the casual ease with which he undid his tie. He worked at a slow, titillating

144

pace. She imagined his hand gliding intimately over her exposed flesh. His touch was warm, gentle, and welcoming. She shivered at the mere thought. Welcome. She would welcome his touch? The idea disturbed her, but not half as much as the heated sensations her daydreaming had ignited.

She spoke, forcing herself to sound in control, but her inexperienced body sent another message to the observant Dragon. "Don't you think we should become better acquainted?"

His shirt was partially open, exposing hard muscled flesh. "I think it would be most unwise of us to wait."

"Why?" she asked. Her wide eyes were drawn to his actions as he pulled the shirt from his trousers, finished opening it, then tossed it carelessly to the carpet.

"Because unwarranted fear can grow, and I don't wish you to become more frightened than you already are."

She took a step backward as though the extra distance would protect her.

"Take off your things, Victoria," he demanded softly.

"No. I will not remove my clothes," she refused, clutching her small purse to her breasts.

His hand snapped forward, pulling the purse from her tight grip and tossing it to the floor. "I meant your hat and gloves . . . to start."

She obliged him by removing her hat. When she was about to start on her gloves, he reached out to assist her. His long fingers gently began to pull the glove from her hand. As he did, her eyes caught sight of the famous tattoo. Her delicate fingers cautiously approached the blue dragon, inching towards it in a mixture of fear and awe. Her hand hovered above it in doubt. Its striking beauty urged her to touch it, yet its fierce power held her back.

"It doesn't bite," Sebastian teased.

He held his arm still for inspection. He wasn't prepared for the bolt of desire that shot through him when her warm fingers caressed his flesh. He responded instantly to her innocent touch and silently cursed himself for allowing her to affect him so.

Victoria was too engrossed with her exploration of the monster to pay any heed to his disturbed condition. She gingerly examined every line and detail. Her finger started at the long curved tail, tracing it slowly, working her way along the blue scales, around the horned head, over the dark eyes and finishing with the flames that shot from his open mouth. She was intrigued by its beauty, yet feared what it represented. Power, sheer brutal power.

She tilted her head back to look into his blue eyes and furrowed her brow at his strange expression. His mouth was closed tightly. Small beads of perspiration lay sprinkled across his forehead. "Do you feel all right?" she asked, her hand gently covering the fierce tattoo.

The sincerity in her voice forced his control to snap. His hand reached out, grabbing her around her slim waist and pulling her flush against him. His mouth claimed hers urgently, primitively, demanding entrance, demanding she respond, demanding her surrender.

His other hand gripped the back of her head possessively, his fingers running through the silky strands of her short hair. He brought her closer as though wanting to merge his hungry body with hers and taste fully of her sweet nectar.

He released her mouth and she whimpered. Her lashes fluttered, heavily drugged by desire, and she trembled, wanting more.

"No," he whispered harshly. "I want to taste you. I want to taste every inch of you."

His mouth feasted on the slim column of her neck. She tasted of soft roses and womanly flesh. The sensual flavor made him hunger for more. He savored the erotic taste. His tongue slid temptingly along her neck, dipping below the ruffled collar.

She quivered in his arms. He felt the rise of her flesh against his lips, tiny bumps that tantalized and teased him. He pulled her toward the bed, gently cradling her as they fell upon the soft quilt.

They lay side by side. His mouth drifted to her ear. He nibbled along the dainty edge as his hand sought the small buttons on the front of her basque. He carefully unfastened each one while his mouth continued to coax her into submission.

His skill as a lover was too much for one so innocent. No thoughts of her greedy uncle invaded her vision. her only thoughts were of the Dragon's touch. It inflamed her. It made her weak. It made her urgent. It made her want him.

Her arms slipped around his shoulders, hesitant, shy, yet needing to touch his flesh. He was warm and hard and it thrilled her.

She moaned when his lips caressed the bare flesh of her shoulder. The throbbing heat that seem centered in the valley of her tightly closed legs raced upward, scorching her soft nipples into a hardened response.

Sebastian was impatient to taste the rosy orbs that sprung to life beneath the thin white chemise. He growled his annoyance at the simple obstruction and grabbed the fine material in his hand, ripping it down the middle to expose the buds that tempted him.

He eagerly captured their ripeness in his mouth, one at a time. His tongue flicked across their peaks, taunting them in erotic play as he reveled in their sweet taste.

Victoria dug her fingers into his shoulder, confused by the strange desire surging through her. She tensed, her fingers digging deeper, when his teeth playfully bit a tender nipple. The soreness still lingered from the confining cloth.

Sebastian felt her slight resistance and raised his head to gently cover her full lips with featherlight kisses. "Did I hurt you, love?" he murmured.

She shook her head rapidly, fearing if she told him the truth he would stop and at the moment, although she could not fathom why, she wanted him to continue his ravishing assault.

He smiled, kissed the tip of her nose, then lowered his head to nip gently at her nipple.

She winced. He slowly raised his head. His midnight blue eyes bore into her questioningly. Her cheeks flushed bright red in embarrassment of his unspoken request.

He realized it was useless to pursue the issue since she was obviously uncomfortable with confiding in him. In time that would change, but for now he would allow her her innocence.

He nestled at her neck, nuzzling the soft skin as his hand traveled with deliberate slowness over her clothing. It slipped across her belly, along her slender hip, down her thigh, and finally rested between her legs.

"You feel so good, love. So very good," he whispered. His hand caressed her, causing a heated friction beneath her clothing.

Victoria moaned and pressed her face to his, seeking what she instinctively knew only he could provide. His hand moved slowly down her leg and slipped beneath her heavy skirt. He ran his fingers along her stocking, traveling up, up, up . . .

"Sebastian!" Victoria screamed. His hand stopped only inches away from the Serpent's dagger.

"What's wrong?" he asked, concerned by her trembling.

"You must stop," she insisted. "We aren't married. This isn't proper."

He was startled by the fear that made her eyes sparkle an emerald green. He wondered if she were recalling her uncle's attack, and if she had lied to him regarding the outcome. 'We will most definitely be married tomorrow. There's no need for us to wait."

"You promised, Sebastian. You promised you would not touch me tonight."

"Yet you will willingly allow me to finish tomorrow what we have begun this evening?" he queried, slowly moving his hand upward.

"Yes," she screamed. "Now stop. Please stop."

He was so stunned by the tears that pooled in her eyes that he removed his hand immediately and brought it up to cup her chin. He tenderly ran his finger along her lower lip. "Do you fear coupling with such intensity that you weep?"

"Yes, yes," she insisted, not caring what he thought her reason were as long as he didn't discover the dagger.

He gently wiped her tears away. "If you fear it this much tonight, you will fear it even more tomorrow."

"No, Sebastian. Tomorrow will be different. I will be away from all these horrible memories, and Beth's death will not be ever so present," she lied, for she had not thought of her departed sister since they had entered the room.

Sebastian berated himself for not thinking of her sister's burial today and accepted her excuse with only a bit of doubtfulness. "I have been inconsiderate. Forgive me."

Victoria was moved by his unexpected thoughtfulness and berated herself for her continued deception.

He sat up pulling her with him. His desire was still strong, but he fought against it. He had no wish to force himself upon her just to satisfy his needs. He wanted her willing and pliant to his touch.

Her small hands fumbled with the torn material, attempting to cover her naked breasts, but Sebastian pushed the clothes away. He bent his head and gently kissed the tender nipples. She shivered at the light brush of his lips, and the instant hardening response they caused.

He lifted his head. "Why does it hurt you?"

Her hands tried to cover her nakedness from his penetrating stare, but he would not have it.

"No," he insisted, grasping her slim wrists in his and preventing her modesty. "I'll have my answer first."

The thought of refusing his simple request never entered her mind, for she feared what might occur if he continued to look at her with such intense hunger. "I used a rough cloth to bind my breasts when I masqueraded as the lad, and its coarse texture irritated me."

He stood, walked over to where he had dropped his shirt and picked it up.

Victoria hastily pulled her basque together.

"I'll see if Aaron has ointment to ease your pain."

"That isn't—"

"It is," he said in a soft demand. "Take the opportunity of my absence to slip into your nightgown. If you aren't changed and in bed before my return I will assume you wish to continue with the consummation of our marriage. Do I make myself clear?"

She nodded, trying to think of a safe place to hide the dagger.

The door closed and Victoria sprung into immediate action. She took the weapon from its hiding place and searched frantically for a spot. She chose the mattress, assuming there would be no reason for him to look beneath it.

It took only seconds to strip off her clothes and shake the wrinkles from the high-necked, long-sleeve nightgown before dropping it over her head and tying the three blue bows across her bosom. She quickly brushed the mop of sable brown curls that refused to fall anywhere but softly around her face and climbed into bed. Sebastian opened the door just as she pulled the covers protectively up to her chin.

She watched him enter the room. A slight teasing smile played at the corners of his tempting lips. He stripped off his shirt and once again dropped it carelessly to the floor.

151

When his hands began to undo his trousers Victoria snapped her eyes shut and slipped beneath the quilt.

His faint mocking laughter filled the room, and she felt a blush creep over her cheeks. The bed creaked from his added weight, and when his hard thigh pressed against her, she took a deep breath and prayed. It was obvious he was completely naked.

She silently berated herself over her strong desire for this man. She felt like a wanton woman. Why, he hadn't even mentioned love, yet here she was willing to abandon herself to his pleasure, not to mention her own.

"Victoria," he said. The demand in his voice jolted her and forced her to peek her head from beneath the safety of the quilt. "We definitely need to discuss your choice of nightwear."

"There's something wrong with this gown?" she asked innocently, since it was her favorite.

"Yes, there's too much of it," he said, smiling wickedly as he casually untied the ribbons secured across her bosom.

"Sebastian," she said, grasping his hand before it could go any farther. "You promised."

"Easy, love," he whispered. "I have some ointment from Aaron that will temporarily relieve your soreness."

She blushed at his mention of her intimate distress. "I'll put it on."

"What? And do me out of the pleasure of touching your lovely breasts?" he teased with a kiss to her cheek.

"I think it would be safer," she smiled.

"I'll be extremely gentle," he whispered, his mouth only inches from hers.

"That's what I'm afraid of."

"I insist."

"You promise to behave?"

"You wound me, woman. I already gave my word."

"Promise," she repeated, still grasping his hand.

He responded with obvious reluctance. "I promise."

She released his hand, knowing the Dragon would never break a promise.

He pushed the light material of her nightgown aside, exposing her breasts. She closed her eyes as his fingers connected with her nipples. He gently massaged the cream around and over her taut orbs.

"You have beautiful breasts, Victoria," he whispered.

His words were spoken with sincerity, and they startled her. Here she was in bed with the powerful Dragon, who was caressing her intimately, and who she was going to marry tomorrow. Yet no words of love had been spoken, no proposal offered, just a command. She suddenly became irritated at his authoritative attitude.

"Sebastian," she began, "it isn't necessary for you to marry me tomorrow. I have provided for myself for over a year, and I can continue to do so."

"By working for Madam Champlain as a scrub boy?" he asked sarcastically.

"No. I can leave San Francisco and begin elsewhere."

"With what? You have no money. Now stop talking such foolishness," he snapped, securing the ribbons on her nightgown.

"I'm not being foolish. You announce to everyone I'm your wife, then tell me we will be married, and

153

never bother to ask if I'm willing, or if I wish to spend the rest of my life with you. And suppose I wish to love the man I marry?"

"Love?" he laughed. "Love is a fleeting emotion best wasted on the young and naive, which I am neither. And you have no choice in the matter. You require protection, and I'm in the position to provide it. I planned to marry someday and since I find myself physically attracted to you, I see no reason not to enter into this arrangement. It's better being shackled to a passionate woman than one who fears the repeated intimate contact of the union."

"Shackled!" she said incredulously. "Isn't it I who shall be shackled to you?"

"I think you will enjoy our shackling," he teased, slipping his hand beneath the cover and searching for the source of her pleasure.

"Stop that," she demanded, slapping his roaming hand. "I've decided against this farce of a marriage. I refuse to enter into such a ludicrous union."

Sebastian's hand darted upward until his fingers hugged her chin in a tight grasp. He leaned over her; his scowling expression displayed his anger. "You will listen closely, Vic. If you try to prevent our union tomorrow I shall lock you in my bedroom and repeatedly make love to you until you are heavy with my child. Then you will have no alternative but to accept my generous offer."

"You wouldn't," she gasped.

"You know damn well I don't make idle threats."

She clamped her mouth shut and refused to speak. Perhaps she could manage to escape before the ceremony.

"Don't even think of fleeing, Victoria," he warned, turning onto his back and pillowing his arms beneath his head. "I'd come after you."

She thought about pointing out the fact that he couldn't find the Serpent, so what made him think he'd be able to find her. But she wisely remained silent.

"Good night, Victoria."

"Good night," she mumbled and turned on her side trying to ignore the presence of his hard muscled thigh pressed intimately against her leg.

Chapter Twelve

Victoria woke to an empty room and immediately took
advantage of Sebastian's absence. She hastily scrubbed
her face, brushed her hair, and donned her black
mourning outfit. She just finished securing the dagger
to her thigh and was straightening her skirt when he
entered.

Sebastian favored her with a teasing grin. "After this
evening, love, I will enjoy watching you dress and
undress in front of me."

Her face turned scarlet. "I'm hungry," she said,
choosing to ignore his remark.

"Aaron's waiting downstairs in the dining salon. We
have just enough time for breakfast before the train
arrives," he said, enjoying the tinge of color to her
cheeks. It was going to be a delight having this bold, yet
innocent woman as his wife.

Victoria picked up her hat and glanced in the mirror
as she placed it on her head.

"Must you wear that?"

"A lady never goes out without covering her head,"

156

she remarked, fastening it in place with a long hat pin.

"Then make certain you purchase a few colorful ones as soon as possible. I hate black on you."

"But I'm in mourning. I must wear it for one year." She couldn't disrespect her sister's passing by wearing colorful clothing; that was unthinkable. Why, it just wasn't done. "What would people say?"

Sebastian checked his pocket watch and replaced it in his vest as though unperturbed by her statement. "I don't give a damn what people say. I refuse to allow our marriage to resemble a funeral. You will wear becoming colors beginning this evening."

She opened her mouth to protest.

"Don't waste your breath, Vic. Beth would have agreed with me on this point."

She reluctantly took the arm he held out as they exited the room, silently cursing his overbearing manner as they descended the stairs.

"Just in time," Aaron said, smiling, as he rose to greet them. "I took the liberty of ordering and everything is ready."

Victoria slipped into the chair Sebastian held out for her and picked up the delicate china cup to gratefully sip the hot coffee.

Sebastian played the host, serving her from the many steaming dishes. Scrambled eggs, fat sausages, sliced potatoes, thick biscuits, and hot gravy were liberally piled on her plate with no protest from her. She was famished. After barely eating yesterday, her hunger was ravenous.

"I was thinking," Aaron said, helping himself to a large serving of eggs and a biscuit smothered in gravy. "Why don't you have that minister friend of yours

157

perform the ceremony? You know, the one who has that mission on Jackson Street."

"Rev. Otis Gibson," Sebastian said. "I'd prefer Judge Connors. Reverend Gibson is heavily involved with helping the Chinese. I'm not sure he'd be open to predating the marriage certificate."

"I don't see why he'd mind when your influence was so instrumental in securing the release of those two Chinese men from jail."

"I know he feels indebted to me, but I don't wish to compromise his convictions."

"I've heard many of the speeches condemning the influx of Chinese," Victoria added. "What did these railroad men expect, that when the railroad was completed they would all miraculously disappear? It was all right when they labored cheaply for them, but now that they wish to enter the job market they're screaming about the foreigners stealing jobs."

Sebastian was surprised by her perception of the current situation. "There are many labor unions in San Francisco that feel the abundance of Chinese is hurting them."

"That's nonsense," she argued. "Why, most of the men in San Francisco wouldn't do the menial work the Chinese are doing. They feel it's beneath their dignity."

Aaron agreed. "That's true, but the Chinese also have been tagged with a bad reputation because of their opium dens and houses of forced prostitution."

Victoria couldn't argue with that. Too many strange stories circulated the waterfront concerning the dangers of opium. She, herself, had seen young Chinese girls fresh off the ships forced into certain unsavory establishments only to emerge weeks later bleary-eyed and in search of a customer.

Sebastian assumed that her troubled expression was caused by the harsh memories she had gathered posing as a lad. It was rough enough for the seamen and the young boys forced to work the docks, but for a woman it was unthinkable. He shuddered to guess what lessons she had learned. "You've seen much working along the waterfront, haven't you, Victoria?"

She released a small sigh; her wide eyes fixed upon her plate as she spoke tonelessly. "I saw many things that I sometimes wish I hadn't."

A tremor raced through Sebastian. She had been lucky playing the little charade, but luck didn't last forever, and it was only a matter of time before her true gender would have been discovered. "It's remarkable you survived on your own for as long as you did. With the Chinese and labor union problems, I'm surprised you found any work at all," he commented.

Victoria was drifting in her memories, recalling the past difficult months, and she accidentally dropped her guard. "Yes, if it weren't for my nightly activities, Beth and I never would have survived."

Sebastian slowly placed the fragile China cup on the saucer, not even bothering to sip the coffee as was his intention. "Nightly activities?"

Aaron also regarded her oddly.

She forced a smile while inwardly trembling. You fool, she silently screamed. *You stupid fool.*

"What were these nightly activities, Victoria?" Sebastian asked, curious as to what a small woman could do at night along the waterfront to earn extra money. The answer he imagined he didn't care for.

"Won't we miss the train? It's getting late," she said,

hoping to divert their attention.

"She's right, Sebastian," Aaron said, checking his watch. "We best get a move on."

The three stood. Aaron walked on ahead. Sebastian slipped his hand beneath her elbow guiding her out and applying pressure to her arm, demonstrating his anger.

She attempted to pull away, but he wouldn't allow it. His fingers dug farther into her skin, and she winced from the added pressure.

"I expect an answer, Victoria, and I won't be dissuaded," he whispered harshly.

The three boarded the train in silence, none seeing the short, pudgy figure spying on them from the train station window. His thick, meaty fingers rubbed at his sore throat while he watched them disappear inside the large vehicle. He'd have his revenge, and it would taste sweet. He licked his lips, tasting not only retribution, but the soft flesh of his niece, Victoria Chambeau.

The trio sat quietly in the velvet, tufted seats. This particular car was reserved for those who could afford the added luxuries, but the amenities were lost on the three occupants. Each were too absorbed in their own thoughts to care about their surroundings.

The train lurched forward as the wheels began to turn, and the perpetual motion soon took on a steady speed.

"What nightly activities?" Sebastian asked once again, his dark eyes fixed upon her face.

He was seated next to her. His knee rested intimately against hers. She could feel the heat of his body through the layers of clothing, and her heart raced

160

recalling his nakedness of the night before. Her body betrayed her, sending color to tinge her pale cheeks. She turned her head, but the Dragon would not have it.

"I will have my answer," he said, then whispered, "and this evening I will satisfy that blush."

She looked at Aaron seated opposite them, praying he didn't hear the intimate remark, but he wore only an expectant stare as though waiting for her to answer.

She couldn't find a reasonable excuse for being on the waterfront at night, only whores and thieves frequented the area at that time.

She held her head up bravely and spoke. "I must decline to answer since my activities were not quite lawful."

Both men openly displayed their shock. Sebastian's eyes widened, and Aaron's mouth fell open.

"What did you do?" Sebastian demanded, fearing she played the whore then stole men's money, a common practice along the coast.

"I cannot say," she insisted, turning her head to peer out at the passing scenery. She hoped he wouldn't pursue the issue until they returned home, giving her more time to fabricate a reasonable story.

Sebastian was losing his temper. Aaron easily spotted all the warning signs: narrowed eyes, clenched fists, and a tightly clamped mouth.

"Sebastian," he said, tapping his friend's arm to get his attention.

Sebastian turned his angry eyes on him.

Aaron continued, not allowing his scathing look to intimidate him. "I think you should pursue this matter in more private quarters," he suggested.

Yes. Yes. Please listen to Aaron, she pleaded silently

161

while continuing her pretense of viewing the scenery.

"Victoria," Sebastian said in a threatening tone.

She turned daring green eyes to him.

"We'll discuss this matter as soon as we return home, and I better receive a satisfactory answer, or God help you."

She held her head up proudly, attempting to display courage while actually feeling relief. At least she had more time to formulate an adequate reponse.

Victoria received an unexpected reprieve upon her arrival home. The two detectives Sebastian had hired to locate the Serpent were anxiously waiting in the study.

"I must see to this matter immediately, Victoria," he said, "after which I will make arrangements for our wedding ceremony this evening."

She released a sigh of relief too soon.

"Don't forget I still expect an answer regarding your so-called unlawful activities," he said, without even a backward glance as he proceeded to his study.

Victoria retired to the room that had once been Beth's, feeling comfort from the familiar surroundings. She began to unbutton her basque when voices drifting up from the front of the house caught her attention. She walked over to the window and pushed the white lace curtains aside to look out.

The two men who she had seen on their earlier visit were talking in excited, raised voices, and tripping over each other as they followed Sebastian to the carriage.

"Yes, sir, Mr. Blood, this sure will make a dandy wedding present for you," one man said.

Sebastian ignored his remark and climbed into the vehicle as though his mind were elsewhere. Victoria wondered what kind of news the two men had delivered that would be such cause for rejoicement.

She shook her head, confused. They couldn't possibly have caught the Serpent, for she was he. So what could it be that had caused the excitement?

Akiko was preparing a hot bath for her when she entered the kitchen. Victoria sat down to join the woman in a cup of tea while the water heated.

"You will be happy with Sebastian-san. He is truly a good man."

"I fear him at times," Victoria admitted honestly.

"It is his way. He was raised in a land where power was a sign of respect. He cannot change his upbringing."

"But there is no love between us," Victoria said, wondering why it disturbed her. She had known of many arranged marriages that had succeeded despite the fact that each person was only fond of one another. Perhaps it was because she was raised in a house where her parents openly demonstrated their affection, and she knew from an early age that they had loved each other. This was the type of union she had hoped for, but now it was only a dream that would never see reality.

"Sebastian-san does not know his own heart. Give him time."

Victoria almost thought the woman was telling her that Sebastian loved her, yet didn't realize it. And that was nonsense. One would surely know one's own heart.

She entered the tub feeling perplexed. She hoped the soothing water would help wash away her problems. It

163

didn't. She recalled how she had instinctively clung to the Dragon for support and protection, and of his kindness to the lad and Beth in their time of need. But most of all she vividly remembered how she responded to his intimate touch. She wondered with much concern if she was a wanton woman . . . or a woman who was falling in love.

Akiko had temporarily placed her in a guest room to prepare for her wedding; only the garments she had chosen for the ceremony remained with her. Her other clothing had been neatly arranged in the master bedroom.

She had been informed that all the arrangements had been made. Judge Connors would arrive at eight to perform the ceremony. Rumors had already been dropped and were circulating rapidly that the Dragon had married two weeks before and had only recently brought his wife to San Francisco. There had been a death in her family, and her presence was required in order to settle the estate.

There was even talk of a dinner party to be hosted by the popular Mr. and Mrs. Fisk in honor of the new-lyweds.

Victoria was stunned by all Sebastian had accomplished in such a short period of time.

"Has Sebastian returned yet, Akiko?" she asked, puzzled by his long absence.

"Yes," she nodded, placing a plate of sliced cold meat and warm bread on the small table near the window. She added a tall glass of lemonade and turned to leave. "He is happy. I think he looks forward to this marriage."

Victoria smiled at the departing woman while considering the reason for his change of mood. She hoped it had helped him forget about her unlawful activities, since she could formulate no feasible reason for her nightly presence along the waterfront.

She remained cloistered in her room preparing herself for her wedding. There weren't many garments to choose from, but she did manage to find one she felt was appropriate, but far from what she would have chosen for this special occasion.

It was an attractive reception dress with a white silk petticoat, puffed lengthwise in the front. An overdress of soft mauve silk opened in front and had a medium-length train in the back. The bodice fit snugly and was of the same mauve color with ruffles running around the neck and dropping down to expose a modest amount of flesh. Ruffles also adorned the long sleeves at the wrist and dainty black slippers finished the becoming outfit.

The soft color accented her dark hair which she allowed to curl riotously about her face, adding only a few sprigs of small white flowers to highlight the mass of curls. The affect was stunning.

She didn't wait to be summoned. She descended the long staircase slowly, hearing boisterous talk and laughter coming from the parlor. She entered the room and all conversation halted.

"Good God, Sebastian. Why didn't you tell me you had found a goddess?" the rotund man with laughing gray eyes announced.

Sebastian fixed his dark blue eyes upon her and with deliberate slowness roamed every inch of her body as though he was stripping off each article of clothing she wore. She shivered at his intimate scrutiny.

His eyes gleamed with wickedness at her obvious discomfort, and he held out his hand, silently summoning her as he spoke. "Judge Connors, may I present Victoria Chambeau. The future Mrs. Blood."

She accepted his outstretched hand as though being drawn into his hypnotic web. She stood beside him, his arm casually resting around her slim waist. She couldn't help but admire his resplendent form outfitted in the finest smoky gray waistcoat and trousers. A white silk shirt was accented by a black vest, and his black tie was highlighted by a diamond stickpin. He looked magnificent, and she felt a sudden swell of pride that this splendid male creature was about to become her husband.

Aaron and Akiko stood as witnesses. It wasn't the wedding she had always dreamed of, but then her life also had turned out vastly different than she had expected.

The ceremony was short. The vows were exchanged. The wide gold band trimmed with diamonds was placed on her finger, and Sebastian leaned over and sealed their strange union with a gentle kiss before whispering, "To a lifetime of happiness, Vic."

Tears touched her dark lashes, spilling out and running down her cheeks. Sebastian tenderly wiped them away with his finger. "You won't be sorry, Victoria. All will go well."

She shut her eyes tightly, forcing the tears to stop. She prayed he would never learn of her secret identity, and that their life together would be happy.

"A toast," the judge shouted, and Akiko quickly

166

produced glasses filled with bubbling champagne.

"To the fortunate man, and to the beautiful woman he was lucky enough to catch," Judge Connors toasted and raised his glass in salute.

"Here, here," Aaron cried, joining in the celebration.

"This must be a happy day for you, Sebastian," Judge Connors laughed.

"Extremely," he remarked. "A beautiful woman becomes my wife, and my search for the elusive Serpent ends."

Victoria froze. Every limb instantly grew rigid with fright. She tried to raise the glass to her trembling lips, hoping the liquor would calm her rising panic. Her hand shook, and she clasped her free one over it. This couldn't be possible. *She was the Serpent.* They had the wrong person, an innocent man, or, worse, a young boy. Probably one of the youths that combed the waterfront desperate for food. Merciful heaven, what was she to do? She couldn't allow an innocent person to suffer for the crimes she had committed.

She spoke in a calm voice, not permitting her fear to surface. "What do you mean? Did you catch the Serpent?"

"I was saving it as a surprise," Sebastian said, expecting her to share his joy. After all, she had known how much he had wanted to snare the elusive fellow. "The Serpent has been caught, and at present is confined to the city jail. But as of tomorrow Judge Connors will release him into my custody for punishment."

"But that isn't fair," she said, fearing the punishment Sebastian would inflict on the boy.

"After what that thieving creature has done to so

167

many men, Mrs. Blood, I feel any retribution the court designates will not be adequate for the heinous crimes he has committed. Therefore, I take great pleasure in turning the fellow over to Sebastian for a just and fitting punishment," Judge Connors finished with a wink at Sebastian.

Victoria realized by the judge's impassioned remark that he had been one of her victims, hence the reason for his strong thirst for revenge. She notice the disagreeable expression on Aaron's face, and assumed he did not condone his friend's intentions.

"What will you do with him?" she asked.

Sebastian smiled and simultaneously raised his glass in a mocking salute. "Why exactly what I promised him, my dear."

The evening she had attacked the Dragon came shooting back in vivid detail, and she recalled his apt description of revenge. Her eyes fluttered several times before they closed slowly . . . and she slumped to the floor in a dead faint.

Chapter Thirteen

"Victoria, Victoria." She heard her name called repeatedly, yet she couldn't manage to rouse herself from the floating fog in which she was drifting. There was a reason she wished to remain in this limbolike state, but she failed to remember why. The masculine voice became insistent, calling her name urgently, demanding her return. She felt herself being forcibly drawn from the comforting cocoon that protected her. Slowly she emerged from the foggy depths.

Her eyes fluttered open and a hazy image of a man floated before her for several seconds before it was clearly distinguishable. She smiled at Aaron sitting on the bed beside her.

"I wish there was sufficient time to approach you on this delicate subject, but Sebastian will return any moment from showing Judge Connors out and I can't wait."

She blinked her eyes several times before furrowing her brow in confusion.

Aaron quietly took her hand in his. "Victoria, you're

the Serpent, aren't you?"

Victoria shut her eyes tightly, wanting nothing more than to return to the safety of her hazy cocoon, but instead she found the courage to face the man who had unraveled her secret identity. "How did you know?"

"I wasn't certain at first," he began, "and when I discovered you were a female I doubted my suspicions, but then all the pieces began to fall into place. Your sister required the exact medicine the Serpent had stolen from me and, of course, there was the fact that he could read the bottle which meant he had some form of education. And every now and then your voice reminded me of someone, but I couldn't quite put my finger on who. When you spoke of your nightly activities the evidence grew, and finally when you fainted I could ignore the facts no more. Only the Serpent would know what Sebastian intended to do to him once he was caught."

"Does he know?" she asked, afraid of the answer.

"No. He is blind where you are concerned and would never imagine you to be the notorious Serpent. I even have trouble accepting it."

"You realize that I must tell him, Aaron. I can't allow an innocent man to be punished for my crimes."

Aaron stood, walked over to the window, ran his fingers through his curly hair, and turned to face her. "He will never be able to accept the fact that you are the Serpent—the one who scarred his thigh and succeeded in besting him. He has too much pride and I fear what his retribution will be."

"Regardless, Aaron, I cannot allow another to suffer because of me."

He shook his head in agreement. "I understand and I admire your courage, but I fear greatly for your well-being."

Victoria tried to force a smile and the weak attempt only managed to distort her features and betray her fright. "He is my husband now; surely he will not harm his wife."

Aaron was about to answer when the bedroom door swung open, admitting Sebastian. "How is she, Aaron?"

He smiled when he saw she was conscious. "You gave us quite a fright, Victoria." He walked around the fourposter and sat beside her.

Her expression remained bleak as she gazed into the midnight blue of his eyes, searching for a small show of emotion that displayed his concern and demonstrated that his heart was not entirely unpenetrable. She thought she caught a glimmer in the deep recesses of his piercing look and she clung to it like a beacon of light in a heavy fog.

"Are you all right?" he asked, reaching for her hand and intimately massaging the soft flesh of her palm with his thumb. "You look pale."

Her eyes fluttered from the suggestive play of his finger against her skin. It teased and titillated in slow circles until her flesh tingled.

"She needs rest," Aaron said, causing Victoria to return to her precarious situation. "The last couple of days have been emotionally draining for her."

Sebastian listened to his friend's advice while he slipped one of the white flowers from her hair. He raised the velvet petals to his lips brushing them across slowly, tainting them with his kiss. He then dropped the intimately caressed petal to her lips and ran it over and over her mouth until she could almost feel his lips upon hers and she opened willingly, tasting the flower with the tip of her tongue.

The light contact of the velvet bud startled her and produced a flash of heat throughout her body. Her eyes flew open and locked with Sebastian's. A wicked grin touched the corners of his mouth as though in promise of what was to come.

"Don't worry, Aaron, I'll take good care of her this evening, and I promise she won't dwell on the sorrow of the last few days."

"Perhaps I should give her a sleeping potion so she will be able to rest," Aaron offered, reaching for his medical bag.

"No," Sebastian snapped, "that won't be necessary. I have the perfect sedative that will allow her to relax and sleep in peace."

Aaron knew his friend intended to make love to his wife tonight, but he feared what his desire would be after he learned of her secret identity. He wanted to warn Victoria to wait until after their union was consummated to tell him, but there was no chance of speaking to her alone.

"Akiko will see you out, Aaron, and thank you for everything," Sebastian said with a curt dismissal.

Aaron fought back the urge to stay and offer support to the young woman who had faced more adversity in the last year than most people did in a lifetime.

A gentle nod and a weak smile told him his presence

172

wasn't necessary. She would face her fate alone.

"I'll check on you in the morning, Victoria," he said, grabbing his black bag and heading for the door annoyed with himself for being unable to offer any other assistance.

"You sound as if you expect her condition to worsen by morning," Sebastian laughed. "Really, Aaron, I'm not the barbarian most people think I am."

"No, you're not, my friend, and I hope you keep that in mind."

Sebastian eyed the closed door for several seconds before turning his attention to his new bride.

"Tomorrow I shall begin a search for a proper lady's maid for you. Until then," he grinned, "I shall be at your disposal."

Victoria pushed herself up until she was leaning against the rosewood headboard. She stretched her arm out, the palm of her hand up as though to ward him off. "Sebastian, we must talk."

He wondered over the guarded stance she took and stood, slipping out of his waistcoat and tossing it carelessly across the chair. He proceeded to unbutton his vest and it joined the coat. "Can't this talk wait until tomorrow? It is our wedding night."

Victoria frantically shook her head back and forth. Her hand dropped to the bed to clutch the quilt in a tight grasp. His disrobing was placing a strain on her heightened emotions. She felt the ripple of anticipation begin in the pit of her stomach and grow stronger, more urgent as he continued to free himself of his clothing.

He pulled his shirt from his trousers and tossed it with his other garments. His chest lay bare to her view and it was like an intoxicating stimulant that filtered through her veins. The thick muscles of his hard chest rose and fell softly with each breath, and she was certain she could hear the steady rhythm of his heart.

She closed her eyes, taking a deep breath. How was she going to tell him that the woman he married and was about to make love to, was the notorious Serpent?

His fingers caressed her cheek suggestively and her eyes opened in shocked surprise at his sudden nearness.

"Victoria," he murmured, leaning over and pressing his lips urgently against hers. His fingers stole upward, gliding along the column of her soft neck as his tongue slipped into the recesses of her mouth, deepening his demand and making his intentions clear.

She never imagined she would experience the desire to mate with a man. After the way her uncle had treated her she had despised being touched by any male. Yet here she was not only wanting, but needing this man to possess her and take her to those heights of pleasure she had often heard the girls at Madam Champlains speak of in giggles and whispers.

Victoria felt the brush of air across her bare back and realized he had unfastened her dress. Soon his hand would brazenly touch her heated skin and she shivered in anticipation.

"Sweet, sweet Victoria," he whispered, slipping his hand beneath the loose material to fondle her full breast.

Sweet, he had called her sweet, but she wasn't. She was the Serpent and it was imperative that he be informed of this immediately.

"Sebastian," she said softly.

174

"Yes," he whispered, nibbling along her neck and slipping down to tempt the tip of her breast with his eager tongue.

"Sebastian, it's important," she insisted, shivering as his moist tongue plunged beneath the material to tease her tender nipple into hardened submission.

He raised his head, his face only inches from hers. His voice held a hint of annoyance as he spoke. "Victoria, I understand your apprehension about tonight, but there is nothing to fear. Trust me. I would never intentionally hurt you. Now, stop this nonsense. We can talk in the morning."

"I can't," she implored. Her small hand reached out to rest lightly upon his naked arm. She covered the fierce tattoo as though in an effort to contain the Dragon's wrath. "Please, Sebastian, we must talk now, and then if you still wish to consummate our marriage . . . I will do so most willingly."

Sebastian sat straight, his back rigid, his senses alert. "Does this concern your nightly activities?"

"Yes," she answered clearly, praying for the strength to deliver her startling news.

He stood. Her fingers lost the light grasp she had on the tattoo and she felt as though he had just slipped through her fingers away from her forever. It was a frightening feeling. It was important for this man, her husband, to understand why she had been forced into the life of a thief. It was important because she was only beginning to realize how much he meant to her. She knew this strange feeling had not materialized overnight. It had grown since the day she had entered this house, a little over three months ago, and she admitted

175

to herself for the first time that she loved the fierce and mighty Dragon.

She prayed that he might someday love her, yet his hatred for the Serpent ran so deep that she wondered if he would be able to accept what she was about to tell him without wishing to exact his revenge.

"I'm waiting," he said impatiently. His arms folded across his bare chest and his dark blue eyes focused intently upon her.

Victoria moved to the edge of the bed, her hands busily trying to push her dress back into place as she spoke. "You recall how difficult it was for me to provide Beth with medical attention."

He nodded, not a muscle flinching on his stern face.

Her fingers fell to her lap locking together to keep their trembling under control. "I tried many jobs, but none paid the kind of money necessary to care for Beth. By accident, I discovered a profession that could provide adequate care for her. Thievery."

She stole a quick glance at his impervious expression and continued before she lost her nerve. "I stalked the waterfront night after night in search of my victims. At first I made a few mistakes, but as my talent grew so did my courage. I wielded my weapon with accuracy and speed, rendering my opponent helpless."

Victoria stood and with her head held high and a flash of the lad's boldness in her brilliant green eyes she delivered the final blow. "I'm the Serpent."

Sebastian didn't speak. He stared at her for several seconds before throwing his head back in a fit of laughter.

Victoria was stunned. He didn't believe her.

176

It took him a few minutes to gain control enough to respond. "My dear wife, I understand your concern for the poor wretched fellow, since you unfortunately have been privy to the release of my temper on a few occasions, but to admit you are he ... Really, Victoria."

He laughed once again at the mere thought of this fragile female being the creature who had instilled such fear into the hearts of so many men.

"Don't you believe me?" came the raspy reply.

Sebastian stilled all movement and glared at the small woman whose familiar voice stirred unpleasant memories. He eyed her critically for several silent moments. "No, I don't believe you, but I do believe you're connected to him in some way. Did you help him bait his traps or did you spread your legs for his pleasure?"

Victoria felt the sting of his words and retaliated. "What's the matter, Blood, does the idea of a woman slicing so close to your manly pride hurt?"

She knew her harsh words were a mistake as soon as they had slipped out.

Sebastian didn't speak. His dark eyes smoldered with anger. His hand slowly moved to the belt at his waist. He opened it and proceeded to unfasten his trousers, his eyes never moving from her face.

Victoria was stunned by his unexpected action. She watched mesmerized as he slipped off all his clothing to stand naked before her. She spun around, too embarrassed to view his manliness.

Her body jerked at the touch of his warm hands on her bare shoulders. He squeezed tightly and forced her

177

to turn and face him.

"If you're the Serpent, perhaps you'd like to inspect the end results of your work?"

She shook her head adamantly, her mouth too dry to speak.

He would not accept her refusal. He shoved her roughly to the bed. Her backside hit the soft quilt as she held her dress from falling and exposing her breasts. She sat up. Her eyes clamped shut, not wishing to view his private parts, nor the scar she had inflicted upon him.

"Open your eyes, Victoria," he demanded hostilely.

She vehemently shook her head. Her eyes locked so tightly they caused a stinging pain in her temples.

His hand grabbed her chin and squeezed unmercifully. "Open them," he shouted, his brutal anger forcing her into submission.

Her head was tilted back and she stared into the stormy blackness of his eyes.

"Look," he whispered harshly.

Her eyes had no choice but to obey. They traveled down his muscled chest, passed his slim waist, over his flat abdomen, to the curly dark hair that surrounded . . . She swallowed hard and continued. His manhood jutted out in stiff protrusion, and she was awed by its size and the power it seemed to represent. She wondered how something so large could penetrate her, and she felt a stab of fear pierce her.

"Have you found your mark?" he asked, a hint of arrogance edging his words.

She looked farther and there it lay, a thick, pinkish scar carved into the hard muscle of his thigh. Without thinking she reached out. Her fingers gently, lovingly touched the healed wound.

Sebastian wasn't expecting that and a bolt of desire shot through him, igniting his passion.

Good God. He had had enough of this foolishness. "Get undressed, Victoria. I intend to discover exactly what you did for the Serpent."

She moved away from him. "You fool. You still refuse to believe me?"

He stormed toward her, stopping only inches from her. "A woman your size bringing a man my size to his knees? Ha!" he spat.

"Of course, a man with your immense physical abilities could never be rendered helpless by little old me," she mocked, walking to stand behind him.

Sebastian was about to turn and demand once again that she disrobe when he suddenly felt the cold steel of a blade pressed warningly between his legs.

"Doubt me once more, Blood, and I'll make ya a woman."

Sebastian experienced a moment of earth-shattering shock. His wife, the woman he thought sweet and innocent, was the notorious Serpent. "Do you recall what I said I'd do to you when I found you?" he asked calmly, not moving a muscle.

"Why do you think I fainted this evening? Although you now can see how impossible your threat was, since I don't possess the anatomy you so viciously swore to cut off." Victoria felt him stiffen. She was mocking him and that stung his pride. Yet he had stood laughing, disbelieving that because of her gender and size she was incapable of being the famous Serpent.

179

"Remove the weapon, Victoria. You've proven your point."

She didn't argue or refuse. He had finally accepted her identity and she complied with his request. She removed the dagger.

It was a mistake. He turned on her with all the fury of a captive animal set free. His large hand reached for the pearl-handled dagger while his other grabbed her narrow wrist.

She struggled against him, but it was useless. His grip was like a manacle firmly locked around her wrist and she only managed to feel the burn of flesh rubbing flesh.

"I thought you'd understand," she said, a spark of defiance lighting her widened eyes.

"Understand?" he asked incredulously. "You expect me to accept my wife's notorious activities with a shrug? Good God, woman, do you have any idea how many citizens of this fair city would love to see you swing from a rope and your carcass left to rot?"

"I did what was necessary," she shouted, watching the way he waved the dagger in the air.

"Pray tell, dear wife, why didn't you just sell yourself? You would have brought a tidy sum."

"I hate men touching me." She realized her hasty statement was a definite mistake.

Sebastian released a low, mocking laugh. "You expect me to believe you abhor my touch?"

"No," she answered, shaking her head, "with you it's different."

"But with other men you hate it?"

"Yes," she replied too quickly. His understanding of

her response was not how she intended it.

"How many men, Serpent?" he asked, raising her arm and bending her wrist ever so slightly backward.

"None, damn you, none!" she screamed, feeling as though her bones were about to snap.

"Shall we see?" he smiled, suddenly releasing her and swiftly running the dagger down the front of her dress tearing it wide open.

She was stunned, but not enough to stand idly by. "Don't touch me," she warned threateningly.

"Not likely," he snapped, further tearing the garment from her stiff body.

She lashed out at him, slapping his hands in a futile effort to stop him.

He laughed at her senseless attempt and tore the last bit of her chemise from her body. She stood naked and without waiting he flung her over his shoulder and walked to the bed. His one hand rested against the soft round flesh of her exposed derriere, and he took great pleasure in making a thorough inspection of the area.

"Stop that," she screamed, pummeling his back.

"That, my dear Serpent," he spat, "is only the beginning."

He threw her down upon the bed, grabbing her hands in his large one and wrenching them above her head. She squirmed in protest over her captivity. He ignored her.

"Sebastian, please, you must understand," she said, trying desperately to wiggle free of his firm grasp.

"I understand perfectly," he answered. "You enjoy rendering men helpless. Perhaps you feel it is in retribution for the way your uncle had treated you."

"No, no. Oh please, Sebastian, understand it was a matter of survival," she begged, choking back the tears that threatened to spill.

Her anguished plea fell on deaf ears. His fingers began to explore her intimately, running over her slender waist, along her silky thighs, to the valley of dark curls tucked snugly between her tightly closed legs.

"You are so beautiful, Victoria, so very beautiful. It is a shame, for I could lose myself within you and never regret it."

His fingers touched the bud of her womanhood lightly, delicate, teasingly, until Victoria begged him in a harsh whisper to stop.

"You don't want me to stop, love," he murmured and kissed her gently on her forehead. His fingers continued downward, forcing her thighs apart as the tip of his finger found her and slid slowly, ever so slowly, within her.

She moaned at the intimate intrusion. His touch felt good, too good, but for all the wrong reasons. "Sebastian, don't."

"Don't?" he mocked dramatically. "You must be used to a man's fingers cradled within you. I'm sure the Serpent had many men rest between her legs in pleasure."

He couldn't have hurt her more if he had struck her in the face. He was trying to punish her. Make her hurt as she had hurt him. Only his pain had been physical. Hers was emotional. She couldn't allow him to do this. She had hoped they could be happy together, but his anger wouldn't allow it, at least not yet. She had to stop him. Stop him before it was too late. She chose the words that she knew would hurt him the most.

"You're right, Dragon. I've wrapped my legs around many a man while they took their pleasure, and enjoyed every thrust."

Her words stabbed him like a sharp knife, just as she had intended. He pulled away from her. His dark eyes stroked her naked body with contempt, anger, and regret.

"When I wish a whore to service me, I'll seek your bed." He grabbed his robe from the chair, slipped into it, and walked to the door, slamming it closed behind him.

Victoria felt the tears stinging her eyes. She had held them back, but they refused to stay locked away any longer. They ran down her face and she turned to bury her sobs in the pillow. He hated her for being the Serpent and now he thought her a whore. What was she going to do?

She cried until her tears were spent. She had faced worse problems, she thought, as sleep tickled her swollen lids. She would find a solution. She would find a way to warm the Dragon's cold heart.

Sebastian paced back and forth in front of the fireplace in his study. He held a glass of brandy in one hand while his other hand raked his dark hair repeatedly.

His wife, a tiny bundle of femininity, was the notorious Serpent and a whore. He shut his eyes against the pictures that blazed before him, vivid pictures of men touching her, caressing her silken skin, hearing that soft moan, kissing those full lips.

He growled like a raging animal and threw the glass into the hearth, smashing it to pieces and sending the amber liquid splashing against the stones.

He braced his hands flat against the mantel and stared into the fireless hearth. He wanted her. He wanted her so badly he could almost taste her silky flesh against his lips.

"Damn her!" he shouted. "Damn her."

Chapter Fourteen

Victoria sat in the large dining room alone. She glanced down the long length of the highly polished rosewood table and at the ten chairs surrounding it. A single setting had been placed for her at one end. White table linen edged in fine lace sat beneath the blue floral china plate and cup. She raised the delicate cup to her pouting lips and drank the soothing tea before releasing an exasperated sigh.

She had hoped Sebastian would have shared breakfast with her. Upon waking she had quickly donned a lilac day dress and had gone in search of him, only to be informed by Akiko that he had gone out earlier and would be returning within the hour.

She raised the teacup to her lips once again and sipped thoughtfully. After last night's confrontation she had hoped they would be able to discuss the matter like adults and reach a solution that would satisfy his pride and her sanity.

Akiko intruded upon her thoughts, urging her to try one of the sweet rolls, warm and sticky from the oven, but she shook her head. She wasn't hungry. She was upset. She needed to resolve this problem now so she could begin to repair the damage inflicted on their already precarious union. If they were going to spend the rest of their lives together then she wished their relationship to contain no animosity.

Voices carried in from the foyer and Victoria knew from the sound that Sebastian had returned with a guest. She forced a smile to surface, not wanting to grant him the benefit of seeing how upset she actually was.

Sebastian entered and the sight of him outfitted in butternut trousers and a dark toast waistcoat tailored to fit his precise measurements flustered her. His perfect clothing which hugged in all the right places boasted his splendid form.

"Victoria," he said sweetly. His face was masked by a radiant smile, yet traced with sardonic undertones. He walked over to her and placed a perfunctory kiss upon her cheek.

"Sebastian, I missed you this morning when I woke," she said with an equally brilliant and phony smile.

Aaron looked from one to the other and refrained from commenting. She had told him, that much was obvious, and apparently he had not harmed her so there was still hope of their union surviving. He ignored their forced pleasantries and joined Victoria at the table without waiting for an invitation.

Sebastian sat opposite his friend and summoned Akiko to bring coffee.

"Is there something wrong with the food, Victoria?" Sebastian asked, noticing her plate still clean.

"I'm not hungry," she answered, pushing the empty

dish away from her.

"Are you feeling all right?" Aaron questioned, wondering if Sebastian had left an emotional scar instead of a physical one.

"I'm fine," she assured him. "I'm just not hungry."

"Perhaps your hunger can be appeased some other way," Sebastian offered, knowing full well she understood his suggestive remark, for her face brightened to a scarlet red.

Aaron quickly interceded, hoping to catch his friend off guard. "So has the Serpent's fate been decided?"

Sebastian didn't flinch a muscle. "Yes, I have chosen a most fitting punishment."

"What gives you the right to judge the Serpent?" Victoria snapped.

"What doesn't?" he snapped back. "I was one of his victims, or need you reminding?"

She turned away. He wouldn't have it and grasped her chin in his hand, forcibly turning her to look at him.

"You have no right," she whispered.

"I have more right than others, dear wife," he said softly.

Aaron coughed lightly, reminding the pair he was there. "Perhaps the Serpent should be allowed to tell his side. Sebastian?"

He released Victoria's chin and frowned, seeing the red mark his firm grip had left. "What is there to tell? He's a thief and a—"

Victoria's eyes popped open. He wouldn't. He wouldn't call her that horrible name in front of his friend.

"And what?" Aaron urged him to finish.

Sebastian stared at his wife. His dark eyes bored into

187

her and she could almost feel his intense glare touching her flesh. "And a liar."

She stiffened in her seat. She was relieved he hadn't called her a whore, but she didn't care to be called a liar. "You're so sure he doesn't speak the truth?"

"Quite sure."

"And what if he can prove otherwise?"

Sebastian grinned, that sinfully wicked grin that always managed to tingle her tummy. "All the Serpent has to do is prove his *innocence.*"

She was no fool. She knew exactly what innocence he was referring to. "His word isn't good enough?"

Sebastian laughed. "Accept the word of a thief? Really, Victoria."

"What if this thief is different?" Aaron added.

Sebastian glared at him and then at his wife. It was obvious Aaron knew his wife was the Serpent. "Then let him prove it," he said and turned his head sharply toward Victoria.

He had challenged her. Openly. Defiantly. He was demanding she prove her innocence or guilt, signing her own fate. He would just sit back and wait. She was angered by his arrogance and lack of understanding. She wanted him to believe her. To trust her. Perhaps to even love her so unconditionally that what she had done wouldn't matter.

"And what if he chooses not to?"

Sebastian leaned close to her. His warm breath teased her cheek. "Then he will be punished."

"A punishment you have chosen, dear husband?"

"A most fitting punishment for the likes of him. One he richly deserves."

"So you say," she said irritably.

188

Sebastian leaned back against his chair. "So I say."

"You underestimate the Serpent's tenacity if you feel he will sit by and willingly accept this punishment."

"He has no choice."

Victoria stood, placing her hands flat upon the table. "As someone once told me, 'There's always a choice.'"

Sebastian stood also, towering over his wife. "In this case there is none."

"I think not, Mr. Blood," she said and turned to leave the room.

"Stay where you are, Victoria. I gave you no permission to leave."

She swung around and Aaron winced at the anger evident in her bright green eyes. "Permission?"

"You heard me," he said and pounded the table with his fist.

Victoria curtsied before her husband and smiled sweetly. "Go to hell, Mr. Blood."

Sebastian was so stunned by her words that by the time he shouted her name she had already left the room.

"Now, Sebastian—"

"Shut up, Aaron," he said and stormed after her.

Victoria was only a few steps up the staircase when her husband grabbed her arm, stopping her. "You have much to learn about being a dutiful wife."

"I don't plan on being a dutiful wife," she said, continuing to display a sweet smile.

"Now, Sebastian . . . Victoria," Aaron said, joining them on the steps. "A little lovers' spat is normal in a marrige. Why not kiss and make up?"

Sebastian pulled her roughly against him. "A perfect solution. Don't you agree, darling?"

189

Victoria didn't have time to argue. His lips seized hers. Harshly. Demandingly. It was as though he was demonstrating who was the stronger—who would have his way. She didn't fight him. She welcomed his kiss, harsh as it was, and when he sensed no resistance his demand turned to a sweet caress. He enticed her mouth with his tongue, slowly, softly, suggestively, until she melted further into his arms.

"Excuse me," Aaron said, reminding them of his presence. They broke apart, staring at him. "Now isn't that better?"

Sebastian looked at his wife and Victoria was angered by the satisfied grin he wore. She pulled away from him. "The only thing that could possibly make me feel better is my dagger stuck through his heart. That's if he has one."

Aaron shut his eyes and shook his head. This match certainly was going to be interesting. He felt sure no one had ever dared speak to Sebastian the way this diminutive woman did. And he wondered if the Dragon had finally met his match.

"I think you better leave, Aaron," Sebastian said calmly.

Aaron looked to Victoria and she nodded as though informing him she was capable of handling the matter. "Very well. I shall stop by tomorrow and see how you both are faring."

As soon as the door closed, Sebastian spoke. "In my study, Victoria."

She grabbed the long length of her dress, lifting it, then her head as she descended the steps and walked into his study.

He closed the door behind them, locking it. The click

of the key caused her to shiver and she fixed a sullen look on him.

He grinned in a sensuously disarming way.

His obvious smugness annoyed her and she itched to penetrate his steely armor. "So did you release the man who those intelligent detectives assumed was the Serpent?"

"He's safely on his way to a faraway port and, may I add, Judge Connors presumes him dead."

"So to everyone concerned the Serpent has met his demise?"

"Correct," he said sternly, "and that is precisely how he will stay. Do I make myself clear?"

"Perfectly. You don't wish your wife stalking the waterfront and slipping her dagger between a man's legs."

"Your sharp retorts will only manage to cause you more trouble, Victoria," he snapped, annoyed by her all-too-vivid description of the Serpent's trade.

She braced her hands on her hips and tossed her head up, sending dark curls bouncing around her face until they settled to delicately frame her creamy complexion. "What can you do to me that you haven't already done?"

He pushed himself away from the desk. "Which brings us to your punishment."

Even though her legs trembled she wouldn't let her fear show.

He stood only inches from her and she bent her head back to look up at him. "You are my wife and shall remain so. You shall perform your wifely duties, including servicing me when I desire . . . but I will never love you. You will be my chattel, my property."

Anger rumbled in the depths of her widened eyes. "I don't need your love," she lied, for she had hoped, prayed that they could set aside their differences and reach a compromise, allowing room for a relationship to take root and flourish, to live happily as man and wife, raise a family and perhaps find contentment and eventually love in each other's arms.

"So you think yourself capable of surviving this relationship without the benefit of love?"

"I have survived much in the last year and can survive more if necessary," she stated proudly, although with a bit of uncertainty.

He never took his dark eyes off her as he reached for a cheroot on the desk, flicked the tip of a match, and casually lit the thin cigar gripped firmly between his teeth. "We'll see, dear wife, for I plan on taking my pleasure with you whenever the mood strikes me. When I grow weary of you, you shall have the comfort of our children to fill your days while I find my pleasure elsewhere."

Victoria felt no defeat, only raging fury. If he thought he was going to use her like a whore then discard her for someone else he was sadly mistaken. But then the Dragon facing the Serpent had forgotten how dangerous the creature's sting could be.

"Your punishment doesn't seem unreasonable. After all, when I've grown tired of you, I shall look elsewhere also."

Her statement shocked him, for he choked on the puff of smoke he had inhaled. "You—you—"

"Victoria, Sebastian. The name is Victoria," she said with a laugh and a sense of victory.

He crushed the cheroot in the crystal ashtray until

there was nothing left of it but shredded tobacco. And when he raised his eyes to her once again she shivered as though an icy hand had run down her spine.

"Your answers are going to do you more harm than good, Vic," he announced in a carefully controlled voice. "Listen wisely to what I'm about to tell you, for I'll say it only once. You will never, I repeat, never, seek another man's bed, for if you do I shall kill you with my bare hands and the man along with you. I won't have you breeding with anyone else or have other hands touch you."

She opened her mouth to protest, but he silenced her.

"I'm not finished. In the future, when I no longer seek your bed, you need only to ask and I shall be happy to *perform* my husbandly duties."

Victoria ached to smack the superiority from his handsome face, but she refrained. There were other ways to tame the mighty Dragon and make him eat his own words. After all, she had mastered the art of thievery. How hard could it be to master the art of making love? To make him want her more than any other woman he ever had, perhaps to even penetrate the cold shield that she was certain encircled his heart.

A half-smile touched the corners of his finely shaped lips. "No response, Victoria?"

"You've made yourself perfectly clear. I see no reason to prolong the battle."

He walked over to her, slipping her small hand in his, and gently massaged the palm with delicate strokes. "You submit easily, Vic. I had thought you would fight your punishment more," he whispered, almost sorry she had relented so easily.

193

She pulled her hand from his reluctantly, having enjoyed his touch. She placed the sensitive palm against his smooth cheek and traced her thin finger along his moist lips with deliberate slowness.

"I shall enjoy you while I can, Dragon," she murmured, "but beware, for the Serpent only slumbers and when released will prove a powerful adversary."

Her mouth claimed his before he could speak and he was so moved by her unexpected response that she almost succeeded in causing him to lose control. He willingly fenced with her darting tongue, reveling in the challenge she had issued him, and he sparred expertly, drinking in all of her sweet taste. He groaned deeply and abruptly pulled away from her.

"Nice try, Victoria, but I'm too familiar with experienced women attempting to seduce me to fall so easily under their spell."

His words were meant to be hurtful, but to his surprise she only smiled and turned to leave the room.

"On second thought, perhaps I'll taste what you offer."

She froze in her tracks.

"As a matter of fact, I was about to bathe and would enjoy the company," he said, coming up behind her, slipping his arm around her waist and propelling her toward the door.

"I—I've already bathed," she stammered, not having expected him to respond to her so quickly.

His light laughter near her ear tickled her skin, sending goose bumps down her arm. "Then we'll share the soothing warmth of the tub."

She didn't have a chance to object. The door was opened and he almost carried her along the floor to the bathing room.

He began to disrobe. "Come, Victoria, show me what you've learned about pleasing a man."

Her fingers moved to the row of buttons on her dress and she slowly undid each one. She had no idea what to do or even how to do it, but she was determined to make the Dragon eat his words. Every one of them.

She stepped out of each of her garments with the skill of an experienced woman. Each dip and turn offered a suggestive, but limited view of her slender body.

Sebastian watched, his hands on his pants. She was a tease, a damn tease, and he intended to do the same.

Her back was to him. Her firm, round derriere faced him as she walked cautiously to the large tub and climbed in. She submerged herself in the water until it covered her shoulders. Only then did she release the heavy sigh that had been trapped in her throat.

"Very good, Victoria. I don't think I've ever seen it done so expertly," he said, climbing into the tub and standing opposite her.

She refused to open her eyes and look at him. It had taken all her nerve to disrobe in front of him. She didn't think she had any left. She wanted to screech at him that she had never done such a thing before. But it was useless. He wouldn't believe her.

"I'm waiting," he whispered so softly that Victoria opened her eyes to see if he was really there. He was.

His muscled arms rested on the rim of the tub as he leaned casually against it. His chest was broad and firm and tapered to a slim waist and flat, hard midriff. A thin line of dark hair began beneath his navel, disappearing into the water below.

"Do you approve?"

Her face turned crimson. She turned away from his mocking smile, preparing to leave the tub. His hands stopped her. They slipped beneath her arms and circled her waist, pulling her back against his wet flesh.

"I like that hungry look in your eyes, love," he murmured and moved his hand up to cup her breast gently.

"Sebastian," she breathed softly.

His name so suggestively spoken ignited his passion even further, making him forget his intentions and thinking of nothing more then tasting every part of her. He spun her around.

Her breath caught in her throat as her wet skin made intimate contact with his. His chest was hard. His thighs were hard. And as his hand slipped beneath the water grabbing her backside and pushing her to him, she felt the strange hardness of his manhood. It felt large and powerful as though it had a will of its own. It pressed against her belly as if demonstrating its prowess.

"Victoria."

Her name sounded like an echo on a breath of wind as Sebastian's mouth calmed hers. It encompassed her so fully, so thoroughly, that his breath was hers and hers was his. It was almost as though they were one.

She moved against him, wanting to, needing to, yet not knowing why. He responded, urging her with his fingers as they dug into her flesh.

His mouth left hers and she moaned her regret. He laughed playfully as his hands slid around her waist and lifted her until her breast was near his lips.

Victoria braced her hands on his shoulders as he captured her nipple with his mouth, swirling his tongue over the hardened bud again and again. She felt his shaft probing at the valley of her legs, pushing, urging her to open to him.

She couldn't stop the heated cries that escaped her lips, or the way she moved against him, demanding him to take her. She didn't know why she responded so wickedly and she didn't care. "Take me, Sebastian, take me," she cried.

Her lustful pleas startled him and in that moment he remembered what she was and what she had done to him. He released her instantly, dropping her into the water.

She rubbed her eyes and coughed as she attempted to right herself. And when she did she looked at him with hurt and confusion.

"Don't play that game with me," he yelled. "You're no innocent. You're a skilled whore."

Victoria's mouth dropped open. What was he talking about? What in heaven's name did she do to make him think that? She didn't understand. Damn, she just didn't understand.

"Nice try, dear wife," he said, climbing out of the tub. "But I've changed my mind. I'm not ready to have you service me just yet."

Victoria watched his powerful strides as he crossed the floor and grabbed the brown robe on the peg, covering himself. "Another time," he smiled and strolled out the door, not bothering to close it behind him.

Victoria released a screeching yell and smashed the water with her fists. He was infuriating. She hated him. Hated him.

She sunk down into the water to her shoulders and

dropped her head back to rest against the tub. She was a fool. She didn't hate him. She loved him. He was stubborn, arrogant, demanding, yet she loved him. And she, even in all her naiveté, thought she had sensed a spark of feeling. A feeling as deep as hers. If she could only make him see the truth. Make him want her as much as she wanted him. But that required skills she didn't possess.

A sudden smile lit her face. She needed a teacher who was a master at the art of seduction. And she knew the perfect person . . . Lola.

Her grinned broadened. "Dragon, you are about to feel the sting of the Serpent's fangs."

Chapter Fifteen

Victoria burst into action as soon as Sebastian left for his office the next morning. He had given her the perfect excuse to leave the house, making her plan even easier. He had informed her that Charles and Harriet Fisk, a socially prominent couple, would be hosting a dinner party for them in three weeks. It was a way of introducing her into San Francisco society. And, of course, the occasion would require a new dress, which meant a visit to the local seamstress and a way for her to sneak in a visit to Lola.

There was one problem. She couldn't parade into the local bordello as Mrs. Sebastian Blood, therefore, she had no alternative but to reactivate the identity of the young lad Vic.

Sebastian had issued instructions to Daniel, advising him to take her to the seamstress and any other shop she wished to visit and then he was to return her home. He was adamant about him not taking her elsewhere.

She had briefly thought of confiding in Daniel, but she didn't wish to be the cause of him losing his longtime position, so she kept the plans to herself.

She waited patiently on the front steps for him to bring the carriage around. She was attired in a lovely violet day dress trimmed in lavender with a matching hat.

Sebastian had given his approval of her choice knowing full well he had had Akiko purposely remove the two mourning outfits she had intended to wear against his wishes.

A sly grin touched her lips as she thought about the patched and worn clothes that were carefully concealed beneath the bustle of her dress. At least that protruding bump was good for something, she thought with a laugh.

Daniel assisted her into the shiny black silver-trimmed carriage and they were off. It didn't take much suggestion on her part to convince the man to go to the local saloon for lunch and a few ales while she was being fitted at Mrs. Havershaw's shop. And it didn't take her long to slip out the back door after the woman had taken her measurements and she had hastily chosen material for the gown.

She hid her clothes in one of the several boxes stacked neatly in the back of the older woman's shop. If she hurried she would have plenty of time before Daniel came to pick her up.

She scurried down the narrow alley stopping only for a second to scoop up some dirt and smear her face before emerging along the waterfront as the young lad known to everyone as Vic.

She breathed deeply, the salty air stinging her nostrils. It felt good. She walked jauntily along the boarded walkway, the sense of renewed freedom lightening her step. She hadn't realized how much she had missed being in charge of her own life, going and doing what she wanted without having to answer to anyone. The last year had bestowed on her more independence than she had ever imagined possible, and she suddenly experienced a tugging reluctance to part with it.

She laughed and kicked at the stone in her path. Perhaps she would continue to visit the waterfront on occasion. After all, it wasn't fair that Sebastian should be allowed to decide her fate just because he was her husband.

She bounced up the steps to the brothel and entered with a wide smile and a spirit full of confidence.

"Vic!" came the shrill call from the top of the stairs.

Victoria took the steps two at a time and threw her arms around Lola.

The fiery redhead squeezed the ragamuffin to her large bosom before leading her to her room. She locked the door behind her and leaned against it releasing a light sigh.

"I heard the Dragon married Victoria Chambeau," she stated, tears blurring her vision.

Victoria couldn't prevent herself from crying. "Yeah, something isn't it? The Serpent marrying the Dragon."

A huge smile filled Lola's flushed face. She walked over to Victoria with outstretched arms. "I'm so happy for you."

The two women clung to each other while a mixture of sobs and laughter spilled from them. They plopped down on the bed together.

"How?" Lola asked, wiping her reddened eyes with her lace hanky.

Victoria used the end of her worn shirt to pat away her tears before detailing the events of the last few days.

"I'm so sorry to hear about Beth," she said, covering the young woman's hands in a sincere show of condolence.

"Thanks, Lola."

"Tell me why you've really come. I sense an urgency to your visit."

Now that she was faced with the prospect of asking Lola intimate questions, she found her courage waning.

Lola grasped her by the shoulders. "Has he hurt you?"

She almost laughed out loud, for he had hurt her in a way she doubted Lola would understand. "No."

"Then what is it?"

She decided to confess all if she were going to be able to convince Lola to help her. The words spilled forth, starting with his discovery of her identity.

Lola listened, her eyes widening every now and then. Finally, when Victoria had finished she said, "So you want to convince him you're not a whore, yet seduce him like one so he never desires another woman."

Victoria shook her head. "It doesn't sound sensible, I know, but what choice do I have? I think if I can pierce the Dragon's armor I may be able to touch his heart."

"Some say he has none."

Victoria laid her hand gently upon Lola's arm. "He has a heart and it's big and soft and tender. And I intend to pierce it."

Lola patted her hand. "I have a feeling you're going to do just that, with my help, of course."

"You will help me?"

"Honey, when I get through with you, the Dragon will leap through fire to get to your bed."

Both women laughed and hugged each other.

"I wish I could stay longer," Victoria said. "But Daniel will be picking me up shortly and I must get back. I'll return the day after tomorrow—that's when I have a fitting. We can start the lessons then."

Lola was about to agree when a thunderous roar filled the house. Victoria froze in place. All color drained from her face as she recognized her husband's angry voice.

"He knows I'm here," she said in a frightened whisper.

"How could he?" Lola asked, making certain the lock was secured.

"I don't know. Perhaps Daniel returned sooner than I expected."

A loud pounding vibrated the walls as well as the door and both women stepped back, away from the deafening noise.

"Let me in, Lola," Sebastian demanded.

"I'm not dressed. You'll have to wait," she called out to him, motioning Victoria toward the window.

"What the hell difference does that make? Let me in!"

"In a minute," she answered, stalling for time. She swung open her closet door and to Victoria's surprise extracted a long, heavy rope.

"For emergencies," she giggled and dropped the curled end out the window. She secured the other end around the brass foot of the bed.

The thunderous pounding continued with curses and threats.

Victoria was grateful that the room faced the back. The narrow alley was always deserted and she slipped over the ledge and held tightly to the rough hemp rope.

"I'll be in touch," she whispered to Lola and began her descent. The palms of her hands soon began to burn from the harsh texture of the hemp as she lowered herself slowly. A sudden jerking of the rope forced her to tighten her grip and stop to look up.

"If you're smart, you'll stay right where you are until I get down there," Sebastian warned, leaning out the window with his large hands firmly fastened to her object of escape.

Panic seized her and the old sense of not being caught returned. She slid the remaining few feet and dropped to the hard ground. She ignored his shouts and the pain in her hands as her small booted feet flew with renewed speed as the thought of the Dragon capturing her haunted her vision.

She ran down alley after alley, jumping over anything in her path including the rats that quickly scurried out of her way. She never once thought of where she was going for there really wasn't anywhere she could hide; eventually she would have to face her husband.

She turned a corner in a flash and collided full force with the sultry Lydia Hodgeson. Yellow feathers drifted in the air and rows of pearls popped free joining the cascading feathers.

"You stupid boy," she screamed, pushing the untidy urchin off her and brushing at the dirt on her dress.

Victoria stood and backed away slowly. A crowd had begun to gather. Attention was one thing she didn't need at the moment.

Two men helped the disheveled woman up. She immediately flung insulting remarks at the lad. "You filthy street urchin, you should be horsewhipped for your impudence. You're nothing but a dirty little beggar not fit to walk the same street as decent folk."

Victoria's temper was smoldering. How dare she berate another when she herself slept with a man knowing she was to marry someone else in September.

The boldness of the lad returned and she marched up to the woman who stood at least four inches taller than she and raised her curled fist to her startled face. "I'm going to say this for your ears only, lady. I may be a beggar, but you're nothing more than a common whore."

Her loud gasp echoed throughout the crowd, sending tongues wagging as to what could have caused such a disturbed reaction from the proper and well-bred Miss Hodgeson.

"You filthy little animal," she screamed and raised her hand to smack the lad's smirking face.

Victoria wasn't about to take anymore. She grabbed the woman's hand and squeezed tightly. "Try it and I'll give you two black eyes," she warned.

Lydia stood motionless. She couldn't risk the chance of having the boy do as he threatened. Why, she'd be confined to the house for weeks unable to venture out for any social function.

The worried expression on her pale face suddenly turned to pure delight and she lowered her hand and skillfully fluttered her long blond lashes.

Victoria was stunned by her reaction although soon she fully understood why.

"Sebastian," Lydia sighed dramatically, "you're just

in time to punish this impudent boy of yours."

Victoria refused to show how much his presence disturbed her. She wouldn't give the damn woman the satisfaction. Instead she turned and artfully resumed the character of the obnoxious lad.

"She was in my way and I ran her down," she announced with a defiant toss of her head.

Victoria was surprised to see a slight telltale sign of a smile at the corners of his otherwise tightly clenched lips.

"In you way?" Lydia repeated in shock. "Why you little liar. You came racing around that corner not watching where you were going. It was almost as though the devil were chasing you."

"Well, now," Victoria said, clearing her throat to speak in the lad's uneducated tongue. "I surely thought that was the bloke who was after me."

Sebastian didn't find her retort amusing, for he shot her a heated glare that warned her not to open her mouth again.

She paid him no heed. The taste of freedom was too intoxicating. "You see, Miss Hodgeson," she began, turning around to face the woman, "this huge fellow suddenly jumped me as I was walking along minding my own business. He dragged me down this rat-infested alley. It's easy to tell rats are around cause you can hear their little feet scurrying about and, of course, there's that piercing squeal they make. Why, one even brushed against my hand when the bloke pushed me to the ground. Want to see?"

She stuck it in Lydia's face for inspection and the woman reacted just as Victoria expected. Her face paled to a ghostly white and her gloved hand flew to

206

cover her beating heart.

The crowd even added to the dramatic moment mumbling words of concern for the poor unfortunate lad.

"Sebastian," Lydia said, "perhaps the boy has suffered enough."

The crowd echoed their approval and several people called out that Miss Hodgeson was a charitable and decent woman. Lydia smiled and accepted her role as a martyr with all the dramatics of a fine actress.

"Your graciousness adds to your beauty, Lydia. There aren't many women who would be so lenient with a boy after what he has done to your appearance. Although may I add no amount of dirt could hide your loveliness," Sebastian said smiling, then lifted her gloved hand to place a kiss upon it.

Lydia blushed appropriately. "Thank you, Sebastian."

The crowd began to disperse, their gossiping tongues clacking about the generosity of the charitable Miss Hodgeson toward a less fortunate soul.

Sebastian reached out and grabbed Victoria's hand, intending to make certain she didn't evade him again. He squeezed tightly and she tried to pull away. He thought her resistance was caused by her wish to flee him, not realizing her hands were raw from the rope and the pressure he was applying worsened the pain.

Lydia brushed lightly at the dry dirt staining her lemon yellow dress. "Sebastian darling, I've heard congratulations are in order. You are now a married man."

"Yes, Lydia," he grinned, wondering what remarks Victoria was about to hear that weren't really meant for her ears.

"You rascal," she grinned, playfully hitting his chest. "You were secretly seeing me while all the time you were married. Is your wife that unattractive, or is she one of those women who believes that her duty is to lie rigid beneath her husband while he exercises his husbandly rights?"

Victoria stopped struggling and Sebastian felt her stiffen.

"She isn't bad to look at. As far as her wifely duties, I have yet to taste all of her talents."

Lydia laughed softly and placed her hand intimately against his arm. "Well, darling, you're still welcome in my bed."

"I'll keep that in mind." He smiled and leaned over to place a friendly kiss on her cheek.

She brushed her lips across his before he pulled away. "I must get these awful clothes off. You should really take the boy home and bathe him, Sebastian. He looks so grubby."

"That's a perfect idea, Lydia," he answered with a wicked grin. "I'll do just that."

Victoria stood silent. Her anger was too near the surface for her to attempt a remark.

"Oh, I almost forgot," Lydia said as she turned to leave. "I shall see your charming young wife at the Fisk's dinner party. I'm looking forward to meeting her, darling." And with a wave of her hand she was off.

Sebastian pulled Victoria along beside him. "I've warned you about keeping you identity a secret," he whispered.

"Everyone around here knows me as the lad Vic, not as the—"

"Enough," he interrupted sharply. "I don't even want to hear his name mentioned."

"You mean she," Victoria corrected.

Sebastian stopped abruptly, swinging her roughly around to crash into his solid chest. He fixed an angry glare upon her as he held her firmly against him. "You will learn to listen to me, Victoria."

She couldn't speak. Her mouth was too dry and her body too attuned to the solid form of her husband.

She ran her small tongue along her bottom lip. The one that was plump and inviting. Sebastian growled and pushed her from him.

"Come on," he snapped and pulled her along. She almost had to run to keep up with his long strides.

She finally managed to speak. "Don't you think people will begin to gossip when the street urchin you hired suddenly disappears?"

"I shall inform everyone that I sent you to live with my father since you craved adventure."

Victoria was angry that he could so easily dispose of the one identity that she felt gave her a sense of freedom. She was about to argue with him when the matter was suddenly settled for her, and in her favor.

"Mr. Blood," Ned Harper called from across the street.

Victoria looked at the short thin man frantically waving a piece of paper in the air.

They crossed the street and stood in front of the Blood Enterprises building while the man ranted on about the message needing to be delivered to the Johnston Warehouse immediately.

"Vic can deliver it in no time," Ned said, handing the paper to her.

Sebastian grabbed the folded note. "The lad has business to attend to for me at the moment. Can't one of the men take it?"

Ned shook his head and chewed at his lower lip while thinking of another solution to his problem.

"I can do it," Vic piped in. "I'll finish what Mr. Blood wants done real quick and then take the note."

"Great," Ned sighed with relief. "It sure is good having you back, Vic. We've missed you the last few days."

He turned to enter the building then stopped and walked back to the boy. "Forgive me, Vic, I've been insensitive. I'm truly sorry over the loss of your sister."

"Thanks," she responded, dropping her head and blinking back a tear. She had been so consumed by her problem with Sebastian that she had pushed Beth's death out of her thoughts.

"All the men are glad you've returned," Ned added.

"He won't be staying," Sebastian informed the surprised man. "Vic feels he needs to get away, so I'm sending him to live with my father in Japan for awhile."

"I see," Ned said, "but that won't be for at least three months so we'll have your help for awhile longer."

Sebastian looked at the man strangely.

"Don't you remember, Mr. Blood? Your next ship scheduled to sail for Japan isn't for three months, and I'm certain you wouldn't trust the fate of such a young boy to any sea captain, but your own."

Victoria wanted to shout with joy. A three-month reprieve! There was no way he could dispose of the lad now.

He noticed her elation and released her hand. "Daniel," he shouted, then turned to Harper. "You're

210

dismissed, Ned, I wish to speak with my driver alone."

"Yes, sir," he answered and hurried away.

"Go with her to the Johnston Warehouse and this time make certain you stay with her. When she's finished, take her directly home. Don't dare make any stops."

"But Ned will wonder why I didn't return," she interrupted.

"Don't push it, Victoria. You will do as I say. I'm angry enough with you over this foolhardy stunt. Go home as I've directed and think about the punishment I intend to inflict upon you for disobeying me."

"Punishment?"

"That's right. I've warned you repeatedly and you still continue to disobey me."

She braced her hands on her slim hips and defiantly tilted her head back. "What are you going to do, beat me?"

"Precisely," he announced calmly and turned to enter the building.

"You—you—you bloody heathen!" she yelled and ran across the street with Daniel in pursuit.

Several curious glances were thrown at Sebastian.

"Have to keep these boys in line," he stated and several heads bobbed in agreement.

He entered the building with a smile. He enjoyed matching wits with Victoria. She was unpredictable. He never knew what she was going to do next and that excited him. He closed the door to his office and sat in his chair.

His heart had nearly leaped from his throat when he had seen her dangling precariously from the rope outside of Lola's window. He hadn't believed his eyes

211

when Daniel had arrived at the office with her clothes tucked under his arm.

Daniel hadn't fully trusted her and had waited outside the alley of the dress shop out of sight. He had followed Victoria to Madam Champlain's and then left to inform Sebastian.

He shook his head, then reached for the pen on his desk. He stopped and turned his hand as his eyes caught sight of a red mark. His palm was smeared with a light coat of blood.

"Damn," he muttered. Why hadn't she told him her hands had been injured on the rope?

He wiped the blood away with his handkerchief. "Wait until I get home, Victoria, just wait."

Victoria was sitting in the middle of the massive fourposter when Sebastian walked in. She had just finished bathing and her complexion was flushed from the heated water. Dark damp curls hugged her face and her long lashes sparkled around brilliant green eyes.

She was tempting, deliciously tempting. Sebastian found it difficult to concentrate on anything but the removal of the peach silk robe that bared one naked shoulder as it rested invitingly along her arm.

He stiffened, thinking how well she played the seductress and how much experience she had had at perfecting her role.

"Are you still angry with me?" she asked. Her voice was soft and gentle.

He ran his finger down her cheek. "No."

He noticed her injured palms cradled in her lap. A jar of cream and several white cloths sat next to her

212

crossed legs. He lifted her hands and examined the raw flesh with a tender, disturbing touch. "Why didn't you tell me you had injured yourself?"

"You never gave me a chance."

"May I bandage them for you?"

His request was simple, yet his purring voice and penetrating eyes suggested so much more that she could only manage to nod her approval.

He returned her hand to her lap. He then removed his butternut vest. His tie followed as well as his cream-colored shirt.

Victoria felt her pulse quicken as he sat down beside her. Her eyes refused to leave his broad chest. The thick muscles, the wide nipples, the flat midriff was tempting, too tempting, and she swallowed the lump that had risen in her throat.

Sebastian smiled, enjoying her uneasiness. He liked her little games. Yes, he liked them very much. He took her hand in his and scooped a generous amount of cream from the jar with his fingers. He rubbed it across her palm lightly, soothing the cream into her tender flesh. He stroked in tiny circles then ran his long fingers up along hers, slipping between them then slowly gliding out to run down to her wrist.

He administered the same treatment to the other hand and by the time he was done she was squirming uncomfortably. He reached across her to get the bandages and his chest brushed her breasts. He heard a sharp intake of breath and hid his smile. After wrapping her hands to the point where she was almost helpless, he placed them back in her lap.

Victoria forced herself to speak, needing to break the spell he had woven. "Akiko told me I need only keep

213

them covered until tomorrow morning."

"Akiko was taught much about healing. You should listen to her."

His finger reached up to delicately brush her lips in a lazy whisper and she shivered. "You want me. Don't you, Victoria?"

His words were unexpected and she fumbled when she spoke. "No. Of course not—I mean, why should I? That is—"

Sebastian grabbed her by the waist and yanked her down flat upon the bed. He half-covered her with his body. "You want me, Victoria. Admit it." He kissed her then, not soft or rough, somewhere in between as though saying, "I'm going to pleasure you slowly, thoroughly, fully."

His mouth drifted to her throat and his tongue teased her pulse. "Tell me, Victoria. Tell me you want me."

She wanted him. She wanted him more than anything in the world right then. And her naiveté forced her to speak. "Yes, I want you."

Sebastian looked into her eyes. He had expected to see the burning passion of a woman gone too long without a man, but was startled by what he saw and abruptly stood, walking away from her.

Before she could speak he left the room, slamming the door behind him. Victoria didn't understand what had happened, or what she had done.

Sebastian sat in the dark silence of his study, brooding. He was disturbed, angry, and confused with himself as well as his young wife tucked upstairs in

214

his bed.

He had wanted to stir her blood, heighten her passion, make her beg for him to touch her, love her. What he had seen in her eyes frightened him, for it wasn't what he had expected.

Her eyes shone brilliantly . . . with innocence and trust.

Chapter Sixteen

"Lola, I'm not sure I can go through with this," Victoria said, sitting in the middle of the woman's bed with her legs crossed, feeling the familiar embarrassing heat rise to tinge her cheeks. She had been blushing a lot lately. It was only her second lesson from Lola, and she was discovering that learning the talents of an experienced woman wasn't going to be easy.

"Of course you can," Lola insisted. "And remember what I told you. It will take time. You must be patient and not rush it. Do exactly as I told you this evening at the supper table and make certain it's an orange you use. It's nice and juicy."

"And if it works?" Victoria asked.

Lola smiled. "A night of surprises for the both of you."

Daniel walked with Victoria, donned in the lad's clothing, back to the office, only stopping long enough for her to purchase a bag of oranges.

"Want one, Daniel?" she asked with a satisfied grin.

"Thanks," he said, accepting the fruit from her a bit reluctantly and shaking his head. "You're up to something. I can tell."

His expression was one of fatherly concern and Victoria felt a sudden need to confide in him. She placed her hand on his arm. "Nothing that will hurt anyone, Daniel. I just want to make certain my husband remains mine."

The black man smiled so widely that Victoria was sure his dark face would crack. She winked at him and he laughed.

"My money's on you, Miss Victoria," he said, peeling the juicy fruit.

"Thanks," she responded, pleased by his words of confidence.

Victoria entered her husband's building, leaving Daniel to enjoy the sweet fruit. She cheerfully greeted the men in the office and offered them some. They all gratefully accepted. They liked the lad and none of them wished to see him leave.

Still having several oranges left, she took one out to give to Sebastian. Raised voices punctuated the air as she approached the Dragon's office. One distant voice spoke in anger and after checking to make certain Ben Shavers wasn't about, she sneaked nearer to the closed door to listen.

"Damn it, Henry. I want the Chambeau place secured and a thorough accounting of all the ledgers and buildings."

"Yes, sir, Mr. Blood," the nervous man answered.

"He's up to something. I can feel it," Sebastian said. "It doesn't make any sense. From all the information gathered, Roland Chambeau was a brilliant business-man. I can't understand him trusting his daughters' welfare and the management of his estate to a man like Tobias Withers."

Victoria strained to hear every word. Was her husband implying that her uncle had somehow managed to gain control of Chambeau property through fraudulent means?

Sebastian's tone changed when next he spoke. "Listen, Henry. My wife has suffered enough hardship. I don't want her to suffer anymore. Do all you can to discover what he has been up to with the profits from the Chambeau holdings. Hire any assistants you need in immediately taking care of this matter and report to me by the end of next week, or sooner if you discover anything important."

"Yes, sir," Henry Atley replied, reaching for his briefcase. "I'll take care of everything."

Victoria hastily knocked on the door, not wanting Sebastian aware of the fact that she had been privy to the conversation. She intended to make some discreet inquires of her own. If Tobias Withers was a crook, she intended to see him suffer for the torment he had brought to her and Beth.

"Come in," Sebastian called.

She entered with a smile as though she had heard nothing.

Henry Atley made a hasty exit with an assurance of his report by the end of next week.

"What took you so long?" Sebastian asked, having sent her on a short errand some time ago.

"A couple of the other men gave me notes to deliver and I stopped at the market. I got this for you," she said innocently, holding the orange out to him.

His spirits soared although he wondered why. She was only giving him an orange. He was glad he had relented and allowed her to accompany him to the office one day a week disguised as the young lad Vic and with the stipulation that Daniel go wherever she did. He had to admit he had succumbed to her persistence only to please himself for he enjoyed having her with him.

She smiled sweetly at him and he wondered how he ever could have imagined her a boy. Even the smudges of dirt which he insisted she place on her face to hide her unmarred complexion did nothing to dampen his passion. He had also demanded she wear a hat, since her hair was beginning to grow and he refused to allow her to cut it.

"Aren't you going to eat it?" she asked, hoisting herself up to sit on the edge of the desk.

He glanced at the round fruit cupped in his large hand and squeezed. He grinned that wicked little grin that tugged at the strings of Victoria's passion. "Yes, love. I intend to enjoy every succulent bite."

Her breath lodged in her throat as his lusty, dark eyes casually roamed over her. She could swear he was capable of caressing her body with those midnight orbs, for her skin prickled with pleasure.

She hopped off the desk. "You will be on time for supper, won't you?"

"Yes, and by the way, I've been meaning to inquire about the gown you're having made for the Fisk dinner party at the end of the week. Will it be ready?"

"One last fitting tomorrow," she answered, not permitting her nervousness over the coming event to show.

He recalled all of her tricks of late and decided to make certain there were no surprises planned. "It isn't black, is it?"

"I wouldn't disobey you," she answered coyly and walked to the door.

One dark brow arched slightly and his fine lips clamped firmly shut contemplating her playful remark. He didn't trust her. "So help me, Victoria, if that dress if black I'll rip it off you."

She turned, clutching her bag of oranges to her chest, a feigned look of shock on her face. "Really, Sebastian, issuing threats you'll never make good on."

He stood, bracing his hands on the desk. "You need your backside tanned."

She smiled and purposely wiggled her derriere in his face, then flung open the door and ran like the wind, leaving her laughter trailing behind.

"Vic!" he screamed, furious at her unladylike display and for igniting his passion with that provocative wiggle.

She paid him no mind. She ran through the large office, past the worried men, who had stopped working at the onset of the commotion.

"Wouldn't give him one of my oranges," she cried, pressing her hat firmly to her head and running straight for the front door. She slammed it behind her with a resounding thud.

Sebastian had followed in his usual long, purposeful strides, but had halted when the door had slammed shut. He caught the look of astonishment mixed with fright on his employees' faces.

"You can have my orange, Mr. Blood," Ned Harper

offered, holding it out to him.

Sebastian eyed the man as though he were daft. Then he smiled, shook his head, and returned to his office.

The men conversed softly as they returned to their assigned tasks, talking about how the small lad could make the mighty Dragon smile.

Victoria took extra pains with her appearance. Akiko helped her bathe, since Sebastian had informed her he still had been unable to locate a proper lady's maid for her. She didn't mind. She was actually relieved, for she enjoyed the Japanese woman's company and didn't find it necessary to hire any further help.

She had sought Akiko's skill with a needle to help alter one of her gowns. The whisper blue satin dress had been fashioned for a young girl. High neck ruffles and long snug-fitting sleeves made it an acceptable garment, but not for what Victoria had in mind.

She had daringly cut the top to pieces, removing part of the sleeves and tightening the waistline. The affect was stunning as well as revealing. The neckline scooped down so low that she was afraid her ample bosoms would fall out with one deep breath. The sleeves brushed the tops of her shoulders and the full blue satin skirt billowed from beneath with mounds of petticoats.

Akiko brushed her hair, permitting the soft curls their freedom. The sable brown strands hugged her neck and fell captivatingly along her forehead and around her ears.

"Sebastian-san will not be able to resist you this night," Akiko said, placing the silver brush on the dressing table.

"I hope not," Victoria smiled, patting a softly scented rose perfume around her neck and down the valley of her bulging bosom.

"You love him, don't you?"

"Does it show that much?" Victoria asked, unable to conceal her feelings for him any longer.

Akiko gently placed her hand on Victoria's arm. "When a woman falls in love there is a radiance about her and you sparkle with it."

Victoria shook her head. "But am I being foolish in believing that it is possible for the fierce Dragon to return my love?"

"Love can tame the wildest beast."

"But if I tame the beast will I win his heart?"

Akiko nodded her head slowly. "The battle is half-won. Don't be fooled by his stubborn pride; search deep within him for the true answer."

Victoria smiled at her encouraging words then stood and impulsively hugged the woman. "I don't know what I'd do without you."

Tears misted in Akiko's eyes. "It is good to have a friend once again."

"Yes, it is," Victoria agreed, feeling the same sense of displacement as the foreign woman who had been removed from her land and customs.

"Come, he will be home shortly and you must be downstairs waiting for him," Akiko said, hurrying her toward the door.

The two women were halfway down the long staircase when the front door burst open, admitting Sebastian and Aaron.

"We have a guest for supper," Sebastian announced

222

to Akiko, failing to see his wife standing off to the right, hidden by the huge crystal chandelier.

"I can't stay long, Akiko. I have a house call to make," Aaron said.

Victoria's moment of distress passed after realizing that her plans for the evening would not be disrupted. She descended the remainder of the stairs to greet them with a titillating smile.

Sebastian had never openly displayed his emotions to anyone. There was nothing that caught him off guard and penetrated the armor that surrounded him, but the sight of his small tantalizing wife outfitted in a gown that would tempt the most celibate of men was too much for his already heightened desire. His mouth fell open.

"Aaron, how nice to have you join us for supper, even if you can only stay a short time," Victoria said, slipping her arm through his.

Her greeting was genuine and Aaron felt at ease even though his friend was obviously shocked by his wife's all too sultry appearance.

"Victoria," Sebastian said, his tone icy and stern. "Don't you think a shawl would compliment your appearance?"

"I'm not a bit cold."

"I didn't ask if you were cold."

"Don't you like my dress?" she sighed dramatically, allowing her plump bottom lip to thrust out ever so slightly.

Aaron stifled his urge to laugh at the coy act Victoria was admirably playing. Didn't Sebastian see how she was using her feminine wiles to tease and tempt him? Was he that much in love with the woman that he was blind to her performance?

Victoria made a grand display of twirling around, billowing the skirt in a cloud of blue satin while her full breasts heaved upward and threatened to spill out.

"I'm so disappointed," she said, coming to a halt beside her husband and innocently reaching for his arm to stop herself from swaying.

Her fingers clung to him and even through the material of his fawn-colored coat, she could feel the strength of him. "I did so want to please you."

He leaned close to her and whispered. "You will please me. When *I'm* ready."

She attempted to pull away, but he held her firm. He was so pigheaded and stubborn. And she was so naive and foolish. This was never going to work. She was wasting her time.

Aaron sensed the change between them and wondered how often they played this game of cat and mouse.

Sebastian forced her arm around his and escorted her to the dining room. Aaron followed.

Supper went well. The conversation was equally weighted among the three of them, especially since the two men were familiar with Victoria's knowledge of the waterfront.

"I tell you, Sebastian, the police in this city are worthless," Aaron complained. "They constantly badger the Chinese, yet turn their backs on other more obvious crime."

Sebastian folded the white linen napkin on his empty plate. "It's the graft. There's too much easy money floating around."

Aaron snorted in disgust. "Perhaps the local wealth

should cease building those palaces on Nob Hill and direct their money to worthwhile causes."

Sebastian gave a hearty laugh. "It is a worthwhile cause to them. It means their standard in this community is well defined."

"That's a laugh," Aaron added. "George Stanton paid me a visit the other day to inquire about his wife's pregnancy, or so he said, since he spent most of the time talking about the home he's building up there. And everyone knows it's his family's wealth that's making it possible. If it weren't for his father's money that man would crumble. He hasn't done a day's work in his entire life."

"If Henry Stanton isn't careful, his son is going to be reduced to manual labor," Sebastian said.

"Then the rumors are true," Aaron stated. "I had heard the older Stanton was speculating too broadly with his investments."

"Far too broadly," Sebastian offered. "And now is not the time. The market crisis in New York is affecting everyone, especially those who speculated as foolishly as Henry did."

Victoria found it the perfect time to inquire about her own inheritance. "My father invested in various ventures, but always managed to make money. By the way, Sebastian, has my uncle provided you with the family accounts? I would like to see how he fared while handling them."

"There's no need to concern yourself with that, love. As soon as my solicitor has settled everything we can discuss what you wish to do with your inheritance."

"As you say," she answered. She had no intentions of forcing the issue at the moment. She'd wait and see, but

225

in the meantime she intended to make her own inquires. She had had her inheritance taken from her once. She wouldn't let it happen again, no matter what her husband thought.

"I must take my leave," Aaron announced, pushing his chair back to rise. "I have already delayed too long and my patient is probably wondering as to my whereabouts."

Sebastian moved to rise, but Aaron halted him with a wave of his hand. "It's not necessary. I can see myself out. Enjoy dessert with your wife."

Sebastian produced a rakish grin and Aaron laughed.

"You will join us again, won't you?" Victoria asked.

"Definitely, Mrs. Blood," he responded gallantly and kissed her hand.

Akiko cleared the table and brought out coffee, tea, a bowl of strawberries smothered in thick cream, and a bowl of fresh oranges.

Victoria reached for the round fruit with the tough peel and placed it on her dessert plate.

Sebastian chose the strawberries and relaxed in his seat to feast on the fruit as well as his wife's revealing breasts.

Victoria felt her courage wane. She recalled Lola's advice about acting nonchalant as though she ate oranges this precise way everyday, but as she began to peel the tough covering she doubted her abilities in being successful in seducing her husband. After all, she was an innocent, even though he thought otherwise. If she were successful, though, he would finally realize she had been telling the truth. The sobering thought pushed her to proceed.

Her slim fingers gently prodded the moist fruit sections apart. With a bit of hesitation she raised one to her lips. She didn't place it in her mouth and bite it. Instead she sucked on it. Slowly, almost languidly, as though she wasn't certain what she intended to do to it. Thrust in. Pull out. Slow. Lazy slow. And each time her lips would caress it.

She stopped with the tip between her teeth and bit the end. The juice squirted out and trickled down onto her chest, running between her breasts.

"How clumsy," she sighed, taking her napkin and delicately patting the crevice where the two mounds of flesh met.

Sebastian had picked up one of the cream-covered strawberries on his spoon and that's where it remained as his hand held it halfway to his mouth. His eyes were fixed upon his wife's outrageous actions. He watched intently as she slid the fruit in and out of her mouth, suckling it with her soft lips and gliding her moist tongue around it as contemplating whether or not to devour it.

He shifted uncomfortably in his seat as she picked up another slice and proceeded to administer the same treatment to it. Her mouth captivated his senses as he watched her play her little game and he felt his loins tighten and ache with the want of her.

Sebastian placed the spoon in the bowl and reached for his coffee, casually sipping it. His eyes never wavered from her mouth as she continued with slice after slice until none remained.

Victoria eased back against her seat, disappointed that she was unable to at least tempt her husband with her suggestive actions. She blamed her lack of success on her inexperience and hoped Lola wouldn't be too discouraged by her failure.

"Are you finished, Victoria?" Sebastian asked in a tightly controlled voice.

"Yes."

"Good," he said, rising abruptly and storming over to stand behind her. He leaned across her, reaching for an orange and the sharp knife. He placed the orange on the table in front of her and raised the knife in the air. He brought the razor-edged steel down in one swift blow, severing the round fruit in half.

Victoria jumped and Sebastian smiled.

He moved to stand in front of her, leaning back against the edge of the table while he held the fruit firmly in his hand. He reached out grasping the back of her neck and held it rigid as he proceeded to squeeze the juice all over her breasts. When he finished he threw the peel on the table and picked up the other half. He brought it to rest right above the valley of her full breasts and squeezed, making certain the sticky nectar slipped down between the firm mounds.

Victoria squirmed.

"Is it traveling down to your belly, love?" he asked calmly.

"Yes, and it will go farther if you don't stop this foolishness."

His dark eyes gleamed in amusement. "But it's doing precisely what I want it to do."

"Why?" she asked incredulously.

"So I can lick every bit of juice off your delicious body."

She closed her eyes. She had accomplished what she set out to do. Could she carry through with it?

228

Opening her eyes, she stood. The juice had traveled downward and nestled on her lower belly. She shivered at the path his tongue would follow.

He stood behind her, his body plastered firmly against hers. His arm wrapped securely around her slim waist, urging her to press into him even more. "It's time, Vic. Truth or tale. Are you prepared to have me discover which one?"

She nodded, unable to speak.

He scooped her up into his arms and took the stairs two at a time. She buried her face in his chest and prayed.

...
...
...
...
...
...
...

Chapter Seventeen

Victoria stood naked. Her heart beat. Her pulse raced.
And she waited. She waited for Sebastian to walk
across the room and touch her. But he didn't move. He
stood still. Dead still. He was naked as well, his body
ready for her, yet he made no move.

His face was expressionless and she wondered what
thoughts danced through his mind. He moved then as
though she had interrupted his concentration. He
walked to the bed, stretched out on his side and reached
out his hand to her.

She hesitated. He was summoning her, letting her
know this would be *his* way. But then he didn't know
that she didn't have the slightest idea as to what to do.

Victoria went to him slowly. Her eyes were wide. Her
lips ripe. And her heart open.

She reached out and he grasped her fingers in his,
gently pulling her down to rest on top of him. She
stiffened at first, feeling the hard length of him, but his
words were reassuring.

"Soft and sticky," he teased in a murmur, kissing her

lips tenderly.

She relaxed against him, trying to recall all Lola had taught. But her mind was blank. She couldn't concentrate on anything, but Sebastian's hands touching her, stroking her, exploring her.

"I want to taste you, Vic. I want to taste all of you."

He lifted her then, just enough to taint her nipples with his lips, sampling her wares before going any farther. They hardened instantly and he smiled before taking the pebble-hard bud into his mouth and enjoying it.

Victoria leaned her head back. He was driving her insane. His tongue was wickedly magic, causing her nipples to ache and the crevice between her closed legs to throb. She felt as though those parts had a life of their own. Pulsing, beating, flowing with the passion of life.

Sebastian lifted her even higher, tasting her belly, licking the sweet orange nectar from her flesh.

She moaned at the exquisite torture he was causing her. Lola had told her, but she had never imagined . . .

Suddenly she found herself beneath Sebastian. His mouth was covering hers, his tongue forcing entrance, his hand cupping the back of her head, pressing her to him.

Alive. She felt so alive.

His lips found her nipples once again while his fingers explored her. She gasped when they sank inside her and for a moment he stopped and stared at her. Slowly his fingers played with her.

His stare continued. He watched her eyelashes flutter, her breathing grow heavy, and her body squirm.

She hungered after him with her eyes and he saw it. He knew she wanted him, needed him. And it excited him even more. He had wanted to take her fast and hard at first, but after looking at her standing there naked, so vulnerable, so lost, he couldn't bring himself to do it. She was ready now, though, more than ready and he intended to delve into her and enjoy every last thrust. She was his, damn it, his.

He stretched out over her, tempting her with the tip of him. He noticed her eyes widen and for a moment he thought he caught a twinge of fear. But then she would show that, for her masquerade was about to come to an end.

He kissed her gently on the lips. He didn't know why, but he wanted to, had to.

He pushed gently at first, easing himself into her. But she was ready, accepting him easily, and she felt good, so good. Her arms circled him, holding him to her, and her legs locked around him. She was waiting for him, welcoming him, and he thrust into her.

He felt her stiffen and heard her groan. He stopped all movement and stared into her eyes.

"Truth," she whispered.

He didn't know what to say, but his body knew what to do. He was gentle as he moved within her, careful not to cause pain, but only pressure. And he did. He felt it in her response. She clung to him, moved with him, climaxed with him.

His name escaped her lips as they hurdled together through the abyss of passion and he liked the way she cried it out with such a driving force, demonstrating her need of him.

Several silent minutes passed before he whispered

softly, "Are you all right?"

"Yes," she sighed, her breathing still heavy and labored.

He gently removed himself from her and she shivered, not wanting him to go. She was grateful when he pulled her into the confines of his arms and held her close. She felt tears near and tried to prevent them from falling, but failed. She had so wanted to hear him call out to her as she had done to him, but he didn't. Lola had warned her it would take time, but she was impatient. She wanted the Dragon's love and she wanted it now.

Sebastian ignored the first tearsdrops he felt fall upon his chest. He never had allowed a woman's tears to affect him. He always felt they used them as weapons to get what they desired. Several more joined the others and he silently swore.

He startled her when his huge hands circled her small waist and lifted her over him. Her soft nipples hardened as they brushed the firm flesh of his naked chest.

"What's wrong?" he demanded. "Did I hurt you that much that it brings tears?"

He did, but not physically, and she doubted he would understand for it even confused her. She shook her head, not trusting her voice.

"Then what's the problem?" he repeated, irritated by his inability to understand her emotions at a time when he felt as though he should.

"I—I guess," she fumbled, searching for a reasonable excuse, "I'm just not use to feeling like this. It's so undeniably wonderful."

Sebastian released a low tortured moan that

sounded like a wounded animal and at first Victoria thought she had upset him with her statement. Then, without warning, he pulled her roughly against his nakedness and held her tightly.

She rested her head against his shoulder, reveling in the intoxicating feel of his hard, warm body molded firmly to hers. It felt so right to be there with him.

His fingers ran up and down her spine, gentle yet demanding in his caress, feeling the silkiness of her skin, and burning a path of passion with every simple touch.

He closed his eyes against the exquisite torture. Damn, but she could unman him. Every word she spoke and every action she performed fueled his desire, and if he wasn't careful she was soon going to find herself forever in his bed . . . and possibly his heart. The unusual thought didn't upset him nearly as much as he had expected it to and he relaxed in his newfound knowledge.

Neither of them spoke and after several minutes passed Victoria slipped off him and from the bed.

"Where are you going?" he asked.

"I need a bath. The juice and your lovemaking," she blushed, "has left me rather sticky."

He laughed and bounded from the bed in one leap. She jumped back, startled by his overpowering size. He reached for his robe on the chair.

"I'll join you," he announced, confident she would not refuse, and she didn't.

The soothing heat of the water was relaxing. Victoria was seated comfortably upon her husband's bent knee. Her head nestled against his moist chest.

They didn't speak and Victoria understood why. He

had watched her carefully when she had washed herself before entering the tub and it was obvious that he desired her.

He finally broke the heavy silence. "I need you, Victoria," he whispered urgently and didn't wait for a response. He stepped out of the tub with her cradled in his powerful arms. The water dripped from their naked bodies. She shivered and he hugged her close.

She clung to him as he walked from the room into the kitchen, along the hallway to the foyer. He stopped and kissed her gently on the lips before proceeding up the stairs.

She peered over his shoulder relieved to see none of the servants about at this late hour, for he seemed not to care if anyone viewed their wet, glistening bodies. He had only one thing on his mind and it appeared nothing would deter him from his course.

He shoved open the ajar door with his shoulder, then slammed it shut with his foot after entering. He deposited her on the bed and scorched her nakedness with his midnight blue eyes.

"I promise you'll find no sleep this night, dear wife," he whispered and produced a wickedly sinful grin before slipping over her.

Morning's first light peeked on the distant horizon as Victoria stood at the bedroom window and looked out. The soft orange glow seemed as though it whispered a silent good-bye to the night.

She pulled the peach silk robe closer around her, hugging her waist. She couldn't sleep. Even though she felt a pleasant exhaustion from Sebastian's lovemaking, sleep eluded her. Her body felt satisfied, content. It was nothing like she imagined. Even Lola's description paled in comparison to the real thing. Or perhaps Lola's prediction was true. She had warned her many times that once she tasted the Dragon, she'd want no other.

She shut here eyes against the thought. She would never want another, but would he? He hadn't even spoken to her of her innocence, admitting he was wrong. He said nothing. Didn't he want to know more? Didn't he want to understand her? Didn't he realize just how much she loved him?

A single tear ran down her cheek. She was a fool. The mighty Dragon loving her, actually caring about her, silly thoughts they were. Silly thoughts.

She jumped as the Dragon's lips touched her neck.

His arms slipped around her, forcing her back against him. "Easy, love. I didn't mean to frighten you."

She didn't speak, afraid her voice would betray her emotions.

"I thought you'd sleep from exhaustion." His hands found their way beneath hers. He shoved them gently aside to slip beneath her robe and slide along the soft flesh of her belly.

Her body instantly responded and she fought the slight quiver in her voice. "I—I'm not sleepy."

"Good," he whispered and ran his hand up slowly to cup her breast. His fingers played with her nipple, delicately, gently, before squeezing it with a light roughness.

"Sebastian," she half-moaned and cried.

"Listen to me, love," he murmured, releasing her

nipple and slowly easing her robe from her body without any protest from her. "There is much I need to say to you."

He pulled her back against him. He was naked and his warm flesh felt good, so good.

His fingers returned to play with her nipple gently, roughly, maddeningly. "I learned the truth tonight. I took your innocence. Now you truly belong to me."

His hand slipped to her belly and his fingers splayed across it, pushing her firmly to him. She felt the potent strength of him pulsating against her.

"You're mine, Victoria. Understand that and never challenge me again."

She wanted to scream out at him, tell him she didn't want to challenge, only to love. But it was too soon, she would wait. She would learn. She would conquer the Dragon with love. She remained silent and moved against him.

He stilled her movement with his hand. "What is this, Victoria, a challenge or desire?"

She knew he was testing her, seeing if she would obey him. She wanted to say it was love that caused her to act as such, but he wouldn't believe her. So she spoke from her heart. "I want you, Dragon."

Sebastian smiled inwardly. By using his infamous name she still challenged him, but so be it. He would enjoy taming her. His fingers crept slowly to tickle the bud of her pleasure.

She moaned once again and he found the sound excited him. He lifted her into his arms and returned her to the bed. He didn't wait. He spread her legs, knelt between them, and lifted her up to enter her.

She winced when he slipped the tip in and he

hesitated. "You're too tender."

His whispered words inflamed her even more. She pushed up, seeking the rest of him, heedless of the soreness.

He attempted to enter her again, watching her face for discomfort. He caught the slight grimace and stopped, pulling away from her.

"No,' she protested, more strongly than she had intended.

He smiled, moved off the bed, and returned—all in a matter of seconds.

He knelt between her legs once again. She jumped when his fingers touched her for they were covered with a cool cream. He worked inside her gently, so gently and lovingly that Victoria swore she would climax against his touch.

He lifted her hips, holding her still for a moment before entering her. He slipped inside her with ease and his slow thrust was her undoing. She moved urgently against him and he answered her demand with that of his own. She pushed. He thrust. And the ancient rhythm began until he collapsed against her, his breathing heavy and his seed spent.

Chapter Eighteen

Victoria carefully opened the narrow drawer of the large desk and slipped out the wide envelope. She didn't have much time. Sebastian was at a business meeting and he had instructed her to remain in his office until his return since Daniel would be accompanying him.

She had a limited amount of time left to use the disguise of the lad Vic to settle her accounts. She still sought Lola's help, intending to make certain she kept her husband in her bed. She hoped to pierce the shield surrounding his heart and hear him declare his love for her. The other matter concerned her property. Sebastian continued to placate her every time she inquired about it. She had had enough. She intended to discover for herself just what was going on.

She glanced at the envelope once again and cautiously removed the contents. After reading only a few lines she plopped down in the large chair behind the desk.

Her eyes repeatedly scanned the material not

believing what she had read. Her uncle had sold most of her father's stocks to Thorndike Enterprises. The money he had acquired for them had gone to pay for improvements to the Chambeau estate, yet she had seen no improvements and surely the furniture he had added wasn't that costly.

The last paper jolted her the most. It was from an attorney her father had hired. It informed Mr. Blood that his services had been secured by Mr. Chambeau to investigate a one Tobias Withers. He was never able to start the investigation for two days later Mr. Chambeau had died in a carriage accident, terminating their transaction.

If her father hadn't trusted his half brother and was having him investigated, then why had he been made executor of the will?

She hastily returned the papers to the envelope and replaced them in the desk. She pulled the knit cap she wore down snugly on her head before rubbing at the excess grime on her face. She had added more dirt recently after receiving several strange inquiring glances. She intended on taking no chances of being recognized.

It was imperative that she begin her own investigation into the matter immediately. She had allowed the problems with Sebastian to take precedence and neglected to make certain her uncle paid for his foul behavior. Well, no more. There was one person who could get the information she needed and she intended to seek his help.

Halfway down the street she realized Sebastian would return before she did, but she didn't allow the thought to dissuade her from her task. She'd form some sort of story to appease him, or at least she'd try.

The sounds of Chinese grew louder on her approach to the waterfront. Their drab black garments were in stark contrast to the plaid sweaty shirts of the loud seamen, but the scene was familiar to Victoria and she felt part of it as though she belonged amongst this strange mixture of life.

A tingle of excitement ran up her spine and her small booted feet scurried along the rough planks ducking and winding her way in and out of the oncoming crowd. She dashed down the next alley on her right and tapped on the door at the end.

She stamped her feet, making a commotion to chase the rats that sat feasting around the barrel where the remnants of the noonday meal had been discarded. They sat for a moment, their beady eyes assessing her before turning back to their meal, unperturbed by her demand.

"Vic, my boy. Come in," the jolly voice called and she hurried inside away from the furry creatures.

"You hungry, boy?" Louie asked, raising the large knife he held in his meaty hand. He brought it crashing down with a solid wack upon the dead fish that lay on the cutting board.

Victoria watched the head fall into the pail beneath the table and recalled the monotonous days of cutting and scaling the fish and feeling as though she would smell like the slimy creatures forever.

"Nah, I ate already, but I could use a favor."

"Sure, boy. What is it?" he said, wiping his bloody hands on his stained white apron.

Vic couldn't help but grin at the large man. In his prime he must have been one tough sailor for he still looked mean enough to break a few heads. His five foot nine inch frame boasted at least two hundred pounds of weight and it wasn't all solid, especially around his protruding gut.

"I need to find out some stuff about a man."

Louie listened carefully as Vic detailed the man's description and provided him with the name. "It's real important," she added.

Louie scratched his gray handlebar mustache. "Vic, I know you're working for the Dragon. How come you don't ask him?"

"This is private business, Louie. This man did me and Beth wrong and I got to right it." She swallowed hard before using Sebastian's revered nickname. "The Dragon don't want me doing nothing about it, and it's a matter of honor with me."

Louie understood. "I know what you mean, but sometimes the cost of revenge runs high. And I don't mean money."

Louie had made himself perfectly clear, but even the thought of bodily harm wouldn't prevent her from her task. "I know I don't look strong, but I can stand my own."

The old seaman shook his head, sure the boy couldn't be dissuaded. "There's a friend of mine who might be able to get the information you want. It'll take time and money."

Victoria didn't mind the money or the wait. She had saved some of her wages and she would use every penny if necessary.

242

"You'll have to meet the fella here at night. I'll let you know when."

Victoria didn't know how she was going to manage that one, but somehow she'd find a way. "Leave the message with Lola. She'll make certain I get it."

Louie nodded. "Now, how about something to eat. You're too damn thin."

She shook her head and laughed as she walked to the door, stopping just as her hand touched the knob. "One other thing, Louie," she said, turning. "Can you get me a dagger?"

His bushy gray eyebrows raised in silent question.

"Just in case," she answered.

"I'll get it," he promised.

"Thanks again." She disappeared out the door with a final wave of her hand.

She hurried along the street, the smell of raw fish clinging to her and leaving a strong odor in her wake.

In her haste to return she failed to be cautious and avoid areas that were known for trouble. Too late she passed an establishment heralded for its troublesome patrons, and it was just her luck to run into one . . . literally.

She bounced off the solid mound of blubber and hit the wooden planks, landing on her backside with a resounding thud. Her eyes caught sight of the sign that hung over the saloon: HADES.

She swallowed her fear and moved with speed and agility to her feet in an attempt to slip past the huge bearlike man into which she had run. He was having none of her hasty departure, though. His hand shot out and grabbed her collar, yanking her backward.

243

"In a hurry, boy?" the man growled, spewing a rush of liquor-coated breath across her face.

Victoria winced and turned her head. "I need to get back to my boss, or he'll wup me." She hoped somewhere in this giant was a heart she could pierce with sympathy.

"And who's ya boss?"

Victoria prayed this was one time the infamous name would help. "The Dragon."

The man turned a fiery red and snorted, his wide nostrils flaring even further. His fat cheeks puffed up until they looked as though they were ready to explode, and his shiny bald head sprung little dots of perspiration.

Vic got the distinct feeling this man didn't particularly care for the Dragon. The next second she was certain of it. In one swift motion he released his hold and backhanded her across her cheek, sending her reeling.

He grabbed her before she could fall and delivered another blow to the same tender spot. Her head snapped sharply to the right.

"I hate the Dragon," he spat, and dragged her into Hades.

"A drink," he demanded with a vicious pound of his mighty fist on the ornate bar. Glasses rattled, men scattered in fright, and the picture of the naked woman hanging on the wall behind the bar tilted.

He deposited her with a teeth-rattling thud on top of the bar and grabbed for the bottle the frightened bartender held out to him.

"Now, Percy, we don't want any trouble in here," the

quaking man began.

"And ya ain't gonna get any," Percy snapped. "Now leave me be."

The huge man guzzled down a good portion of liquor straight from the bottle, part of it dribbling from his mouth onto his blue sweat-stained shirt.

"Drink," Percy demanded, pushing the bottle to her lips when he had finished.

"Don't want none," she cried, her mind swimming with ways to escape.

"Drink," he screamed and forced the bottle to her locked lips.

She had no choice but to open her mouth for fear he would cause more damage with the bottle than with the liquor. The fiery liquid scorched a path down her throat and into her belly. When he finally pulled the bottle away she coughed and sputtered and thought her burning stomach would revolt.

"I hate the Dragon," he repeated once again.

Her head spun and her face ached, and she prayed Sebastian was searching for her, for she saw no avenue of escape.

The burning liquid was forced upon her again only this time it went down without much irritation and didn't taste as bad as before.

"Do you like working for the Dragon?" Percy asked, taking another generous swig from the bottle.

Vic wasn't feeling any more pain. As a matter of fact, she felt pretty good. "Nah, he's a real bloody bastard."

"Why do you stay with him?" he asked. "You're small, but you've got guts. You're not afraid to stand up for yourself."

"I owe him," she hiccupped and reached for the bottle, taking a generous gulp.

"What'd he do for you?"

"He took care of my ill sister and helped me give her a decent burial," she answered and, without knowing why, she began to cry.

"He even bought her a real fine coffin with brass handles and had her sent by train to the family plot." She wiped the tears away with her worn sleeve and winced when she connected with her swollen cheek.

The large man's eyes misted with tears. "I had a sister. She was real good to me. She died too."

"Ahhhh, that's a shame," Vic consoled, placing her small hand on his broad shoulder.

"No one understands how it feels unless they lost a sister themselves," Percy lamented. "You're a good lad and the Dragon was good to you. You do owe him."

"Why do you hate him?" she asked, followed by a hiccup.

"He refused to hire me on one of his ships because I got drunk and busted up this here saloon. He said I couldn't hold my liquor."

"Well, can you?"

He rubbed his bald head in thought and swallowed a generous gulp from the near-empty bottle. "I guess not, and you know something? If he hadn't refused me I wouldn't have been here when my dear sister died."

Vic stared at the teary-eyed man.

"Maybe the Dragon ain't so bad after all," he grumbled.

"He's still a bloody bastard," Vic laughed and slapped her leg.

Percy joined her in her drunken gaiety and before long they had the entire saloon roaring with laughter.

"I tell you, Daniel, I'm going to kill her when I get my hands on her." Sebastian paced back and forth in his office. He had returned only moments before to discover her missing, and his temper had ignited into a full-blown rage.

He had repeatedly warned her of going off without Daniel's protection, but she was too obstinate to listen. Now she was going to pay.

"I don't even know where to begin to look," he yelled. "She could be anywhere—in trouble, hurt, or . . ." He refused to voice his fearful thought. He didn't want to think of the consequences if someone along the waterfront had discovered her gender.

"Should I start searching, sir?" Daniel asked, hoping Victoria was visiting Lola, but not wishing to inform his angry boss that his wife frequented a whorehouse.

"Yes, you're familiar with some of her favorite haunts. Perhaps—"

Sebastian never finished; loud, boisterous voices carried through the door from the outer room, interrupting him.

He flung the door open and marched out to see what the commotion was about. He stood in stunned silence; even he couldn't hide his shocked expression in seeing his small wife tucked under Percy English's huge arm. What was even more strange was that she was laughing, singing, giggling, and carrying on as though she were . . . drunk!

247

"There's the bloody bastard," Victoria yelled and followed her declaration with a hearty laugh.

Sebastian's dark eyes took on such a heated glare that every man he passed as he stormed to the front of the room turned pale and clamped their mouths shut.

Percy stood the young lad up and attempted to let go of him, but every time he did, the boy would sway precariously. Finally he grabbed him by the back of his britches and steadied him.

"See, I told you he ain't so mean," Victoria said to Percy. She tried to take a step forward and was halted, by what she didn't know.

She tried again and again until she sputtered, "Hey, who's got hold of my drawers?"

The men in the office couldn't contain themselves any longer. They burst into fits of laughter.

Sebastian braced his hands on his hips and swung around. One scathing look silenced them.

"See? See the way he scares people?" Victoria said, poking Percy in his thick gut.

Sebastian directed his question to the large man, who he recalled had a penchant for strong spirits. "Since he's too inebriated to give me a straight answer, suppose you tell me what happened and begin by explaining how he got that vicious bruise on his face."

Victoria bravely stepped forward, but her foot found thin air since Percy continued to hold her britches. "Bloody hell, Percy, let go of me so I can tell the bastard what happened."

Percy wasn't sure what to do. He could tell by the Dragon's murderous expression that the boy was in severe trouble, and he felt responsible, for he had developed a fondness for the bold lad. "I'll tell him, Vic."

"Nah, I'll tell him, after all it was me that walked into that stupid door," she said, exaggerating a wink and causing herself to moan from the pain it brought.

"And did you also drown yourself in a bottle of liquor?" Sebastian asked, grabbing her arm and nodding for Percy to let go. He did and Vic sprang forward, crashing against the steel-hard form of the Dragon.

"I took the lad into Hades for a drink," Percy said. "Didn't know he wasn't use to strong spirits."

"You took him into *Hades?*" Sebastian repeated, not believing his own ears.

"Yup," Victoria smiled, attempting to stand straight, but finding the task difficult even with Sebastian supporting her.

"Percy, I want the truth and I want it now," Sebastian shouted, furious at the unlikely story being told.

"You quit yelling at my friend," Victoria demanded, swinging her small fist in his face.

"Percy," he said in a bone-chilling tone that made the large man shiver.

He wasted no time in telling the Dragon the whole truth and adding his sincere apology since he discovered what a likable lad the boy was and he didn't want to see any harm come to him.

Victoria poked at Sebastian's hard chest with her finger as she spoke. "Don't you dare yell at him or hurt him."

"It's not him I intend to hurt," he whispered harshly

near her ear.

"You're going to give me that wuppin' you keep promising me, aren't you?" she wailed, tears springing to her bloodshot eyes. "You're going to beat me till I can't sit."

"Stop it, Vic," Sebastian ordered, sensing the liquor was finally taking its toll.

"Oh no, Percy! You've got to take me with you. He's going to beat me," she pleaded, turning her head to beg his help.

"Stop it, Vic," Sebastian demanded, shaking her roughly and only managing to make her cry louder.

"You don't know what happens when he strips—"

Victoria never finished. Sebastian lifted her swiftly and flung her over his shoulder with such a thrust that it knocked the wind from her.

"Percy, I suggest you leave and never, I repeat never, show your face around here again," Sebastian warned.

"But the lad?" he dared ask, concerned for the poor boy.

"The lad is my responsibility as well as my burden. And I owe you no explanation of his punishment."

Percy knew when to leave well enough alone. The Dragon was too powerful to cross and he wanted to continue to sail the seas. One word from this man and all that would swiftly come to an end. He left without muttering another word.

"Daniel, the carriage," Sebastian yelled, turning to face his men. His quick spin caused Victoria to feel as though she couldn't stop twirling.

"Say your bood-byes now, gentlemen, for Vic will not be returning here."

They shouted their regrets and wished the boy luck. When Sebastian turned around once more, Vic raised her head and waved jubilantly to them. "Don't worry, men, you can't keep a good lad down. I shall return."

The men laughed and Sebastian delivered a vicious wack to her backside.

He dumped her into the carriage and she scrambled to the seat opposite him and rubbed her tender derriere. "You bloody—"

"Don't dare say it, Victoria," he warned with a menacing look that frightened even the drunk Vic.

She threatened him silently with a murderous glare, her courage strengthened by the generous amount of liquor she had consumed. He understood what caused her defiance and chose to ignore it. All he wanted was to get her home and rid her of that awful fish and liquor odor.

The carriage bumped along and with each rocky movement Victoria's belly lurched. She felt as though she were on a rough sea voyage and all she wanted was to safely reach land.

She never felt so relieved in her life as when the carriage halted in front of the house. Sebastian stepped out and turned, his large hands circling her waist and lifting her out. She didn't protest. The spinning in her head had worsened and she feared her ability to stand on her own.

His arm remained firm around her midsection as he guided her into the house. She felt as though she was walking on a cloud for her feet seemed to be treading on air.

251

He shouted for Akiko, issuing orders to prepare a bath.

Victoria's stomach churned and churned and grew close to erupting. "Sebastian," she said softly and when he didn't answer, she raised her voice. "Sebastian!"

He turned, his dark eyes a mixture of anger and concern.

She didn't understand why, but a lone tear slipped from her cheek and she was barely able to voice her dire condition. He wasted no time in lifting her up into his arms and bolting for the kitchen.

Victoria didn't think it was possible to feel as sick as she did. "I'm dying, Sebastian, I'm dying," she moaned, bending over the arm he had wrapped snugly beneath her breasts and staring into a now-empty bowl.

"You're not dying, love," he soothed, gently wiping her brow with a cool, damp cloth.

Memories of the past few hours flooded her mind and she rested her head back against the solid wall of her husband's chest. "Sebastian, I'm so sorry for my awful behavior."

He smiled, recalling the defiant stance she had taken in his office. "I had a feeling you would be."

"I didn't want to drink that horrible liquor, but he forced me."

"I know, love," he murmured. He shook his head, admonishing himself for allowing her to retain the identity of the lad. He never should have permitted it. "Your days as Vic Chambers have just ended."

She felt too ill to argue with him and remained silent.

252

"Sebastian-san, the bath is ready," Akiko said, standing in the doorway. "Shall I summon Dr. Samuels?"

Sebastian shook his head and stood, bringing Victoria along in his arms. "Just send a message asking him to stop by sometime tomorrow."

"Oh, Sebastian, please don't move me; the room is still spinning," Victoria cried, grasping his neck and burying her face in the comforting softness of his silk shirt.

"You must have a bath, love. You can't possibly crawl beneath the covers of our bed in this condition," he teased, tenderly kissing her swollen cheek.

"I don't think I can manage. I have no strength left."

"I'll take care of it for you."

She wasn't too ill to understand his intentions and she shivered at the thought of his hands touching her naked flesh.

He stripped her quickly, sitting her on the small stool as he gently sponged her body with the softly scented water, vanquishing the awful odor of raw fish. His deep blue eyes captured hers as though holding her prisoner as he glided the soapy sponge along her silky throat, over her arms, around her flat belly, and up across her full breasts. He continued in a slow, deliciously tormenting motion, thoroughly saturating every inch of her nakedness.

He forced her to stand and she obeyed. He slipped the sponge by her tightly locked legs and one quirk of his dark brow warned her he would brook no opposition. She relented and regretted it instantly. His purposely slow, languorous strokes sparked her heated passion even further and she released a low moan.

Sebastian cursed and threw the sponge in one of the empty buckets. He roughly pushed her back upon the stool and rinsed her soapy body thoroughly before lifting her up against him, totaling disregarding his soaked shirt. He carried her to the large tub and deposited her inside.

Victoria rested upon the small stool, closing her eyes as she relaxed in the steamy comfort, hoping the water would soothe her aches as well as her passion.

She was drifting in a light slumber when Sebastian joined her a few minutes later. He pulled her gently into his arms and she willingly nestled against his solid form.

He ached to delve into her sweet depths and he knew moments before he could have easily done so. Yet a sudden concern for all she had been through haunted him, for he didn't wish to worsen her ill condition.

His fingers tenderly pushed back the wet curls that hugged at the purplish bruise. What had driven her to disobey his orders? Why did she risk his wrath and visit the waterfront? What secret was she harboring from him?

She moaned, interrupting his thoughts, and pressed against him as though seeking comfort. His arms tightened around her, offering what she sought.

She slipped into an even deeper slumber, content in his embrace, and he doubted he would be able to wake her. He carefully rested her on the stool, bracing her sleeping form against the wooden structure.

He wrapped his dressing gown around himself, fastening it tightly to his wet body. He called for

254

Akiko's assistance and she appeared just as he lifted his still-sleeping wife from the tub. The servant tucked a large towel around the woman.

"Bring a supper tray to my room, Akiko, and a pot of hot tea in case she should wake," he ordered before leaving the room and carrying his lightweight bundle upstairs.

He ate alone and watched her well into the night, but she didn't budge. Finally satisfied that she rested comfortably, he climbed into the massive bed, curled his large naked body around her small one and settled into a contented slumber.

Chapter Nineteen

Victoria slowly opened her eyes to the sunlight streaming across her face and instantly clamped them shut. The shaft of pain that shot through her head brought a wave of nausea to her stomach. She opened her mouth to moan and felt as though a layer of cotton lined it.

She tried moistening her lips, but her tongue was too dry. She attempted to turn on her side to see if Akiko had left any water on the nightstand and immediately regretted it. Her head pounded with the resounding noise of a hundred clamoring hammers hitting steel. She released a woeful moan that sounded almost like a howling dog.

"That bad?" came the teasing voice of her husband.

She refused to open her eyes and meet the familiar glint of humor that would be staring back at her.

"Go away," she demanded in a strong whisper.

Sebastian ignored her order and sat on the bed next to her. He placed his cool hand on her forehead after pushing back the silky brown curls that rested there.

His dark eyes tightened in rage. His lips became a thin line upon spying the purplish bruise that covered her high cheekbone just below her eye. The color had deepened considerably since last night.

His finger delicately caressed the tender area over and over, as though attempting to erase the mark he felt was caused by his selfishness and stupidity. If he hadn't wanted her presence at his office, and the antics of the lad, this never would have happened. but he had wanted her near him. His insatiable appetite for her had grown beyond reason and he enjoyed seeing her garbed in the lad's clothing, especially knowing that the slender curves hidden beneath the ragamuffin appearance were his for the taking.

He pushed the alluring thought from his mind and spoke in a soothing tone. "I have something that will make you feel better."

"Nothing will make me feel better," she moaned, keeping her eyes shaded with the palm of her hand from the sunlight that insisted on piercing her closed lids.

His strong hand grasped her delicate wrist and yanked it away from her face. "You will sit up and drink this concoction Aaron insisted I give you, then you may return to wallow in the misery of your well-deserved hangover."

Her eyes instantly snapped open, wincing at the horrible pain the fast jerking motion had caused. "Well-deserved hangover?" she repeated incredulously.

"You heard me," he said, placing two large pillows behind her head and gently lifting her to rest against them.

"How do you come to the conclusion that I deserve this?"

"You, my dear wife, disobeyed me and that was a definite mistake on your part." He handed her a tall glass filled with a bubbly liquid.

"Drink," he commanded.

"No! My stomach will never hold it down," she informed him with a hint of her old boldness.

Sebastian was glad to see her rebellious side returning. "Drink it," he repeated much more strongly.

She pursed her lips together like an irate child who was intent upon refusing medicine from her parent. She folded her arms stubbornly across her chest and the simple act of defiance only managed to irritate Sebastian further.

"Victoria," he said in a deadly calm voice. "You can either drink this foul-looking concoction, or I can make your backside ache ten times worse than your head."

"You wouldn't dare," she gasped, her head vibrating from the thunderous pounding.

"By now I thought you would have learned there isn't anything I wouldn't dare do," he smiled confidently and held out the tall glass to her.

She mumbled beneath her breath and grabbed the drink, sloshing the liquid over the rim and onto the covers.

"Good girl," he cajoled as she raised it to her lips.

She stopped and for a minute contemplated tossing it in his face, but the scathing look he directed her way warned her of the dire consequences of that rash action. She tilted the glass and downed the liquid as fast as she could, hoping she wouldn't make a fool of

258

herself once again and lose the contents of her protesting stomach.

"Now rest, and when you're feeling better come to my study. I fear we must discuss this matter of Vic and bring his antics to an abrupt end for his safety as well as my sanity."

It was well after twelve when Victoria was finally able to rise. She had to admit that she felt much better thanks to the horrible drink Sebastian had forced on her. Her head barely pounded and she found, to her surprise, that she was famished.

She hastily slipped into a copper skirt and an ivory lace blouse that rose high on her neck. She secured a lovely cameo pin, which she had purchased at Mrs. Havershaw's shop, at her throat and brushed her hair until it shone with its dark sable brilliance.

Her hair had grown considerably and she was finally able to pull the sides up with combs while allowing the back to fall in a mass of riotous curls just touching the base of her neck.

She took one final look in the mirror and stuck her lower lip out in a pout. The bruise on her face marred the ladylike quality she intended to present to Sebastian. She had hoped she could convince him that she was a demure young woman capable of handling anything, including the disguise of the lad for another few weeks. She had to be able to keep her appointment with Louie and his friend when the time came, and she couldn't do it as Mrs. Sebastian Blood.

She pinched her cheeks gently, causing a slight blush of pink and added a generous amount of lilac perfume to her wrists and behind her ears.

She hastily made her way down the long staircase

stopping for a moment to admire the view of the San Francisco Bay from the oval window. Its sweeping beauty never failed to take her breath away, or lift her spirits, and she descended with an air of confidence.

"You look much improved." Akiko smiled at the foot of the stairs.

"And I feel much improved," she agreed. "As a matter of fact, I'm famished. Would it be a bother to ask you for a small meal?"

Akiko shook her head. "You are mistress here now. Whatever you wish just ask for. The staff is here to serve you."

"Sebastian wishes to speak to me, so as soon as I finish with him I'll join you in the kitchen."

Akiko attempted to protest.

"Please," Victoria said, preventing her from continuing by holding up her hand, "I can't bear to sit in that splendid dining room built for so many people. It is absolutely desolate eating in there by myself."

Akiko bowed her head in concession. "I will await your presence in the kitchen."

Victoria knocked on the heavy door and waited until Sebastian bid her to enter. She opened it and walked in, assured of her ability to sway his decision regarding the lad Vic.

Several minutes later the house rang with the sounds of their warring voices.

"I will not permit it," Sebastian shouted, slamming his tightly clenched fist on the top of his desk, jarring the many items that covered it.

"And what if I refuse to listen to you?" she replied with a haughtiness that infuriated an already raging Sebastian.

"As I promised you on another occasion, I'll lock you in my room, strip you of your clothing, and fill myself with you until your belly is swelling with my child."

Victoria gasped at his audacious remark. "You—"

"Don't bother, Victoria. You know damn well that I would, as a matter of fact." He grinned broadly, leaning back in his chair, and placed his arms behind his head. "You may already be with child."

"Sorry to disappoint you, lord and master, but I'm not," she snapped, when actually she wasn't certain. The possibility hadn't crossed her mind.

"Too bad, it would have saved me from continuing to share your bed." The harsh words were out before he could stop them. And he soundly cursed himself upon seeing the devastating effect his hurtful remark had on her.

The color drained from her face and her shoulders appeared to droop in defeat. So he only wanted to get her with child, that was why he stayed in her bed. And like a naive fool she thought she was beginning to win his heart.

"I will do my best to see that your seed finds its mark, for then I will not have to put up with your touch that I abhor and detest," she calmly announced. She boldly tossed her head up in defiance as she had done so many times before and walked regally toward the door.

No one could tell from her outward apperance what inner turmoil she was experiencing. She intended to pay a visit to Aaron and see if there was a possibility that she was pregnant, then he would have no excuse to continue to make love to her, a task that obviously repulsed him. And she would still manage to find a way

261

to retain the lad's identity, if only for the meeting with Louie.

Sebastian was furious with himself. He had no intention of leaving her bed even if she were with child. His ache for her was unrelenting and he intended to satisfy himself within her if it took the rest of his life. Perhaps the anger he seemed to constantly direct at her should be directed at himself. He was fighting the odd sensations he felt toward her. He was acting irrational, something he rarely did, yet when she was near, he found it impossible to think straight, or act reasonably.

He realized her declaration was made in anger, but his own choler refused to allow her even that small concession.

She reached for the brass knob and turned it only to have the door slam shut with a resounding crash.

"Shall I demonstrate how you detest my touch?" he murmured. The flat of his hand was braced against the heavy door while his powerful body blocked her from doing anything but turning to face him.

She retained her outward composure, but inwardly she feared what her traitorous body would do if he dared carry out his threat. "It isn't necessary," she managed to whisper.

"But I think it's very necessary," he corrected her. His hand reached up to fondle her full thrusting breasts beneath the lacy blouse.

A light tap at the door interrupted them, but Sebastian continued to caress the fleshy mound, deriving great pleasure from forcing her soft nipples to respond to his incessant demand.

"Go away," he commanded.

"But, Sebastian-san, she has not eaten all day and—"

"I will not repeat myself, Akiko," he snapped, angry that his authority was being challenged.

Victoria closed her eyes in despair. There was no way Akiko would disobey the Dragon . . . no way.

His hand that was braced against the door slipped down to the nape of her neck, gripping the slender, lace-covered column and drawing her nearer to him.

His mouth clamped down on her open lips as she was about to protest and his tongue forcibly demanded entrance. He thrust and sparred with her until he took command and delved into the familiar territory that belonged to him.

Sebastian pressed his imposing body forward, forcing her back against the closed door. He braced himself firmly along her slender form.

She could feel his hardness and it fired her blood.

His other hand slipped around her narrow waist, hugging it tightly, while he continued his assault on her emotions.

Her body surrendered against her better judgment. Her small hands curled possessively around his neck, holding firm to his strength and giving in to his passion. Her willingness fueled his own heated desire and his hands slid sensuously down her back, cupping her buttocks and grinding against her in a lazy, suggestive motion.

She moaned his name repeatedly, burying her head against his chest as he continued to torment her.

"So you abhor my touch?" he whispered.

It was as though he had thrown a bucket of ice water in her face. She pushed frantically at his massive chest, wiggling in his arms in an attempt to free herself.

"Stop," he shouted, "or I shall toss you on the floor

263

and finish what I have started."

She instantly ceased all movements and he laughed.

Victoria hated the mocking laughter he always flung at her when he assumed he had won. She forced her head up and stared into the cold dark blue of his eyes.

"Release me," she demanded.

"Do you concede that you do not abhor or detest my touch?" he asked, pressing warningly against her in reminder of his intentions if she failed to answer truthfully.

She bit at her lower lip, struggling with the fierce desire to deny the obvious, but chose the wiser course. "I concede."

"Good," he whispered and lowered his lips to tenderly feast on hers: sweetly, undemandingly, thirstily.

Her body continued to tingle and when he released her, she shivered.

"Cold?" he asked with a hint of sarcasm.

She shook her head, not trusting her voice.

"Go eat, Victoria," he commanded, "and remember, the lad Vic is gone forever. Don't you dare let me catch you dressed as him again or I shall carry out my threat. Do you understand?"

"Perfectly," she responded and turned quickly to leave, fearing her mouth would retaliate and the war would begin again.

Sebastian collapsed in the high-backed leather chair behind his desk. His heart continued to race erratically and his manhood throbbed to the point of near explosion. He had punished himself more than his wife. He had set out to demonstrate exactly how his touch affected her and in the end he had proven to himself

264

that she was the nectar he would never tire of drinking.

But she was also a bundle of defiance. The year on the waterfront had given her a taste of freedom that she didn't wish to relinquish and in a way he couldn't blame her, yet there was no way he could have his wife running around the waterfront as a boy, escorted or unescorted. He also didn't trust her. He intended to have Daniel keep an extra keen eye on her for she was bound to do something.

He smiled, a deliciously warm and sensuous smile. "Give me an excuse, Vic, just give me an excuse."

Chapter Twenty

Stunning, exquisite, beautiful. The words rushed into Sebastian's head as he halted in the doorway of the bedroom and admired the breathtaking image of his wife standing in front of the full-length mirror.

He had warned her not to wear black and she had obeyed him. She was attired in a creamy white silk creation. The bodice dipped teasingly low to tempt and tantalize the gentlemen's eyes. The sleeves barely touched her shoulders before puffing out to the middle of her arm then hugging her wrists where they ended in points, a pearl teardrop gracefully touching the back of each hand. The waist fit snugly, demonstrating the slimness of her figure. The full skirt possessed two layers, the first gathered up in four spots where they were secured with small bows of the same color.

But it was the intricate beadwork that made the gown so unique. Small pearls and sparkling crystal beads adorned the bodice and the bottom layer of the skirt. They glittered and winked as though announcing to all that the wearer was worthy of such a creation.

Sebastian tried to still his rapidly beating heart and his growing passion, for although the gown was lovely, it was his wife who had given it life and he wanted nothing more than to remove the garment and bury himself deep within her.

He curtailed his emotions as he watched Victoria's hand gently touch the soft curls that fell around her face. She almost looked as though she didn't believe it was her and he felt compelled to reassure her.

He walked over to her and stood behind her. The top of her head barely reached his chest. "My God, but you're beautiful."

The sincerity of his words startled her, for he sounded as though he actually meant it.

"I have something for you." His hands reached in front of her placing a two-strand pearl necklace around her neck. Her eyes widened as she caught sight of the round gold circle that held a cluster of tiny pearls in its center and fastened the strands together. It rested just above the valley of her breasts and was a perfect accompaniment for her gown.

"Sebastian," she sighed, stunned by his generous gift. "I've never owned anything so beautiful."

He leaned over and gently kissed her cheek. "This is only the beginning, love."

She couldn't believe her ears. Did he actually care for her?

"You are Mrs. Sebastian Blood now. I can't expect you to be seen without the jewels and clothes befitting your station."

His words stung more than if he had raised his hand against her. She had thought he presented her with the gift because he cared for her. How foolish she felt.

267

Sebastian watched the startling impact his statement had on her and he silently cursed himself. He had purposely bought the damn pearls to please her, yet when he saw that look of delight in her eyes that touched his heart, he had blindly struck out at her.

"Yes, my station. I forgot," she mumbled and let her fingers drop away from the pearls that moments before had brought her so much pleasure.

He felt a sudden urge to make amends. He didn't wish her to feel anything but happiness this evening. He leaned over and ran his warm lips delicately down her neck, nipping playfully as he came to her bare shoulder. His intimate caress had the desired affect. Her body swayed as though drugged by his touch and he slipped his arm around her slim waist, hugging her to him. His teeth nipped and teased the creamy flesh of her shoulder, making certain his bites were gentle so no bruises marred her lovely skin.

Her body answered his subtle demands, pressing suggestively against him. He knew full well if he continued they would never make it to the dinner party.

"You will be the most exquisite creature there this evening," he whispered, reluctantly placing a last kiss on her neck and promising himself to finish later what he had begun.

Victoria sighed, not really anxious to meet the cream of society. She studied Sebastian in the mirror as she stepped aside. He looked splendid. The black formal attire was tailored perfectly to his large frame, hugging just the right places, accentuating his solidly built form.

"Are you ready, love?" he asked, holding his hand out to her.

She nodded and reached for him.

He grasped her hand firmly. "Come, let us introduce the Dragon's lady to San Francisco society."

Charles Fisk had made his fortune in the gold and silver mines and was one of the wealthiest men in the city. He was also one of the few men who held the distinction of being honest. His wife, Harriet, was a plain, simple woman who with the onset of prosperity decided to indulge herself. They had just completed building a stunning home on Nob Hill.

"Sebastian, this looks like a palace," Victoria whispered, stepping from the carriage. Her eyes drank in the palatial splendor of the four-story home. Turrets and balustrades abounded and Victoria felt as though she had just stepped into the past.

"Good, then it is only befitting that my princess have her debut here."

She smiled. "And will the prince pay homage to his princess this evening?"

"Princess, the homage I intend to pay you later tonight will take your breath away."

She blushed profusely and he released a hearty laugh.

"You're terrible, Sebastian," she scolded with a playful tap to his arm.

He took her hand. "Come, I have a feeling you and Harriet Fisk will get along famously."

The incessant chatter all but halted when the couple entered the ornately decorated parlor. A soft, rotund woman with gray hair moved toward them. A tiara of diamonds sat on her head and the array of diamonds and sapphires that dripped from her neck and ears startled Victoria.

"Sebastian, you naughty boy, marrying and not even telling anyone. You should be ashamed of yourself," the woman teased with a playful wink.

Sebastian smiled. "Victoria, may I present our hostess Harriet Fisk."

Harriet didn't give anyone a chance to speak. "Well, of course she knows I'm Harriet. Who the hell else would have the nerve to reprimand the Dragon?"

Victoria waited for Sebastian to explode. She had never heard anyone call him by that name to his face, but to her surprise he just grinned and winked at the audacious woman.

"Now, dear," Harriet said, taking hold of Victoria's arm. "You must make certain you keep an eye on every woman here tonight, for they're likely to stab you in the back as soon as they're given a chance. They absolutely hate you for stealing the most eligible and handsome bachelor around."

"The honored couple has finally arrived," interrupted a chuckling voice.

Victoria wasn't surprised to see that Charles Fisk resembled his wife in size and weight. They made a perfect pair: happy, carefree, and obviously still in love with one another after twenty-five years of marriage.

"Glad to meet you, Mrs. Blood," the rotund man said, reaching for her hand and shaking it heartily.

"Victoria, please," she said, instantly liking the man's unpretentious manner.

"Victoria," he repeated. "Well, son, you certainly are going to have your hands full tonight keeping all the

270

dandies away from your charming wife."

"I don't think there'll be a problem, Charles, since I don't intend to leave her side."

Harriet poked her husband in his ribs with her elbow. "So, it's still like that for you two?"

"Go on with you," Sebastian teased, "Charles has told me all about your insatiable appetite."

The woman roared with laughter. "Yup, the old guy just can't keep up with me."

Victoria couldn't help but join in the laughter. She had never met anyone as outspoken as Harriet, and she instantly liked the brash woman.

"Darling, you've finally arrived," came the familiar purring voice.

Victoria didn't have to turn to see who it belonged to. She'd recognize that mewing tone anywhere.

"Victoria, may I present Lydia Hodgeson," Sebastian said.

Victoria turned and the woman's eyes flashed open. Several tension-filled minutes passed before Lydia spoke. "You know, you look vaguely familiar. I could swear I've seen you somewhere before."

"Nonsense," Harriet snapped. "And besides, you can't monopolize the couple's time. There are too many others who wish to meet them."

Lydia opened her mouth to protest, but Harriet had already carefully maneuvered the couple away from her.

"She's a pain in the—"

"Harriet," Charles warned in a strong whisper, "you promised you'd watch your mouth tonight."

"I forgot, deary," she said sweetly. "Would you mind

getting me a glass of punch, honey? And, Sebastian, you get some for Victoria. I'm sure she must be parched."

Sebastian seemed reluctant to leave her side.

"I'll take good care of her." Harriet smiled and when the two men were out of sight she continued as though she hadn't been interrupted. "That woman's a pain in the ass, so watch yourself around her."

Victoria couldn't help but smile as the matron rattled on about this one, pointing out that one, and being extremely explicit in her likes and dislikes toward them.

A tall, lanky man approached them with a short, plump woman trailing him like an obedient puppy.

"Victoria, may I present George Stanton and his wife Myra," Harriet said, introducing the odd pair.

"A pleasure to meet you," Victoria said smiling, and the woman's thin lips quivered slightly in response before she dropped her eyes to the floor.

"My wife is extremely shy," George said and received a disgusted snort from Harriet.

Victoria understood better than anyone why the woman acted as she did. She recalled Lola describing the man's perverse pleasure for inflicting pain on the women at the brothel. It seemed that he practiced his sadism on his wife. Bruises were visible on her neck, although the high ruffles hid them fairly well, and Victoria hadn't failed to notice the bruises around her wrists. The woman wasn't shy, she was frightened.

"May I say, Mrs. Blood, you honor San Francisco society with your beauty," George complimented.

His eyes feasted on Victoria's breasts and she moved

272

uncomfortably in her seat from his all too lusty stares.

"You may say it once, Mr. Stanton, but never again," came the stern warning. All heads instantly turned to stare at the Dragon.

George backed away, not wishing to offend the powerful man. He wasn't foolish enough to believe he could best the Dragon in a fight, but everyone had a weakness and he had just discovered the Dragon's. One day the information might prove useful.

The remainder of the evening progressed without incident until the twenty guests were enjoying their dessert and Lydia startled everyone with her outburst.

"Now I know where I've seen you."

Victoria looked to her husband, who was seated directly across from her, for help. His face was expressionless, yet his dark eyes held her spellbound and the slight nod of his head told her not to worry.

"You look exactly like that street urchin Sebastian has working for him."

The room hushed and tiny patches of whispered conversation began to circulate the long table. Victoria tried to prevent herself from blushing, but it was impossible. The hated heat rose to tinge her cheeks and she fought to keep her eyes focused on her husband.

Sebastian concentrated on easing his wife's distress and circumventing the problem that the babbling woman had managed to create. He tried to silently convey his ability to handle the delicate situation to his wife before turning his attention to the matter.

Victoria was able to produce a weak smile and the small show of strength enabled him to proceed.

"Your perception for resemblance is remarkable,

273

Lydia," he began. His calm voice was a soothing intoxicant to the people seated around the table as they listened intently to his explanation. "I had thought to keep the lad's identity a secret and spare Victoria's family any shame."

Lydia toyed with her sapphire necklace, amused by the distress she was causing the young woman.

"You see, the boy is a cousin to my wife. His parents find it difficult handling him. He's an obnoxious little fellow, determined to do as he pleases. They asked me to see to his upbringing."

Harriet took it from there. "How absolutely marvelous of you, dear Sebastian. There aren't many who would take a problem child under his wing and help him on the road to a better life."

"Yes. Here, here, Sebastian," Charles added. "A most charitable act."

Several others voiced the same opinion and before long the whole table was echoing their appreciation of Sebastian's show of decency toward the wayward lad.

Victoria found herself resenting every word, for the lad had reason for acting as he did. She was sure none of these people were even remotely concerned about the boy.

Sebastian caught the glint of anger in his wife's eyes and he prepared himself for the tongue-lashing he was sure she would deliver when they entered the carriage.

He was surprised and a little disappointed when she remained silent during the short trip home. He had found he enjoyed sparring verbally with her and wondered why she refused to upbraid him for speaking ill of the lad.

274

Victoria entered their bedchamber and retired behind the Oriental folding screen to disrobe. It was something she had never done before and the small act of defiance irritated him.

He pulled roughly at his formal tie and listened to her huffs and puffs as she tried to unfasten the numerous pearl buttons that ran down the back of her gown. He stepped toward the offending screen and stopped. If she wished to be obstinate about it, then let her manage on her own.

Victoria struggled to undo the tiny buttons, popping a few as she fumbled awkwardly with her hands behind her back. She was furious with him. How dare he talk of Vic that way when he knew full well he was speaking of his own wife?

Sebastian remained silent while he stripped off his evening clothes. He watched as her dress was flung out from behind the screen to land on the chair. Petticoat, stockings, and corset followed, and his imagination ran wild.

Damn her for hiding from his view. He enjoyed watching her disrobe. There were times she still felt awkward around him, although he couldn't fathom why. He had touched and kissed every inch of her delectable body, but every time she began to undress before him a little sprinkle of pink would brighten her cheeks and she'd quickly turn away from him. Of course, he appreciated the view from either side so it didn't really matter.

What did matter was that she was being un- reasonably and contrary. He had set down the rules regarding their relationship and he intended to see that

275

she followed them. He still sought her bed and she better damn well be available to him when he desired her company.

He angrily flung the last remnants of his clothing onto the chair and slipped beneath the silk quilt, pulling it over his lower torso as he pushed up the pillows behind him.

Victoria emerged a few minutes later attired in a nightgown that covered almost every inch of her body. Even her slim neck and trim ankles were invisible to his view.

"Take it off!" his low, growling voice demanded, furious at what the garment represented. She was all but telling him that there would be no intimacy between them this night.

"No," she adamantly refused.

"Take it off, or I'll rip it off."

Victoria stood her ground, bracing her hands on her hips in defiance and spit out the words she knew would only fuel his anger. "I don't wish to make love tonight."

He leaned forward, the white embroidered pillows falling to the side. A heartless expression settled in his dark eyes and he fixed a blood-chilling stare upon her. "Take it off, and I don't intend to repeat myself again, Victoria."

Her legs wobbled traitorously beneath her gown and a sudden chill ran up her spine, sending goosebumps to cover her legs and arms. She wanted so much to fling out a refusal, yet his expression warned her that that would be a most unwise decision.

She attempted a different approach. "I—I'm tired."

"No, you're angry," he corrected her. His hardened

expression showed no trace of softening.

She wanted to tell him to go the devil, but she had a feeling he was friends with the devious creature. She tried another approach. "Then if I'm angry there is no sense in our making love, for it will be most unpleasant."

"To you perhaps, but not for me," he informed her callously. "Your body is an outlet for my passionate needs. It isn't necessary for you to like me as long as your body accepts me and of course we both know the answer to that."

If she had had her dagger she would have stabbed the insufferable, arrogant fool. Here she was trying to find a way to keep him in her bed and make him fall in love with her and he was speaking of carelessly using her for his own passionate fulfillment. Well, she'd show him how much her body willingly accepted him.

She pulled at the ribbon that held the nightgown together near her throat than slipped it up and over her head, baring her naked body to him.

"That's much better, Victoria," he said without emotion, yet inwardly he cursed himself for being an idiot. He wanted to hurt her for her show of defiance, so he lashed out at her where he knew it would hurt. He could almost feel the heart-wrenching pain he had caused her, yet his pride blocked any form of apology or admission of regret. Instead, he reached out for her, hoping to show her how he really felt.

His touch was light and gentle and it unnerved her. She had thought he would be demanding and excessively aggressive, then at least she would have a reason to deny him. But this, this was torture, and she

277

wondered if she could endure it without surrendering.

His large hand tenderly cupped her breast as his mouth descended to suckle on the rosy orb and linger there as his hand continued down along her waist. She was kneeling in front of him on the bed, her head tilted backward away from him as his hands squeezed her buttocks pulling her toward him.

Her heated flesh connected with the hard muscled core of his stomach and she struggled, fighting the fire he had managed to ignite easily in her.

He felt her reluctance and understood the reason, but refused to let her go. His fingers reached up, nestling in the soft curls that framed her head. He grasped a handful of her silky hair while his other hand gripped the firm flesh of her backside. He pulled her toward him, yanking her head forward and claiming her mouth with a soul-wrenching kiss.

She tried to break free from his possessive hold, but he was too powerful and his tongue . . . his tongue explored her mouth feverishly: delving, twisting, and mingling with her own while sending shafts of pure pleasure reeling through her veins.

"Don't fight me, Victoria, don't fight me," he whispered breathlessly as he left her mouth, pulling her head back and tasting the slim column of her exposed neck.

She struggled once again, but with less enthusiasm and he felt the difference. He slipped his hand between her legs, entering the soft nest of her womanhood and forced a moan from her lips.

"So soft, so wet, so ready," he murmured, raining kisses on her flushed face.

She felt his hardness pressing against her and she attempted one last show of resistance.

He wasn't expecting it and her head escaped his light grasp.

"No," he yelled. His large hands reached out for her, grabbing her beneath her arms. "You will not deny me nor yourself this pleasure."

Victoria was too stunned by his sudden movements to realize what he intended. She cried out in shock as he impaled her in one swift motion. She sat immobile upon him, her hands braced on his broad shoulders and her eyes wide with surprise.

He released a growling laugh, biting playfully along her lower lip that had fallen open from shock. "Ride me," he whispered demandingly.

She blushed profusely and buried her head against his hard chest.

"Ride me, Victoria," he commanded again.

She couldn't bring herself to move. "I can't," she murmured.

"Yes, you can, love," he cajoled and slipped his hands around her waist to demonstrate how.

She gasped when he began, but after several minutes she followed his lead and moved. She didn't recall when his hands had slipped away or when he had leaned back, full length upon the bed. She only knew it felt too glorious to stop.

Higher and higher she went, soaring out of control until she screamed his name over and over, finally collapsing against the length of him, spent from her furious ride.

His hands snared her body, lovingly soothing her

dampened flesh with his caress and whispering softly in her ear, "So perfect, so beautiful, all mine."

He never thought it was possible to feel so fulfilled, yet she had driven him to dazzling heights and his descent was earth shattering. How could one small woman make him feel so good? Even after knowing she was the Serpent, the one who had so viciously slashed him, he still wanted to possess her with a fierceness that was frightening. He had thought to control her with passion, yet unknown to her, she was the one who held the reins of control, for he knew without a doubt he would not seek another's bed. His body was quenched by her and his thirst ran deep. This young vulnerable woman was his . . . and he loved her.

Chapter Twenty-One

Victoria was breathless and exhausted from the last two months of the social whirlwind. Harriet Fisk had come to call on her several times for tea, bringing a host of friends in tow. In turn, they all invited her to tea at their homes, or out for a day of "socializing," as they termed it, although to Victoria it was downright gossiping.

She often wondered if her catapult into the social world of San Francisco was due more to her husband's doings than from the women.

It didn't really matter at the moment, for there were more important matters that required her attention. She was going to see to one this afternoon with Daniel's help, and the other would be taken care of tomorrow when she saw Aaron.

She had informed Sebastian that her afternoon would be occupied with a shopping spree and he seemed pleased, yet she sensed an undercurrent of annoyance.

He had been acting rather strangely lately. She

almost thought he was waiting for her to defy him and disappointed when she didn't. The last few weeks she had been the perfect wife always obeying, never questioning his commands, and always pliant to his touch, which didn't take much doing. Every time he glanced her way, or teasingly kissed her neck and whispered naughty things to her she melted. He made love to her not only with his body, but with words and looks as well. She shook aside the disturbing feeling her thoughts were creating and wondered if her plan of distraction was really working. She wanted him to believe her the docile wife so when the time came for her to meet with Louie's friend he wouldn't suspect anything.

She furrowed her brow, pondering over her wifely perfection role, for it seemed to irritate him. He frequently taunted her with cutting remarks as though forcing her into a fight. One day she had actually burst into tears when he scolded her for some minor irritation she had caused him. If she hadn't, she would have surely scratched his midnight blue eyes from his head for he had infuriated her.

The small act had caused him to storm from the room with a snort of disgust. That was the first night he had not sought her attention in bed and it disturbed her.

Victoria continued to wait patiently in front of the house for Daniel to bring the carriage around. She slipped on her creamy beige gloves and smoothed the material of the high-necked apricot day dress she wore. She straightened the jaunty little beige hat with attached veil on her head and gazed at the clear azure sky.

The fall weather had brought the usual dry wind and it brushed at the tendrils that hugged her face. It was a glorious day and she was finally going to see Lola and discuss more important things than who just bought what and who was taking a trip where.

Daniel smiled at her as he helped her into the carriage. She returned the gesture, knowing the large man was relieved she wasn't going to meet Lola at the brothel, or that she wasn't disguised as the lad. Poor Daniel. She was quite trying to him at times.

The black shiny carriage rolled away from the boisterous city, leaving the smells and sounds of the thriving civilization behind, and entering the beauty of a less populated area.

Victoria loved the hills with their preponderance of lush trees and foliage. A wide array of wildflowers dotted the landscape in profusion, filling the air with a multitude of fragrances, her favorite being honeysuckle. Its rich, sweet scent always managed to outshine the others.

Lola was waiting for them in the arranged area and the two women hugged each other with joy before strolling arm and arm anong the quiet beauty of the hills.

"You look fabulous, Victoria. Being the Dragon's lady has done wonders for you."

Lola's reference to her as the Dragon's lady sent tingles of delight along her arms.

Lola noticed her pleased reaction. "So, you like being the Dragon's lady?"

"I like," Victoria grinned broadly, and the two women laughed.

Their conversation turned to matters at hand and

Victoria spoke at length of the last two months.

"And you say he seems annoyed and irritated by your wifely perfection?" Lola asked, after listening quietly.

"Yes, terribly annoyed."

"Yet he stills seeks your bed?"

"Only until he gets me with child," she added with a touch of sorrow.

"And has he got you with child, Victoria?" Lola queried, catching the despondent note in her speech.

"I'm not certain. I have an appointment with Dr. Samuels tomorrow and then I'll know for sure."

"Don't tell him if you are," Lola ordered.

"What?" Victoria responded, startled by her demand.

"Oh child, don't you see he loves your independent, defiant nature. You challenge him where most women pacify him. Where other women do as he commands you do the opposite. You ignite his sense of adventure. With you his life is not dull, it's exciting."

"But he shouts and rants and raves when I disobey."

"And how does he make love afterwards?"

Victoria was about to speak then stopped. His lovemaking had taken a different turn since she had become docile, and although she still enjoyed it, it lacked the fire and lust of their previous unions.

"My God, child, don't you realize the Dragon loves you?"

Victoria was stunned. "He doesn't love me."

"Don't be a fool, Victoria," Lola laughed. "The man hasn't sought another woman's bed since your wedding. He refused to attend Lydia's wedding to save you any further embarrassment. He has spent every night

284

wrapped in your arms, and you tell me the man isn't in love with you? Poppycock!"

Victoria felt nothing but confusion. Could what Lola said be true? Could the Dragon really love her?

Lola sensed her doubts. "Release the lusty woman that resides in you, Victoria, and you'll find the Dragon not only stays in your bed, but also your heart."

Victoria's face lit with a brilliant smile. "Perhaps I'll do just that."

Lola squeezed her arm reassuringly. "You won't be sorry. Now down to business. Louie contacted me. The meeting is for next Thursday evening at his place. He said it took longer than he had thought to get the information and he doesn't think you're going to like what his friend has discovered."

Victoria's eyes widened in surprise. "Did he give any hint as to what the information was?"

"Just that things aren't what they seem to be, but don't ask me what he means by that. I only deliver the messages. I don't decipher them."

"Miss Victoria," Daniel called from atop the carriage. "We better be going."

"One minute, Daniel," she shouted back. "Did he mention anything else?"

Lola nodded, her brown eyes full of concern. "He has the dagger you asked for. Why do you want it, Victoria?"

"For emergencies," she explained. "I have no intentions of reactivating the Serpent." She knew that was what her friend had assumed and she wanted to put her fears to rest.

Lola released a sigh of relief. "Good, for a minute I was worried."

"No need to be. Why in heaven's name would I ever want to do anything so foolish?" she laughed and the two woman walked to the waiting carriages.

The next afternoon Victoria sat in Aaron's comfortable office waiting the results of her examination. She fiddled with her lilac gloves, twisting and turning them in her perspiring hands. When still he didn't enter she stood and walked around the small clean room. Prints of the San Francisco area graced the stark white walls and one wall contained floor-to-ceiling bookshelves stacked with medical books.

Victoria ran her finger back and forth across the thick leather bindings and felt as though she would burst if Aaron didn't show up soon. She had been delaying this visit as long as she could, hoping her suspicions were wrong. Although it seemed unlikely, Sebastian had made love to her almost every night since that first time. It wasn't that she didn't want his child. She wanted his baby more than anything. She had grown to understand him more and more of late. She realized his outward expressions didn't always portray his inward feelings. She needed time to dig deeper and touch his heart. But if she were pregnant, he would leave her bed. She couldn't let that happen, for if it did, he would slip through her grasp, away from her forever.

As though he sensed her distress, Aaron entered and smiled.

"I'm pregnant, aren't I?" she stated flatly.

Aaron was puzzled by her obvious unhappiness. He had known Sebastian wished a house full of children and that the news would delight him.

"Yes, Victoria, you are," he answered, adding, "Is

286

there some reason you wish you weren't?"

Victoria walked to the wooden chair, facing Aaron's desk, and sat down on the edge, her back stiff and erect. "I must ask a favor of you, Aaron," she said, purposely ignoring his question.

He didn't care for the way she spoke and he hoped there wasn't going to be a problem that would force him to confront Sebastian. "What is it?" he asked, leaning forward in his seat and folding his hands to rest upon the top of his desk.

"I don't wish to break the news of the baby to Sebastian just yet."

"Why?" Aaron demanded sternly.

Victoria met Aaron's troubled eyes for the first time since he had entered the room. She was surprised to see annoyance fixed in them. She sighed before speaking, realizing he had assumed wrongly.

"Oh, Aaron, I want so much to try to right things between Sebastian and me before telling him he is about to become a father."

Aaron smiled in relief. For a minute he was afraid she was going to announce she didn't want the baby. "You won't be able to hide it for very long."

Her hand automatically flew to press against her flat stomach. "Will I begin to show so soon?"

Aaron spoke reassuringly. "You're a petite woman. I'd say in about another month your abdomen should begin to protrude and I rather think Sebastian will notice the difference."

"Then a month is the most time you're giving me before I must tell him?"

Aaron frowned. "Actually, I'd prefer you tell him immediately, but since you feel so strongly—"

"Oh, I do, I do," she insisted.

He grinned at her haste to reassure him. "I'll give you the month, Victoria, but if you don't tell him by then, I'll take the matter into my own hands."

"Thank you, Aaron," she smiled gaily, slipping her gloves on and standing. "When do you wish to see me next?"

"Next month will be soon enough and I expect to see Sebastian with you," he added as a reminder of his warning.

"Yes, doctor," she answered obediently.

Aaron's voice stopped her before she reached the door. "One other thing, Victoria. If you attempt any of your antics, that seem to delight your husband, you will void our agreement and I shall inform him immediately of your condition."

She furrowed her brow recalling her meeting with Louie, then quickly recovered herself, but not before Aaron caught the troubled frown that flashed across her face.

"I'll be careful," she announced cheerfully and with a wave of her hand she slipped out the door.

Aaron didn't care for the way she phrased that. It was as though she intended to do as she pleased, yet add extra caution. He'd have to inform Akiko to keep an eye on her and with that he turned to write himself a note.

"Victoria, I wish to speak with you," called Sebastian as she passed the study.

She had just divested herself of her hat and gloves and was about to join Akiko in the kitchen for tea when his shouting command had stopped her. He had been a bear lately. It was almost as though he wanted her to defy him and yet he constantly warned her against disobeying him. She shook her head before entering. She needed to retain her docile state until after this meeting with Louie, then watch out, Dragon, because you're in for a surprise, she silently told herself.

"Yes, dear, what do you want?" she asked soothingly.

Sebastian winced. Where was the spitfire woman he had married who had lit his days and ignited his nights? She had become like all the other simpering females and it irritated him to think that he had forced the change. He had asked Harriet Fisk to introduce her to other woman and include her in their activities. Now all she ever spoke about was her shopping excursions, social visits, and the latest fashion. Gone were their conversations of the Chinese labor problems, graft, and politics. He missed arguing his point with her for she had proved an intelligent opponent.

"Sit down," he demanded. An irritating tone edged his command.

She obeyed, biting back the snappy remark she wished to hurl at his arrogant, handsome face. She paused a moment to study the fine lines of his strong jaw, his tightly pursed lips, and his smoldering blue eyes. He was annoyed all right, but there was one other emotion prominent and Victoria was finally gaining the experience to detect it.

It was passion, a lusty, fiery passion that meant he wanted to strip her bare and take her with a savage need that never quite satisfied him until he filled her two or three times. This was what Lola had cautioned her on, fearing she was incapable of keeping him content. Yet Victoria had discovered that her own need equaled that of her husband's.

"Victoria."

His deep, resounding voice startled her and her eyes widened in pure innocence, focusing her attention on him.

He soundly cursed himself while gazing at her cherry pink lips which begged to be caressed and her high full breasts which seemed to him to plead for his tongue to pleasure them. Why did he allow her presence to disturb him so? He had taken her with a soft and gentle touch last night. And now he found himself wanting, no, *needing* to take her with a brutish demand. The painful ache in his loins only heightened his temper, and it was evident in his snappish speech.

"Why have you turned down every woman who has applied for the position of your personal maid?"

"None seemed to have the qualifications that I require," she responded, failing to add that she needed someone who wasn't going to run to the mighty Dragon with every little inappropriate thing she did. In other words, she required someone who would be faithful to her.

"And pray tell, my dear, what are those qualifications?" he asked, leaning insolently back in his chair.

Victoria decided to add to his mounting irritation, why she did not know, but the temptation was too much for her to pass by. "Oh," she sighed dramatically, "I require someone skilled in arranging hairstyles, and aware of the latest fashions, and able to help me plan social gatherings, and . . . Oh, you know what I mean, Sebastian. After all, we are an important part of San

Francisco society and I do so want to make a good impression."

Her little act had the desired effect. It irritated him all the more.

"Very well, Victoria, since you find it impossible to make a small decision on your own, I shall make it for you. I've been advised of a woman who is in need of such a position and comes with the exact qualifications you wish. A personal friend of mine had employed her, but no longer requires her services. She shall start tomorrow."

Victoria had a rather strange feeling about this woman. "Who was her previous employer?"

Sebastian seemed to derive great pleasure in answering her question. "Lydia Hodgeson."

Victoria rose to her five foot two inch height and held her head erect. "You are mistaken, sir, if you think I will employ that woman's personal maid."

Sebastian stood to his full height of six feet four inches and walked around the desk to stand directly in front of her.

"I didn't ask your permission. I have already secured her services and the matter is closed."

Victoria had all she could take. She released all her pent-up frustration from the last few weeks of acting the docile wife.

"Bloody hell you will!" she screamed, slamming her small hands on her hips to stress her point.

Sebastian was so shocked by the unexpected outburst that for a moment he stood speechless, leaving the way open for her to continue.

"I refuse to have that woman in my house," she ranted. "Let her stay with that blasted bit—"

"Don't even think of saying it, Vic," he warned. "I have secured the woman's services and she arrives tomorrow. You will act accordingly or I will—"

"Tan my bottom?" she taunted. "Oh, yes, I've heard that often enough—ever since I entered this house. Well, Dragon are you waiting for the courage to carry out your threat?"

His lips tightened, his jaw clenched, and a smoldering heat centered in the blue-blackness of his eyes. Her heart sank. She had made a mistake, a definite mistake, but she refused to admit it or back down.

"The Serpent's tongue is like a whip," he said calmly, too calmly.

"And you might as well add deadly," she smiled sweetly, swinging her slim hips provocatively as she walked over to the fireplace, hoping she would be able to make it to the door before he lost complete control.

"Are you perchance suggesting that I'm less of a man because I didn't make good on my threat?"

Victoria sweepingly admired the width of his shoulders, his narrow waist, trim hips, and the other amenities that lay beneath his well-tailored clothes. No, he certainly wasn't less of a man, but she wasn't about to tell him that since he had so rudely hired someone of whom he knew perfectly well she would not approve.

Instead, she chose to push him even further, again wondering why. "My, my, a man that actually carries his brain in his head instead of between his legs."

She thought for certain he would bellow steam from his nose, spit fire from his mouth, and grow horns from his head, his rage was so great. She paled.

"You leave me no choice, love," he responded,

enunciating each word carefully.

Her heart raced wildly, yet she portrayed a vision of complete calm which annoyed Sebastian even more.

"First, my dear husband," she cooed, "you'll have to catch me." With that she dashed from the room.

Sebastian was caught off guard, a rare occurrence, and she heard him release several oaths as he finally followed her.

Akiko halted in the foyer, a bundle of linens stacked neatly in her arms, watching Victoria fly past her with a raging Sebastian close behind.

"Don't disturb us for anything," he commanded, speeding past her as a wicked, teasing grin covered his handsome face.

Victoria didn't have time to slam the door shut. He was directly behind her and as she tried to swing it closed he pushed against it with his mighty strength, sending it crashing against the wall.

He took two steps into the room, grabbed the heavy door and heaved it closed with a resounding slam that sent echoes reverbrating throughout the entire house.

"Strip, Victoria," he demanded in an icy tone.

She shivered. This time she had done it. This time she had pushed him too far. She opened her mouth to protest.

"Don't waste your breath, love, for once I'm through delivering that much promised spanking, I intend to demonstrate just how much of a man I am."

She stamped her foot on the carpet and attempted to speak. "I wo—"

"Shut up and strip," he bellowed, sending another shiver down her spine.

Victoria found her hands obeying while her mind

293

continued to defy. "You can't do th—"

"We've been through this numerous times. I do as I please," he calmly announced. He unbuttoned his shirt and pulled it carelessly from his pants. His broad, hard chest that had pillowed her head so many nights came into view as his hands reached to unfasten his belt.

She frantically searched for a way out. Failing to see any other than apologizing, she decided to face her fate—until she remembered she was pregnant.

She couldn't allow him to make good on his threat. He might harm the child. She had to swallow her pride for the sake of the unborn baby. She had to apologize.

She was standing in her pale pink petticoat. Her fingers toyed with the dark pink satin ribbon near her breasts.

"Sebastian," she began slowly, hating what she was about to say. "I wish to apologize for my childish outburst. I don't know what got into me."

Her simple admission knocked the wind from him. He couldn't believe that just minutes ago the old fiery Victoria had returned, the one who had ignited his blood to boiling. Now all of a sudden the simpering one was back. What in the world was going on?

"Are you telling me that you're sorry for the way you spoke to me and that you will willingly accept Miss Simmons as your personal maid?"

She fought back the urge to spit her refusal in his face. Now he would have someone else to watch over her. "Yes, that is what I am saying."

"Fine," he snapped and reached down, angrily fastening his trousers. He then grabbed for his shirt.

Victoria was stunned. She had wanted to prevent the spanking, but not the intimacy she was certain he had intended. His denial of her placed the bee back in her bonnet. Actually, she felt more like a hornet whose nest had been rattled.

She had recalled something Lola had told her, and without thinking she flung it at him in the bold lad's uneducated tongue.

"Having trouble getting it up, Guv?"

Sebastian stood deadly still and turned an infuriated glare on her. His eyes sparkled carnal black, his lips locked so tight they turned a deathly white, and his fists clenched dramatically at his sides.

Victoria took two steps backward.

"Keep going, Victoria, you're headed in the right direction." His fingers deftly unfastened his trousers as he approached her.

She continued backing up. Her wary eyes watched his every movement. He stepped out of his clothes, tossing them carelessly to the carpet, and when he stood before her completely naked she blushed. It was obvious he wasn't afflicted with that particular problem.

His fingers clamped firmly to her chin and forcibly raised her head up. "After I finish demonstrating what we both already know, Mrs. Blood, you will explain fully where you picked up that delightful little phrase."

Victoria smiled, catching the lusty humor that lighted his eyes.

"Damn, love, but you ignite my soul," he whispered harshly before claiming her mouth with a hot and hungry kiss.

Her head bent back with the force of his passion and his hand clasped the back of her head, drawing her to him. His tongue was a precise sword wielding its

295

expertise and Victoria met his thrust with her own wanting, needing to taste him. Her arms circled his warm naked back. Her fingers tingled against the feel of his hard corded muscles.

He playfully bit along her lower lip, nipping and teasing as he continued down the column of her smooth throat, lingering on the small, rapidly beating pulse and tasting her life force so sweet beneath his lips.

He didn't stop as he drew her to the bed. Sitting on the edge, he pulled her between his spread legs and ripped the remaining clothes from her body.

"Sebastian," she scolded in a murmur.

"I'll buy you ten more so I can rip them as well," he growled before his hungry mouth captured one thrusting rosy bud.

She moaned as he suckled at her breast, relishing the intense pleasure he was causing her. She ran her hands through his dark hair, pulling him closer as though wanting him to take more and more.

He feasted greedily, like a man who had been deprived for too long. His hands ran down along her spine, cupping her firm buttocks and kneading the tender flesh.

"Sebastian," she groaned, and in one swift movement she was lying on the bed beside him. His hands urgently sought her womanhood, sliding into the soft moistness and driving her to the brink of insanity with his masterful strokes.

She tried to recall the advice Lola had given her in an attempt to gain some control, but Sebastian held tightly to the reins of their lovemaking. He was the master, guiding and controlling, and she was the pupil, following and obeying.

"Touch me, love, touch me so you can feel the strength of me," he demanded in a hoarse whisper.

Sebastian drew her hand to him and she clasped her small fingers firmly around his throbbing shaft, amazed at the intense pleasure she derived from its velvety touch.

"Guide him, love, show him where your need is so great," he cajoled, rising above her, his hands braced on either side of her head. "Show him," he ordered sternly, as though he were in agonizing pain.

She obeyed, not because he ordered, but because she wanted to show him how great her need of him was. She directed the long, hard, pulsating length of him to her. She felt the tip of him at her entrance and moaned.

"Meet him, love, come up and meet him," Sebastian demanded softly, bending to tease her aching lips with light delicate strokes that left her begging for more.

"Meet him," he commanded and thrust inward as she rose upward.

Victoria released a sharp yell at the quick penetration, but Sebastian captured her protest in his mouth and silenced her with his tongue.

Her arms swung around him and her body responded in kind to his wild driving thrusts.

He reluctantly released her mouth, pulling several seconds on her lower lip with his teeth as though not wanting to part with her. He hovered over her like a giant predatory animal, his hands returning to brace themselves on either side of her once again.

"Wrap your legs around me, Victoria."

She followed his instructions without hesitation and his wild thrusts deepened as she locked her slim legs around his waist. He rode her hard, fast, and furious, and she loved every minute of it.

He growled out his command for her to join him in a hurtling release. He urged, demanded, ordered her to obey and she did, exploding in a blind fury and when she thought it over he shouted, "Again, Victoria," and thrust into her once more with a mighty force, sending her reeling into a mindless release that rocked her soul, touched her heart, and made her scream out his name.

Chapter Twenty-Two

Martha Simmons sat stiffly on the edge of the white damask covered chair, her back rigid, her head erect. She didn't glance left or right, but kept her violet eyes fixed upon her new employer as he spoke.

"Victoria sometimes engages in certain activities unsuitable for a young lady of her social status," Sebastian said. "I expect you to keep me informed of her social calendar as well as any other plans that might enter her pretty little head."

Martha nodded. He wanted her to spy on his wife. If she didn't need the position so badly she would tell him to stuff it, but that was impossible. Lydia Hodgeson had dismissed her abruptly, announcing that she intended to hire a French maid while in Paris. Now Martha was stuck. Her sister's husband had died just six months before, leaving the widow with six children. Martha had been helping her feed the large brood and her generous contributions at least kept them from starving.

She had never married. Now that she was fifty-five

she wasn't likely to meet the man of her dreams, but her nieces and nephews helped fill the lonely gap and she wasn't about to see them turn to the streets for want of food.

"I'm glad we understand each other, Miss Simmons," Sebastian said, nodding to Akiko who had been standing quietly near the door. She hastily departed after his silent command.

"Victoria will join us momentarily. I had wanted to speak with you first to make my instructions clear."

"I understand perfectly, Mr. Blood," she answered. Another man who doesn't trust his precious wife, she thought, although it was perfectly acceptable for the man to have his dalliances, but heaven forbid the woman should.

Sebastian studied Martha Simmons intently. She had not moved since her arrival. She sat stiff and straight. Her full frame was attired in a nondescript gray day dress, matching hat, gloves, and short cape. Her light gray hair was tucked neatly under a small lavender chapeau. Her soft violet eyes held a hint of sensitivity. She was perfect, more then he had hoped for. Now Victoria wouldn't be able to make a move without his knowledge. He would finally be able to stop worrying about her getting into trouble, or worse, getting hurt.

His eyes strayed to the open door, catching sight of the object of his thoughts. His breath tugged in his throat and a tantalizing heat whispered across his body as it always did when he caught sight of her.

She looked elegant in the apricot day dress trimmed with an array of soft green ruffles and bows. It gave her creamy complexion a gentle peach glow.

"I'm so sorry to have kept you waiting, Miss Simmons," Victoria said, extending her hand and smiling brilliantly.

Martha Simmons rose instantly and just as quickly sized up the small bundle of femininity who stood at least four inches shorter than herself. This one had spunk and something else that glittered from those wide luminous green eyes—mischief! Goodness, but this little woman was going to be a delight to work for after that horrid Lydia Hodgeson.

"It's a pleasure to meet you, Mrs. Blood, and may I say I am looking forward to working for you."

Victoria wasn't certain, but she thought she caught a hint of admiration in the woman's eyes. Perhaps it would prove beneficial to have a faithful lady's maid after all.

Sebastian smiled, feeling confident he now had everything under control. He graciously dismissed himself from their presence, allowing them time to become better acquainted. He walked with purposeful strides from the room, experiencing a sense of elation over his small victory.

Victoria watched him depart. His lighthearted grin, the regal tilt of his head, and that sauntering walk all pointed to one thing. He thought he held the upper hand. Well, she'd see about that.

"Miss Simmons," she began.

"Martha," she corrected politely.

"Martha," she repeated, locking her arm with the older woman's and directing her toward the settee. "Let's get to know one another."

301

Martha smiled. Yes, this position was definitely going to prove to be interesting.

"Dinner party next Thursday?" Victoria frowned. She hadn't planned on this obstacle. "Perhaps the following Tuesday evening would be more suitable."

Sebastian was busy sifting through a stack of papers that lay before him on the desk and didn't sense her apprehension. "No, Thursday is perfect for everyone and I've already extended the invitations. I feel it is about time we reciprocated for all the affairs we have been to lately."

"Damn," she muttered without thinking.

Sebastian glanced up at her. "What was that, love?"

"Fine, Thursday will be fine," she answered and turned to leave.

"Victoria," Sebastian said softly and she turned. "Is there something wrong? You seem irritable lately. Aren't you feeling well?"

"I'm a little tired. Too much social life," she laughed and waved his remark away with her hand as she hurried from the room.

"Martha, Martha!" she called, racing up the stairs. The woman appeared instantly. "I need to speak with you."

She grabbed the older woman's hand and rushed down the corridor to her room, slamming the door behind her.

Martha was breathless by the time she sat in the chair. "Whatever is the matter, Mrs. Blood?"

Victoria paced nervously back and forth in front of the woman, wringing her hands in frustration. She was

302

going to have to take the chance and confide in her. She had no choice. She stopped pacing. "Martha, I need your help."

The woman grinned and leaned forward in the chair. "Whatever you say, Mrs. Blood." And Victoria smiled.

"Akiko, I must meet with this man tonight. I have no choice. He has the information I need. Unfortunately Sebastian chose this evening for the dinner party so I had to devise a plan," Victoria explained.

"There will be trouble," Akiko stated flatly.

"Nonsense, everything is planned right down to the last detail," Martha said.

Victoria released a weary sigh and rested back against the embroidered pillows on the bed. "You must understand how important this is to me, Akiko. I must find out what my uncle has been up to. It is the only way to save what little is left of the Chambeau holdings."

"All will go well, you'll see," Martha added, pulling the coverlet up over Victoria's chemise-clad body. "Now, you rest until the dinner party tonight. You've been looking a little peaked lately."

Victoria smiled at the older woman's maternal fussing. She had been right about Martha Simmons. In the last few days the maid had proven it. She confided in Sebastian only what Victoria had instructed her to. Actually Victoria thought the woman delighted in supplying Sebastian with inaccurate reports.

Martha ordered Victoria to sleep before leaving the room to attend to other matters. Akiko remained.

"She does not know you carry the Dragon's child?"

303

Akiko asked.

Victoria shook her head and grinned. "No, and neither would you if you weren't so perceptive."

"The signs are easy to read. Tiredness, morning illness, the material of your gowns stretched across your growing breasts. I am surprised Sebastian-san has not noticed."

"Fortunately for me, he hasn't," Victoria sighed, suddenly feeling weary. "If all goes well this evening then Vic will exist no more."

"Why don't you seek your husband's help in this matter?"

"I fear Sebastian would keep certain information from me, not tell me the complete truth in order to spare my feelings."

"He doesn't wish to see you hurt."

"That's why he would tell me only what he thought necessary. I want to know everything. I want to know about the money—"

"He would not keep that from you," Akiko interrupted.

Victoria agreed with a shake of her head. "You may be right, but I wish to know why my father left our guardianship to a man like Tobias Withers. It just doesn't make sense. I don't know if Sebastian would tell me that."

"He would spare you the pain."

"No, Akiko, I don't want that. I've been through much and if greed is the reason for it, I wish to know."

Akiko shook her head. "I pray all goes well for you this night, for I fear the Dragon's wrath if a problem arises and he discovers you jeopardized his unborn child's life."

Victoria shivered as Akiko closed the door. Her hand slid to rest on her flat belly. She would never allow any harm to come to the babe, but if Sebastian did catch her on the waterfront disguised as the lad and learned of the expected child, his fury would hold no bounds.

Victoria felt like a fancy bookend at the bottom of the long table while her husband attired in his dinner finery at the other end completed the set. The glittering guests sandwiched in between were the novels. She smiled at her ridiculous conception and glanced around at the array of chattering people. Judge Connors and his wife Grace, a woman who definitely enjoyed her place in society; James Philips, a local banker, his wife Beatrice, and their daughter Charlotte, a young woman of about nineteen whose tongue managed to spread society's latest gossip at a startling rate and who definitely required sincere help in finding an appropriate husband; Martin and Catherine Wyndell, a wealthy couple who helped aspiring artists and whose dignity and elegance charmed all who met them; and, of course, Charles and Harriet Fisk, her favorites.

"You must attend Corrine's tea Wednesday, Victoria," Grace Connors said, tapping at her diamond and pearl necklace as though attempting to draw attention to the ornate piece. "It is an important social event."

"Bulldwaddle," Harriet Fisk said with a wave of her chubby hand as though dismissing the statement as preposterous.

Victoria smiled, accustomed to the woman's outspoken behavior, yet still amazed at the wealth of gems that constantly dripped from her. Tonight she wore a preponderance of diamonds and emeralds.

"Harriet, really," Grace scolded. "If you insist on speaking so . . . so outrageously, the women will stop inviting you to the affairs."

"Not likely, honey," Harriet chuckled. "My money pays for far too much in this city for you to even think of eliminating me from your intimate group."

Victoria hastily intervened before the confrontation could go any further. "That is an absolutely beautiful necklace, Grace, wherever did you get it?

The woman smiled broadly and proceeded to explain in great detail how she came about the gaudy piece.

Victoria grew restless. The time was drawing near and she hoped all would go as planned. She had taken a chance and included Harriet in her plan, but she wasn't sorry. She was certain the woman would carry her part out perfectly and she did.

As the steaming bowl of soup was placed in front of her, Harriet waved her hand dramatically to stress the point of her story and the hot liquid spilled all over Victoria's bodice and onto her lap.

Sebastian sprung from his seat and was at his wife's side in seconds. Everyone stood offering their help and talking incessantly until—

"Everyone sit down and shut up," Harriet demanded.

The guests seated themselves instantly, but Sebastian remained by his wife's side.

"I'll summons Martha," he said.

"Nonsense," Harriet interrupted. "I caused this

306

unfortunate mess. I'll help her." She didn't give Sebastian a chance to reply. She wisked Victoria out of the seat and to the door.

Victoria only had enough time to turn her head and assure her husband she'd be fine. His disarming smile caused a pang of guilt to sting her, but she still proceeded with her plan.

In minutes she was transformed into the grubby ragamuffin Vic. Harriet and Martha giggled and fussed like schoolgirls instigating a prank. Akiko stood silently by the door and Victoria could hear her warning whispering in the recesses of her mind. *If the Dragon finds out . . . If the Dragon finds out . . .*

She got out of the house without difficulty and headed straight for the waterfront. Time was of the essence and she could not even spare a second. Harriet could only keep Sebastian at bay for about twenty, possibly thirty, minutes, the usual time it took for her to dress, after that he would certainly demand his wife's presence.

Louie was waiting at a corner table with the man when she came barging in, completely out of breath.

"I don't have much time, Louie. Is this the guy?" she asked breathlessly.

The stranger leaned forward, his face marked by years of hard living and his brown eyes alert to all around him. "I got your information. You got the money?"

Victoria pushed the mound of coins toward him. He counted them and, content he hadn't been cheated, slipped them into his coat pocket.

"Tobias Withers is dead," he stated flatly.

Victoria was stunned. "My uncle died?"

307

"Yup, two years ago."

Victoria shook her head. "That's impossible. I saw my uncle a couple of months—"

The man didn't allow her to finish. "He isn't your uncle."

Victoria was not only stunned, but confused. "What do you mean?"

"The man that's passing himself off as your uncle is Albert Thorndike."

"Thorndike Enterprises," she whispered, recalling the name on the letter she had read in her husband's office.

"I'll explain," the man offered, sensing her confusion. "Albert Thorndike is a notorious thief and swindler. Somehow he got hooked up with your uncle and when he discovered how much the man's half brother was worth he decided to take matters into his own hands."

"What are you saying?" Victoria asked, frightened by what the man was implying.

"I don't have proof, but I got it on good authority that Thorndike murdered your parents after getting rid of your real uncle."

Victoria had thought there was nothing more that could possibly shock her after all she had been through, but she was wrong. She sat in silence, a cold sweat tingling her body.

"I'd be careful if I were you, lad. He's a real nasty man. I wouldn't put anything past him. He's the type that would kill his own mother for a price."

Victoria's eyes grew cold and hard and she stood, leaning her small hands flat upon the table. "Well, Thorndike made a big mistake, 'cause I'm gonna gut the bastard."

The man was too startled by the young lad's declaration to respond.

Victoria turned to Louie. "You got the other thing I asked for?"

"Yeah," he whispered, and slipped the dagger from under the table into Vic's small hand.

"Thanks for all your help, Louie," she said, taking the weapon from him and leaving as hastily as she had arrived.

The stranger laughed and smacked Louie on the back. "That kid's got a big pair."

Instinctively Victoria headed back in the same direction, her mind in turmoil over the vicious greed of one man and how it had destroyed her family. Her father must have suspected something to have hired an investigator. Perhaps he had been trying to locate Uncle Tobias. After all, the man had written to them regularly and had sent gifts on her and Beth's birthday every year, except . . . Except the year before her parent's death. She felt a sudden sadness for the man who she hadn't remembered all that well, but who her father had spoken of so often and with such kindness. He had befriended a man and trusted him, and that man had destroyed her entire family.

She picked up her pace. She was angry, so very angry, and if she didn't vent it somehow, she thought she would explode.

"Hey, kid, what you doing out so late?"

Victoria stopped dead in her tracks and looked at the small group of boys standing on the corner. There were four of them ranging in size from extra small to large. She felt a momentary twinge of fear, then threw her shoulders back and approached them with brave defiance.

"I don't answer to nobody."

"Oh, yeah?" the larger one said with a hint of challenge and stepped off the wooden walkway.

Victoria recalled the baby nestled comfortably in her womb and prepared to defend the child as well as herself.

Sebastian sat staring stoically at Harriet Fisk as his other guests enjoyed the meal. She fidgeted in her seat and her eyes kept stealing glances toward the doorway as though anxiously awaiting someone's arrival.

"It is taking Victoria rather long, isn't it, Harriet?" he asked, causing the woman to almost jump out of her seat.

"Yes, yes, it is and I best go see what's keeping her," she said, and sprang from her seat like a tight coil.

"Sit, Harriet," Sebastian commanded and the woman obeyed without question. "I'll see to her myself *this* time."

All the guests remained silent. Their eyes alternately focusing on Harriet and Sebastian, as though waiting for an explosion and it came.

The commotion at the door startled everyone, but when Akiko announced that the police wished to see Sebastian regarding the lad Vic, Harriet turned a sickly white and Sebastian mumbled several foul remarks beneath his breath.

He stormed to the foyer, his guests trailing in his

wake, not wanting to miss any delicious part of a scandal.

Sebastian didn't see Victoria anywhere and his heart caught in his throat. He felt his limbs go numb and his heartbeat accelerate as he studied the three officers standing grimly near the door.

"Mr. Blood," the taller officer said, stepping forward, "is there a young lad named Vic in your employment?"

Sebastian nodded, fearing if he spoke he would shatter his barely controlled emotions.

"Well, lad, show yourself. He isn't going to bite you," the officer said with a wink to Sebastian.

Sebastian released his breath, not realizing he had been holding it. He watched as Victoria's face peeked out from behind the rotund policeman.

"Come here, Vic," he commanded, but Victoria refused to budge. "Come here," he repeated in such a threatening tone that the large man stepped aside leaving the small boy to face the Dragon alone.

Sebastian's deep blue eyes almost turned obsidian from seeing the disheveled appearance of his wife. Her oversized shirt was torn at both shoulders. Her knuckles were smeared with a mixture of dirt and blood, and her lower lip was split and bleeding, sending a steady stream of blood dripping onto her shirt.

"Come here," he repeated once again, only this time through gritted teeth and with a minimum of control.

Victoria stepped forward, tossing her shoulders back and holding her head up in defiance. She stood before him and wiped the blood on her sleeve. "The bunch attacked me for no reason."

Sebastian narrowed his eyes into dangerous slits and

she wisely remained silent.

"What happened, officer?" he asked, not talking his eyes off his wife.

"A group of boys attacked him near the edge of the waterfront. They were doing quite a job on him when we arrived, although I have to admit the lad can hold his own, even though he is puny."

Sebastian directed such a murderous glare at the man that he stepped backward away from the offending look as though it could hurt him.

"Vic, go to your room and stay there," he ordered.

She was about to protest when he grabbed her arm and pulled her against him. "Shut up and do as I say."

She shook her head and he released her, pointing toward the stairs. She followed his direction, not turning to look at the guests who were watching the exchange with a great deal of pleasure.

When she reached the top Martha was waiting, but she silenced the woman with a hand before she could speak and listened as Sebastian saw the police officers out and made apologies to his guests.

"He'll be coming up soon, Martha. I think it would be best if you weren't present."

"But I—"

"I insist," Victoria said, not allowing the woman to protest any further.

Victoria retired to her room, closing the door behind her, knowing it would be futile to attempt to lock it. He would only break it down.

She sighed gratefully when she spied the pitcher of hot water waiting for her on the dressing table and quickly slipped out of her tattered clothing. She hastily scrubbed herself, ridding her face and hands of the dirt,

312

grime, and blood. She covered her cleansed body with a soft pink silk robe and brushed her hair until it shone, then she sat on the bed and waited for the Dragon.

The door opened and he entered. He remained silent as he removed his jacket, waistcoat, and tie, tossing them on the chair near the fireplace. He unbuttoned his shirt and pulled it from his trousers, then turned on Victoria with all the fury of an avenging demon.

"Where the hell are your brains?"

She attempted to answer, but he wouldn't allow it.

"You little fool. I've made it more than clear that Vic is to exist no longer, yet you constantly disobey me and do as you damn well please."

Victoria attempted once again to defend herself, but his bone-chilling voice halted her words.

"You pushed me too far this time, Victoria."

She shivered and pulled her robe more securely across her breasts.

He ran his fingers through his dark hair and turned, silently cursing beneath his breath. She had almost been lost to him. His heart still beat at an alarming rate. He had thought for a moment, a frightening moment, that she had met with some foul end. He never imagined he could hurt so much, feel so much pain, ache with such emptiness, yet he had. For a few seconds he had felt it all. He realized then how very much he loved her.

He tore his shirt off and threw it on the floor, then turned and walked over to her. She pushed herself back upon the bed, hoping to gain a safe distance from him, but he would not have it. He reached out, grabbed her arm, and dragged her to him until both his hands held her small body prisoner against his naked chest.

313

"You stupid little fool," he whispered harshly. "Don't you know how it made me feel to think that you may have been hurt or killed? That I would never see your lovely face again, never hold you in my arms and taste your sweet passion, never see you swell with my child, or watch you grow old with me. My God, Victoria, don't you know how very much I love you?"

Her mouth fell open and he claimed it with a hungry passion that seared her soul. *I love you. I love you.* The words tumbled in her head as they both fell back upon the bed, his hands reaching out, pushing away her soft silk robe. His mouth found her breast and he captured one taut peak and feasted with an urgency that heightened her own need.

He needed to feel the warmth of her flesh and know she was real, here in his arms, safe. He needed to taste her, all of her, and he needed to love her, over and over and over.

Her fingers grasped his dark hair and pulled his head up toward her mouth. "Tell me again. I want to hear you say it again."

"I love you," he murmured and kissed her. "I love you."

Her fingers whispered across his lips as he spoke, as though trying to capture his words and hold onto them. A lone tear slipped down her cheek and he caught it with the tip of his tongue.

"Don't every doubt my love, Victoria. It is too strong and it shall bond us throughout eternity."

"Sebastian," she cried. "I love you so much."

His face remained expressionless for one moment and then he gently touched his lips to hers. "Show me how much," he whispered, and Victoria smiled.

Their sweat-glistening bodies burned with the fiery passion their overwhelming need had ignited. they tossed and tumbled, bit and nipped, until their naked flesh begged for fulfillment.

"I need you now, love," Sebastian demanded. "Now!"

He covered her with his length and entered her swiftly. She cried out, but not in pain, in pleasure.

He leaned over her, his arms braced on both sides of her and she clasped each taut, muscled forearm with her hands. He tossed his head back and moaned as she wrapped her legs around his buttocks locking him to her.

"Victoria!" he cried out and she pushed against him harder and harder until . . .

He called out her name over and over as he tumbled in the silky aftermath of their pleasure.

Several silent minutes passed as they both lay quiet against each other.

"My lessons finally paid off," she whispered with a contented smile after regaining control of her breathing.

"Lessons?" he questioned, gently slipping off her and pulling her to rest against him.

She ran her finger playfully across his chest. "I asked Lola for help in keeping my husband confined to my bed and my bed alone."

"You little witch," he laughed, although he felt a deep tug at his heart that she should care enough to go to such extremes.

She abruptly sat up. "You do intend to stay in my bed exclusively, don't you?"

He smiled, a wickedly sinful smile. "And what if

I don't?"

Victoria knew he was teasing and grinned. "I'll just have to keep taking lessons from Lola until I get it right, unless, of course, you'd like to take over as teacher."

He pulled her roughly to him, swinging her small body across the length of him. She felt his hardness and swallowed the lump that lodged in her throat.

"I'll take over the lessons, sweetheart, and as far as this bed goes, it shall be occupied solely by you and me until our dying day."

Victoria flung her arms around his neck, raining kisses upon his face, "I love you. I love you. I love you."

She stopped and stared at him in bewilderment and he raised a brow in silent question.

"There's one thing I don't understand. How did you know of the child?"

"What child?" Sebastian asked.

Pink tinged her cheeks. "You had said you feared never seeing me swell with your child."

"I meant when you became pregnant," he answered and felt his stomach flutter.

"Oh," was her only reply.

"Do you carry my child, Victoria?" he asked sternly.

She bit nervously along her lower lip. "You're angry."

"You haven't answered me. Why should I be angry over such joyous news," he said, raising his voice with each word.

She pulled away from him. "Because you'll think I risked our unborn child's life by what I did tonight."

Sebastian sat up. "Are you with child, and damn it, give me a straight answer."

"Yes," she shouted and tossed her head up.

He ran his fingers through his hair in frustration for the second time that night. "Damn it, woman, you're impossible."

"You're not pleased about the child?"

Sebastian shook his head and pulled her into his arms. He pressed his hand flat upon her stomach. "I prayed your body would bear the fruit of my seed. I want our child very badly, but I might have lost the child as well as you this evening and that I could have never lived with."

Victoria pressed her hand against his cheek and he turned his head and kissed her palm. "Promise me that Vic will exist no more. Promise me, for your safety as well as our child's."

"I promise," she murmured and caressed his lips with hers.

He moaned and they fell back upon the bed together, tumbling into the intimacy of lovers.

Chapter Twenty-Three

George Stanton relaxed in the garish parlor at Madam Champlain's, waiting for Rosy. He enjoyed the buxom woman with hair the color of straw, especially since she never complained when he asked her to perform certain acts. He excited himself by recalling his last visit with the woman and squirmed uncomfortably in his seat, hoping it wouldn't be long before she could service him.

He glanced across the room and watched the antics of a short rotund man with one of the girls. He was playfully squeezing her buttocks as though sampling the merchandise. He moved on and sampled more of the girls until he collapsed in the chair next to George.

"Lively bunch," he grinned, his heavy face thick with perspiration.

George nodded his agreement.

"Tobias Withers," he said, stretching his hand out to George.

"George Stanton," he returned, accepting it.

"George, I wanted to speak with you about a

proposition," Tobias said.

"Proposition?"

"Yes, there's a business deal I'm putting together. It's a rare opportunity to make a good deal of money."

George was accustomed to being approached by men looking for investors. Those familiar with him knew it was his father who controlled the purse strings, and that he had no money of his own with which to speculate. Evidently this man was new to the area, so George decided to play along for awhile. "And how much of an investment is required?"

"That's the best part. It won't cost you a cent."

George leaned closer to the man, his interest piqued. "It won't cost me anything, yet I'll still make money?"

Tobias signaled one of the girls for a drink then turned and favored George with a self-satisfied smile. "That's right."

George rubbed his chin thoughtfully. "This opportunity, is it legal?"

Tobias laughed and slapped his knee. "You're a smart man, Stanton, too smart to fool. So, are you interested?"

"Let's discuss it, then I'll let you know."

"Fair enough. I hear you know the Dragon."

"A casual acquaintance."

Tobias nodded slowly and leaned over next to George, glancing about to make certain no one heard him. "In that case you won't mind when we kill him."

George sucked in his breath.

"After we get his money, of course," the fat man added.

"But how?" George asked, half-seriously considering the absurd idea.

"Leave the details to me."

"But—"

"We'll discuss it more tomorrow."

"Yes, but—"

"All set, honey?" Rosy called from the doorway, her arms stretched out eagerly.

"Go! Go! Enjoy yourself," Tobias urged. "She looks mighty inviting."

George walked over to Rosy and whispered something in her ear as he squeezed her buttocks.

She smiled at Tobias and beckoned him with her finger. "Want to join us?"

Tobias got out of his chair as fast as his overweight body would allow. He slapped George on the back and laughed. "Yes, sir, I knew you were the right man for the job."

Several hours later the two men emerged from the establishment in high spirits.

"I knew I was wise in coming to you with this," Tobias smiled. "You've provided me with more information then I had hoped for. The Dragon and my niece shall both receive a fitting punishment for what they have done to me and you, my friend, will receive a just reward for helping me."

George smiled. He'd finally be able to pay off some of his mounting gambling debts without his father's knowledge. Lately the old man had refused to help him, insisting money was tight and he couldn't afford to carry his son's debts for him.

"Shall we meet here tomorrow, say around four?" Tobias asked. "I'm interested in finding out some information about a thief known as the Serpent. Then we could share Rosy once again. My treat, of course."

"Fine with me," George agreed. "But you're wasting your time with the Serpent. He's dead."

"That's not what I heard," Tobias said, smiling.

"Lola," Rosy called, knocking on the door.

"Come in."

"I need to talk to you," Rosy said, rubbing at the bruises on her arms.

Lola patted the bed. "George Stanton visiting again?"

Rosy nodded and sat down. "Yes, and there's something I think you should know."

The two women sat talking on the bed for almost an hour. When they finished, Lola hastily scribbled a note and sent it off, hoping she'd get an immediate response.

Sebastian sat in the leather chair by the fireplace. His dark brooding eyes stared at the amber liquid that sat untouched in the crystal glass. He seemed deep in concentration, yet when Aaron entered the study he sprang up and cast him an anxious look, as though expecting unpleasant news.

"She's fine, Sebastian," Aaron assured him promptly. He had never seen such a worried expression on his friend's face before and he felt relieved to know the man was actually allowing his emotions to surface.

Sebastian swallowed a generous gulp of the fiery liquid and returned to the chair. "Help yourself, Aaron."

321

Aaron filled a glass and joined him.

"I thought perhaps that scuffle she was in last night may have done some serious damage to the child," Sebastian said, finally voicing his fears.

Aaron smiled. "Victoria is strong."

"But tiny," Sebastian added quickly.

Aaron shook his head. "Yes, that has crossed my mind more than once."

"You expect a problem with her delivery?"

"I didn't say that," Aaron said, not wanting to upset his friend, but wondering if her small size would present some difficulties.

"You don't have to say it," Sebastian snapped.

"Look, Sebastian, I have no idea how Victoria's delivery will proceed. Every woman is different and I'd be a fool to judge this early in her pregnancy."

Sebastian released a sigh. "Well, I'll make certain she gets plenty of rest and no strenuous activities."

Aaron laughed. "Why do I feel you are about to take on more than you can handle?"

Sebastian grinned like a satisfied cat. "Because she's so damn unpredictable and downright stubborn."

"And you love her."

Sebastian's expression grew serious. "Very much, my friend, very much."

Sebastian had spent the last two days home, making certain Victoria rested and recovered fully from her small altercation. She had all but thrown him out of the house that morning, insisting she'd do fine without him.

322

He still didn't trust her. He was certain, given time, she'd be up to something again.

"The report is ready, sir," Ben Shavers said, entering the office.

Sebastian listened intently as Ben outlined the latest information on Tobias Withers.

"It seems that he's been spotted several times at Madam Champlain's with George Oliver Stanton. Like seeks like," Ben added before handing the folder to Sebastian.

"I don't trust either man," Sebastian said, scanning the papers.

"And rightly so," Ben agreed. "Could be that they're up to something."

"I guarantee they are. Both men are in dire need of money, a situation that can make the most honest man turn dishonest."

"True, true."

"Tell the investigators to continue. I want them to look into Wither's background. Where he came from before Santa Clara. And before that. Victoria mentioned he traveled excessively. See what they can find out."

Their conversation was interrupted by a knock on the door. Ned Harper handed Ben a note that had just been delivered.

Ben raised his brow while reading it, then handed it to Sebastian. "From George Stanton."

Sebastian smiled, but it wasn't a pleasant one. "They finally made their move."

"Then I should return the message with your willingness to meet with Mr. Stanton this afternoon?"

"By all means. Actually I'm looking forward to it."

Victoria was impatient to meet with Lola. The note had been explicit as to the importance of the matter, yet her husband had refused to return to work until he felt certain she was all right. Under other circumstances she wouldn't have thought twice about having him around, but the urgency of the note upset her. She had to find out what was wrong.

She had taken the chance and asked Daniel to drive her to the brothel. He had shaken his head adamantly telling her it was no place for a lady. She had then informed him he could take her, or she'd find another way of getting there, going along without his protection. He had instantly relented.

She was taking a chance going there as Mrs. Blood, but she didn't have a choice. There was no time to set up a meeting elsewhere. If Sebastian found out, which she was almost certain he would, she'd just have to face the consequences. She laughed lightly to herself. She had faced many before and some had proven quite enjoyable.

The carriage stopped and Daniel helped her out.

"I won't be long, and don't worry so," she said, seeing the troubled frown he wore.

"I'll be waiting right here. *Right here!*" he stressed, pointing where he stood.

"Wonderful. If I need you, I'll scream."

Daniel's eyes almost popped from his head. He quickly stepped in front of her, blocking her path.

She raised her hand to his chest. "I'm only teasing, Daniel. I'll be fine."

He reluctantly moved out of her way. "Right here!" he shouted.

She waved her hand and continued walking toward the brothel.

Lola was waiting when she entered and hurried her up the stairs to her room, ignoring the stares of the girls they rushed by.

"What is it, Lola?" Victoria asked.

"Tobias Withers has been here several times."

Victoria stiffened. "Have you—"

"No," Lola snapped. "I couldn't after what you've told me of him. He's been sharing Rosy with George Stanton."

"Sharing?" Victoria asked. "You mean both at the same time?"

Lola smiled. "We haven't gotten to that part of your education yet."

"I don't think I want to."

"No, I don't think the Dragon would approve. Anyway, it seems the two men discuss things while . . . well, they discuss things."

Victoria felt the tingle of her fear prick her skin. "What have they been discussing?"

Lola hesitated a moment then spoke. "You and the Dragon."

Fear evaporated to disgust. "While they're . . . they . . . That's horrid."

Lola reached out and touched her hand. "That's nothing, Victoria, and it doesn't matter at the moment. What does matter is that they spoke of involving the Dragon in a business deal."

"That's nonsense. Sebastian would never—"

"Know," Lola finished.

Victoria looked puzzled.

"Think about it. Staton goes to your husband with a business proposition and sets him up for Withers."

Victoria frowned. "Sebastian isn't stupid. He would never fall for such an obvious plan."

"Right again. He'd expect it and go along with it to get to Withers."

Fear returned, raising her flesh. "And Withers would arrange another accident. But how would he get Sebastian's money?"

"He wouldn't, but then he's after revenge this time, not money."

Victoria sat down on the bed. "Why would Staton help him if he wasn't going to get anything out of it?"

"Because he's a fool, and Withers knows it. He's using him and probably will dispose of him after it's over, but Stanton's too stupid and greedy to see it."

"I love Sebastian, Lola. I can't lose him. I won't."

"Are you going to tell him what's going on?"

Victoria shook her head. "No, he'll tell me not to worry about it."

"Well, he is capable of taking care of himself."

"Yes, so I've been told numerous times, but I've seen what Withers can do."

"But what can one small woman do against him?"

Victoria smiled. "I can make certain I gather enough information to present to my husband and the authorities." She didn't bother to add that if there was a way she could dispose of the devious man herself she intended to do just that.

"And I'll help."

"I was counting on it," Victoria said. "Do you think Rosy would help."

"Without a doubt."

"Good," Victoria said. "Then this is what we'll do."

"So, Mr. Blood, as you can see for yourself this is a rare opportunity for one with the capital to invest," George Stanton finished.

Sebastian sat behind his desk staring at the man. He couldn't believe that the man was such an idiot. Even someone with a simple mind could see what he was up to. Did Withers really assume that the Dragon was stupid, or was he issuing a subtle challenge? He would play along for awhile, watch and see, then he'd decide what to do.

"Yes, Mr. Stanton, it does sound promising, although I'd like a few more facts and figures before committing myself."

George was elated. "Of course. It will take a few weeks, naturally."

"I'm in no hurry."

George stood. "Good. The gentleman concerned will take care of everything."

Sebastian nodded. "When can I meet this gentleman?"

George pulled at his vest. "He'll be arriving in San Francisco in a few months. Now I really must go. I'll be in touch."

Sebastian was amazed at the speed in which Stanton exited the office. So Withers intended to take his time, but why? He'd have to make certain he kept an eye on him. And his wife as well. He'd instruct Daniel to watch her carefully.

There was a knock on the door and Daniel entered.

"You're just the man I wanted to see," Sebastian said, waving him in.

Daniel approached cautiously. "There's something I have to tell you."

Sebastian stood, walked around his desk and pushed his coat back as he braced his hand on his hip. "What has she done now?"

Sebastian was home. Victoria was certain of that since the door had been slammed so hard the walls shook. She remained on the settee, reading her book, looking like the perfect wife when he entered.

"Madam, do I have to tie you to our bed to make certain you behave?" he shouted, walking in the room and stopping in front of her.

Victoria closed the book and slowly raised her eyes, her gaze traveling the length of her husband. "Sounds as though it could be entertaining."

Sebastian swore beneath his breath and stepped back from her. Her suggestive remark hit its desired target. He instantly though of her naked on the bed, her arms and legs spread wide and tied to the posts. The wicked scene inflamed him.

"You'll do wise to watch your tongue, woman."

Victoria sighed and tried to look contrite. "Yes, that was shameful of me, but Lola has spoken of how some men enjoy the idea of a woman helpless beneath them, leaving the way open for them to do whatever they wish."

He thought of her again, naked on the bed, touching her, kissing her, teasing her to new heights of passion. "Enough," he shouted, storming toward her and

328

forcing her back against the settee.

His arms pinned her there and his dark eyes bore into her. "Cease your prattle, madam, or I shall demonstrate exactly how it feels to lie helpless beneath a man."

Victoria attempted to show that his words didn't disturb her, but they did. She couldn't help but picture him rising over her imprisoned body, doing all those deliciously wicked things she did so love.

"I can't believe it. For once you're actually obeying me."

Victoria didn't bother to correct him. He would only find it amusing to know she found it impossible to speak at the moment.

He stepped back. "Now that I have your attention, what in heaven's name were you doing at Madam Champlain's this afternoon?"

"Daniel," she mumbled.

"Of course, Daniel. Do you think the man is going to cover for you like Martha Simmons?"

"Martha is—"

"Faithful to you," he finished. "It didn't take me long to realize that."

"She is working out better than I thought."

"Enough of Martha," he said. "We were discussing your visit to a local brothel."

Victoria stood, feeling more confident on solid ground. "Don't tell me you're worried what people will say?"

"To hell with what people think," he yelled. "You could have been hurt."

"But—"

"No buts, Victoria. You're carrying my child. You

329

will act accordingly and do what women do that are with child."

"You mean stay home and sew baby clothes?"

"I suppose that is one of the things women do while they wait for the birth of their child."

Victoria couldn't believe he was serious, but one look at his stern expression told her he was. The thought of being confined to the house for months was unbearable. "I have no intentions of sitting home everyday and twiddling my thumbs, or sewing."

Sebastian caught the defiant fire that gleamed in her green eyes. He knew that obstinate look all too well. "You are not, I repeat, are *not* going anywhere without my permission."

"Is that an order, dear husband?"

"A warning, madam."

"I shall endeavor to heed it then."

"A wise decision," he said, "although you'll understand if I have my doubts."

"You know me well, husband," she said, walking over to him and toying with the buttons on his black vest.

He slipped his fingers beneath her chin, pulling it up. "What were you doing at the brothel, Victoria?"

His strong voice told her he expected a direct answer. And she gave it. "I went to see Lola."

"Why?"

She understood he wanted the truth. If she had wanted to see Lola that much he would have made arrangements for them to meet. Therefore, this meeting was made in haste and he wanted to know why. "She needed to speak to me. She was upset."

"About what?"

"It's personal, Sebastian."

He stared at her for several silent moments then nodded. "You better be telling the truth. And you better not pull anymore stunts like this." Why did he feel as though he were repeating himself?

"I'll be good."

He slipped his arms around her waist and lifted her up against him. "I've heard that before."

She wrapped her arms around his neck and brushed her lips over his. "Trust me."

He teased her back, nipping at her lips with his. "Not likely."

His body reacted instantly to their playfulness. His lips trailed kisses to her ear and he whispered, "I think it's time for another lesson."

Victoria shivered from the goose bumps his kisses had caused. "What lesson?"

He whispered in her ear, detailing it all vividly, descriptively, outlining everything down to her shivering climax.

She clung to him, her breathing heavy, her body ready.

"Do you want me to do those things to you, love?" he asked, lifting her into his arms.

"Yes," she murmured in the crook of his neck.

Sebastian carried his tiny wife out of the room and up the stairs, locking the bedroom door behind him.

Chapter Twenty-Four

Sebastian discovered as the months passed that Aaron had been correct. His tiny wife was too much to handle. She did as she pleased, but in such a way that never openly disobeyed him.

"I forbid it," Sebastian said, slamming his fist on the breakfast table and rattling the china and silverware.

"Sebastian, really. I'm not some porcelain doll who will break if roughly handled and it's only a carriage ride to inspect Harriet's orange grove," Victoria said calmly.

"Madam, are you blind, or haven't you noticed that you've rounded considerably in the past four months and shall deliver my child in only two months' time?"

Victoria patted her protruding stomach and smiled. "He's quite safe."

"And he shall remain that way, for you will not be taking a carriage ride to inspect orange groves."

"Sebastian, you're being overly protective."

"Yes, Victoria, I am and for a good reason. While other women wait patiently for the birth of their child in the confines of their homes, content with their sewing and embroidery, you are out visiting your friends along the waterfront."

Victoria's eyes widened in disbelief. How in heaven's name did he find that out?

"Aha! So it is true," Sebastian said, pounding the table once again.

"You tricked me," she retorted, attempting to get out of the chair, but having difficulty.

"Don't bother, Victoria. I intend to spend the entire day with my wife."

His self-satisfied grin irritated her, but she was more annoyed with herself. She hadn't been as discreet in her dealings as she had thought. The investigation into Albert Thorndike was progressing nicely, and today she was to receive further information. Now that meeting would be delayed.

"Very well, Sebastian, whatever you say."

Sebastian furrowed his brow. Obedience: that was out of character for her. She was definitely up to something. And he was almost certain it had to do with her uncle. His investigation had turned up startling information, but he had been afraid to present the facts to Victoria for fear the shock would cause a miscarriage. Now he was beginning to wonder if she knew as much as he did. If so, why was she keeping it from him?

She still had that indomitable pride and he hoped she wasn't seeking her own avenue of revenge, for her uncle was much more dangerous then she realized.

"Will you be working in your study all day?" she asked.

"No, I thought we'd spend it together."

"Doing what?"

"Whatever you'd like to do."

She smiled. "I want to make apple cookies."

Sebastian's dark eyes bored into her. He knew what she was up to. She hoped to frustrate him enough to allow her time to herself, then she'd sneak off and to hell with the consequences. Well, she was in for a surprise.

"Apple cookies it is. When shall we start?"

Victoria was stunned, but proceeded in her attempts to make her husband wish he hadn't stayed home this day.

She was amazed, though, at Sebastian's skill in the kitchen. He cut, blended, and baked like an expert.

"Where did you learn how to cook?" she demanded with an irritated stamp of her foot.

He leaned across the table and wiped the smudge of flour resting on the tip of her nose. "My father's concubine taught me."

Victoria's mouth dropped open and Sebastian popped a warm cookie into it.

While she chewed the delicious treat, he explained. "I was forever in Nikko's way, following her around like a lost puppy. I suppose it was because I never had a mother and always longed for one. Nikko filled that void. She treated me as though I was her child and that included helping her bake cookies, although I don't recall apple cookies being on the top of her list."

"Is she still with your father?"

"Yes, and I wouldn't be surprised if they showed up here in a few months. Once he receives the letter informing him he is about to become a grandfather there'll be no stopping him or Nikko."

Victoria smiled. "I'd like to meet both of them."

A jumble of raised voices interrupted them and Sebastian went to see what was causing the commotion.

He returned only seconds later. "There appears to be some sort of trouble at one of my warehouses. It's imperative I see to it at once. Promise me you will remain in the house."

Victoria sensed his apprehension and didn't wish to cause him any further worry. "I promise. I'm rather tired anyway. I think I'll take a nap."

Sebastian stepped forward and gently placed his hand protectively on her rounded belly. "Aren't you feeling well? I could send for Aaron."

His obvious concern for her touched her heart and she covered his hand with her small one. The warmth of his skin tingled her nerve endings and she recalled that it had been several days since they had been intimate. She missed their tender lovemaking and suddenly felt the need for him.

"Come home soon," she whispered and squeezed his hand.

He tilted his head to the side and studied her flushed face as though making certain of her intentions. When her cheeks reddened even further he laughed and leaned over to kiss her. "I will definitely hurry, love."

She playfully pushed him away. "You better."

Victoria found the house quiet after his departure. She had thought to make him sorry he stayed home, yet here she was miserable that he had abandoned her.

She roamed the downstairs rooms, disheartened by the solitude. Akiko and Martha had gone to the market. Daniel was with Sebastian and the two young girls that worked in the kitchen were off for the day.

335

She was totally alone.

Victoria took a book of Shakespeare's sonnets from the library shelf and nestled on the settee to read. Her mind kept focusing on her husband, however. Since the night he had declared his love for her, life had been one large dream.

He wrapped her in love and made every day special and she loved him more and more. She had never thought her feelings could run so deep for a man, or that she could hunger for a man's touch as she did for the Dragon's.

She giggled thinking of his infamous nickname and the reason for it. She had grown to love that fierce tattoo and marveled at the show of power it always struck in her every time she viewed it.

Sebastian Blood belonged to her, body and soul, and she would let no one take him from her. A shiver ran down her spine as though warning her of some unforeseen force that held a different opinion and she promised herself to make certain her investigation of her uncle was quickly resolved.

Victoria returned the book to the shelf unread and was about to go upstairs to rest when there was a pounding on the front door. Frightened that something might have happened to Sebastian, she hurried to answer it.

"What do you want?" Victoria said. Her voice was full of icy contempt as she viewed Tobias Withers standing before her.

His round, full body seemed stuffed into his apparel and Victoria couldn't help but sneer at the way his starched collar bit into his fatty flesh.

"I thought a visit to my dear niece was in order," he

grinned, stepping around her to enter.

Her body froze in anger for a moment, then she became concerned. He mustn't know she was alone. "There is no reason for you to visit."

"Now, my pet—"

"I'm not your pet. I'm not your anything," she screamed, "not even your niece." The words were out before she could call them back and she bit at her tongue for being so stupid. She hadn't wanted him to know she had discovered his deception, at least not yet.

"So, your little investigation has proven fruitful."

Victoria stiffened and held her head high. She would not allow her fear to show, even though his bulging brown eyes glared at her with that same hideous look as the night he had attacked her.

"Never afraid, are you, Victoria? Well, this time you should be. My plan would have gone smoothly if it hadn't been for you. Your sniveling uncle was easy to dispose of and even your parents' deaths were no problem," he laughed. "But you, my dear *niece,* have proven to be a thorn in my side which I intend to extract."

Victoria felt her blood boil. She was no longer frightened, she was angry. Her mother and father's deaths were not necessary. Their lives were taken from them by a sick madman and she had every intention of seeking revenge.

Tobias's hand snapped forward and grasped her wrist in his. "This time you will not escape me. This time you will pay for destroying all my hopes and dreams."

"Your hopes and dreams?" she spat. "Why, you're nothing but a short fat turd who needs to be squashed beneath my foot."

"You—you—" Tobias sputtered, while his face glowed like a shiny apple. He yanked her wrist, dragging her farther into the foyer.

She clawed at his hand, attempting to break free. "My husband will return soon and then you'll be sorry."

"Your husband should be dead by now," he announced with a satisfied smile.

"Dead?" she repeated in a hushed whisper, as though speaking loudly would make his statement true.

"Give me more credit, dear. You don't really think I would show up here without making certain your husband wasn't taken care of first."

"No!" she yelled and pulled with such a fierceness that her wrist slipped from his grasp. She ran into the parlor, searching for anything that would be useful as a weapon and cursed herself for not having her dagger at hand.

Suddenly she was yanked backward, his arm planted firmly around her protruding stomach. She felt her breath evaporate and a pain cross her lower abdomen and she worried for the baby's life. If she allowed herself to believe his ridiculous statement then the child was the only part of Sebastian she had left. She pushed the thought from her mind and swung her small fist backward, connecting with his nose.

Tobias released her immediately. "You bitch," he yelled, covering his bleeding nose.

Victoria wasted no time. She ran past him, but he was quick and reached for her dress as she flew by. He caught hold and pulled at the bottom, causing the material to grab at Victoria's feet and send her

338

tumbling to the floor.

She shielded her stomach with her hands and twisted so her back would take the impact of the fall. He was on her instantly, straddling her legs with his heavy weight and capturing her fists with his meaty hands.

"I intend to have my fun with you before I slowly snuff the life from you." He laughed.

She struggled, but it was useless. A pain centered in her belly and she swallowed the fear that she was about to lose Sebastian's child.

"Now, my dear niece," he said sarcastically and tore at the bodice of her dress.

Memories of that horrid night he had attacked her came flooding back and filled her with anger. She had lost much because of this man and she still might lose more. She struck out wildly; punching, hitting, and scratching wherever she could land a blow.

The pain in her belly continued, but she ignored it, determined to fight for her survival as well as the child's. Her hand hit his nose once again, sending blood spraying out.

"Damn you," he shouted and attempted to grab her hands.

She moved too fast, still striking out.

The front door crashed against the wall and Tobias looked up in shock as the Dragon charged full speed at him. He resembled a demon from hell. His dark eyes glared so brightly and his face was so contorted in anger that Tobias closed his eyes and prayed.

The short man was lifted off Victoria with the ease of a feather being plucked from a chicken. He was slammed against the wall by the one hand Sebastian had firmly planted around his neck. His feet dangled in midair and Tobias was certain he was about to relieve himself.

"I'm going to take great pleasure in disposing of you, Withers," Sebastian sneered. "Do you know how many ways of torture the Japanese have devised?"

Tobias groped at the powerful hand that held him and for the first time in his life he prayed for a quick death.

"Sebastian," came the low moan.

Sebastian turned to see a pale Victoria holding her stomach while fighting to rise.

"You sonofabitch," he yelled and slammed his free fist into Tobias's face. The man crumpled to a heap on the floor.

Sebastian lifted his wife gently into his arms and when she moaned and buried her face in his jacket, he cursed the man in rapid Japanese.

He thanked God over and over for having Aaron accompany Akiko back from the market. They both entered the house as Sebastian was climbing the stairs. Aaron quickly followed his friend.

"Please, Aaron," Victoria pleaded, grabbing his arm after Sebastian placed her on the bed, "please don't let me lose the child."

He smiled reassuringly and patted her hand. "Your too stubborn and strong to let this little mishap affect the baby." He prayed he was right.

Sebastian refused to leave her side. He removed her clothes and slipped her into a nightgown while Aaron hurried to retrieve his medical bag from the carriage.

An extremely upset Martha Simmons was directed to boil water and Akiko joined Aaron to assist him.

Sebastian was wiping Victoria's face with a cool

340

cloth, removing the spots of blood that had dripped onto her from Tobias's bloody nose when Aaron and Akiko entered.

"The pains have eased," he announced with a smile.

"But haven't gone entirely?" Aaron asked.

Victoria reaffirmed his question with a nod.

"That's bad?" Sebastian said.

"Not necessarily," Aaron responded and opened his bag, "but I would like to examine her. So could you please leave us alone for a few minutes?"

Sebastian's eyes darkened and he was about to deny his friend his request when Victoria's small hand touched his face.

"I'll be all right," she whispered.

He kissed her hand and with much trepidation left the room.

Sebastian damned himself when he descended the stairs to see that Withers had vanished. He had the house and grounds searched, but the man was gone. In the morning he would have his investigators track him down and then . . .

"Sebastian, I'm telling you she's fine. Just make certain she rests for the next few days and if the pains don't return there should be no problem," Aaron said, trying for the third time to convince his friend that his wife was not in labor, or that it appeared she would be anytime soon.

"I will be able to reach you at home if the need should arise?" Sebastian asked.

"Yes," Aaron assured him. "Now get some rest. You look worse then Victoria."

"I will rest after I discover who was instrumental in starting that fire in my warehouse."

"Fire?"

Sebastian leaned back in his chair and rubbed his throbbing temples. "Nothing to worry about. Fortunately my men were on top of the situation immediately. It's funny though, I would have been there today if I hadn't decided to stay home with Victoria. Strange, isn't it?"

"Too strange for my liking," Aaron added. "You should report this to the police."

"There's no need. I know who's responsible."

"Who?"

"Victoria's uncle, but he's not her uncle."

"What do you mean, not her uncle?"

Sebastian expelled a heavy sigh and proceeded to detail all the information his men had gathered on Tobias Withers, not knowing that his sleeping wife had discovered the startling news weeks before.

Sebastian eased his naked body beneath the covers of the bed and rested himself against the length of his wife as she lay sleeping on her side. He placed his hand protectively across her stomach and waited. It wasn't long before the baby let his presence be known. He smiled over the wonder of the movements that told him his child was safe and warm inside Victoria. He rubbed her tummy softly as though commanding the baby to rest and he did. The movements stopped and both mother and child slept.

He nestled closer to her warm body, slipping his large leg between her small ones and recalling the fear that had consumed him today when he thought he would lose her and the child. He had every intention of having the house guarded as well as Victoria. He would take no chances while Withers was still at large.

Victoria stirred, moaning softly.

"I'm here, love. No one will hurt you," he whispered tenderly in her ear.

She pressed against his hard form, seeking the comfort and protection she instinctively knew she'd find and slipped once again into a contented slumber.

The following day was cloudy and promised rain. Victoria felt the gray sky matched her somber mood. She had risen late and found Sebastian out. Akiko assured her he would return shortly and that he left explicit instructions that she was to remain in bed and rest.

The room had become like a prison to her and she sought the coziness of the parlor. She had remained in her lace nightgown, slipping her peach robe over it.

Akiko had brought her tea and biscuits, but she had no appetite. She couldn't stop her thoughts from drifting to yesterday when she thought she had lost Sebastian and possibly the child.

Her hand went protectively to cover her stomach. The pain had eased, then stopped all together. She was relieved when Aaron had informed her she was fine and not about to give birth.

It was frightening to think of life without Sebastian. She smiled, thinking of how easily she had become accustomed to him. His bickering, his orders that she behave appropriately, his insatiable desire for her, were all the reasons why she loved him so very much.

She recalled the sensation of his warm, hard body

against hers last night. It felt so safe, so protective, so good. It was almost as if she curled up in him he would be the shield that would prevent all hurt or pain from harming her. And the funny part of it was that she knew he would do it if he could.

A tear sprang to her eye and she wiped it away. This pregnancy was making her cry so easily lately. Another tear found its way out. She wiped it again, harshly reprimanding herself to stop. It didn't work. Another tear followed, then another, and another.

Sebastian entered the house. The first drops of rain sprinkled across his dark hair and the black material of his jacket. He was about to go upstairs to check on his wife when Akiko informed him she was in the parlor.

His brow raised in annoyance and Akiko quickly explained that Victoria had felt confined in the room and wished to rest in the parlor.

Sebastian gave a quick nod and walked to room. He heard soft steady crying as he placed his hand on the knob of the partially opened door. The gentle sobs tore at his heart.

Her head was drooped almost to her chin and her hand covered part of her face as though trying to catch the tears.

Sebastian sat beside her and tenderly pulled her into his arms. She sought his comfort instantly, burying her face against his shirt and continuing to cry.

He tried to soothe her with soft words, but they didn't help. He rubbed her back, hoping if he allowed her to shed her tears she'd feel better, but still she cried. Finally he became worried that she would make herself sick.

"Vic, if you don't stop crying, you'll drown the both

of us."

Victoria was touched by the use of the lad's name and his playful teasing. She raised her face to him and spoke in Vic's uneducated tongue. "I'll cry if I want to."

Sebastian smiled, pleased that he had broken through to her, but then he noticed the cloud slip over her face once again and her bottom lip begin to quiver.

He carefully lifted her to sit across his lap and pressed his lips to hers before he spoke. "What's troubling you, love? Tell me so I can make it all better."

Her lip continued to tremble, but she fought the tears that threatened. "He told me you were dead."

Sebastian's expression grew serious. "Who told you I was dead?"

"Yesterday. Tobias told me you were dead. I was so frightened that it was true. And then when the pain started I was so afraid I'd lose your child too. Then I'd have nothing that was part of you left."

Sebastian could almost feel her anguish. He had experienced the same feeling about her the night the police had brought her home. At that moment he wanted nothing more than to wring the life from Tobias Withers for having caused her so much pain.

He kissed her softly as though she were a delicate flower that would fall apart from being touched. "I can't say I will never die, for death is inevitable, but it will take more than a man like Tobias Withers to bring me down."

"But he's so cruel and evil," she said, grabbing his hand and squeezing it.

"I know, but I'll take care of everything. Don't worry. You need only concern yourself with keeping you and the baby healthy and happy."

Victoria opened her mouth to protest. "No, love," he continued, "in this you will finally listen to me." He kissed her lips once again, more strongly this time, demanding a response.

His hand stole up to fondle her breast, warm and full with milk. It weighed heavily in his hand and he couldn't stop himself from leaning down, pushing the material aside, and tasting it.

Victoria felt his lips against her nipple, gentle and kind as he suckled it. She ran her fingers through his dark hair. It was soft and silky to her touch as it glided between her fingers.

She moaned from the pleasure he was giving her.

He instantly stopped. "I've caused you pain?"

"Yes."

"Where?" he asked, his hand covering her stomach.

"Here," she whispered and placed his hand between her legs.

He ran his hand up beneath her gown and felt her readiness, warm and wet against him. "I'm sorry, love. I should never have started this. We can't—"

"Why?" she asked, her eyes full of disappointment.

"After last night it wouldn't be wise."

"But Aaron said nothing of abstinence yet."

"I know, but last night—"

"That was last night. This is today and I feel fine."

"But—"

"Feel me, Sebastian," she murmured, caressing her face next to his. "Feel me. I'm ready for you."

His fingers moved within her. "Victoria, this isn't wise—"

"Good, that feels so good," she moaned next to his ear, nibbling along it.

346

"Victoria," he tried one more time.

"Taste me," she whispered. "Taste more of me." She pulled his head to her breast and he didn't resist.

Several mintues later she was naked on the floor, writhing beneath him. Sebastian hovered above her, careful not to bring her pain, only pleasure. They moved together, escalating higher and higher until they both shattered in unison and tumbled into the silky aftermath of contentment.

Sebastian pulled her against him, throwing her robe across them. "Victoria, will you ever obey me?"

She smiled sweetly and kissed him. "Always, darling, always."

The Dragon's laughter echoed through the house, causing the servants to nod their heads and smile.

Chapter Twenty-Five

Sebastian helped Victoria into the carriage and climbed in after her. "I don't see the necessity in this."

Victoria fussed with the rose-colored cape she wore, covering her well-rounded stomach. "I've told you. Mrs. Hobart makes the most stunning baby clothes and I wish to purchase a few more things for the baby before his arrival."

"And I told you I could have had the woman come to the house so you wouldn't have to bother yourself with this trip. You are only a few weeks away from delivery. You should be home resting."

Victoria slipped her arm around her husband's and squeezed. "But the weather is beautiful, Sebastian, and I just couldn't resist getting some fresh air."

He placed his large hand over her small gloved one. "I understand, and I shouldn't complain. You have been good lately, not running here or there, just entertaining friends for tea or lunch."

Victoria smiled sweetly. If he only knew that those visits were an elaborate subterfuge . . . Harriet had volunteered to be the messenger, picking up notes from Lola and bringing them to Victoria, who in turn would give her a message back. It was working out rather well. All she needed now was the time and place the two devious men planned on meeting with Sebastian.

"Victoria, are you listening to me?"

His words burst upon her thoughts and she patted his arm in reassurance. "I was just thinking of how I will be glad when all this is over."

"So will I. It upsets me to see you labor so with the burden of carrying the child."

Victoria wasn't thinking of the child, but she allowed him to think such. "Sebastian, don't speak such nonsense. Carrying the child is not a burden. Actually I quite enjoy it."

"Enjoy it?" he asked with a pleased smile.

"Yes," she and directed his hand to lay across her belly. "It's so wonderful to feel him move inside me, first a flutter and then a light kick. And now with strength. To know that we gave this small bundle life because of our love for each other fills me with such contentment and happiness."

Sebastian leaned down and kissed her gently. "I love you, Victoria, so much at times that it pains me."

She touched her finger to his lips. "I don't want our love to pain you."

"But it does," he whispered, "for my need for you is so great that when we're apart I ache for your nearness and when we're close I want to be within you forever. I can never seem to get enough of you."

"And I you," she murmured and lifted her lips to meet his.

The carriage halted and Daniel opened the door.

"That's enough of that," Harriet said humorously. "After all, that's what got her into her present condition."

Sebastian laughed and stepped out, helping his wife. "Can't help myself, Harriet."

She poked him in the arm with her elbow. "Well, at least we know you two are going to have plenty of babies."

"Are you sure you'll be all right?" Sebastian asked, helping her to adjust her cape over her tummy.

"I'll be fine. Harriet and I are going to shop at Mrs. Hobart's and then take tea with Catherine Wyndell."

"Promise me if you grow tired, you'll have Harriet return you home immediately."

"Oh, go on with you, for heaven's sakes," Harriet scolded, shooing him with her hands. "I had six children and worked the damn mine up until the day before I delivered each one. Women aren't made of glass, although some act as though they are, silly twits. Victoria, fortunately for you, isn't one of them. Now get on with your business."

Victoria looked to her husband and reassured him with a smile and whispered, "I promise."

Sebastian climbed into the carriage with a bit of reluctance and was off.

"Men," Harriet said, shaking her head. "Sometimes I wonder why God made them, then I recall how I got pregnant and have to agree they're here for a good reason."

Victoria was still laughing as they entered Mrs. Hobart's shop.

*　　　*　　　*

350

"Your appointment with Stanton is in twenty minutes," Ben informed Sebastian as he placed a pile of papers on his desk.

"I'll be glad when this matter is settled."

"You're worried Mrs. Blood will discover the truth about her uncle?"

Sebastian sighed heavily and leaned back in his chair. "Yes, and with her delivery only a few weeks away I don't want to take the chance of what news like that could do to her."

Ben agreed with a nod. "Who would have believed that Withers isn't Withers at all, but instead a man called Albert Thorndike."

"And," Sebastian added, "that he had Victoria's uncle killed as well as her parents. It would be horrible for her to learn of this just now. I have to wait until the time is right."

"Definitely," Ben insisted. "After all, she's in a delicate condition right now and not able to handle things rationally."

Sebastian doubted that, but kept his thoughts to himself. "Let's get these papers cleared up so I'll be ready for Stanton."

Victoria flipped through page after page of designs for baby clothes while Harriet thumbed through the material. To anyone around they looked like two women busy discussing a wardrobe for the soon-to-be-delivered baby. Anyone close enough to hear them would know otherwise.

"Lola says next Thursday and I don't like where they've set it up," Harriet said.

351

Victoria smiled and pointed to a design. "Where?"

Harriet nodded her approval with a wide grin. "The waterfront around midnight."

"But that's so obvious. Stanton and Withers must realize Sebastian would be aware of their plans."

"Withers yes, Stanton no; he's too stupid. And they intend to have Stanton meet Sebastian around ten and take him to a local club then make some inane excuse about how the other gentleman was delayed and they'll now have to meet him down on the waterfront."

"I can't believe how Withers has convinced Stanton to go along with this ridiculous scheme."

"Money." Harriet said. "Stanton needs money something terrible. The creditors are on his back and his father has absolutely refused to cover his gambling debts. He's providing for Myra and the little girl she delivered last month, but will no longer support his son's gambling habit."

"So he's blind to the truth?"

"And it just may kill him."

"How shameful."

Harriet stopped fiddling with the material. "Victoria, what do you plan to do with all this information?"

"I was going to inform my husband and make certain he didn't plan on playing the hero by facing the two men alone."

Harriet sighed. "Good, then there's something else I think you should know."

"Mr. Blood, so good to see you again," George said with a phony smile.

352

Sebastian directed the irritating man to a seat and made himself comfortable in his chair behind his desk. Stanton was becoming more annoying with each visit. The fool actually assumed he was going to succeed in this idiotic plan. "All the papers seem to be in order, but I'd still like to speak to Mr. Thorndike personally before I proceed."

"Yes, yes, I can understand your misgivings in entering this agreement before meeting with Thorndike, but time is extremely important in a business matter such as this. Since this is just the first portion of your investment it would make sense to proceed and not wait. After all, according to the contracts you don't have to invest any further if you choose not to."

"Granted, but I prefer to meet the men I deal with before I sign anything."

George fussed in his seat. He needed the money and he needed it now. Damn the Dragon for his obstinacy. Now it would be necessary to follow the plan Withers had outlined. "If you really insist, although—"

"I insist, Mr. Stanton."

He didn't like the way the Dragon's dark eyes stared at him. "Well, Mr. Thorndike is a busy man, but I could probably arrange for a meeting one night next week."

"That sounds acceptable."

"Are you sure you won't—"

"No, Mr. Stanton, I won't change my mind."

"Very well. Shall we say next Thursday evening around ten?"

Sebastian nodded and showed the man to the door, not bothering to shake his hand.

He leaned against the door and thought of the

coming meeting. Stanton probably didn't know Withers was actually Thorndike. They probably planned to have Stanton take him to an isolated spot where he would be forced to sign the paper, or so George thought, when actually Withers had all intentions of doing away with Stanton and the Dragon.

But what of Victoria? What had Withers in mind for her? The thought disturbed him, extremely so. That was one of the reasons he refused to take all the information he had gathered to the police. He feared Withers would be freed, especially if he had the money to pay off the judge who would try him. No, he had no choice but to settle this himself so Victoria would be safe.

Sebastian wondered if his wife was finished at Mrs. Hobart's shop. It was close to the time she was to meet Catherine Wyndell for tea. He recalled the eating establishment where they were to meet and smiled.

"Ben," he called swinging the door open, "I'm going to Dr. Samuels's office and see if he'll join me for lunch. I'll be back in a couple of hours." He paused a moment. "On second thought, I may not return until tomorrow."

"What is it, Harriet?" Victoria asked, feeling the baby move slightly. She patted her belly to calm him down.

Harriet hesitated a moment, then spoke. "Withers plans on murdering Sebastian."

The baby kicked Victoria with such force that she yelped.

"Are you all right?" Harriet asked, watching the way

Victoria's hand held her stomach.

"Yes, fine. The baby just seems more active than usual."

"I shouldn't have mentioned this—"

"No. I had assumed that was Withers's plan, but to hear my assumption verified was still a bit of a shock." It also made her realize she would have to take matters into her own hands. She would need to hire someone, someone who would make certain Withers never got the chance to touch her husband.

"Victoria, you're not thinking of—"

"Don't be silly, Harriet. In my condition what could I possibly do?"

"Don't know, but I'd say you'd sure in hell try."

Victoria smiled. "Don't worry. All will be taken care of."

"Victoria, darling, whatever are you doing out of the house in that ghastly condition?"

It wasn't necessary for Victoria to look at the woman to know who it was. "Lydia, I didn't know you had returned from France."

"Only for a short time then we'll be off again." She smiled and picked up the material to inspect.

"Don't tell me you're expecting a little one, Lydia?" Harriet said smugly.

"Heavens no. I hate the creatures. And what nine months of carrying one around does to a woman is pathetic. Losing your shape, marks all over you—oh, the thought just makes me sick."

"Then why are you in Mrs. Hobart's shop? She only caters to babies."

Lydia dropped the material on the table. "I'm going to visit Myra Stanton and naturally I must bring a gift

355

for her new daughter. It wouldn't do to arrive without one."

"Nope, wouldn't be proper at all," Harriet agreed.

"By the way, Victoria, how is your husband? Excited about the event?"

Victoria favored the annoying woman with a pleased smile. "He's thrilled and so attentive to me. He just can't do enough."

"How nice," she said, her voice edged with disappointment. "Well, I must decide on my purchase and be off. Myra is expecting me soon."

"We must be going ourselves," Harriet said, standing.

Victoria rose with just a small amount of difficulty, but she didn't fail to see the look of disgust on Lydia's face. It was a shame the woman was so selfish, but just as well she didn't like children, since Victoria was certain she'd make a horrid mother.

Lydia walked away with a farewell wave and Harriet busied herself with her cape.

Victoria turned to retrieve hers from the chair when through the window her eyes caught a scene across the street.

She watched as Withers spoke to a man, smiling, nodding, and patting him on the back several times as though pleased with what he was telling him. Victoria didn't move. There was something familiar about the man Withers spoke with, although she couldn't see him clearly since his back faced her. She could have sworn she'd seen him before.

The two conversed for several minutes, then Withers handed something to the man and he slipped it into his coat pocket. Withers walked away and the man turned.

Victoria's breath caught in her throat. The baby kicked in excitement and she felt a cold sweat creep over her. The man facing her was the doctor who had taken care of Beth. He knew her as Vic Chambers. If Withers discovered that information, what other information had he uncovered. Did he know she was the Serpent?

If he knew he would use it against her. She could be sent to prison, away from Sebastian, away from her baby. The evil man would succeed again in robbing her of all she cherished most. Fear and anger rushed up to stab her heart and Victoria dropped to the floor in a dead faint.

"She should have been here by now," Sebastian said, tapping his finger on the gold-trimmed plate in front of him.

"She probably got so caught up in buying for the baby that she lost track of time," Aaron offered, stirring the sugar in his coffee.

"Catherine is here waiting." He nodded toward the woman who was seated several tables away and was busy speaking with a friend.

"She doesn't seem at all perturbed by Victoria's tardiness. Now stop worrying. I swear some men are worse than their wives during their pregnancies."

There was a commotion at the entrance to the dining area. A small boy was yelling to let him pass and the head waiter refused the little urchin entrance.

"I gotta see the doc. Let me go."

Aaron immediately stood and Sebastian followed.

"Doc, a lady's collapsed over at Mrs. Hobart's. A

357

Mrs. Fisk told me to fetch you in a hurry. When I got to your office, they told me you were here," the boy panted.

With the mention of Harriet's name, Sebastian flew out the door. Aaron followed quickly behind him.

Victoria was still on the floor when the two men entered. Her eyes were just beginning to flutter open. Harriet was bent down beside her, fumbling with the buttons at her high-necked dress.

Sebastian hoisted Harriet out of the way, dumping her like a sack of potatoes to the side. He gently lifted Victoria's head to rest in his lap while his fingers hastily unfastened the buttons part of the way down the front of her dress.

Aaron instructed the other startled women to step aside and Mrs. Hobart took over from there, directing all of them away from Victoria except for Harriet.

Aaron felt Victoria's abdomen, and finding nothing there that warned of labor, he softly called her name.

She opened her eyes slowly, having difficulty focusing on the faces surrounding her.

"Is she all right, Aaron?" Sebastian asked, protectively laying his hand across her tummy.

"She's fine, probably a bit too much activity in one day for her."

Victoria heard Aaron's words and knew she was in for it now. "I'm fine," she said in a soft whisper.

Sebastian's nostrils flared and his lips tightened.

Aaron caught the signs of his friend's temper flaring. "She needs rest and no further excitement."

Sebastian caught the jest of Aaron's words. He was telling him to calm down for the sake of his wife's condition. He did so instantly. "Have you completed your shopping, love?"

"Yes, Sebastian," she said and attempted to sit up.

He held her firm. "Stay and rest a minute, then I'll help you up."

She did as he asked, nestling against his strong legs.

"I suppose tea with Catherine is out?" she said jokingly.

His lips curled up slightly, just slightly. "Definitely."

"We can go tomorrow," Harriet offered.

"No, she can't," Sebastian stately firmly. "She's not going anywhere until after the birth of our child and Aaron's approval. And don't even think of fighting with me about this, Harriet."

Harriet clamped her mouth shut.

Sebastian helped Victoria up and sat her in the chair.

"Did something upset you?" Aaron asked, knowing her to be in excellent health and wondering if something else was responsible for this fainting spell.

Victoria shivered, recalling the doctor's face and the consequences that could follow. Her eyes fluttered lightly again and her hand went to her stomach. "I don't feel at all well, Sebastian."

"We better get home," Aaron said, worried by her pale complexion.

"My carriage is waiting outside," Harriet said.

Sebastian buttoned his wife's dress and tied her cape around her. She made an effort to stand, but found her legs weak and sought Sebastian's arm for support. He instantly gathered her into his arms and carried her from the shop.

She rested in Sebastian's lap on the ride home. Aaron attempted to question her further, but she informed him she just wasn't up to it at the moment.

Both men were startled by her declaration and fell silent.

Harriet left the two capable men to look after Victoria, promising that she'd return tomorrow to see how she was feeling.

"I think it would be wise for me to give you a quick examination," Aaron said.

"It really isn't necessary. I feel tired that's all. Some sleep and I'll be just fine," she argued.

"Aaron's the doctor," Sebastian said sternly. "He'll be the one to decide what's necessary."

"Sebastian, really, it—"

"I won't have anything happening to you or the child because of your stubbornness. Now you will do as he says."

Victoria was in no mood to argue with him. She just wanted to be left alone for awhile so she could determine what was necessary to protect herself from Withers. "Fine, Sebastian. Help me upstairs and I'll change. Then Aaron may proceed with the examination."

Sebastian was shocked. "You mean you're actually going to do as I tell you?"

"Yes, of course."

"What are you up to, Victoria?"

"Nothing."

"You have to be up to something. You never give in this easily."

Victoria sighed and attempted to rise out of the chair in which Sebastian had placed her. He instantly felt contrite about arguing with her and reached out to help her. "I'm sorry, love."

"Oh, Sebastian, so am I. So am I," she cried and buried her face against his chest.

He was startled by her words and held her tightly to him. He had the distinct feeling she wasn't apologizing for today and he wondered what was causing the grief he heard in her voice. "Come, I'll help you change."

She leaned against him as they walked to the steps, but when she looked up she sighed and lifted her tearful eyes to him. "I can't."

His heart felt torn. Why did he feel she wasn't speaking about climbing the steps? He scooped her into his arms and took the steps slowly, cradling her to him.

She relished the feel of him. His strength, his power, the heavy beat of his heart, all told her how capable he was of protecting her.

She nudged her face against the side of his neck and he placed a kiss on her forehead. "You're safe, love, you're safe."

A lone tear slipped from her eye and she prayed he was right.

"How's your face?" George asked, beginning to take his clothes off and join Tobias and Rosy on the bed.

"It's fine. You should see the other fellow though," Tobias laughed, slapping Rosy on the rear.

"You should be more careful when you go out at night. Too many unsavory characters about," George warned and sat on the bed.

"So is our little deal all set?"

George frowned. "He wouldn't sign the papers, just like you thought. Wants to meet with Thorndike first."

"Did you arrange it?" he asked, pulling Rosy against him.

"Told him just like we discussed it. Thursday night,

ten o'clock." George smiled as he watched Tobias cover Rosy with his heavy body. "You don't think we'll have trouble with him signing those papers, do you?" he asked uncertainly.

Tobias shook his head, unable to speak since he was too busy enjoying Rosy.

"I really need that money. Damn, creditors won't leave me alone." George stopped then as he watched the two writhing on the bed. Tobias squeezed and bit and slapped just like he liked to do. Pain and pleasure, it felt good, real good. He grew more excited as their tempo increased and so did Tobias's slaps.

George grinned, thinking of his turn and how his problems would all come to an end soon, very soon.

Tobias's thoughts were similar to George's only as he felt himself burst into Rosy it wasn't thoughts of money that filled his head. It was the satisfaction of seeing the fool on the bed next to him lying quiet in death beside the Dragon.

"Feeling better?" Sebastian asked, placing the silver serving tray with tea and sandwiches on the table near the window.

"Much better," Victoria said from the bed where she sat propped against numerous lace-trimmed pillows. After the examination and Aaron's assurance that all was fine, she had gratefully fallen into a deep sleep.

"I thought you might enjoy a light supper since you weren't feeling well."

"Tea and sandwiches are fine. I'm really not all that hungry."

He sat beside her on the bed, fussing with the covers

around her. "Victoria, if there's something troubling you, you only need tell me of it."

Victoria wanted to tell him so very much, but she was afraid. Afraid for him, afraid for her child, and afraid for herself. Withers had stolen more than material things from her, and she wasn't about to let him take anymore.

Sebastian saw the doubt and uncertainty in her eyes. "When you're ready, love," he murmured and kissed her gently.

His thoughtfulness touched her heart. She caressed his face with her fingers. "I love you, Dragon."

"You mean you don't fear the fire I roar," he teased playfully.

She smiled and kissed his cheek, his chin, his lips. "Your roar of fire sparks my passion for you."

"Then I shall roar more frequently."

She giggled and threw her arms around his neck. "I do love you so."

"And I love you, Victoria, very . . . very . . ."

His words trailed off as his lips touched hers and they kissed, holding onto each other as if they parted they would never come together again.

Chapter Twenty-Six

Victoria stood by the large oval window watching the night fog creep over the bay, until with a sudden intensity it rushed forward to envelope the wooden and brick buildings, sealing them with its misty shroud.

She recalled the nights she had reverently prayed for the foggy cloak to aid the Serpent in her task. And it did, as though the strange mist could hear her sobbing pleas and understand. It surrounded her with comfort, protection, and the anonymity she required to pursue her work.

A woeful sigh escaped her lips as she continued to focus on the night while a powerful arm slid around her waist just above her protruding stomach to pull her back against the solid form of her husband.

She smiled and gently laid her small hand across the dark material of his sleeve as the back of her head sought the comfort of his chest.

"You should be resting," he whispered, his warm breath tingling the tip of her ear.

She shivered and laughed. "Only if you join me,

dear husband."

Sebastian grinned at his diminutive wife's boldness, but his body responded as she knew it would. "You are cruel, my love. Your time is too near for us—"

Victoria didn't permit him to finish. "There are other ways," she murmured seductively.

"Lola schooled you too well in the art of love," he teased, knowing full well he wanted nothing more than to scoop her up into his arms, carry her to their bedroom, and become lost in the intimate pleasure he knew he would find there. But that was impossible, not because of her pregnancy, but because of a meeting that must take place that night.

Her soft suggestive voice threatened his resolve. "It wasn't Lola who taught me what I want to do to you tonight, dear Dragon."

It was Sebastian's turn to shiver and for sanity's sake he pulled away from her. "I must go out," he answered sternly, causing Victoria to spin around to face him with wide, frightened eyes.

"Where? Why? You promised you'd stay close by because of the babe," she pleaded, her hand instinctively covering her well-rounded stomach.

Sebastian could almost taste her fear and wanting to alleviate it he smiled and playfully tapped the tip of her nose. "A man cannot even go out with his best friend for a few drinks and conversation?"

"You could have that here," she demanded, the tight set of her mouth displaying the determination to keep him home. She knew his destination and she knew she had to keep him home with her tonight.

He forced a smile, for she was too perceptive. "Aaron and I have some business to attend to."

"What kind of business?"

Sebastian studied his wife's taut stance and the brilliant green of her eyes. She knew, damn it, she knew, but how?

He reached out and grasped her arm, then gently slid his other arm around her back to softly propel her up the steps and down the hall to their bedroom.

She slipped from his grasp as they entered and walked to stand near the window.

"You know about your uncle, don't you?" he asked with a murderous glint in his eye, for she had disobeyed him once again by continuing to seek information concerning Tobias Withers.

"My uncle is dead and you damn well know it," she said, placing her hands firmly on her hips.

Sebastian's anger mounted. His fear of losing her was so great that it consumed him like a flame burning inside. He had never experienced a strong desire to kill someone as he did toward Tobias Withers or, as they both knew now, Albert Thorndike.

"I wanted to spare you the pain until it was over, finished, complete, until I could come to you and tell you the scoundrel had paid for his crimes."

Victoria felt her heart skip several beats and she took a deep breath against the pain, the pain of knowing this strange, evil man had robbed her of her family and against the pain of knowing her husband loved her so much he would even sacrifice his own safety.

Tears slipped from her tightly closed lids and she silently cursed her inability to control her emotions lately.

Sebastian stepped toward her, but her eyes flew open and she held her hand up, warding him off. "I refuse to

366

allow you to leave this house tonight."

Sebastian grinned and took two steps toward her.

She waved her hand, warning him to stop. "Don't laugh at me. You're not going anywhere, do you understand?"

His grin broadened and he took several more steps toward her.

"Sebastian, Sebastian," she cried, until her pleas were silenced by his mouth upon hers.

Sebastian glanced down at his sleeping wife. It was ten o'clock and they had spent the last hour and a half pleasing each other in ways that brought a satisfied smile to the Dragon's face. He slipped his hand beneath the quilt and gently ran it over her bare, round tummy as though his touch offered the babe and his wife protection. He then kissed his slumbering wife on the cheek, pulled the quilt up to her neck, and exited the room in haste before he changed his mind.

Akiko was waiting for him at the foot of the stairs, his black evening cape in her hands. "She will be angry when she wakes and finds you gone."

"Tell her I went to meet Aaron."

"She will not believe me."

Sebastian shook his head. "Don't let her leave this house tonight, Akiko."

She nodded, for his statement was more a plea than a command.

Sebastian climbed into the carriage and Daniel directed the horses away from the house and toward the waterfront.

In seconds the dark interior of the carriage was lit by

a spark of light, then followed by the soft glow of the tip of the thin cigar Sebastian had lit. Tonight he had a meeting with George Oliver Stanton on what was purported to be a business matter, but which Sebastian knew to be a trap, a trap that Albert Thorndike had arranged. If all went as the Dragon had planned, this evening would find the two devious men taken care of permanently.

"What do you mean, he's gone out?" Victoria demanded of Akiko thirty minutes after being wakened by a frightening dream.

"He went out with—"

"Don't lie to me," Victoria said, shaking her head and slipping anxiously from the bed.

Akiko held her robe open for her since Martha Simmons had been given the evening off to visit with her sister and her family.

"He is in danger, Akiko, I can feel it. This night will only bring sorrow if you fail to tell me where exactly along the waterfront he's gone."

Akiko watched the petite woman pace back and forth in front of the window in worry. Her hand was placed on the small of her back rubbing the nagging backache that had begun only moments before.

Victoria stopped her relentless pacing and glared at the Japenese woman who had become her friend. "I know he feels he can handle any matter that comes his way, but I fear for his life tonight and I want to be near him if he should need me or if—"

Victoria let her words trail off. She wouldn't voice her fears, she couldn't, and she was sure Akiko understood the fear she felt.

"I hear and see many things," Akiko began and Victoria listened closely. "He wishes no harm to come to you, yet he does not take the precautions necessary to protect himself as he has done so many times before. His thirst for revenge is too great and he thinks with his heart not his mind."

Victoria sighed, realizing she was the cause of his strange behavior. "Tell me so I may help him," she pleaded.

Akiko nodded. "He does not know that I know of his plans, but as I said, I hear and see many things."

Twenty minutes later Victoria was slipping her dagger into the side of her worn boot then stepping back to examine herself in the mirror. She smiled. The Serpent definitely looked funny with a protruding stomach. Even the large shirt and baggy pants with which Akiko had provided her could not hide her advanced pregnancy. She grabbed the woolen cap from the table and shoved her hair under it as she pulled it down around her forehead and ears.

"The dirt," Akiko announced, shuffling into the room with a bowl. She helped Victoria place the grime on her pale face. The Oriental woman stopped, sensing something was amiss.

"Do you feel well?" Akiko questioned.

"Of course," Victoria said, assuming her backache was caused by the position in which she had been sleeping and would disappear soon.

Akiko nodded, seeing no reason to doubt her and followed her down the steps and to the back door. "I told the Dragon I would not allow you to leave the house tonight."

Victoria grinned that bold audacious grin of Vic Chambers. "You aren't letting me leave, it's Vic that's scurrying off into the night."

Akiko bowed her head slowly as in reverence to the woman's determination. "Be careful, Vic," Akiko said and closed the door on the dirty face.

Victoria felt a chill race through her body, but pushed its fearful significance aside and headed for the waterfront.

The distant foghorn called out its alarm to the vast emptiness of the bay, warning the ships of the fog's danger. It sounded particularly strong and powerful tonight as though it sensed the danger stalking the docks.

The Serpent felt it with each woeful blast as she slid silently along the buildings to slip behind the stacked crates for protection. She leaned back against the tall stack and held back the moan she wished to release. The backache had grown in intensity and was now a nagging pressure in her back and lower belly. She had thought for a moment that it might be the baby announcing its arrival, but she had three weeks before that blessed event and her inexperience pushed the unlikeliness of an early delivery aside.

Akiko had informed her of the exact spot, but wasn't sure of the time. Victoria, was, though. She had promised Akiko she would stay well hidden and not reveal her presence unless absolutely necessary.

She slid down along the wooden slots that comprised the crates and gratefully sat on the hard cold ground relieving, only slightly, the pain in her back. Her waiting began as it had done so many times before, only this time it was her husband's footsteps and voice she listened for.

Sebastian drank and laughed with George Stanton until the man was well into his liquor. George finally informed him that the gentleman had been detained on the waterfront and they were to go there to meet him.

The Dragon nodded and George's muddled brain assumed all was going as planned and that the Dragon wasn't as intelligent as he had first thought.

Sebastian climbed into the hired carriage, having dismissed Daniel hours before and instructing him to follow close-by in case he was needed.

"Fool," Sebastian muttered beneath his breath.

"What? What was that?" George asked, his head beginning to spin.

"Fools," Sebastian said. "Only fools, thieves, and murderers venture to the waterfront at this late hour. Perhaps you are one of these men, Mr. Stanton?"

George's cheeks flamed and he sputtered and muttered until his tongue finally found the proper place and he spoke coherently. "No, no, of course not, Mr. Blood, just a businessman with a deal of great value for one like yourself."

"Like myself?" Sebastian questioned sternly.

"Wealthy, wealthy, I mean," George answered nervously.

Sebastian grinned. It would be a pleasure to teach this fool a lesson.

The carriage left them standing in the heavy mist with the foghorn blaring, the water lapping at the

371

docks, and the distant sound of a drunken man singing the praises of a certain well-known lady.

"Shall we proceed?" Sebastian said, extending his hand for George to lead the way.

"Yes, yes, by all means, proceed," George said, stumbling over his words and feet as he walked into the dark night and the trap that would finally slay the mighty Dragon.

"He said he'd be here around twelve, I'm certain of it. Probably be only a minute now," George said, backing slowly away from him.

Sebastian sensed the other man's presence before he saw him, but not before the gun was placed firmly in the small of his back. Damn, he thought, but didn't allow it to upset him too much. He knew he could easily disarm the fool.

"Walk," the voice commanded gruffy and Sebastian did so, while a stumbling George Stanton followed.

"This was too easy, you fool. Are you sure he doesn't have help close-by?"

George wiped his wet brow with is handkerchief. "No, no, I'm certain he came alone."

Albert Thorndike dug the gun into the Dragon's back, relishing the feel of the power he held over the large man. "Pretty sure of yourself, aren't you, Dragon?"

"Yes," was Sebastian's only reply, but was said with such conviction that both men shivered.

"Well, you made your first and final mistake," Thorndike informed him.

"You think so?" Sebastian asked and turned around before the man realized he had moved.

Thorndike delivered a stinging blow to Sebastian's

face and was surprised to see the man didn't even flinch when his meaty fist connected with hard flesh. "I'll kill you if you move again, then I'll have the pleasure of tasting that dandy little morsel of womanly flesh you so proudly call your wife."

His remark had the desired affect. Sebastian stiffened.

"Let's get this over with," George whined. "Make him sign those damned papers before you kill him, then you can do as you like with that woman as long as I get my money."

"You'll get what you deserve," Thorndike shouted to Sebastian.

"Not if I can help it," came the raspy voice that brought a frightening chill to George, an angry scowl to Thorndike's face, and caused the Dragon's temper to soar.

"You're dead," George said, shaking where he stood and wondering who the Serpent would choose as his victim.

He found out seconds later.

"Then it must be my ghost that's got my dagger placed so close to your manly pride."

Sebastian's midnight blue eyes glared with fury. And Thorndike seized the opportunity for his benefit.

"Your husband doesn't seem to like your nightly trade, Victoria."

George gasped. "Victoria, the Serpent? Impossible."

Victoria sliced the man's trousers and pressed the blade against his moist skin.

"It can't be, can't be," George squealed. "The fellow is too skilled with a blade."

"Tell him, Victoria, or I shall dispose of your

husband," Thorndike warned, pushing the gun against Sebastian's chest and forcing him to move away from George.

Sebastian wanted to wring his wife's neck. He could have had both men well taken care of by now, but her stubbornness . . . he stopped in mid-thought. It wasn't her stubbornness that caused her appearance here tonight, it was her love for him. Just as his love for her had brought him here so had hers. He smiled, but vowed to give her a sound tongue-lashing for frightening him, for he had no doubt he could get them out of this little predicament.

"You always seem to get your way, *Uncle,*" Victoria said. She bit her lower lip after the words were out, for the pain in her belly had grown in intensity. She had known for the last thirty minutes that she was in labor. She had not planned to show herself, but when Thorndike had hit Sebastian she couldn't prevent herself from moving. He had taken away too many people she had loved and she wouldn't allow him to do it again. Even if it meant delivering the baby on the waterfront.

"The Serpent, a woman?" George said and yelled the next minute as he felt the blade once again slice his skin.

"She cut me, she cut me!" he screamed.

Sebastian smiled and Thorndike shouted, "Shut up, you stupid fool."

"I'm bleeding, I'm bleeding."

"You'll bleed a lot more if your friend doesn't release my husband," Victoria warned.

"Release him, release him!" George screamed.

Thorndike smiled. "Really, dear niece, you think I'd

let a whining fool like him stop me." And with that Thorndike directed his gun toward George and fired.

George looked with wide-eyed shock at his chest, covered the hole that was streaming blood over his hand, then collapsed to the ground.

"One less to worry about," Thorndike said without emotion.

Sebastian took a step toward him, but Thorndike pointed the gun at Victoria. "Please, it would give me great pleasure to see her die before your eyes."

Sebastian froze.

"I'm going to carve your heart out and feed it to the fish," Victoria said calmly.

Thorndike grinned. "That was one thing I always admired about you, your tenacity to survive, no matter what the consequences, but I'm afraid this time it is impossible. You must die."

"Not before I kill you, Thorndike," Victoria stated, flipping the dagger over in her hand to grasp the blade.

"Really, dear, the bullet would certainly hit you before you could release that blade."

"Shall we see?" she said calmly.

Sebastian paled for the first time in his life. The little fool was playing with death and there she calmly stood announcing to her adversary that she intended to see him die before she did. He had had enough. It was time he brought to a halt the danger she had placed herself in.

He was about to step forward when Victoria's words stopped him.

"You killed my parents, forced my ill sister to live the last year of her life in fear, and forced me to turn to thievery. There is one thing, however, that I do wish to

375

thank you for, *Uncle,* and that is that I met a man who I love more than I ever dreamed possible."

She held the dagger's blade firmly in her fingers and raised it in the air.

Sebastian realized at that moment she was prepared to forfeit her life for his and he released a yell that reverberated along the waterfront.

Everything happened within seconds after that. Victoria released the blade, Thorndike fired the gun, and Sebastian delivered a blow to the man's nose that forced the bone and cartilage to pierce his brain and cause instant death.

As Thorndike crumpled to the ground, so did Victoria. Sebastian froze for several seconds before he ran to his wife's side.

Fear licked at every pore in his body and he prayed to a god he even wondered existed to spare his wife's life. She was doubled over as though kneeling in prayer, her head almost touching her round belly. He lifted her face gently and caught his breath as he gazed into her wide, tearful eyes.

"The baby," she whispered hoarsely.

"He's been hit," he said, his hand instinctively searching for blood.

She managed to shake her head. "No, he wants to see his father for himself."

Sebastian was stunned. "You're in labor? The bullet missed you?"

"Yes to both questions."

He didn't know whether to feel relieved or not, although he didn't have much time to ponder his indecision. The moan Victoria released chilled him to the bone and he whistled for Daniel who he knew was nearby.

He scooped her carefully into his arms and she rested her head against his chest. "I want to see for myself," she said in between deep breaths.

"See what?" he demanded, feeling her belly contract with another pain and wanting desperately to get her home.

"See that he is dead."

He shook his head. "I don't think—"

"Please," she moaned, "I must see for myself."

He understood her need to see her enemy dead and walked over to where his body lay. She looked down at his bloody face and saw that Sebastian had done what she had wished to do, but as Sebastian turned to walk away she saw her dagger. It had pierced Thorndike's heart and she smiled.

In minutes the house was in an uproar. Sebastian was screaming for Akiko and Martha Simmons. Daniel had been informed that his position in the Blood household hung precariously unless he brought Aaron to the house immediately.

The large black man had smiled at Victoria and she had winked as he cracked the whip in his hand and drove the horses out into the night.

Sebastian was informed that Martha had been granted the evening off and wouldn't return until the next day.

"What the hell am I paying her for?" he yelled.

"Sebastian," Victoria said calmly as he placed her on the bed, "You were the one who told her she could have the time off."

Sebastian growled like an angry bear and proceeded to help his wife undress. After several fumbling attempts and unbearable pain, she instructed her husband to wait downstairs for Aaron.

"I refuse," he said adamantly.

Victoria grabbed her belly and doubled over. "Sebastian, please see if Aaron has arrived yet."

The distraught man flew from the room and Akiko smiled. "It wasn't time for another contraction."

"I know," Victoria grinned, "but he was making me nervous. Now, please help me into my nightgown before he returns."

The first bright light of dawn was peeking over the horizon and Sebastian still paced the foyer floor. Back and forth he had walked for hours after Aaron had insisted he was doing his wife no good, for every time she was in pain, Sebastian would wince and threaten Aaron's life if he didn't do something for her.

He had expected screams as her labor advanced, but he had heard nothing but low moans and it frightened him. He looked up and without stopping to think, charged up the stairs. He was about to knock on the door when Aaron swung it open.

"Perfect timing, Sebastian. Come meet your son."

Sebastian walked into the room. Victoria was braced up upon two lace-covered pillows, her face pale and tired, but her smile radiant. He leaned over her and kissed her gently on the cheek. "Are you all right?"

"I feel wonderful," she said and looked down into her arms. Sebastian's glance followed and there, nestled in a blanket in her arms, was his son. He was

378

small, wrinkled, and pink, but the top of his head held a patch of raven black hair.

"Isn't he beautiful?" Victoria asked with a smile.

Sebastian felt a lump rise in his throat and he had to clear it before he spoke. "Yes, he's beautiful."

"Don't you like him?" Victoria asked, suddenly fearful that he was not thrilled with his son's birth.

Aaron and Akiko silently left the room as Sebastian sat next to Victoria on the bed. He placed the palm of his hand against her face and spoke in a strong whisper as though it hurt him to speak. "I was frightened that I might lose you and the child. I couldn't bare to think of life without you, Victoria."

She pressed her warm face against his cool hand. "There's no need to worry about that any longer. I will be by your side forever."

"And my bed," he said, recalling the words he had hurtfully flung at her so many months before.

"Forever," she murmured and he sealed her declaration with a kiss.

Epilogue

Early evening settled along the waterfront bringing with it the first shades of dusk. The fog hovered out along the bay, rolling in ever so slowly as though waiting for someone.

Victoria stepped down from the carriage, her hand clasped firmly in her husband's. She looked out over the bay as they walked along the wharf.

"It's so peaceful," she whispered, as though paying reverence to the calm scene.

"Not many people see its beauty," Sebastian said, sensing the same strange feeling of contentment as his wife.

They both stood quiet a moment, listening to the water lapping along the wharf, the cry of the gulls, and the blast of the distant foghorn.

"It's time to let go," Sebastian said, knowing what what his wife was about to do was difficult for her.

"I know," she murmured.

Sebastian handed the pearl-handled dagger to her. She took it, feeling more than just its coldness. She felt the warmth of life. The shiny blade had helped her survive among the harsh realities of life, had helped her provide for her sister, had given her a taste of freedom, had brought her and her husband together, and in the end had helped her achieve her revenge.

It was a trusted friend, a friend she felt reluctant to part with, yet she knew it was time. It was time to say good-bye.

Sebastian covered her hand with his. The blade was warm from her touch and he understood her need to cling to it one last time. "We have each other. The Serpent is no longer necessary."

A tear tickled at her eye. "It's hard to say good-bye to a friend, especially one so loyal."

"I know, but there are times friendships must be severed, even when we don't want them to end."

Victoria nodded. The Serpent was no longer. The night she had raised her weapon against her uncle was the night the Serpent had died. Now the burial was necessary.

Sebastian released her hand. She stepped forward to the edge of the dock, glanced down into the darkness of the water, and raised her hand over it.

"Good-bye, Serpent," she whispered and released the dagger. Water splashed on the bottom of her dress as the shiny object was swallowed into the dark depths of the bay.

She turned and with tears glistening in her eyes walked into her husband's outstretched arms. He held her tightly for several moments before they returned to the carriage.

Sebastian experienced the stirrings of desire for his wife as he assisted her petite form up and into the carriage. The baby's birth had not diminished her beauty. As a matter of fact, it had enhanced it. And if he didn't seek her bed soon he was going to go completely insane.

He climbed in beside her and they were soon off at a slow, leisurely pace.

Victoria watched the way her husband moved his powerful body restlessly in the seat. She had known for the last few days that his forced celibacy was taking its toll. Of course, she hadn't informed him that she had seen Aaron that morning. He had advised her that all was well and she and Sebastian could resume their intimate relations. She had wanted to surprise him this evening, make a special occasion of it. A candlelight supper, small talk, suggestive glances, touches, and finally he would take her upstairs and make love to her all night. That's what she had planned, but she suddenly found herself impatient.

She shifted her body so it pressed against him and moved so her breats swept invitingly across his chest as she pretended to look out his window. "It's such a lovely evening."

"Yes," he mumbled, squirming uncomfortably in his seat as the ache in his loins grew unbearable each time her breast brushed against him.

She brought her face just inches from his, her soft cheek whispering near his. Touching, yet not touching. "This time of the day is so peaceful."

"Yes," he snapped.

His sharp retort didn't disturb her. She actually enjoyed it since it warned her she was achieving the desired results.

"Ahhh," she sighed heavily, and pulled her shoulders

back while forcing her chest out. "It feels so good to be out along the bay once again."

The sigh did it. It reminded him of the satisfied sounds she made after he'd—

He grabbed her by the shoulders, swung her across his lap, and kissed her soundly. She tasted deliciously moist and sweet.

"I've missed you," she murmured, when he finally tore his mouth from hers.

He smiled sinfully and claimed her mouth once again.

He tasted her like a starved man unable to quench his appetite. Her arms came up around him, circling his neck.

His hand slid along her back, down around her slim waist and over her round derriere. He pulled at her skirt, forcing it up so his hand could slip beneath it. He glided across the silky stocking that covered her leg and slipped farther and farther up until his fingers found their way to the warmth between her legs. He touched, teased, tormented.

Sebastian growled in annoyance at the garment that blocked his path, and cursed it soundly. He could feel her readiness beneath it, moist and hot against his flesh.

"Sebastian," she moaned and turned her lips to his. Their kiss was hungry and urgent.

"I want you, Victoria. God, how I want you," he whispered harshly near her ear.

"And I you, my wicked Dragon," she answered. "Please, make Daniel hurry."

"But—"

She silenced his protests with her fingers pressed

gently upon his lips. "I saw Aaron this morning. Everything is fine."

His eyes narrowed. "You knew earlier and waited until now to tell me?"

She shook her head, smiling like a little girl who had just parted with a special secret.

He grinned at her disarming response. "Do you know what I'm going to do to you for making me suffer?"

"What?" she asked playfully.

"I'm going to make love to you all night. I'm going to touch you, Victoria. Especially here." His fingers tore at the material and in seconds his fingers slipped inside her and she was lost.

"That's not all I'm going to do," he said, brushing his lips with hers. "I'm going to taste you, every inch of you—your nipples, your belly, your—"

"Sebastian," she cried against his mouth.

"Tell me, Victoria, tell me how much you want me."

She took his face in her hands. "I want you, Dragon. I want you so badly it hurts."

He kept her on his lap as he leaned over by the window and stuck his head out. "Daniel," he yelled, "if we're not home in five minutes, you're fired."

Daniel laughed and snapped the reins. The horses bolted, the carriage sprang forward, and the Dragon's lady smiled.